I Love Bill

I Love Bill

And Other Stories

Wang Anyi
Translated by Todd Foley

Cornell East Asia Series
an imprint of
Cornell University Press
Ithaca and London

Number 214 in the Cornell East Asia Series

Copyright © 2023 by Cornell University

First published 2023 by Cornell University Press

Library of Congress Cataloging-in-Publication Data

Names: Wang, Anyi, 1954– author. | Foley, Todd, 1983– translator. |
    Zhang, Xudong, 1965– writer of foreword.
Title: I love Bill and other stories / Wang Anyi; translated by Todd Foley.
Other titles: Wo ai Bi'er. English
Description: Ithaca: Cornell University Press, 2023. | Series: Cornell
    East Asia series; no. 214 | Summary: "In two novellas and three short
    stories, Wang Anyi describes various aspects of life in modern China,
    centered mainly around Shanghai, Xuzhou, and northern Jiangsu
    province"—Provided by publisher.
Identifiers: LCCN 2022055701 (print) | LCCN 2022055702 (ebook) |
    ISBN 9781501771057 (hardcover) | ISBN 9781501771064 (paperback) |
    ISBN 9781501771071 (epub) | ISBN 9781501771088 (pdf)
Subjects: LCGFT: Novellas. | Short stories.
Classification: LCC PL2919.A58 W41613 2023 (print) |
    LCC PL2919.A58 (ebook) | DDC 895.13/52—dc23/eng/20221209
LC record available at https://lccn.loc.gov/2022055701
LC ebook record available at https://lccn.loc.gov/2022055702

CONTENTS

FOREWORD

Xudong Zhang

Readers of this collection need no reminder that reading literature in translation comes with rewards as well as challenges, which together make the experience both exciting and frustrating, often tantalizingly so. At best, reading the translation makes one wish to speak the foreign language and know everything there is to know about the country, society, or culture in which the work originated. At worst, it leaves us embarrassed or humiliated by the elusiveness of deep understanding or the simple absence of genuine interest (the familiar "Give me a reason to read this!" or "In an ideal world . . ." readily comes to mind), as the blunt alienness and strangeness of the text, presented in our own language, fail to resonate morally or aesthetically even for the most curious and open-minded—or "tolerant" or "promiscuous"—among us.

However, for a dedicated student of modern China or an initiated reader of world literature, a certain kind of educated tentativeness or undecidedness might be precisely the right place to start, as the reading process usually benefits from a starting point conditioned by doubt rather than conviction, and by a sense of wonder rather than certainty. If reading translated literature only drives home the idea that reading is but venturing out, leaping forward, and groping in the dark, then what could facilitate this individual journey practically and methodically would be a commonsensical, even pedestrian, discussion of the context by a so-called specialist. However, this could be only in the sense of a local tour guide, whose job is no more than pointing out a few highlights in the wealth of information that can be easily accessed and assembled either in print or on the internet.

Arguably the single most important realist novelist writing in China since the late 1980s, Wang Anyi has had a long and productive career that defies popular labels and ready-made critical or literary historical categories. Commonly (and unthinkingly) referred to as "the most prominent woman writer in contemporary China," her energy, strength, technical prowess, and wide-ranging presentation of sociopsychological actualities often surpass and overwhelm her male peers, upending the gender hierarchy still prevalent in Chinese literary circles, as well as Chinese society at large. In terms of critical acclaim and media exposure, only Mo Yan (the 2012 winner of the Nobel Prize in Literature) and Yu Hua (whose *To Live* might be the most read contemporary Chinese literary work outside mainland China) might be said to be in the same league. While most prominent literary works by leading Chinese writers draw upon the rural experience and concentrate on small-town China as the anchor and background of an unfolding Chinese story (as tragedy or comedy; as the epic, poetic, or prosaic tales of mundane everyday life; or as History with capital "H"), Wang Anyi is and has always been a decidedly urban writer, though some of her early stories were based on her relatively brief personal experience as a "sent-down youth" (*zhiqing*) during Mao Zedong's Great Proletarian Cultural Revolution (1966–76). The forefront of literary exploration and experiment in the Era of Reform and Opening (1979–2012) is characterized by a penchant for formal innovation and aesthetic intensity, which inevitably privilege a style informed and inspired by Modernism as an international movement. Yet Wang Anyi has always retained her artistic, even political, identity as a realist writer, though her realism is always as ambiguous and idiosyncratic as it is willing and able to absorb other styles and formal–technical strategies. Indeed, calling Wang Anyi a realist is tantamount to lending realism an afterlife and a new vocation in the Chinese context, as her persisting literary productivity and innovation eventually force her readers to face realism once again, often at the end of many stylistic paths. Meanwhile, her ability to mingle this mode of writing with numerous currents both historical and contemporary, and above all her determination to appropriate and integrate those external elements into a single method, has foregrounded her distinctive narrative voice. In turn her voice characterizes and sustains that method of realist mimesis (imitation, representation) of reality. Indeed, various labels, images, and categories bestowed to Wang Anyi's work, while not always entirely misleading, can only become meaningful entry points into her literary space when understood as different aspects, moments, and temporary motifs and intensities of the integrated and holistic mimetic architecture of her writings.

Even though Wang Anyi writes entirely in Chinese and for a Chinese audience, and has been shaped most intimately, and in an overdetermined way, by Chinese literary scenes, institutions, and social milieu, it can be said, without any hyperbole or irony, that Wang Anyi might be more readily and precisely recognized and analyzed in a world literary context by tracing her literary genealogy in the European realist and postrealist traditions. If we allow that even the crudest analogy across time and space can be helpful in establishing points of relatability, comparison and resonance, if done guardedly, one is tempted to say that she should be read as a worthy inheritor of Jane Austen for her intuitive insight into the socioeconomic power relations in personal and romantic entanglements, as well as in terms of her elaborate experimentation with indirect free speech as a narrative tool to organize complex, even chaotic, historical experience in momentous flux. One might equally be tempted to suggest that Wang Anyi, whose energetic, all-encompassing, and devouring style is seen as equally if not more "masculine" than her peers, should be more productively compared to Balzac, whose conservative politics as a monarchist never get in the way of his clear-eyed observation of French capitalism and the sociohistorical drama it undergirds. Wang Anyi, a self-styled "daughter of the People's Republic," routinely declines praise that compares her to the leading stylists of the (fleeting) Chinese bourgeoisie, such as Eileen Chang of the 1940s. In doing so, she issues no apology in response to the whispers about her red lineage (both her parents were prominent communist "cultural workers"). This can also be read as a tacit response to the critical interpretation of her work as postrevolutionary melancholy, whose flip side might be construed as an unconscious nostalgia for Mao's China in which she grew up. At the same time, she is also confirming her literary identity as an inheritor of European realism, which, in the postrevolutionary, postsocialist ideological atmosphere of the Chinese 1980s, 1990s, and the first decade of the twenty-first century, may inadvertently stand out as against the grain of history and thus radical, at least culturally speaking, or in terms of taste (that is, "conservative" in the context of post-Mao China).

To the short list of her literary ancestors (Austin and Balzac), one may want to add Flaubert and Zola in terms of a naturalist attention to ever-swelling details; Tolstoy in terms of the narrative and quasi-religious ambition to present and comment on social dynamism and stasis, with all their relational complexities and entanglements; Chekov in terms of the intimate and even-handed presentation of small, helpless folks hanging in the balance of everyday life while going through profound moral torment; or, as a case in point that realism as a style and genre can be stretched almost endlessly before reaching a breaking point, Agatha Christie, whose detective stories and melodramas of modern life appear to strike a deep chord in Wang Anyi's own literary vision, solving problems and unpacking secrets by being observant and nosy, chatty but unsentimental, and by writing logically and analytically so that reality itself is set to show its own reason and unreason, truth and untruth. To this list, one could also add any number of ephemeral or lingering influences or flirtations with various schools, movements, artistic tastes, or genres, from modernist stream-of-consciousness or absurdity to nonfiction, but only as a heightened mode of narrative and social commentary, and often still along realist lines, including that now largely extinct tradition of "writer as intellectual."

All these analogies, influences, and genealogies can only be distracting and misleading if not situated within the context of the post-Mao vicissitudes of Chinese literature and Chinese society. But here, too, realism as a concept, method, and artistic practice proves to be as expansive and supple as it is resilient, something that has guided Wang Anyi through successive periods of socioeconomic and cultural upheavals. For instance, in her early career, she was often grouped in the "returnees" (from the countryside to the city) and thus a writer of "scar literature" (*shanghen wenxue*). However, her stories about the "sent-down" youths returning to their native big city are never only or even mainly about recounting the bitterness or hardships of a whole generation's rural exile. Rather, those early works tend to gravitate toward the narrative representation of a collective experience derived from the shocking encounter with the Chinese countryside, as well as an equally shocking re-encounter with the big city in which the protagonists feel lost and alienated. Her most acclaimed works in this period tend to show this double encounter and alienation with fresh realist sensibilities and an intimate treatment of experiential and psychological details. They include "Life in a Small Courtyard" (小院琐记, 1980), "The Destination" (本次列车终点, 1981), and *Lapse of Time* (流逝, 1982). All this led to a twofold (albeit repressed and curtailed) bildungsroman, which helps explicate the hidden engine and ambition of Wang Anyi's writing from the very beginning of her career. The bildungsroman as a major genre in nineteenth-century European literature never panned out in modern China, for obvious sociohistorical and cultural–political reasons. However, as a moment of converging possibilities, it leaves a profound trace in the development of Chinese realism, before or after the onslaught of Modernism. For most of the 1980s, as Wang Anyi steadily established herself as an important literary presence in the Chinese literary scene, she was increasingly categorized as a member of the "Searching-for-Roots" (*xungen*) movement, exploring the cultural or group-psychological backgrounds that determine individual behavior, often offering a "deep-structure" explanation of some genetic flaws. As a literary movement and expression of social ideology, the Searching-for-Roots school constituted one of the literary wings of the general neo-Enlightenment thrust of younger-generation intellectuals in the first decade of post-Mao reforms. The excavation project, while aiming at a historical and anthropological understanding of the slow-moving collective experience, is only a matter of concentrating aesthetic and symbolic capital in the realm of culture so as to promote the radical modernization processes, albeit from a more technically competent, professionally secured fashion, with an eye on the "march toward world literature" as not only Chinese writers, but also as contemporary writers. Even though some of Wang Anyi's better-known stories and novellas available in English, such as *Baotown* (小鲍庄, 1985) and *Love on a Barren Mountain* (荒山之恋, 1986), were produced in this period, it might be fair to say that she was only an absentminded participant in this trend.

Wang Anyi first found her distinct, unmistakable voice in her work of the early 1990s, with her novella *The Story of an Uncle* (叔叔的故事, 1990).

In retrospect, what makes this novella significant is not its devastatingly unflattering portrait of the self-serving, narcissistic, skill-less Chinese intellectuals, but rather the fact that with its publication, she had gained complete moral, aesthetic, and intellectual independence vis-à-vis the older generations of Chinese writers and intellectuals by charting an unwavering stylistic and representational path for herself. The decade that ensued witnessed the unstoppable rise of Wang Anyi to literary stardom all the way to the peak of contemporary Chinese literary production, which has come to be read and judged in an increasingly globalized symbolic space. After all, as a literary decade, the Chinese '90s coincide with the socioeconomic passage culminating in China's entry into the World Trade Organization at the end of 2001. This would pave the way for China's epochal ascendance as the "workshop of the world," which, in retrospect, might be a more important historic watershed than the September 11 terrorist attack on the United States. The international "Shanghai Fever" (*Shanghai re*) is a case in point. The rediscovery of Shanghai as an enclave of global capitalist history and colonial modernity in the late 1990s and early 2000s played an important role in helping to shape the ideological landscape and aesthetic (in the original sense, that is, relating to senses) taste and expectations of Chinese society with its emergent urban consumer masses.

Literally and symbolically, Shanghai as a "world picture" now contributed to a latent political unconscious and explicit public rhetoric and policies (i.e., neoliberal economics) in China during the turn of the century, threatening to dislodge the state-sanctioned institutions and daily realities from their older, conventional discourse (centering around socialism and nationalism, for instance), before relocating or reinserting them in the chain of events of global capitalist expansion. The fact that Shanghai was the only city in mainland China capable of nostalgically and sentimentally returning itself as a moment and locale back to a purported universal history, therefore, anchors it as a focal point of global imagination. Wang Anyi's most acclaimed novel, *The Song of Everlasting Sorrow* (长恨歌, 1995), no doubt anticipated and to some extent prefigured this upcoming tide, but only "unconsciously," either in the form of endless descriptions of grainy details and intimate vignettes of urban forms of everyday life, or in a more elevated, sometimes sublime, painting of the city as allegories of collective experiences underpinned by class, gender, and apocalyptic events. The fact that the novel's most intense and prevalent mood or affect as "unnamed emotions" (Fredric Jameson) is mourning and melancholy sets her work apart from the usual suspects and proponents of the ideologically driven "Shanghai nostalgia"; it also, interestingly, sets in motion various kinds of realist impulses and techniques that permeate the novel, from melodrama to cold-blooded economic calculation. Little wonder that the 1990s turned out to be the most splendid chapter in Wang Anyi's writing career, in which her realist exposé of the intricate interiors of Shanghai everyday life cuts deeply into sociogeological layers of modern Chinese history, whose internal tensions and contradictions are sedimented and fossilized in its most developed metropolis. To the extent that Wang Anyi lends a narrative voice, a cognitive perspective, and aesthetic form to this repressed temporal–spatial structure, she can be properly regarded as the foremost urban writer of modern China. The prevalent historiography of modern Chinese literature, however, still turns to the countryside in search of a credible mode of realist literary production, if only to follow the official history of the Chinese Revolution unfolding along the triumphant strategy of laying siege to the cities from the countryside. Rooted in and flourishing along with thick urban experiences, however, Wang Anyi's realism marks a deviation from that modern Chinese literary orthodoxy but conforms to the normal and classical experiences of realist development in Europe, North America, Russia and, to a lesser degree, Japan.

As a method, such realism proves equally capable (i.e., in its subtlety, intimacy, power, and expressiveness) when turning to rural and small-town experiences with their attendant in-between characters and behaviors. Some of the best stories and novellas Wang Anyi has written so far fall into this socio-experiential space of in-betweenness and ambiguity. A few of the very best from this select group are showcased in the present collection, including "The Troupe" (1997), "Match Made in Heaven" (1998), and "A Girls' Trip" (2003). The locales of these stories vary, including provincial towns and mountain villages, but they are not so much fixed and isolated spaces as corridors of complex socioeconomic, political and cultural interactions and mediations (between different classes, social backgrounds and statuses, political–ideological stands, cultural habits, etc.). They provide an ideal situation for realist storytelling and problem solving, showing an embedded rational interest in revealing—by means of following and imitating—the concrete steps of the characters' action, argument, and reasoning; "A Girls Trip," for example, borders on a detective story and a road movie all at once. Of the stories selected here from this period of hyperproductivity and formal inventiveness, only "I Love Bill" is nearly entirely urban in terms of its setting, imagery, and the density of human interactions (save the last scene of the female protagonist's escape from the correctional institution and into the mountains). But one should remember that this decade in Wang Anyi's career is, then, as now, overshadowed by *The Song of Everlasting Sorrow*, which remains the definitive story of Shanghai as romance and allegory, and tragedy and melodrama, all at once. The urban complexity, intricacy, nuance, and sensual excesses are not only remarkably presented in many other stories and novellas, notably *Anecdotes from the Cultural Revolution* (文革轶事 1993), but also reinforced by her rich, panoramic, and stylistically deliberate essay production with titles such as "The Women of Shanghai," "The Western-Style Buildings in Shanghai," and "The *Longtang* [small alleys] in Shanghai."

The explosive energy and dazzling innovativeness of Wang Anyi's writing in the 1990s propelled her into the following two-plus decades with unabated productivity and an ever-growing list of awards, both domestic and international. Commenting on her entire career would be premature and at any rate exceeds the scope of this introduction. Suffice it here to observe the general dynamic of her stylistic development as a singular complex of repetition and difference, subversiveness and restoration. It would not be misleading to characterize her more recent writings as revolving around Shanghai, but it is also obvious that Shanghai as represented by Wang Anyi has also experienced increasing and heightened degrees of "deterritorialization," a term used by the French philosopher Gilles Deleuze to describe the movement of form or substance to vacate the space and property it occupies in order to be reconstituted as both the self *and* something else. In Wang Anyi's novels, stories, essays, and critical writings of the 2000s and 2010s, Shanghai has morphed into its awkward adolescence as a story of intellectual education (*The Age of Enlightenment* [启蒙时代], 2007), its premodern origins and myths (*Heavenly Scent* [天香], 2011), or its neighboring regions as metaphors of its suspension and oblivion (*Nameless* [匿名], 2016). From such a distance, her realist style seems to have gained a new momentum, velocity, and intensity in its mimetic capturing of a historical reality now held as an object and totality. Remnants of her earlier style, particularly of the melodramatic variety, have all but disappeared, replaced by an ever tighter and denser narrative design that operates on the level of an unending, holistic, even metaphysical indirect free speech. In *Heavenly Scent*, a "historical novel" set in the late Ming era (late sixteenth and early seventeenth centuries), we see the work of embroidery, a kind of "valueless" female labor confined to the inner chamber, becoming value-added products in the social sphere (but not yet "commodities" in today's sense) before morphing into works of art and, ultimately, work as such. Culminating in a mimetic figure of productivity and feminine bond, such a vivid and multidimensional figure stands as an allegory of the work of literary production engaged in by a twenty-first-century woman writer; or, rather, the work of writing presenting itself as the allegory of a historic and collective productivity and human unity commensurate with the epic experience of Chinese industrialization and commercial activities beyond—or at least oblivious of—the reach of the imperial state.

If the potency of Wang Anyi's storytelling has found its more rigorously conceptual expression in her latter-day work, thus conducive to an emergent discussion of "realism after modernism" in China (with the country or system itself being a curiously anachronistic case of "capitalism after socialism"), then the now classical period of her work, embodied by the most celebrated stories written in the 1990s, may constitute an "ideal type" of contemporary Chinese literature as an art form, which momentarily finds "perfect"—concrete, immediate, and vivid—sensual appearance for its often distressed and warring, but always searching, ideas. The rapidity of change in China may be dizzying, but it nevertheless has left behind some records and artifacts that contain within their formal and aesthetic properties something more durable and serene, upon which one can dwell and contemplate. For everyone who takes an interest either in China or in literature, the stories by Wang Anyi, carefully selected and beautifully translated by Todd Foley in this collection, are something one should not want to miss.

Greenwich Village, New York
July 2022

Translator's Preface

For the past several decades, Wang Anyi (王安忆) has stood as one of the most highly regarded writers in China, producing a long list of award-winning works generally noted for both their subtle realism and their poignant depictions of women's perspectives in times of historical transition. As one of the major writers to emerge in the early years of the post-Mao reform era, Wang Anyi's consistent output has served as a unique sort of literary bridge into the twenty-first century. Her roles as president of the Shanghai Writers' Association and vice-chair of the Chinese Writers' Association only affirm the influential position she continues to hold in the contemporary Chinese literary scene. Yet despite her critical acclaim and vast oeuvre, only a small selection of her work is currently available in English translation. By far the most significant among these is her 1995 novel *The Song of Everlasting Sorrow* (长恨歌), translated by Michael Berry and Susan Chan Egan and published in 2008; more recently, Howard Goldblatt's 2019 translation of her 2000 novel *Fuping* (富萍) has been a welcome addition. Taken together, these novels showcase much of what Wang Anyi does best: *The Song of Everlasting Sorrow* masterfully examines the residues, transformations, and afterlives of a pre-socialist petty-bourgeois Shanghai society, which tenaciously persists and reimagines itself as the city struggles through the subsequent Mao and post-Mao eras. *Fuping*, however, examines Shanghai from a different perspective, focusing on the paradoxical relationship between the city's identity as modernity itself and its human foundation of regional migrants, who bring with them a shared sense of rootedness in a proximate yet completely external history and culture that stretches all the way back to an unspoken, romanticized, and imaginary memory of premodern Yangzhou.

In 2016, Wang Anyi spent the spring semester as a writer-in-residence at New York University, where I was lucky enough to help organize a series of workshop discussions led by Professor Xudong Zhang. Every two weeks, we would meet to discuss a selection of Wang Anyi's works chosen by the author herself; the stories in this volume are taken from that list. Beyond that, and on a more practical note, the stories here offer a broad range of Wang Anyi's literary output in relatively short, digestible forms that are well-suited for use in the classroom. They have also been selected with the general reader in mind, offering immediately accessible and engaging works like "I Love Bill" (我爱比尔) and "A Girls' Trip" (姊妹行) alongside a more experimental novella like "The Troupe" (文工团), which is made all the more challenging by its very specific social and historical context. *The Song of Everlasting Sorrow*, with its pages of subtle introductory description of Shanghai's *longtang* alleyways, requires the unfamiliar reader to make a significant initial investment; many of the stories in this collection hit the ground running, inviting a more serious intellectual engagement to develop naturally along the way.

A major hurdle for Wang Anyi's works in translation is their understated depictions of mundane daily life, filled with oblique references to specific times and places in a pared-down, chatty language. "I Love Bill" (1996), which may be taken as the cornerstone of this collection, offers something that more successfully overcomes these barriers of translation by taking the issue of cultural translation itself as a central focus. The engaging plot centers on Ah San, a young university student in Shanghai who drops out of art school to pursue a romantic affair with Bill, an American cultural attaché. While their relationship seems stilted and hollow from the very beginning, each is deeply attracted to the cultural imaginary the other represents. For Bill, Ah San is the mystical Chinese culture he studies and reveres, while Bill embodies the enticing global cosmopolitanism in which Ah San yearns to participate. Set during the mid-1990s, "I Love Bill" captures the anxieties of this particular historical moment in China's economic and cultural transition with superlative poignancy, and it explores the nature of an emerging cosmopolitan imaginary as part of China's evolving encounter with the West. No other work of Chinese literature, to my knowledge, captures the particular tensions of this transitional period so well. Yet at the same time as the story carries this specific historical significance, it handles the issue of cross-cultural exchange in a way that continues to be universally relevant and accessible: The types of cultural barriers between Ah San and her boyfriends are quite common and rudimentary, but the self-reflection and questioning they ignite within her raise fundamental questions of existence and belonging in the modern world.

Striking an entirely different tone, "The Troupe" relates the narrator's memories of her time in a provincial cultural workers' troupe (*wengongtuan*) around the end of the Cultural Revolution in the 1970s. This novella, written in 1997, loosely follows the gradual demise of the troupe through its unsuccessful efforts to negotiate a variety of shifting factors, such as competing with other troupes, pleasing the local leadership, recruiting the proper talent, finding appropriate materials, and selling enough tickets. Rather than following a coherent central narrative, the piece consists of a series of rich descriptions of several aspects of the troupe, which serve as section headings. The narrator's recollections are full of minor contradictions and ambiguities that mirror her conflicted attitude, which seems to hover between a warm nostalgia and lingering disgust. While the cultural workers' troupe was a specific form of government-appointed labor during a very particular period, "The Troupe" expands the context of its existence in a way that connects it to a longer history and a broader geography—though only the narrator's memory ties it to the present. Her reflections begin by tracing what she surmises to be the residues of Liuzi opera, the traditional local operatic form, through the troupe's older members who performed it before the Cultural Revolution. Although the city of Xuzhou, where the troupe is based, is portrayed as an uncultured outpost in the undesirable northern reaches of Jiangsu province, its proximity to Qufu, the birthplace of Confucius and origin of Liuzi, infuses it with a romantic sort of historical and cultural importance. The novella ends by describing the layout of the surrounding counties, thereby inscribing the troupe as part of the enduring physical and cultural geography. Without prioritizing a central plot, this work stands apart for its innovative narrative style, which experiments with a realist depiction based around the imperfect intersections of history, memory, geography, and subjective experience.

"Match Made in Heaven" (天仙配), published in 1998, is a substantial short story that focuses on the contested status of a revolutionary martyr. In the remote mountain village of Xia Kilns, a young, unmarried man is tragically killed in the process of digging a new well, and his parents are overcome with grief. To ease their suffering, the village head suggests posthumously marrying their son to an anonymous young woman who died decades earlier after turning up in the village as a gravely wounded soldier. However, when an old veteran cadre unexpectedly comes to town looking for the soldier's remains, the village head finds himself caught between his official obligations to his superiors and the moral and emotional responsibility he feels toward the parents who lost their son. The story is a touching and often humorous examination of the competing value systems that coexist in modern China, and the unexpected ways they can come into conflict with one another.

"A Girls' Trip" (2003) is another page-turner concerned with conflicting yet overlapping value systems that end up coming to a head in a rural village. Fentian and her friend Shui are a couple of fun-loving country girls who set off to visit Fentian's fiancé in the city of Xuzhou, but along the way they end up kidnapped and sold off as brides. The conflicts that arise as the two women struggle to escape their situations highlight the often-unanticipated moral, political, and ideological tensions surrounding this very real social problem—a problem that made international headlines in January 2022, when reports surfaced of a trafficked mother of eight kept chained in a shack in the outskirts of Xuzhou, the very setting of Wang Anyi's story. But beyond this, the story also perceptively updates and casts in a new light a series of the most common binary oppositions to be found throughout modern Chinese literature, including country versus city, tradition versus modernity, official versus unofficial, and individual agency versus fate.

The shortest story in this collection is "The Rescue Truck" (救命车, 2007), which is about half the length of the other two short stories. It describes a young boy's bout of typhoid fever and his family's experience as his illness fluctuates in severity. The narrative is framed by the boy's memory, beginning with the last thing he remembers before falling ill, and ending with his return to consciousness as he goes home from the hospital. While the story subtly depicts the perspectives of different characters and manipulates the overall perception of time, the narrative voice maintains a consistently objective distance that some critics characterize as "pure description." The inclusion of this relatively short and simple story serves as an excellent example of some of the basic components of Wang Anyi's particular art of realism, which are developed into more complex narrative forms in this collection's other works.

Translating these stories has presented me with the obvious problem—how could I presume the ability to convey Wang Anyi's works in English? I have gotten through only by reminding myself that on some level, the task is always doomed to fail. The fact that, in translation, the highest ideals must immediately coexist with an imperfect practical reality is stultifying, but also freeing. I have done my best to approach this task as a literary scholar and teacher, identifying what I see as the works' core literary and philosophical elements and remaining focused on transmitting these to students and readers in English.

At times, this has involved slight deviation from the conventions of standard English. For example, I maintain Wang Anyi's avoidance of direct dialogue, which some English translations, very understandably, insert into her works. Wang Anyi often relays speech by embedding it into the text, set off by a colon. While this is not an uncommon practice in contemporary Chinese writing in general, I feel this has major implications for the narrative distance Wang Anyi employs in her particular style of fictional realism. In the late 1980s, she consciously turned away from writing direct dialogue, which had certain ramifications: Rather than an immediately accessible presentation of reality, we are instead presented with an ambiguously mediated narrative voice. In a story like "I Love Bill," this is crucial. Ah San's idealized imagination of her Western boyfriends is not based on direct, objective reality, but rather a mediated version of it that is always already, to some degree, interpreted. Furthermore, in a more transparent reality, much of the dialogue would presumably take place in English, yet the narrative voice has already translated it into Chinese. In my view, therefore, the narrative presentation of this work is tantamount to demonstrating one of the story's most compelling ideas: how problems of translation, mediation, and interpretation can undermine presumptions of a universal modernity.

Another characteristic of Wang Anyi's writing is her particular construction of paragraphs, which often lead up to a final, poignant sentence or statement that crystallizes the paragraph's overall sentiment and connects it to the rest of the work in a particular way. Sometimes, the paragraphs get very long. While on the whole I have maintained the integrity of her original paragraphs, in the interest of accessibility, the longest ones, which occur in "A Girls' Trip" and "The Troupe," have been split into two.

Finally, Wang Anyi generally narrates from a neutral, nonjudgmental perspective, which often involves the use of a simple, common diction at key moments in the stories. Even something like the title "A Girls' Trip" might stand as an example of this. While my English translation risks sounding lighthearted and frivolous, the original title offers no interpretive judgment of what this trip (or "travel") is like. While it starts out fun, some really terrible things happen—but is it necessarily only a tale of woe? The challenge I found with this characteristic of Wang Anyi's writing was to maintain a simplistic neutrality in English while not devolving into a flat-sounding artlessness. Above all, I always tried to avoid words that might sound better, or more appropriately "literary," in English, if it meant inserting a certain judgmental implication that was not in the original. As a result, parts of the translations may seem overly plain or awkward, but my intent was to maintain Wang Anyi's unadorned neutrality over and above superficial aesthetic preferences of English that are external and unrelated to the original.

I am deeply grateful to Wang Anyi for not only allowing me to translate these stories, but also for her consistent willingness to sincerely engage in discussions of her own work in our biweekly workshops. I would also like to thank our co-organizer Shiqi Liao, the participants in these workshops, and those who participated in two related conferences at Duke and NYU, for helping to shape my own understanding of Wang Anyi's writing. The International Center for Critical Theory (ICCT) has provided me with crucial support in the project, both in material terms and for enabling me to present my work on Wang Anyi's writing at a number of international conferences. Two peer reviewers of the manuscript offered excellent insights and suggestions, and I am especially grateful for

Kirk Denton's careful attention and keen editorial eye. Many thanks also go to Alexis Siemon at Cornell University Press for helping this volume become a reality. I would never have been able to undertake this project without the help, mentorship, and guidance of Xudong Zhang, who has always been ready and willing to assist with anything, answering the most petty and technical of my translation questions while couching them in his singularly insightful and illuminating interpretations. Perhaps even more importantly, he has also managed to make this daunting and sometimes disheartening task fun and enjoyable. The same goes for Wenjin Cui, whose help and friendship has also been crucial for my completion of this project; her willingness to answer my text messages whenever a question would arise proved to be an invaluable and incomparably convenient resource. Finally I'd like to thank Patricia Foley, Larry Foley, and Lou Johns for their crucial support and patience. Sharon Ostfeld-Johns has made her mark on this volume as my most trusted reader and consultant, and I dedicate these translations to our children, Cliff and Pepper.

I Love Bill

I Love Bill 我爱比尔

A cypress tree appeared among the gently rolling hills ahead. It remained in view for a long time, for a while to the left, then to the right. Everything else was covered in fields of short tea shrubs, without a single person visible. The sky was vast, with only a few clouds. As the bus rumbled down the dirt road, Ah San looked at the cypress tree through the bars on the window and thought to herself: Actually, it all started with loving Bill.

That was ten years earlier, when Ah San was still a second-year art student in college. Back in those busy, vibrant days, Ah San and her classmates went to all sorts of exhibitions, concerts, and plays, from which they would draw fresh inspiration. They were always looking for a good time, wanting to see things for themselves, and possibly also try them. Ah San's major was fine art, and she got together with some artists from outside the university to organize an exhibition. It was here that Bill appeared.

The two other artists involved were her former painting teacher and her doting older brother. Both were about ten years older than her and had grown up during the Cultural Revolution. A feeling of resentment was unavoidable in their paintings, alongside a critical awareness. By contrast, people were drawn to Ah San's carefree watercolors for their aesthetic character. During the discussion session, Ah San's voice trembled as she explained that she painted simply out of happiness, which further intrigued people. She received quite a bit of attention. But of course, when the exhibition was over, it was all forgotten. The important part was Bill.

Bill was an American cultural attaché. The consulate always paid close attention to cultural events, so it was only natural that a young, energetic figure like Bill would turn up at Ah San's tiny exhibition. With his chestnut-colored hair and cheerful eyes, dressed in jeans and a striped T-shirt, Bill was the typical image of an American youth from the movies. He introduced himself as Bi Herui. This was the name given to him by his Chinese teacher, and he was clearly very proud of it. He told Ah San that her paintings had an avant-garde character, which thrilled her. In clear and precise yet rudimentary Chinese, he said to her: Actually, we don't need you to tell us anything; we saw what we needed, and that's enough. Ah San replied: I also only want what I need. Bill's eyes lit up, and he extended a finger and pointed forcefully, saying: That's the thing—if you go after what you want, everybody wins.

With this brief exchange they were connected, and both felt very happy.

Bill asked Ah San how she got her name.[1] Ah San replied that she was the third child in her family, and she had been called that ever since she was little. Now, she adopted it as her pseudonym. Bill said he liked it. Ah San asked Bill the meaning behind "Bi Herui," and he gave her a rigorous explanation: It's an auspicious name, with the character "he" (和) coming from the phrase "may harmony be taken as the highest principle," and the character "rui" (瑞) coming from the phrase "a timely snow promises a bountiful year." Ah San laughed as she watched these set phrases come out of Bill's mouth. Bill laughed, too, and added: I like this name. Ah San had the feeling this young diplomat was a little stupid—tease him, and he responds very earnestly; laugh, and he does too. She couldn't believe how easygoing he was, as if he were always fine with everything. She could also see that he didn't really want to be called Bill, yet she couldn't bring herself to call him Bi Herui, which sounded too inflated. So she said

---

1. Literally, "Ah Three."

to him: If you want me to use your Chinese name, then you have to call me by my English name. Bill asked what her English name was, so she quickly made one up: Susan. That's no good, said Bill, there are too many of those. Why don't I just call you Number Three? Ah San realized Bill wasn't quite as naïve as he seemed.

Just as he loved his Chinese name, Bill loved China: Chinese food, Chinese characters, Chinese opera, Chinese faces. Like many Chinese people, he had a bike, which he would ride fully merged in the flow of traffic. Now, with Ah San beside him wearing a backpack and riding a women's racing bike, it was as if she were following him to the ends of the earth. Actually, the two of them were riding so wildly it was as if they were racing. They ended up going to get a drink at a hotel café, the kind of place with a snobbish atmosphere. After a while, Bill went to the bathroom, leaving Ah San sitting there by herself. A woman approached her rather unwillingly with a drink menu and said: We only accept foreign exchange certificates.[2] Ah San remained stoic and didn't reply. After Bill returned and sat down across from her, the waitress returned but avoided Ah San's eyes. Ah San found it laughable. After a while, a bubbly woman came by and struck up a lively conversation with Bill, casting Ah San aside. Once again, she found it laughable. As she listened to Bill continue to sing the praises of China, she thought to herself: Your China is not the same as my China. She never expressed this thought, though, and instead only continued to encourage Bill's love for the country. She introduced Bill to some Chinese folk art, including local Shanghai opera and Jinshan peasant art. She took him to the island pavilion in the middle of the lake at the city god temple, and to Zhou Village to see the local dwellings dating from the Ming and Qing dynasties.

Zhou Village really fascinated Bill. Under his large frame, the small stone bridges seemed like a miniature world. As he walked over them, he attracted several people who followed behind. One was an old woman, who tugged on Ah San's sleeve and asked her knowingly: What country is he from? America, Ah San replied. The woman scrunched up her mouth and said, disapprovingly: A few days ago three British people were here,

---

2. Foreign exchange certificates were issued by the Bank of China from 1979 to 1995 and were the only form of currency foreigners in China were permitted to use.

and the camera they had was bigger than his; it was the kind you carry over the shoulder. At that point, Bill was chatting with two small children. They were telling him that the kitchen in the home of a certain local family had a river running through it, and boats could pass directly into it. Bill let them lead the way. The two small children walked in front, while some other children mocked them and threw rocks. Just as the pair were about to retreat, Bill took charge of the situation. He turned around and invited the other children to come along, which caused them to blush and then back off. After lunch, Bill and Ah San again appeared on Zhou Village's famous twin bridges. By that point, people were already getting used to them, and one person even asked if they had eaten yet. Although they had originally only planned on a day trip, they lingered on in the peacefulness of the afternoon. As the sun began to set, casting a golden glow on both the water under the bridges and the smoke from cooking fires, Bill was even more reluctant to leave. He listened to the shepherds singing their evening songs.

They decided they would leave the next morning.

The Zhou Village inn also probably dated from the Ming or Qing dynasties. It was structured with wooden partitions, and when the second-floor windows were opened, you could look down to see the street market along the river, much like the sprawling classical painting *Riverside Scene during the Qingming Festival*. Their rooms shared a partition, and they each stuck their heads out of their windows to chat and enjoy the view. The evening rays were very delicate, and the ripples on the water were evenly distributed in fine lines, like threads of silk. Bill recited "The Peach Blossom Spring," but Ah San didn't listen or offer a response. She was thinking of other things. Later, when the sky had become dark but the moon had not yet risen, and there was not even a glimmer of light, the two sat together for a while in one of their rooms. The mood turned gloomy, even tinged with a bit of regret. They each searched for topics of conversation in an effort to lighten the atmosphere, but, finding no success, they eventually went their separate ways to bed. Before turning out the lights, Ah San heard three knocks on the partition, so she responded in turn. This served as "goodnight," and in that moment it produced a feeling of mutual intimacy. Ah San woke up sometime during the night to discover that her room was very light, and she raised her head to see the moon illuminating the sky over Zhou Village. Bill is just on the other side of the partition, she quietly thought to herself. She could almost hear him breathing. But when she held her breath and listened carefully, all she could hear was the distant sound of a TV program. Only then did Ah San realize that it wasn't actually very late. In the morning, she got up and wandered around by herself. After strolling for a bit, she saw a figure standing still in the morning fog. As she approached, the person turned around and smiled at her—it was Bill. They both felt that being apart for the night was like being separated for years.

The trip to Zhou Village drew Ah San and Bill closer and established the basis for a relationship. Previously, they had merely been like two professionals forming a friendship. Now, as they once again sat at a bar having a drink, each knew the mood had changed. At one point, Bill ordered something new, and he wanted Ah San to taste it. As he extended the glass toward her, Ah San stretched out her neck and puckered her lips to touch the edge of the glass. Suddenly she raised her eyes to meet Bill's, and for an instant they both froze. In that moment, something important occurred.

Ah San had a pair of catlike eyes, which she would often squint to gaze out through thin little slits. Then, all of a sudden, she would open them, revealing them to be quite large and round. This allowed her to take on a sort of Oriental mystique. As her eyes now fixed upon Bill from behind her drapelike bangs, Bill's heart skipped a beat, and he was seized by a feeling of tenderness. The first time he hugged her and felt her small, soft, seemingly boneless frame, he thought it was almost as if she had turned into a cat with nine lives. When he told this to Ah San, she merely asked: Why nine lives? In the West, said Bill, we say that cats can die nine times. Ah San replied: Dying once is enough for me. Hearing this, Bill went to kiss her. He discovered her lips and tongue also contained an element of mystery, as if they were at once both open and closed. It was difficult for Bill to suppress his excitement; he wasn't sure how to handle Ah San. He had not expected that embracing this enigmatic body would be so tantalizing. Ultimately, though, he recalled the Chinese perspective on female chastity. He remembered a Chinese teacher who had once discussed the *Biographies of Exemplary Women* with his class, and it had left an awe-inspiring yet terrifying impression on him. As a result, he forced himself to calm down.

Ah San, who had gotten her hopes up, also calmed herself, but she felt uneasy. Had she done something wrong that made Bill lose interest?

Perhaps she had not taken enough initiative. They were both a bit withdrawn for the rest of the day, as if they each had something on their minds. When it came time for them to part, Bill rubbed Ah San's head, giving her the sense that he still had feelings for her. When she returned to her campus dorm that day, she sat under the mosquito netting and closely examined her body. Her investigation did not reveal any problems. In the shadowy lamplight, she appeared flawless and pure. Yet this also involved a contradiction, as it clearly indicated her inexperience. Is this what had tamped down Bill's excitement? At any rate, her body was eager to learn. She stretched out her legs, speaking to Bill in her heart.

The next day, Ah San got started on a new painting, which looked like a sketch of a mural. She drew a featureless woman with hair that covered her face and flowed down to become a lush cluster of small flowers, and a large pink flower assertively blooming from her private parts. Against a field of dreary, crablike bluish green, the pink flower appeared especially beautiful and tender. A week later she was finished with this new work, which she named *Ah San's Dreamland*. On a weekend afternoon when everyone else had gone home, Ah San invited Bill over to her dorm to show it to him. After he had looked at it for a while, he asked her a question.

I understand this painting has to do with sex, he said, but where does your perspective on sex come from? Because I know that Chinese people don't have this kind of attitude toward it. So it must be Western, but I know you've never been to the West, and I'm probably the first Westerner you've ever known. Ah San answered him: This painting isn't about sex. Bill seemed unable to switch topics and continued down this dead end: Maybe you don't think it is, he said, but in your subconscious, it definitely is. Ah San just laughed: You've got it backward—it's consciously about sex, but subconsciously, it's not. This answer confused Bill, and he forgot his original question. Then Ah San took a piece of silk clothing from the bed and used it to cover the white dress she was wearing. Let me demonstrate for you Chinese people's idea of sex, she said. She proceeded to grab a nightgown from her classmate's bed and use it to cover the silk garment, and then added a third item. Covered in these layers, all hanging at different lengths, she moved toward Bill and lifted her head to look him in the eyes: Now, she said, show me what sex is for a Westerner. Bill gazed at her for a bit and then went to remove her clothing, taking off everything down to her white dress; then he hesitated. But Ah San seemed expectant, indicating it wasn't over yet. So Bill went ahead and took off her dress.

Finally, Ah San said: Do you understand? A thousand rivers flow into the sea—this is my answer. Only then did Bill remember his question, although it had already been resolved. A cushion of art and theory had made up for Ah San's lack of experience, making Bill feel she was at once both naïve and worldly. Her body had a childlike quality, yet was so strong and supple, and she was provocative in a tactfully indirect way, which left a deep and lasting impression. Bill was beside himself.

When Ah San's body melded into Bill's, her mind was still her own. At one point she was seized with fear and felt that disaster loomed, but then pleasure returned. At any rate, it was extraordinary. The storm had passed, and her mind was quite clear. She saw fresh blood on her lower body, and she discreetly pulled a towel over it so Bill wouldn't see what had happened—the thought of which had never occurred to him. When she was alone that evening, Ah San felt a sharp pain, but it filled her with a sense of happiness. She savored it as a souvenir.

Later, Bill told Ah San that he was beginning to understand the ability of Asian people to experience sex, which was more sensitive and meticulous than that of Westerners. For instance, he had once seen some examples of classical erotica from China and Japan, and the subjects in them were always clothed during sex. Although it sometimes appeared quite heavy and cumbersome, it was still extremely arousing. Ah San described this as a splash of red in a field of green appearing more vibrant than a whole sea of red. The conversation moved on to the clothing of different countries, and both agreed that the back of a woman's neck exposed by the open collar of a Japanese kimono was more titillating than a Westerner's bikini. They then proceeded to make love in their clothes. The constraint tested their patience and made their desire surge that much higher. At several points as they stood facing one another, Bill would reach his hand into Ah San's clothing, the movement of its layers making her heart flutter. The small body underneath the clothing didn't know what spot awaited his next move. It was like an arrow drawn back tightly on a bowstring—had Bill ever experienced anything like this before? This can't be a person, he thought. It must be a phantom!

Rather than actual sex, Ah San was now more interested in creating the atmosphere. She employed a number of tricks, one after another. For a late bloomer like Ah San, her own desire was beside the point, and her only thoughts were on how to make Bill happy. When she was with the blond-haired, blue-eyed Bill, she had the dramatic feeling that everything unreal became real. This enabled her to realize an imaginary world, all thanks to him. She couldn't let him lose interest and go; she had to hold onto him at all costs. Ah San knew that when it came to making love, she could not compare with her blond-haired, blue-eyed rivals. There must be rivals vying for Bill, she thought, yet when she imagined them she didn't feel any jealousy. She felt she could overtake them with a different approach. Bill had once said to her: You're the most unique. Ah San was sensitive to the fact that he had not said "you're the best." She knew there was a difference, but she was unsure of how to overcome this gap. She would just have to try another approach.

They would usually make love on the weekends in Ah San's dorm. One time they rented a hotel room, but in that kind of place, Ah San was unable to practice her art. The room was too clean and orderly, and there was nothing available for her to get creative with. There was a bathroom, of course, but this was a whole other issue. Ah San became completely passive. She stood under the showerhead without knowing what to do, getting soaked by the water. When Bill handed her a towel she felt a twinge of excitement, but it was quickly tamped down by a feeling of dejection. Bill never took Ah San to his place, and Ah San prudently never asked, although it secretly bothered her. The dorm, however, had its merits: it was Ah San's domain, where she could do as she pleased and let her imagination run wild. Winter came, and because there was no heat in the dorm, they made love under heavy blankets. These were all fresh, new experiences she shared with Bill. As the afternoon light filtered in, she felt slightly dispirited, yet she also sensed they depended on one another.

A foreigner so frequently going in and out of a student dorm naturally attracted the attention of the school authorities. First the head teacher, then the dean's office, and finally the campus security department came to talk with Ah San, asking her to strictly uphold the school's code of conduct while also attempting to figure out the situation with Bill. Ah San didn't say a word, either to them or to Bill, but she quietly set about renting a private apartment off campus. The university was located in the south of the city, and to the south of that was a place called Huajing Village, where the villagers all grew chrysanthemums for a living. In recent years there had been a building spree, but the housing supply had outstripped demand, so the extra apartments were rented to people from the city with nowhere else to live. So, Ah San went to Huajing Village and rented an apartment. When Ah San got settled in and brought Bill to her new place, it was during the time when the villagers were drying the chrysanthemums out in the sun. In front of each door stood drying racks, all covered in white chrysanthemums. Walking past them, they entered Ah San's building and went up to her room on the second floor. Warm sunlight shone on the curtains, and the air was filled with the astringent scent of the flowers, making Bill feel drunk. Ah San had set up the room rather strangely: A double mattress was placed directly in the center, covered by a mosquito net that hung from a hook on the ceiling fan and flowed down to the floor. That's where they made love.

Later, Bill had Ah San sit on his knees so they were facing one another. When she was naked Ah San looked like an underdeveloped young girl, her arms and legs so thin it looked like if they were bent, they'd break. Her neck was also very slender, and her skin was as thin as a sheet of paper. Bill knew, however, that the heart inside this small paper person held a great warmth, and this was what he could not let go. He stroked her hair, thin, soft, and smooth as silk, and said softly to her: You're so different! It was as if her body had been created from some other type of material—a material so light and weak, yet in no way inferior. It was truly a marvel. Ah San looked at Bill and thought of an Albanian film she'd seen as a child called *The Bronze Bust*. Bill was the bust. Albanian films were the only Western films available in those days, so it had left a deep impression on her. She stroked Bill—it really was as if his muscles and bones had been forged out of bronze. But she could also tell from his eyes that the heart within this hard statue was soft and tender. As they looked at one another, they both felt as if they weren't really human—like they were detached from reality, both figments of the imagination.

At one point, Bill said to Ah San: Although your appearance is entirely that of a Chinese girl, your spirit is more like a Westerner's. This was the answer he had come up with for Ah San's mystique. Ah San smiled and said: I don't understand what a Western spirit is. Bill had no immediate response and thought for a moment before saying: Chinese people emphasize "the Way," but Westerners place importance on the "human." Ah San told him about the play *Autumn River*, in which a nun yearns for the mundane world and goes down from the mountain to seek shelter among the people. Bill listened intently and then approvingly exclaimed: It sounds like this story took place in the West. Ah San gave a snort of contempt: Everything good is in the West! Bill was once again flummoxed by her and wasn't sure how they had reached this point. But he did feel there was a misunderstanding between them; he was just unable to locate the crux of it. Ah San needed to be clearer on this than Bill, since it presented her with a troubling contradiction: She didn't want Bill to see her as a Chinese girl, but the reason Bill was attracted to her in the first place was because she was a Chinese girl. It was this paradox that made her behavior appear so indecisive. It also drove her to try her best to find a point of confluence between China and the West, one she might then use to mediate her contradictions.

Recently she had developed a keen interest in the choreographed fighting in Peking opera. She said to Bill: If we could somehow represent the characters' movements in *At the Crossroads*, what kind of painting would it make? She noted some of their specific movements and used traditional colors to paint the contours on a piece of white silk, which she presented to Bill on his birthday. Bill liked it very much, and used it as a scarf to wrap inside the collar of his down jacket. They then went to a buffet at a newly opened hotel.

It also happened to be Thanksgiving, so it was quite crowded. Most of the people were Americans, including several of Bill's coworkers, who waved from separate tables. Ah San had done her makeup in an exaggerated manner that day, and under her jean jacket she wore a men's chunky wool sweater that hung down to her knees. Below that she had on woolen tights and low cotton boots. Her hair was up in a bun, with some wispy strands hanging down. At first sight she looked like a classical warrior, and she attracted no small amount of attention. When the waitress came over to light their candle, she looked Ah San over with a penetrating glance so sharp it seemed capable of peeling away her skin. The waitresses at these places all had such fierce eyes. Ah San couldn't keep herself from smiling a little too broadly and producing some superfluous English. When she went up with Bill to get some food, she chatted with him the whole way, pausing only as she made her selections and then lingering for quite a while. Finally, she chose a small piece of cake and stuck a candle in it, which she had Bill blow out as she said: Happy birthday! Bill's head was spinning, and he stared at her and said: You're so weird. Ah San was sensitive to the fact that he had not said "You're so beautiful."

It was night when they left the hotel, walking down the street in one another's embrace. Ah San snuggled into Bill's down jacket like a little kangaroo. The sound of their playful laughter drifted up and down the empty street, and they each felt as if they were walking on air. Feigning surprise, Bill asked: Where are we? Manhattan? Bangkok? Kuala Lumpur? The Vatican? When Ah San heard this, she was so filled with happiness that she nearly forgot where they actually were and began fabricating her own bizarre-sounding place names. All of a sudden, Bill pushed Ah San away from his chest, took two steps back, struck a fencing pose, and said: I'm Zorro! Ah San responded immediately by putting her hands on her hips: I'm Carmen! They took turns fencing and bullfighting, zigzagging along the street. The streetlights cast strange shadows of them on the ground. A pedestrian walking past stared at them, and then turned back for another look. Neither of them noticed or cared; they were focused only on their own happiness. After frolicking for a while, Ah San once again burrowed into Bill's jacket. This time, they both calmed down and walked along quietly. Occasionally they raised their heads to gaze up at the dark blue sky, which was partially obscured by the crisscrossed branches of the trees. The air was sweet.

Bill started talking about his childhood. His father was a senior diplomat who had been posted to Africa, South America, and Asia, and Bill's childhood had been spent in these places. Ah San asked: Which place is your favorite? I like them all, Bill replied, because they're all different and unique. Ah San couldn't help but think of how he had said she was unique, and she felt hurt. So she forced him to come up with an answer for which place he liked best. Seeming to read Ah San's thoughts, he hugged her tightly and said: You're so unique. This time, Ah San put forward an unprecedented question: Bill, do you like me? I like you a lot, Bill replied. Because he responded so readily, Ah San wasn't quite satisfied, feeling that the moment she had so long prepared for had passed by so simply. Next time, she thought, I'll say the word "love." Bill would surely be more serious about love! Yet she hesitated about whether or not it was appropriate to ask about "love." Did their relationship have anything to do with "love?" Ah San wasn't sure what Bill thought; she didn't know what she herself thought.

After Ah San rented the apartment in Huajing Village, she saw less of
Bill. One reason was that it was too far, and another was that it was awkward for a foreigner to keep showing up in a peasant village. Each time he
went, it was a major commitment. Sometimes they even disguised him, allowing them to stealthily enter Ah San's room while avoiding the discomfort of the villagers' stares. After such difficulty getting inside, they would
often want to linger, sometimes remaining all afternoon and into the evening. Ah San was painting scarves for a silk factory at the time; each one
was different, and each cost ten yuan. Sometimes the four walls of her
room were hung with scarves that supposedly recorded the contours of
fight sequences from Peking opera. Their flowing lines encircled them as if
they were in the middle of a whirlpool. Other times, scarves that had not
yet been painted and were still pure white hung on the walls, while chrysanthemums bloomed outside on all sides of the building. This made their
bed appear like a giant funeral coffin. Ah San laid on Bill's chest, thinking
to herself: Even if I died now, I would still be happy. After night fell, Bill's
facial features gradually became obscured, but his silhouette grew more
distinct, like a statue of a Greek god. Ah San found this arousing, and she
kissed him. On his large frame, her kisses seemed weak and fragmentary,
making her wonder if she could ever win Bill's love.

You're my thumb, said Bill. Ah San was taken aback. She thought to
herself: Why not say I'm his rib? With these kinds of thoughts following
one after the other, Ah San became a bit shy, and she repaid Bill's affection with an increased indifference, like a form of repentance. Although
this now prevented her from broaching the topic of "Do you love me?"
she could still further explore the realm of "like." She asked Bill what
exactly it was he liked about her. Bill gave it some serious thought and
then replied: Your modesty. When Ah San heard this, the smile on her face
unconsciously fell. Bill continued: Modesty is a noble virtue. To herself,
Ah San said: It's not a virtue I like; out loud, she said: Thank you, Bill.
Her words were a little sarcastic, but Bill was too earnest to perceive it.

After Bill left, Ah San remained in the room. She didn't put on any
clothing, but painted her scarves in the nude, one stroke after another,
in order to pay the rent for this seldom-used room. When she thought
of the virtue that Bill had bestowed upon her—"modesty"—she couldn't
help but cry. Choking with sobs, she applied the paint here and there
all over her body with trembling hands. She was upset, but didn't know

whom she could vent her anger toward. Toward Bill? Bill honestly liked her modesty—how could she take it out on him? Then she would take it out on herself! To look at her, she seemed to have transformed into a calico cat—a brokenhearted calico cat.

These days, Ah San had been skipping a lot of class. Between painting scarves to earn money and spending time with Bill, she didn't have enough time. These two activities consumed most of her energy, and she always had to get enough sleep. Sleep was now how she used most of her daylight hours. She curled up alone on her big mattress, her ears filled with the sounds of the neighbors' voices while sunlight and shadows played over her face. She would usually begin to stir as the sky gradually darkened. Her lower eyelids were a greenish purple, and small bluish veins crawled up the base of her nose. If she were going to see Bill, she would have to spend a long time on her makeup. She started applying her makeup thicker and thicker, her small face becoming totally covered in colors. This was especially the case for her lips. The more she traced over them the bigger they became, until they became thick, sexy lips, bright red and glistening. Ah San was slightly nearsighted, and the light in her room was not quite bright enough, so she ended up with heavier makeup than she realized. She almost looked as if she were wearing a mask. Her clothing was also exaggerated. Maybe she would wear a broad-shouldered, batik-print suit covering a skintight white leotard. Or maybe a padded jacket with a high collar that buttoned up diagonally from the chest, paired with a long skirt that dragged on the ground and clunky, square-heeled leather shoes.

Then a school official came to talk to Ah San, informing her that she still had a year until she could graduate, and that she must diligently attend her classes. The next day, without a word to anyone, Ah San withdrew from the university. After that, she was never seen on campus again. One evening before the summer break, she quietly returned to her dorm to retrieve some things she had left there. A girl who lived in the same building saw her and didn't recognize her at first, but after a minute she was shocked to realize who it was. Seeing that she was gathering up her belongings and was about to leave, she asked Ah San if she knew. Knew what, Ah San asked. Knew that the school had expelled her, the girl replied. Whatever, Ah San said with a laugh—although her expression was a little downcast. The classmate offered to see her off, and Ah San didn't refuse. They walked through the deserted campus, each casting their own shadow under the streetlights. Ah San wasn't particularly close with this classmate, but they both seemed to be feeling a bit sentimental at that moment, so they continued to walk on in silence. All of the surroundings that had accompanied Ah San for the past three years were obscured in the dark, just waiting there in the shadows. Then, Ah San simply said: Why don't you head back now? Ah San continued walking for a bit, and then turned her head to find her classmate still standing in the spot where she had left her. She waved at Ah San once more.

Ah San didn't tell Bill about being expelled from school, which carried with it some pleasure of self-persecution. Her family, who lived in a neighboring province, also never found out. For a while she holed up in Huajing Village, painting scarves and sleeping. Even Bill thought she had left the city. This went on for about two months. Once again the drying racks were set up and the white chrysanthemums were spread out. The village was immersed in the scent of the flowers, and their petals floated in the air. Ah San sat alone in her room, far removed from the outside world. Bill was also very far from her. She painted a batch of plain scarves as if they were ink paintings. The only colors were black and white, and they hung on all four walls, like a meditation room. Subsisting only on bread and water, she also seemed to be meditating. When she finally ventured back out into Huajing Village, she was as thin and pale as a ghost. She was dressed in a white silk mourning gown over a white silk bodysuit, and the ensemble was cinched at the waist with some strips of white silk fabric. Her makeup was also incredibly light, and around her eyes she had used a smoky gray; her lips and fingernails were red. Her shoes were made from color-blocked patches, with white uppers and red tips that suggested red polished toenails. This was how she appeared before Bill.

Bill was shocked at Ah San's transformation. He didn't know how she had undergone such an astonishing change. He stroked her skin, and wasn't sure what it was made of—it scorched the palm of his hand. He didn't understand anything. This was a million miles from the flesh of the young woman with whom he had been so intimate, and he sensed a certain danger lurking behind that Oriental mystique. Yet his desire was ignited—there was something apart from her body that he found attractive. There seemed to be some kind of tragic element, as if they were facing a precipice, which infused his passion with a shocking force. This time, they were in the room of Ah San's friend, a divorcée who had knowingly lent her the keys. The friend's things were strewn all around them, along with photos of smiling women they didn't recognize and the scent of unfamiliar toiletries and cosmetics. All this gave the feeling that they were in some kind of trap. Bill had never experienced a woman so deathly thin as Ah San. Her chest and buttocks were nearly flat, and her ribs protruded like a washboard. It was not her body he was craving, but some kind of spiritual element. The clothes Ah San had removed lay in a snow-white pile, and her lipstick had been smeared all over her body from Bill's kisses, as if she were covered in bleeding wounds. The sense of danger grew stronger.

From somewhere in the empty courtyard of a distant apartment complex, the creaking sound of a swing set could be heard.

Bill gradually calmed down and looked to Ah San at his side; only now could he begin to recognize her. Ah San, he asked, what have you been up to these days? Thinking about something, said Ah San. What is it? Bill asked. Ah San said: It's . . . I love Bill. She turned her face away when she said this, and remained with her back facing him. A long time passed and the room had begun to darken, but neither of them had moved from their original positions. Finally, Bill spoke: As our country's consular officials, we are not permitted to fall in love with girls from a communist country. More time passed, and the sound of the swings quieted. Bill was nearly asleep. Dreamlike images passed through his mind that made it seem like he had returned to his hometown in the American heartland, where he had attended middle school among those boundless cornfields. Suddenly he woke with a start and discovered that it was already dark outside and Ah San was getting dressed. Her face had been washed clean, and her hair had been freshly combed. I'm really sorry, Ah San, he said. Ah San laughed dismissively: Bill, why are you apologizing? This gave Bill the feeling that he had become irrelevant. But what had just happened?

Bill and Ah San's relationship went on as if nothing had happened. Bill introduced Ah San to two tutoring jobs, one for Chinese and one for traditional painting. Her students were the children of some American CEOs, and the pay was not insignificant. Because she wanted to give a good faith effort, she was quite strict, but the children were uninterested, and even the parents encouraged Ah San to loosen up a bit. This was especially the case for the boy studying painting, who would gruffly seize the brush in his freckly hand and give it a full dunk in the ink. With a single stroke, the rice paper would be soaked, while the child's parents stood alongside praising him: Great job! So Ah San was happy to loosen up. Both families lived in the Qiaohui apartments behind the bustling Huaihai Road. Outside the building it was noisy and chaotic, but passing through the doors was like entering a different world. The air was completely different and smelled of a mixture of cheese, coffee, and vegetable oil, along with the scents of foreign toiletries and the slight odor of the wool carpeting. Now with these two sources of income, Ah San's economic situation improved significantly, and she began looking for a room in the city.

Eventually, she found a place in an old-style apartment block. It was a room in an apartment, the owner of which was away visiting relatives in America with no clear date of return. The arrangement was for partial rent in exchange for housesitting. In the larger portion of the apartment lived a nannylike woman, who was also responsible for looking after the place. Every afternoon she invited over some people with nothing better to do for mahjong, and they would stay well into the night. Because she and Ah San were each violating a certain taboo, they didn't have much to do with one another, and when they saw each other they didn't even exchange words. Ah San gave up her room in Huajing Village.

Now it was much more convenient for Bill to come visit. The location was much livelier than Huajing Village, and Bill often came during the day, when the city noise was at its height and there was a constant flow of people and traffic. The curtains were an old velveteen fabric with many loose threads hanging down, and merely bumping against them would cause a cloud of fuzz to float in the air. The floor was creaky and carried the scent of cockroach droppings, which gave everything an old, outdated feeling, as if year in and year out it all just sat there like this—a slightly nauseating thought. Ah San gave herself the task of dressing up the place. She bought a heap of silk scraps and made them into a dozen or so cushions, all pleated in an old-fashioned style. She placed them everywhere—on the bed, on the sofa, on the armchair. She bought a set of men's satin pajamas and wrapped herself up in them. Bill reached his hand inside and said: I can barely find you. When they made love in the soft, slippery satin, it seemed as if a hundred years had passed. The parents of one of Ah San's students had given her a coffee pot, so she brewed finely ground coffee, filling the room with a fragrant yet bitter scent. The owner of the apartment had an old-fashioned record player that had been broken for many years and that was stored under the bed. Ah San got it out and found someone to fix it, and with some effort it could be used to play some old, grainy-sounding music. Americans could never resist the allure of history; a half-century's worth of nostalgia was enough to captivate them.

They now found a new game, in which they once again played characters and changed their voices. This time they dressed up as ghosts that haunted old houses and produced strange sounds. When they looked at each other's faces, they couldn't see the real person at all. They thought to themselves: This is all so crazy! They were never very far from this "crazy." It wouldn't work with any other person; it had to be the two of them, Bill and Ah San. Sometimes they would stand naked in front of the window and hold one another. Lifting up the corner of the curtains, they would look over at the building across the street and wonder what was going on behind the darkened windows. Did it have anything to do with them? Although it was in the center of the bustling city, this world surrounded by old curtains and old wallpaper felt even more isolated than Huajing Village. Heading out and going to a brightly lit restaurant, they both had the feeling there was no going back. From across the table, Bill reached over and placed his hand on Ah San's and they stared into each other's eyes. Their gaze seemed permeated by the stale darkness of that old apartment, and it contained something profound.

If America changed its diplomats to China, Bill would have to leave her, but he didn't think about it. He felt only that he and Ah San wanted each other, and that they were very happy—this was the American notion of sexual equality. So Ah San kept herself from thinking about it too much. She told herself: I love Bill, and that's enough. She really thought she was happy—just look at her dance! Everyone watching applauded her spins, and she returned their applause. Whenever Bill said something funny, she laughed hysterically. When they were leaving, she climbed on Bill's back like a monkey and made him carry her. After a little while she got down and they switched positions. Ah San couldn't budge with him on her back, so he had to spread his legs and walk a few steps himself. As they walked along, Bill sang his university's fight song. Ah San was so happy! Surely no one could ever have as much fun as she and Bill.

But who knew what it was like when Ah San was alone?

In this gloomy apartment, everything was dilapidated. With such a high ceiling, when Ah San laid on the floor under a pile of pillows, it was almost as if she didn't exist—Ah San herself forgot that she did. She could lay there like that all day without eating or drinking, in an ambiguous sleeplike state. Without Bill, there was no Ah San—she both existed and achieved happiness because of him. Only on his account was this apartment infused with life; otherwise, it was no different from a grave. The white chrysanthemums of Huajing Village were now very distant. Back then, her love for Bill had been relatively mild; now it had turned much sharper. Ah San had a doll that wore denim overalls and had messy blonde hair like a haystack. Its hand was stuck in its pocket, and the headphones of a Walkman hung on its ears. On its back, she wrote "Bill." This was not to curse him, like traditional Chinese voodoo, but rather, to love him.

Bill's vacation was coming up, and he would leave in about ten days. I'll miss you, Ah San, he said. Ah San blurted out: Are American diplomats allowed to miss girls from a communist country? As soon as she said it, she regretted her pettiness. To her surprise, however, Bill laughed. He didn't detect Ah San's sarcasm, nor did he think of what he had once said to her. I already miss you, he said with a laugh. Ah San became more annoyed. Bill's heart must be so pure that it doesn't contain a trace of resentment, she thought. He might be older than her, but he was more childish. But such a big, grown-up child was so adorable! Ah San buried her face in his chest. The thought that they had grown so close but would eventually have to part suddenly delivered her an emotional jolt, and she immediately began to cry. Bill thought they were tears of happiness, and he started to get excited. This time, Ah San whimpered from start to finish, and Bill's excited panting mingled with her whimpering. His face became soaked with Ah San's tears, and her heartache also transferred to him. He also wanted to cry, but he thought it was out of happiness.

Before Bill returned to America for his vacation, the consulate was having a big cocktail party to welcome the ambassador, who had come down to Shanghai from Beijing. Ah San went along to join in the fun. As soon as she entered, she spotted Bill wearing a black suit and smiling broadly as he stood in a receiving line. His hair was smoothly combed and his face appeared bright and fresh. When he shook Ah San's hand and said "welcome," she felt as if they were meeting for the first time. Ah San was again dressed unconventionally, this time wearing lantern culottes with a pair of cloglike sandals, a wide silk scarf wrapped around her bare shoulders, and wooden "pearl" earrings. Her hair hung straight down to her waist and was clasped by a string of wooden pearls. Bill snuck away from his duties long enough to come over and say: You're really beautiful! This did not make Ah San feel any closer to him; on the contrary, it only made her feel further away, as if it were just part of his diplomatic pleasantries. As she watched the handsome and talented Bill socialize, she was intoxicated by his every movement—he was so good-looking! With a glass of white wine in her hand, Ah San stood by a table of hors d'oeuvres and waited for the welcome ceremony to begin. People stood around chatting in twos and threes, and there were also some people there by themselves, like her. She kept to herself, and no one paid her any attention. At this point, Ah San experienced a slight feeling of disappointment.

Although the last rays of the setting sun had not yet disappeared beneath the horizon, the lawn under the balcony was lit up all around. More and more people arrived, and it gradually became crowded. She recognized a few people from the art world. One of them, looking surprised to see her, asked: Ah San, you haven't left? To go where? Ah San asked. Everyone said you went to America, they replied. Ah San responded only with a laugh as the friend went on to tell her about this and that person who had gone to America. As they were talking, a small wave formed in the crowd as someone new arrived. It was a tall, thin woman dressed in a black skirt suit. Although she had an elegant appearance, she was waving her arms and talking loudly in a shrill, piercing voice, which made her seem a little crass. She was clearly a familiar face among that crowd, and many people came by to greet her. Soon a small group had clustered around her, like satellites in orbit. Ah San's friend told her she was a famous author, and that anyone who could gain entrance to her sitting room could also obtain a foreign visa. The Author brushed past Ah San as if there were no one there, leaving behind a heavy scent of perfume. Her laugh was piercing. The crowd followed her as she went, and even Ah San's friend joined the group. Only after they had gone by did Ah San see that across from her was a row of chairs containing a pair of former movie stars. With thick makeup and gaudy outfits, they sat there eating discreetly from their little plates. Others lingered around with plates in their hands, dressed casually for the most part, and looking indifferent—it was clear that they were from the tech world and had little interest in anything else. Ah San watched Bill from a distance as he stood in the middle of the lawn under the balcony, chatting with what appeared to be several female study abroad students.

The crowd gradually concentrated on the lawn. Now that the sky had grown dark, the outdoor lighting seemed brighter. The Author was also out there, and had become a center of attention. Inside the reception hall, only a few academics and old movie stars remained, along with Ah San. The greeters in their white uniforms casually got up, talking and laughing as they slipped across the freshly waxed floor. Someone's plate tipped, and an oily spring roll plopped on the ground; it was then picked up and returned to the plate. Ah San once again caught sight of Bill. Just then someone came over and started talking to her, asking her where she was from and what she did for a living. She recognized him as another consular official, although it wasn't Bill. At first she started giving some mechanical responses, but gradually she became more interested and started asking some questions in return. The official responded politely and then suggested they move out to the lawn to drink some champagne, where the table was. Once he had escorted Ah San into the crowd, he took his leave. Ah San realized he was making sure she didn't feel ignored—this was the work of a diplomat. Bill shuttled back and forth among the crowd, busy with the same task. Ah San's mood had been lifted a little, and she felt calm enough to go strike up a conversation with someone. She had a lively character by nature and her spoken English was very good, so before long she became quite a dynamic figure. Even the Author noticed and shot her a few glances. When the cocktail party was coming to a close, Bill came over to Ah San's side and asked with a friendly smile: Did you have fun? Lots of fun, Bill, she answered. She said goodbye to Bill and left the consulate. It was already rather late as she walked down the tree-lined street in the damp night air, but she didn't feel like stopping. She continued to walk, and all of a sudden she began to sing.

After that, Bill left.

Ah San and Bill had arranged that every week at a certain time she would wait at a friend's place for his call. The friend's place was just an empty art studio without a single piece of furniture, and the phone was just placed on the floor. Ah San sat on the floor hugging her knees and staring at the phone, which remained silent. The appointed time came and went, and still nothing. Ah San stared at the phone so long she began to feel it was a strange looking contraption—what even was it? She suddenly felt it was totally pointless. She didn't understand what this phone's relationship with Bill could be; and furthermore, what was so interesting about him? Did "Bill" even exist? Laughing, she rose to her feet, only to discover that her legs had fallen asleep and lost all sensation. After dragging herself forward a few steps they felt a little better, and she was able to walk out of the room. She placed the key under the doormat and left.

Sometimes Ah San felt a distinct longing for Bill, and she would revisit the places they had been together. But things were no longer so clear. Where was he? Everything looked the same as it had before, only there was no Bill. She had forgotten what his face looked like. Every foreigner she passed on the street was Bill, yet none of them were. She looked around her room in that old apartment. Scattered everywhere were someone else's belongings, the traces of a stranger—what did they have to do with her? Wasn't she only there because of Bill? She'd dropped out of school and was now all alone in this place—wasn't it all because of Bill? But what even was Bill in the end? She answered herself: Bill was a bronze bust.

Two strangers came knocking on her door that day, one relatively young and the other a bit older. Ah San asked suspiciously if they were looking for her. Yes, it was definitely her they were looking for. Their manner was friendly but determined, so Ah San had no choice but to let them in. After taking their seats, they told her they were from the Ministry of State Security, and that they wanted to ask her about the situation with Bill. Ah San told them that Bill was a private friend of hers, and she had no responsibility to give them a report. The older one said that Bill was an American government official, and that they had the right to find out about his activities in China. Ah San said nothing. The older one softened his tone and said they had no ill intentions, nor did they want to meddle in her private life. They only hoped she would consider her sense of duty as a Chinese citizen. Her relationship with a diplomat, Bill, had attracted attention, and there had to be a story behind it; naturally they had a right to ask. Ah San remained silent, and so did the two visitors, who simply waited for Ah San to open her mouth. After a long silence, Ah San said: There's nothing between Bill and me—there's really nothing. Shaking her head and choking up with tears, her voice went hoarse and she felt a sharp pain penetrate her gut. She believed what she'd said was not one bit wrong, not one bit. Between her and Bill, there was, really, nothing.

Not long afterwards, Ah San moved out of the room in the old apartment and rented a new place. It was along the river in Pudong, in one of the first buildings erected in this newly planned district. Only a few people had moved into the entire building, and the rest of the apartments remained empty. In the evenings, only those few windows were lit up; the rest were dark. The path leading up to the building was even more lonely and silent. Coming here after tutoring at the Qiaohui apartments in the noisy city center was like entering a different world. But who even cared? There was no Bill, so nothing else really mattered. Counting the days, Bill should have returned by now, but he wouldn't be able to find her; there was also a good possibility he would never even try. She just couldn't imagine Bill going by himself to that old apartment and ringing the bell, and then waiting for that nannylike woman to get up from her mahjong table to open the door for him. No, Bill wasn't such an ordinary figure. Ah San had decided to end their relationship; she couldn't impede his future as a diplomat. With this decision, she felt a slight joy of self-sacrifice. But then another thought quickly followed: What is there between Bill and me? There's nothing between us, so I can't say I've sacrificed anything.

Without Bill, the days passed one by one. The silk factory had plenty of her scarves and wanted to move in a different direction. Ah San was tired of painting them anyway, so she was happy to quit. Just then, some of her artist friends were getting together to put on an exhibition. She hadn't done any serious painting for quite some time, and she had a lot of fresh ideas, so she decided to redouble her efforts and enthusiastically threw herself into the task. As she stretched the canvas across the frame and affixed it with tiny nails, one by one, she was surprised to discover how familiar it felt and how nimbly she worked, as if by second nature. The joy of work swelled up within her, and Bill became an abstraction not even worth mentioning. The brush spreading over the canvas preoccupied her with the concrete details of her task, and everything else was secondary. If it weren't for rent and daily living expenses, she would have also quit her tutoring jobs. Now, when she finished up the lessons, she would race back to Pudong thinking of the unfinished painting that awaited her. There was a bit of warmth in her heart after all.

Ah San gazed at the lonely cypress tree on the hill and said to herself: Even if it had all stopped here and gone no further, everything would be fine.

She thought back to that time when her friends once again started coming over to her place, eating bread and canned food and drinking beer and Coke as they discussed the exhibition. Such freedom in those days! But now . . . she stared at the bars on the window and sighed. She had really taken things too far. What was her relationship with Bill? She never saw him again, and she never heard anything, either. Although the families she tutored for were Bill's friends, foreigners never asked about each other's private affairs; if you didn't bring it up yourself, the other person never would. Two years later, in the Author's sitting room, she heard that Bill had been transferred to South Korea—so seeing him again was even more out of the question. Ah San thought back to how she had received the news with an air of indifference. She honestly couldn't tell if she really loved Bill or not.

That Christmas Ah San still sent Bill a card, although she didn't sign her name or write a return address. She didn't know what he would think receiving such an enigmatic Christmas card. The exhibition that year fell through in the end. The main organizer had pulled out to go to France. While walking down the street, an older French woman had stopped him to ask directions, and she happened to run an art gallery; she recognized his talent and moved him to France. Actually, he was the only person to pull out, and it wouldn't have mattered that much. What mattered was that once he left, everyone else lost interest, as if they had all just seen their luck wave them goodbye. Of the foreigners walking down the street, young and old, you could never tell which of them could turn out to be your next patron. After the exhibition fell apart, Ah San's room was piled high with new works, most of which involved thick, heavy blocks of color concealing human forms, streets, and buildings. They were mysterious and eerie, and had the characteristics of all twentieth-century art—that is, the abstraction of form and concretization of thought, which made it all look vaguely similar. Ah San had seen and heard a lot in these past few years, and her thinking had expanded, but without practice her skills had become rusty. As a result, the obscurity of her figures gave an exaggerated feeling of abstraction, while the focused nature of her thought brought a certain clarity. It all appeared intense and penetrating, although certain aspects were lacking in execution and seemed a bit insincere. Sometimes Ah San would sit facing a painting for a long time and become confused, asking herself: Whose work is this?

By the time these paintings had accumulated a thin layer of dust, someone came. It was a local art critic. His articles were nothing much and his critiques were indecisive, but because he wrote a lot he had gradually become an authority. He was now acting as an agent for a Hong Kong art dealer, which allowed him to shape public opinion while also making inroads in the market. He came to Ah San's apartment in Pudong, looked at her paintings, and immediately bought one. He also engaged her in a discussion, which began with the question of why she made art. Ah San said she did it out of happiness. This was the same thing she had said years before, but now, having undergone careful reflection, she said it with more certainty. The Critic said: It's strange. You say you do it out of happiness, but your paintings convey pain. Ah San smiled and said: You mean you don't even understand this? Happiness and pain are in essence the same thing—they're both feelings on the verge of hopelessness. The Critic asked why this was, and Ah San smiled again: You mean you still need a reason? When things happen, they exist, and existence is reason. The Critic delved further: Why do things happen this way and not that way, and what exactly is the difference between this way and that way? Ah San said maybe there's a difference, maybe there isn't. Then they talked about whether or not there are concrete connections between things. The Critic thought that on the surface there aren't, but essentially there are. Ah San had the opposite opinion, saying that on the surface there are, but essentially there aren't. The Critic then circled back around and said: If everything is so isolated, how can happiness and pain be the same thing? This caught Ah San off guard.

Their conversation skipped around and never really got anywhere, although they both found it very interesting and even inspirational. The Critic recalled how timid Ah San had been when she first appeared on the scene, and he felt that she had since matured very quickly, to the point where they could now discuss theoretical questions. Where had she been getting her inspiration? As Ah San and the Critic talked, her thinking gradually became clearer. What she had at first seen as a confused regression in her new works, she now felt was what she really wanted to say. It was all so natural and spontaneous.

Two weeks later, Ah San received a check made out in American dollars. It was like a certificate confirming that her painting had entered the global currents and been accepted by the international establishment. Ah San was no longer an isolated local artist.

After that, the Critic became a frequent visitor. When they had finished philosophizing, he made Ah San paint, supervising her like a foreman. At one point, the mere sight of paint sickened her. But just when she thought she would secretly take the day off, the Critic came knocking. Suffering through this peasant-style labor saved Ah San from floating around in her rambling thoughts and rescued her from ennui. Her life became hectic, and she had goals. Her tutoring jobs had ended by now; she had fulfilled her duties, and the families were leaving China to return home. Ah San focused all of her energy on painting and looking at paintings. She rushed from one exhibition to the next, and even visited her friends' studios to see their new work and hear their new ideas. In class Ah San was never seen as an outstanding student. Now, though, her discussions with the Critic and her success selling paintings allowed her to see her talent.

How much paint Ah San splashed around during this time! She grew tired of painting those puddinglike blocks of color and the objects hidden in them. Instead she began to paint multitudes of lifelike, miniature people, bunched together like sardines and distributed over an intersection or a high-rise building on a reverse-perspective plane. It was incredibly time-consuming and tedious, and Ah San painted as if it were embroidery. The initial results were quite arresting—after being unable at first to clearly locate any person or thing in the painting, discovering this vivid and life-like scene was truly a joyful experience. These miniature people were all well-formed, deliberate, and completely adorable. They also conveyed the peace in Ah San's heart. Some disruptive things had happened, leaving in their wake a mood of thoughtful discretion. Time trickled by as she painted these small figures. Sometimes after a long stretch of painting, Ah San would raise her head to find that the sun had already set. Whistles from the ferryboats drifted over from the river, lending the evening a sense of timelessness.

Then the Hong Kong art dealer arrived and had the Critic introduce him to Ah San. It was only upon meeting him that Ah San realized he was actually an American who did business in Hong Kong. He didn't really understand art, but after conducting some research, he had predicted that after a certain number of years, works produced by the younger generation of Chinese artists would find a large global market. He accordingly made an acquisition plan, which involved specifically going after the works of unknown artists. What he wanted were Western-style paintings, not traditional Chinese ones. This was also part of his prediction—he felt that the craze for Chinese painting and folk art was only temporary, and that it didn't indicate Chinese artists had really broken out into the global market. Only those artists who worked with oil paints and had grown up with Western concepts could assume such a role. Ah San was one of them.

He invited Ah San and the Critic, along with an instructor from a foreign languages institute who could serve as an interpreter, to the Peace Restaurant for dinner. They had a wonderful time—the candles were lit, some old-time jazz was playing, and at a neighboring table a tour group from Western Europe sang along with the music. Ah San's eye's filled with tears as she looked out over the scene, dimly lit by the dispersed light, and she thought: It would be so much better if this American man, sitting in front of her and clumsily grabbing at things with his chopsticks, were Bill. This kind of evening seemed like a holiday, in what country was unclear. Ah San loved it. The American was a good bit older than Bill, well on his way to becoming an old man—but once he got a little alcohol in him, he became very lively. He liked to tell jokes, and when he finished one he would stop and look around to see everyone's reaction, like a small child who had done something good and was waiting for praise from the adults. His appearance had none of the shrewdness of a businessman; he even seemed to possess some of the romantic innocence of a poet. Although he was a little old, his spirit had not diminished; he was like a character in one of Shakespeare's comedies. It was as if their whole race had been specifically molded for a romantic drama. The only downside to the evening was the Critic's nervous discomfort. When he saw that Ah San could speak English so well and converse directly with the American, he began to worry that Ah San would ditch him as an agent and sell her paintings directly to the American herself. So the Critic insisted on making the interpreter translate every word Ah San and the American said. There were some jokes that weren't that easy to translate, making the interpreter hesitate, but the Critic would stare anxiously at his mouth as if some gold nuggets were about to come dropping out. Actually, everything Ah San said was about something unrelated.

The next day, the American came to Ah San's studio, the Critic and translator naturally following behind. When the American saw Ah San's paintings, the frivolity of the previous evening's dinner was completely wiped from his face, and he appeared serious and critical. He didn't say much to Ah San, but posed several questions to the Critic. Ah San listened off to the side. The American's questions had nothing to do with painting or art, but they demonstrated his knowledge of the market. These paintings are almost no different from Western ones, he said. If you covered up the signature, people could definitely take them for the work of an American artist, so how are they supposed to attract attention in the market? The Critic replied: For a young Chinese artist to have traveled the long road from the Western Enlightenment to the modern era in the span of ten years is in itself something worthy of attention. More forcefully, the American said: But what I mean is, if you covered up the signature, what is it that would make people pay attention to this work over another? In the West, there's already so much of this kind of painting. As he spoke, he took the painting Ah San had just finished—one of crowds at a department store—and placed it in front of him. Then he said: This could easily be taken as a painting of New York. Nowadays in our city, said the Critic, there are a lot of fancy hotels, and once you go inside you could be anywhere in the world. The American followed up: Yes, but once you leave—no, you don't even have to leave—if you just stand by the window and look outside, you can see that this is definitely not just any place in the world. It's China. Ah San couldn't help but secretly admire this American; he certainly wasn't as simple as he looked. He then concluded: At the end of the day, what Westerners want to see in a Chinese oil painting isn't the West. It's China. The Critic said dejectedly: What about batik prints from southwest China—aren't they more authentically Chinese? The American gave a magnanimous smile and said: We've already talked about this.

When the American came this time, he didn't buy a single one of Ah San's paintings, but he told her he thought she was talented and that he would still buy something from her. Later on, the Critic complained to Ah San that the American had gone back on his word. He had been interested in modern paintings from young Chinese artists at first, but now he was asking for something different. Ah San, however, said she understood what the American meant, it's just a bit awkward—when she takes up the palette knives, she has a different way of thinking; it's a problem of integrating form and content. The Critic wanted her to explain a bit more, so Ah San said: When I use a calligraphy brush on good quality *xuan* paper, my thoughts become concise and implicit. I'm writing an essay through subtraction; my world is Chinese and built upon brevity. But a canvas and oil paints make me see a world built on increase through addition; this world is exactly the opposite of the Chinese world—in the former everything is clearly visible, while in the latter everything is concealed. The Critic couldn't help but nod. Ah San continued: Chinese thought is like an inscription in bronze, while Western thought is an embossment. The Critic said: Then can you use palette knives to make an inscription? Ah San didn't answer. She felt she'd come close to the heart of the matter, but she couldn't quite get there—something had caused her thoughts to spring back.

This, however, did not stop Ah San from continuing to paint. She was determined to take a new approach. She made a lot of rubbings of stone inscriptions, carefully examining the strokes of the characters, as well as the marks of erosion. The ink in Chinese paintings isn't just black, she thought—it's a thousand different colors all together. So when she used colors, she did her best to make them strong and brilliant. Isn't Chinese art characterized by elegance? She would demonstrate elegance through garishness—wasn't there some room for this in the Chinese conception of art? She made room with her complicated jumbles. She believed these two extremes must have something in common. Her following paintings took shape with these thoughts in mind. There were still chunks and lines of color, taking tablet inscriptions as the basic form, with careful brush-strokes that were textured and looked like Hunan embroidery woven in all sorts of different colors. As soon as she finished one, even she would be surprised—but she was in no hurry to go display them, preferring instead to wait until she had painted enough to line her walls the whole way around. Then she would invite the Critic over to receive his guidance.

Ah San was now slowly but surely making a name for herself, and when foreign consulates held events, they would often send her invitations. She obviously never went back to the American consulate. She struck a match off the invitations they sent her, and as they slowly burned, it was as if a smiling consular official, ready to greet her in a black suit, appeared before her eyes—Bill. Actually, by this point Bill had already gone to Korea.

At these events, a crowd of people would form around her, giving her a status similar to that of the Author. But unlike the Author, she didn't have to make a show of herself, talking loudly until she was hoarse. She was young and nicely made-up, and she'd had some success in selling her paintings; on top of it all, her English was excellent, so she was naturally quite appealing. At first she could sense the hostility in the Author's eyes, accompanied by her redoubled efforts to exaggerate her position and prestige. Ah San couldn't help but feel pleased by this, knowing it was all directed towards her, and that it meant she had the upper hand. Then, the Author started cozying up to her. As soon as she went up to Ah San, it was like seeing an old friend—she complimented Ah San's skirt and bracelet, and introduced her to the people she knew. Naturally, Ah San was very friendly and asked her advice on a few things. In the blink of an eye, they became good friends, standing shoulder to shoulder before going entertain their respective groups. Several times after that they brushed by one another and exchanged knowing smiles. When the party was over, the Author invited Ah San to come over to her place.

The Author lived in the Western district, on the first floor of a foreign-style residence with a private garden. The garden wasn't big, but it was very neatly kept, with a few trees and a tiny bit of lawn. On that particular day she was throwing a masquerade ball, where everyone was supposed to come up with their own costume and also bring something to eat. Colored lights were strung on the branches of the trees, and a couple of beach chairs were set out. The Author was dressed up like a black swan, walking around in tight black pants as she greeted guests. Her husband went along with things by wearing a paper mask over his eyes and a sword at his waist—he was probably Zorro—as he busily rushed around. Ah San dressed up as a cat; actually, she just wore a paper crown on her head with a tail cleverly attached to her butt and dragging behind her, but this made the Author very grateful. Aside from a few foreigners dressed up as Chinese people from the Qing dynasty and a German guy wearing a Red Guard uniform, the rest of the guests were either not in costume at all, or they had missed the point and dressed up very nicely, with most of the women wearing formal floor-length gowns. To call it a masquerade ball was not entirely accurate.

As Ah San looked over the room full of people, she thought of something a friend once said to her: Anyone who could gain entrance to the Author's sitting room could also obtain a foreign visa. This explained the room's elite atmosphere. What sorts of figures were in attendance? There was a movie star; there was an opera soloist; the person playing the piano in the corner was an accompanist from the dance academy; there was an incisive essayist who had a column in the evening paper; there was a descendant of however many generations from Confucius, which was considered a real rarity in Shanghai; there were the offspring of prominent figures in the business world; and there was a young official from the municipal government, who had driven himself there in a car.

As the evening progressed, they started with drinks and then moved on to dinner. As they ate, a program kicked off with singing, storytelling, jokes, magic tricks, and people making spectacles of themselves. The party reached its climax and everyone started dancing, while some people went out to the garden to chat. As they talked, a line of people holding onto each other's shoulders came wiggling out through the French doors and circled around them. Ah San was the last person in the train, and the person at the head came around to grab hold of her tail. The colored lights in the trees began to sway, and the shadows in the garden became less defined. The train eventually became a bit disorderly, with people stepping on each other's feet, until one person finally stumbled over a chair and fell down. This helped wrap things up in the garden, and everyone started filing back inside.

The Author suddenly clapped her hands and asked everyone to quiet down so she could make an announcement. The cassette player was stopped, and the talking and laughter subsided. She pulled out a young woman who had been standing behind her and said: Next week Laura will be going to America. Everyone began clapping enthusiastically, and a jokester rushed over to the piano and began banging out the melody of "The Star-Spangled Banner." This young woman with the English name "Laura" now became the center of attention, and a crowd of people gathered around and peppered her with questions. A few words and phrases related to the visa officers at the American consulate reached Ah San's ears—there was a man who was easy to deal with, and a Taiwanese woman who wasn't; was it possible to avoid the woman and go on the days when the man was working? Ah San had perked up her ears to listen when someone suddenly pulled her tail. She turned around to discover it was the Author.

She handed Ah San a plate of cake and said quietly: Laura looks young, but she's actually over thirty—she hasn't had a boyfriend since returning from Yunnan, where she'd been "sent down," and she hasn't had much luck with work, either. She's going to America on a student visa, and her future is uncertain. The Author's face had broken out in a sweat, causing some of her makeup to run, and her complexion was a bit sallow; she looked tired. She devoured her cake like a starving beast, coating the corners of her mouth with white cream. She continued: Laura's father graduated from St. John's University, and their family was very rich, but after the Cultural Revolution they lost everything and were never able to get back on their feet. Then, using the spoon she was holding, she pointed to the German man dressed as a Red Guard: What's this Nazi asshole playing at? Not understanding what she had said, the "Nazi asshole" smiled and raised his glass toward them. Both smiled back. Ah San suddenly felt that she liked this woman. The Author swallowed her last bite of cake and wiped the corners of her mouth, and with an expression that showed she was once again rallying her forces, she took her leave of Ah San and went off to start brewing some more shenanigans.

Just like that, Ah San became one of the Author's most honored guests. Whenever she threw parties, she and Ah San would prepare for them together. Ah San was young and had studied art, so she had a lot of tricks up her sleeve. One time she devised a game—in addition to some food, each guest was also to bring a sentence written on a slip of paper. There were three requirements for this sentence: It had to specify a person, a time or place, and what they did. For example: Ah San, after eating dinner, painted a painting; Laura, on the bed, cried; Charlie, on the ice, went running. These sentences were then each cut up into three parts and gathered up. The game began and everyone sat in a circle; first the "person" parts of the sentences were distributed, and then the "when or where," and finally the "what they did." Everyone was once again holding a complete sentence, but this time they were all new creations with funny results. For example: Ah San, on the bed, went running. Beforehand, Ah San had encouraged some of the younger guests who liked to stir things up to write some crazy sentences in order to produce more shocking results. Each new sentence brought gales of laughter that nearly brought down the roof. Some of them made fun of people who were there, some mocked people everyone knew, and others ridiculed well-known government officials. When Ah San's turn finally came to assemble the three slips of paper in her hand, she read the result, but she was unable to produce any sound. Everyone held in their laughter and waited, thinking they were about to be presented with a particularly outlandish one—this was the orchestrator of the game, after all. After a long pause, Ah San began reading word by word: Bill, on a certain poetic evening, seeks Ah San's love. This was a real-life drama injected into an evening of fun; everyone was a bit disappointed, and there were a few polite laughs. The person in charge collected the strips of paper once more, shuffled them like cards, and then passed them out for a second round.

By the time the party was over it was already after midnight. Ah San didn't go home, but curled up on the Author's sofa for a few hours until the sky became light. Quietly she rose without disturbing the Author or her husband, who were both fast asleep in the next room. She grabbed a piece of cake and downed a cup of coffee, both of which were left over from the night before. After such a wild night there hadn't been time to clean up, and everything was a mess. The strips of paper from the game were still spread out on the tea table. She gathered them up, stuffed them in her bag, and quietly shut the door as she left.

There were only a few people on the morning ferries, and the steam whistles reverberated through the wide open space between the water and the sky. The sun had not yet come up, and a thin mist hung over the river's surface. Ah San's thoughts were a bit muddled, and she didn't quite know why she was headed home just then. Her ears were filled with the sounds of the river's waves, one after the other. The Pudong district gradually appeared before her. She stepped onto the dock. The sun rose over the horizon, and suddenly everything became radiantly illuminated. Ah San, though, felt tired—her eyes burned with a lack of sleep from the night before.

When she got back to her room, she bathed and changed her clothes, and then pulled the curtains shut and climbed onto her bed. The sunlight shining on the curtains made it look a bit like evening. Sitting there cross-legged, she pulled the strips of paper out of her bag, separated them into three piles, and played the game by herself. She selected out the strips of paper in order, put them together, read the sentence they made, and then shoved them aside to make the next sentence. Everything around her was completely calm. The few sounds she did sometimes hear in her building were absent—everyone who worked was at work, and everyone in school was at school. Ah San quietly arranged the strips of paper, waiting for that sentence to appear: Bill, on a certain poetic evening, seeks Ah San's love. She knew she wouldn't get it, but what would the other sentences be? Finally, the name "Bill" appeared; then it was "on the beach"; and finally, just two words: "goes swimming." What did this mean? Ah San asked herself. She gathered up the strips of paper and threw them off the bed. She yawned and began to feel drowsy, and before she could even get under the covers, she was sound asleep.

A new style of painting had quietly begun appearing in the art world—poster art. It took some of the most popular images of the time and carefully and realistically reproduced them, while making a few small changes. For example, DaVinci's *Mona Lisa* would get the two strokes of Hitler's mustache added to it. This type of poster art passed through intermediaries like the Critic and made its way to collectors overseas. The skills of realism required for this style made the artists hunker down to intensely practice up on their basic skills. Then this poster art moved on to photographs from the news, using the same methods to make slight changes, which made the element of political satire more prominent. It was as if Ah San had just woken up to discover this new direction. She felt like she had arrived late on the scene—how could she catch up and not be left in the dust? She ran from studio to studio and found that they were all brimming with excitement, finally marking an end to the previous period of apprehension and confusion. People were either anxiously making art or talking about politics. Lots of political jokes and rumors were circulating through the grapevine, and these became their creative materials. The most successful among them was a young instructor at the art institute, whose work had already been published in a Hong Kong periodical with its own special introduction. This artist, who was originally from the countryside, had an extraordinary imagination, creating scenes that hilariously melded Chinese history with modern society—for example, figurines of Qin dynasty terra-cotta soldiers as the spectators of a soccer match, with Confucius as the goalie and Rummenigge taking a penalty kick. He stayed in his messy, single dorm room painting around the clock, barely remembering to eat or sleep. The room smelled of paint and sweaty feet, along with instant noodle seasonings. He was effectively using his life of rural hardship to create a new artistic wave and march out into the world.

After running around to all of these studios, Ah San at first came away feeling a bit muddled, but then she slowly began drawing out the main points. Actually, all of this absurdity came from one main idea: the disordering of time and space, people and events. She looked through her old paintings—those tiny figures at the department store and the intersection—and decided to work from here to develop a new concept. She struck a new tone that was pretty and lifelike, and the results looked like they were on American Kodak film. Not only did these small figurines consist of all sorts of living creatures, but those in the most eye-catching positions were all figures of importance: They consisted of political figures, movie stars, celebrities, and religious leaders, from ancient times to the present, hailing from China and all over the world. All of their images were extremely familiar—they were constantly circulating in the media, and symbolized the trends of history and society. These figures were out on the streets then and there, busying themselves with the common trifles of their daily lives. Aside from biting satire, the paintings also conveyed a sense of something quite moving—it came from the careful and perceptive depiction of daily life, through a warm and gentle understanding only a woman could have. The Critic, however, was hesitant. He felt there wasn't enough critical edge, and that they were full of vulgar, commercial pleasure. He was unable to admit that in his heart the paintings moved him because many works find success by contradicting those very feelings. But in the end he decided he would still try, because who knows? These Americans could be so unpredictable.

A steady stream of weird paintings came flowing toward these dealers, and even they weren't quite sure what to make of them. Their critical abilities were under assault, and sometimes they had no choice but to ask the artists themselves for help. They would bring one artist to go look at the paintings of another artist, and vice versa, taking their opinions as consultations. At the same time, many artists were dispensing with dealers all together and engaging directly with the art market themselves. Moreover, some professional agents from overseas had been infiltrating the art scene, and they were naturally more experienced. Very quickly they crowded out those agents who had only recently gotten into the business; they didn't even need their help getting introduced to the right sources. As soon as they got to whatever hotel they were staying in, artists would appear at their doors. News of their arrivals spread like the wind. Unsurprisingly, the predictions of that American based in Hong Kong were pretty good; actually, it had all happened even faster than he'd anticipated, and within just two years the market had greatly expanded. Now, after these two years, he was shifting his attention toward Vietnam and Cambodia. The prices of paintings in Mainland China were far from what they had once been, and they were still being driven up further—even the most unqualified artists were asking outrageous prices, and would only take American dollars at that. Some of his old clients, including Ah San, would occasionally mail him photographs of their work, but with the sensitive nose of a businessman, he could smell that these works were becoming too trendy and commercialized, no longer possessing that innocent naiveté he'd once seen as their greatest asset. So now this art dealer and his pioneering spirit gradually and quietly moved out of Shanghai.

Things got very exciting. More artists joined the ranks of those able to sell their paintings, and the competition grew fiercer by the day, enveloping their workspaces in an atmosphere of anxiety. Some artists took the initiative and closed their studios to outside observers in order to prevent anyone from imitating the results of their own explorations. The new innovations all had characteristics that were easy to copy, and everyone was desperate to be the first. The day a new intervention was made was the same day it was buried, with a whole pile of similar paintings produced that drowned out its originality. Everyone was impatient and working as fast as they could. The poster art style had already become replaced by actual posters. These old posters, which came from who knows where, were cut up and pasted together to form new works, the stains and creases lending them an abstract meaning with unknowable depths. So collages became popular, and artists laid down their brushes, took up scissors, put their heads down, and got to work.

Everything depended on inspiration. A sudden inspiration had the potential to bring enormous success. Other than that, there wasn't much rhyme or reason. Theoretical discussions like the ones Ah San and the Critic once had were now not only irrelevant, but unnecessary. Now it was just like sitting in meditation: People felt anxious, but good ideas just wouldn't come. That rural kind of hard work and diligence was no longer of any use—the young instructor had already left his job, taken up a camera, and gone out traveling on a bicycle, leaving this noisy city behind him.

In the building where Ah San lived, workers were constantly coming in to do renovations, and the clanging and banging went on all day long, with all the weird sounds of hammer drills and electric planers. Ah San had no choice but to clip a Walkman at her waist and cover her ears with the headphones. But this wasn't enough—she still got a headache from all the noise. To really get away from it, she had to go out; there wasn't much she could do in her room anyway, and it had already been quite some time since she had done a painting. It seemed like everything she should paint, she'd painted—what was she supposed to do now? She had already gone through several periods when she had lost sight of her goals, but each time she would reach a turning point, opening up a sunny new vista. She believed this time would be no different, so she didn't feel as worried as she had in the past. But when would the next turning point come? She couldn't force it, so all she could do was wait.

Ah San's building was surrounded in all directions by a construction zone, where new buildings were constantly springing up from the leveled ground. In no time at all, it became a large-scale residential neighborhood. As Ah San walked along the dirt paths that skirted the construction sites, looking down at the tips of her shoes as she went, she noticed that she was trampling some grass and tiny flowers into the mud. Another spring had come, she realized. The sparse yellow flowers of the winter jasmine swayed in the chilly breeze. The heavy dampness in the air was also a sign of spring. Ah San's mood lightened, and she felt a little better.

When she came to the end of the dirt road, she was in no hurry to turn around. Instead, she walked right into the section of land that had just been cleared. A small village factory had just relocated from the site, and the tire tracks from the graders and other vehicles were still visible in the dirt. Just then, Ah San noticed a strange image on the ground: a dozen or so knitted gloves lay squashed in the mud, creating a pattern of evenly distributed crisscrossing lines, with little braided flowers lending them a crude sort of elegance. Ah San stopped in her tracks, and as her eyes lingered on the sight, she thought: This is truly a case of wearing out your shoes in search of something, and then finding it by chance when you least expect it.

Ah San withdrew from the empty lot, then turned around and walked back. She understood what she wanted to do. There was once again a whole pile of things waiting for her, and she had to get busy.

Ah San's studio became a manufacturing workshop. She would concoct a kind of mortar out of her paints and oils and spread a thick layer over the canvas; then, before it dried, she would haphazardly sling on a knit glove or sock, press it in, and then slowly peel it off to leave its impression. The details of their distribution and overlap depended entirely on her arbitrary tosses. The final products gave the impromptu feeling of a Chinese ink-splash painting, as well as a certain fatalistic philosophy;

they also gave the sense of a game. Some socks and gloves would end up getting thrown in the same place, while others would nearly miss the painting entirely—this was fate. Ah San called this collection *Labor*. The contradiction was intentional—they were clearly playful, yet she called them "labor." As soon as these paintings emerged from Ah San's studio, they began circulating among the artist community. For a short period afterward, a swarm of similar works appeared. Of course, the styles of the impressions were all unique, and they were done in all sorts of colors and designs; some showed even more ingenuity. The painting that garnered the highest price in Ah San's collection was two square meters and covered with sharp impressions left by bricks, stones, tiles, and other debris; its title was *Primitive Society*. A close examination would have revealed this as the source of all Ah San's painting. But everyone was busy and impatient—who had time to really get to the bottom of things?

Of course, there were also times when Ah San built upon the primary sources of others—those collages, for instance. Her own take was to use calendars, so she collected some with pictures of beautiful women and set to work. So, on the matter of originality, her accounts couldn't be so neatly settled.

Ah San's impressions in paint actually opened up a new path, which was a turn toward sculpture. Gradually, people were no longer content to merely make impressions on the canvas, and the actual objects themselves began to take center stage. Old rags and worn-out shirts began to appear on paintings, along with even bigger things like tea kettles, aluminum pots, tongs, and straw hats. The items became more and more varied. These sorts of works presented commercial art collectors with some difficulty. At the same time, however, some art dealers started reporting back good news to certain artists about their commercial success overseas. Holding an international exhibition was every artist's dream.

Ah San started hunting around for this kind of opportunity. She mailed photographs of her work to the cultural departments of a number of foreign consulates, as well as to some dealers she knew. She knew full well this would not yield any results, but it was better than nothing. A short while later, she launched a second assault. She cut out the middleman and dealt directly with the dealers, arranging their accommodations and accompanying them to go look at paintings, go sightseeing, and buy things. This is how she met the French art dealer Martin. Martin had a gallery in a small town in eastern France near the border with Germany, and he didn't know much about China. Ah San was the first Chinese artist he'd met.

Martin's town was rather out of the way, with a population of several thousand. The gallery had been established by his grandfather. As it was for many French people, art was simply a part of his life, not seen as some superfluous luxury. The gallery had two floors: The first floor was the owner's private collection, while the second floor featured rotating exhibits. In the past, Martin's family had never expected it to earn any money—it was just part of the family's assets, which at the same time provided their town with some culture. By Martin's generation, however, the situation was a little different. He had gone to college in America and studied communications at a west coast university. He was ambitious, but also sensible. Returning to the peaceful seclusion of his hometown made him want to do something to connect it with the rest of the world. He decided to use the gallery for that.

Just as the church provided Europeans with their first lesson in Western art, Martin's first insights into Eastern culture came in Chinese restaurants. Those soaring, magnificent cathedrals, with their imposing beauty and decorations so garish they were elegant, accorded with Martin's appreciation of extravagance. Chinese food was also rich and colorful, and had its own ornate style. In stark contrast, the yellow-skinned faces of Chinese servers were uniformly stiff, cold, and expressionless; under the resplendence of the tasseled lanterns, they were a bit like figures in a Ingres painting. When Martin was studying in America, he met a student there from Mainland China—after meeting him, and another few twists and turns, Martin had now arrived here, in front of Ah San. By this time he was twenty-four, three years younger than her.

Martin was tall and thin, and his neck and wrists stuck out quite a bit from his buttoned-up collar and cuffs, making him look like a middle schooler who had just gone through a growth spurt and couldn't find any clothes that fit. His white skin had been turned red by East Asia's summer sun. In an attempt to cool down he was constantly drinking Coke, which would cause him to burp and then say "sorry." Even though he had been to Paris, New York, and Los Angeles, the crowds and chaos of Shanghai still shocked him. As soon as he left his hotel he would lose his bearings, so he'd spent the two days prior to meeting Ah San holed up in his hotel room watching TV. So when Ah San appeared—speaking fluent English, no less—Martin immediately felt like he had come upon a familiar face in a distant land. They left the hotel and went all over the place. By the end of the day, Martin was thoroughly sunburned.

Strictly speaking, Martin was really a country bumpkin who hadn't actually seen that much of the world. He kept right on Ah San's heels, afraid he might get lost. When it came to spending money, he was also quite stingy—they would always eat at one of those little hole-in-the-wall restaurants and then return to his hotel before dinner, shaking hands and saying goodbye in the lobby before Ah San was dismissed. It was hard to say how much he understood about art, let alone how much he really enjoyed it. Ah San was particularly surprised that he had basically no opinions on Western modern art, and even seemed a little bit ignorant of it. This made her feel more confident when she was with him. After she'd accompanied him around the city for three days, she took him over to Pudong. As the ferry gradually pulled away from the riverbank, Martin stood on the deck looking back at the buildings clustered along the Bund and said: It looks a bit like the Seine. It was only then that Ah San realized Martin was a young man from France.

When Martin looked at Ah San's paintings, his expression became thoughtful and serious. Up until this point he'd remained rather shy and timid, having felt dependent on her. He sat on the floor, and Ah San put a painting in front of him; after a while he lightly flicked his can of Coke, indicating he was finished, and Ah San switched the painting with another one. He didn't utter a peep, nor did he take a drink of his Coke or burp; he just concentrated on the painting. Ah San couldn't help but feel a little uncomfortable. She restrained herself from looking into Martin's light blue eyes, which seemed to contain something fatalistic. She had not initially thought of Martin in that way, but now things were a little different. This grandson of a French gallery owner had a natural grasp of art, though he was unable to put it into words. Starting from Michelangelo, the history of European art ran through his people's veins—like someone with rigid morals making clear distinctions between right and wrong, they could clearly appraise the authenticity and value of art.

By nine o'clock in the morning the sun was already blazing hot, and the electric fan was busily oscillating around in a futile attempt to dispel the heat. A patch of sunlight shone directly on one side of Martin's face, which was dripping with sweat, though he didn't realize it.

He had seen all of the paintings. He took a drink of his Coke, and then another, and then finished the rest of the can. When he raised his head to look at Ah San, that shy expression of dependence had returned to his face. He said: Do you have any more paintings. The words delivered Ah San a jolt. No, she stiffly replied. Martin lowered his head, looking as if he had done something wrong but with no way to make up for it. You're very talented, he said after a pause. But painting is not like this. Ah San nearly began to cry, and then she almost started laughing. He had never painted anything himself, she thought, So what was the basis for this judgment? In a sarcastic tone, she asked: Really? What should painting be like? Martin raised his eyes, bravely looked directly at Ah San, and very honestly said: I don't know. Once again, Ah San didn't know whether to laugh or cry. But deep down in her heart, in a well-hidden place, she knew Martin was a little bit right—and that was precisely what made her feel afraid and under attack. She was sitting on the floor as well, but in a different corner. Hot air gradually seeped into the room, and the breeze from the fan was hot, too. Martin reached into his backpack and pulled out a can of Coke, but just as he was about to pull back the tab, Ah San stopped him. I'll get you a cold one, she said. She got up and went to the refrigerator to get them each a can. When Martin took his from her, he flashed a clever yet innocent smile. Ah San felt embarrassed she'd been angry.

I'm as hot as a dog, said Martin as he stuck out his tongue and panted. Ah San responded in a huff: You're a dog that bites people. They both laughed. They each began to feel a sense of mutual understanding, which seemed to bring them closer together. For lunch that day, Ah San made instant noodles, to which she added two eggs and a handful of garlic sprouts. After lunch they felt a bit sleepy, and they dozed off in their respective corners after some intermittent conversation. They had made it through the hottest part of the day, and now that the sun had moved further to the west, the air became a little less suffocating. The sound of a tamping machine started up in the distance. Finally, the glow of the sunset appeared on the horizon. It was first concentrated in a ball, which then began to break open and spread its rays across the sky, filling it with magnificent colors. This looks like the sky in my hometown, said Martin. He then proceeded to describe what it was like there: winding cobblestone streets lined with small shops, umbrellas, and ice cream vendors.

Customers could ring a bell, and the owner would come out to do business. The town had a central square where farmers would come early in
the morning to set up stands for selling produce and flowers. On evenings
during holidays, young people would come out and dance in the square,
and a town band organized by the locals themselves would play music,
which would go on all night long. Almost everyone there knew each other;
their families had lived there for generations, and some people had never
left. You know, Martin said, France and China are the same—they are
both old countries with people who never leave, which allows us to maintain a sense of home. Finally, after he moved on to talk about his family's
gallery, the two of them fell into silence.

After a while, Martin said: Where I'm from, we're all a bunch of country folk, and we like things that are original. Things that are original?
Ah san asked, but she felt a sense of what it meant as she spoke. Martin
stuck his hand out in front of him and grabbed the air. It's whatever
I can feel with my own hand, he said, not what other people have told me.
Ah San also stretched out a hand and touched the wall beside of her: What
if you're feeling the thing next to it—does that count? That would require
us to use our hearts, said Martin, and the heart is more powerful than the
hand. What about the brain? asked Ah San. Is the imagination necessary?
We must imagine things that are original, Martin replied. A bit confused,
Ah San asked: So whatever can be touched by the hand, and also imagined, is something original? Martin laughed, and his sunburned face suddenly glowed with a pure light: What our hands can touch is something
original for us; what we imagine is something original for God.

Now, Ah San felt like she and Martin had grown further apart—a giant
had come between them, and that was God. This gave them an essential
difference. For Martin, everything was simple and clear, but for Ah San, it
was all muddled and confused. She couldn't help but envy Martin, but she
knew she could never be like him, and that made her sad.

That evening, they took the ferry over to Puxi and found a noodle
restaurant deep in a winding *longtang*. The restaurant was located in the
sitting room of a traditional *shikumen*-style residence, with a table set
out in the courtyard and a light with a metal shade illuminating the front
door. Above the restaurant and on both sides people were going about
their daily lives—all of them had eaten dinner already and were watching
their TVs, which were all on different channels; the racket from the TVs

mingled with the whirring of their electric fans. People had moved their wooden benches out into the *longtang* to enjoy the cooler air, and they were either chatting or playing chess. At the restaurant, each person was eating a bowl of noodles with shredded pork and vegetables, and for those who wanted beer, the owner would send one of the neighbor's children to go buy some at the *longtang's* entrance. The customers would clink their glasses and exchange a knowing smile. That day, even though there was no definitive outcome, Ah San and Martin felt very content. They had become friends.

When it was time for them to part ways on the Bund, Ah San, like always, held out her hand for a shake, but Martin said: No, we should do it the French way. As he said this, he moved in toward Ah San and kissed her on each cheek. She watched as his long, thin frame bent over and squeezed into a small Xiali car, which then drove away and melted into the light of the streetlamps at dusk. Ah San didn't return to Pudong, but instead turned around and hopped on a bus headed into the city.

The air conditioning was on in the Author's home, and as soon as Ah San entered she felt a penetrating coolness that made her feel at ease. The Author was home alone watching TV in her pajamas, and she asked Ah San why it had been so long since she had stopped by—had she been off on some adventure? Ah San didn't say anything but instead downed glass after glass of water; the noodles she had just eaten contained too much MSG, and she was only just now feeling the effects. When she finished drinking her water, she put down her glass and asked the Author a question about religion: Where is God? The Author responded jokingly: You're asking me? Maybe I should ask you. Ah San felt a little embarrassed, like she was putting on some kind of act. This was the great thing about the Author: She was never fake. The Author then continued to press Ah San on whether she'd had some adventure. Ah San really wanted to talk with her about Martin, but as soon as she opened her mouth, what came out was Bill. Did you know Bill? she asked. That cultural attaché at the American consulate? Of course, said the Author, he was transferred to South Korea ages ago. I was with him for a while, said Ah San. How else could my English have gotten this good? It's all thanks to him.

The Author became serious and listened attentively. Ah San's eyes flashed with excitement as she told about her love affair with Bill, almost as if she were telling a story about someone else. From time to time she would repeat the phrase: *How should I put it?* She really couldn't find the right words to realistically describe this romance in a way that sounded convincing. It all sounded like she was describing a play—only the very end was believable, when Bill said: Consular officials from our country are not permitted to fall in love with girls from a communist country. This part was absolutely true, and because of that, the Author believed Ah San's story.

When Ah San had finished talking about Bill, a feeling of emptiness suddenly took hold of her. With a sense of dread, she thought to herself: She was now left with nothing at all. What if nothing new ever happened? Or what if she really was able to forget Bill? Feeling depressed, she curled up on the sofa and didn't say any more. She was tired from running around in the heat these past few days, and her throat had begun to hurt. Afraid she was getting sick, she asked the Author for some herbal tablets. As the Author gave her the medicine, Ah San looked up at her with pitiful eyes and asked: Do you think I'll be able to leave some day?

The Author pressed the tablets into Ah San's hand and returned to her seat: Leaving, what's so great about leaving? After a pause, she softened her tone and said: Ah San, I've got two phrases for you—if you try to grow flowers, they won't bloom. But if you randomly stick a willow twig in the ground, it will grow into a huge shade tree.

The next day, Ah San went to Martin's hotel. Martin was already waiting in the lobby, and when he saw her, he happily rushed up to greet her. By the end of that day, Ah San felt that Martin had grown a bit closer to her, and she was touched. Martin grabbed her hand and asked where they were headed. He felt that Ah San had the authority to arrange everything for him. At first, she had intended to keep Martin from meeting any other artists, but after yesterday, she changed her mind. She knew that Martin didn't really enjoy these kinds of artists—he was different from the other art dealers she had met, and there was no need to monopolize him. Furthermore, Martin had spent so many francs to come to China that she felt she should let him see a few more things and not seem so petty. So she announced to Martin that today they would go look at paintings by some other artists. With that, they set out.

How did Martin compare to Bill? Ah San asked herself. In this region, with its tall, lonely cypress trees dotting the hillsides, Bill and Martin both seemed so hazy and indistinct. It was as if they were just two ideas with no real form. Ah San shifted her body, feeling tired from sitting so long on the bus with such monotonous scenery. Then she noticed that the two female labor reform prisoners sitting across the aisle from her had strange smiles on their faces. Unthinkingly she followed their downward glances and saw one of them secretly making an obscene gesture. Ah San felt sick and averted her eyes. In fact, though, while she was in the detention center, she had already gained some idea of the life that lay ahead of her, and she had prepared herself.

Through the darkness, Martin's eyes appeared. There were no other blue eyes quite like them. Bill's eyes were that typical, deeper color of blue, like the kind written about in poetry, but Martin's were so light they were nearly transparent. Both men were tall and sturdy, but Bill was very well proportioned, as if each part of his body had undergone rigorous training to make it develop perfectly and evenly. Martin, on the other hand, was like a tree that had just sprouted directly up from the ground—a bit gangly and crooked, but very strong. Bill was naturally more handsome, like a Hollywood star, while Martin was closer to nature and something more essential. It was as if Bill had grown from an embryo in a test tube, while Martin was the fruit of a thousand generations. But it was precisely because Martin was such a natural being that Ah San felt they lacked a certain mutual understanding. His attraction was also based on this unfamiliarity. Bill's world was big, open, and exciting, while Martin's was peaceful, remote, and isolated, and the road to get there was much more winding.

Their love blossomed in their final three days together. Their relationship could definitely be considered love. Each of these three days they grew closer to one another. This was especially true for Martin—because he knew they would part, the feelings he showed were even stronger. Ah San was more optimistic because she placed more hope in her efforts. She stayed the night in Martin's room, the "do not disturb" sign hanging on the door from evening until the following afternoon. Martin was just traveling, and he knew this love would never lead to anything. He was always clinging to Ah San and saying "I love you," as if love could save everything. Ah San thought about how long she had waited for Bill to say these words, but now she was hearing them from Martin—the people and the circumstances were all different. In her heart, though, she was still happy. She believed in love, and if it didn't happen with Bill, it was because what Bill felt for her was not love—but, "Martin loves me."

They loved each other in every way; then they became tired and fell asleep. Sometimes Martin would open his eyes and gaze at Ah San's Chinese face in the dim light filtering through the curtains. It was small and delicate, her dainty nostrils fluttering imperceptibly, making the flat outline of her face suddenly come to life. He thought of the Chinese restaurant in his faraway hometown, where there was a traditional ivory carving of a beautiful woman. Chinese faces are particularly suitable for sculpture—among their subtle features lies a feeling of purity that is understated, yet profound. He really loved her—he couldn't keep from kissing her. His kisses woke her up, and they became entangled once more—it was never enough.

Despite their three nights together, Ah San still felt her romance with Martin was primarily on a spiritual level, which maintained a particular sense of purity. They slept in each other's embrace like a big sister holding her younger brother, and they held hands in the same manner as they strolled down the street. Martin's large hands revealed his devotion. He was clumsy, and because he knew he was clumsy, he was always trying to be careful. Simply based on his hands, Ah San knew: "Martin loves me." Looking at his excessively gangly limbs, Ah San couldn't help but tickle him; this made him start thrashing around like someone who had just fallen into the water, and he ended up knocking everything nearby onto the floor. Ah San laughed and said: There's an old saying in China—a man who fears tickling fears his wife. I'm not afraid of any wife, Martin replied with a laugh. I'm afraid of Ah San. Hearing this, Ah San's heart sank. Just as her thoughts had turned elsewhere, Martin went to tickle her, but did not get the expected reaction. He felt a bit disappointed, but coming into contact with Ah San's body made him gentler. He embraced Ah San and looked into her eyes. Those eyes, like the delicate carvings of a sculpture, wore an ambiguous expression he could not understand—this moved him, and he once again began to feel sentimental.

He held Ah San, and Ah San held him—they both felt impassioned, but their reasons were different. Martin was embracing a moment, but Ah San was embracing her whole life. Martin wondered how he could feel so strongly for this Chinese girl, even when her painting was so completely misguided. Ah San wondered how this French guy made her want to try once more to be an upstanding person—if he destroyed her views on art, she could just stop painting. One knew that everything would eventually come to an end, while the other wondered if everything was about to begin—yet the bitter anxiety they felt was the same. As Martin looked at Ah San, he felt like she was drifting further and further away from him, like an illusion he could never grasp. As Ah San looked at Martin, he seemed to be growing closer to her—she saw him in her life; she couldn't live without him. Ah San, said Martin, you're my dream. Martin, replied Ah San, you're my reality. They each slightly misunderstood what the other said, immersed in their own thoughts and worried by their own feelings.

The sun gradually set, and then gradually came up again, slowly collecting its light from one fixed point in the room and transferring it to a different one; despite the curtains hanging over the window, it was still able to shine through. It was enough to bring tears to the eyes.

As Martin's departure drew near, it finally came time for him to pack his suitcase. His things were spread out all over the room, but were gradually gathered up until there was no longer any evidence that Martin had ever stayed there. His razor, his cologne, his sneakers, his shirts—they all got stuffed into two large suitcases that stood by the door. These two bags had lots of extra space left over, and were still rather empty. All of a sudden, Ah San said: Pack me in your luggage and take me with you! I'd rather bring you with me in my pocket, Martin replied. Martin thought Ah San was just saying something sweet to express her reluctance to see him go, but Ah San pressed the matter further. Taking his hand, she said in a trembling voice: Martin, take me with you—I want to go to your hometown because I love it—because I love you.

Her speech was a little jumbled, but Martin understood. His eyes grew sober, but were still filled with sincerity. He grasped Ah San's tiny hands and moved them right in front of him, carefully examining the blue veins running under her translucent skin, and then said: Ah San, I love you. Hearing this, Ah San moved herself a step closer to him, raised her head, and anxiously looked up into his eyes. His eyes were so light they were nearly colorless—just what did they contain? But Ah San, Martin continued, I've never imagined living with a Chinese woman; I'm afraid I wouldn't be up to it. Why? Ah San immediately asked. She knew it was a stupid question that wouldn't lead anywhere, but she still very much wanted to hear his response. Martin thought for a while and said: Because I just wouldn't be able to. This was Martin's attraction: His answers were extremely simple, so simple that they reached the truth.

Ah San lowered her hands, and Martin also let them drop. Now, they each felt a disappointment they couldn't articulate—a beautiful memory hadn't yet taken shape before it was smashed to pieces. Each misread the other's thoughts; the mutual understanding they'd once had now became a misunderstanding. They both felt a bit wronged, but neither said anything. Then they fell into silence. Their final moments together were passed in this silence. At this final juncture, Martin's trip to China became too unbearable to recall, with the depressing feeling that it had all suddenly been ruined. For Ah San, the pain nearly extended to her whole life. She thought: If Bill couldn't be with her, fine, it was because he didn't love her; Martin loved her, but he couldn't be with her, either—what was wrong with her?

Finally it was time to leave, and they once again embraced tightly. But they both felt the hollowness of the action. It was as if each of them recognized their obligations at that moment: They needed to put a period at the end of this romance and bring it to an amicable close. They were each determined not to let their disappointment show, yet when they exchanged a passionate kiss, deep down they felt exhausted. As soon as they parted, they each felt relieved of a heavy load. Ah San didn't even go with Martin to the airport; she simply watched him get into a taxi from the entrance of the hotel and waved goodbye. She was almost anxious to get away from him. But this was only in the moment, and a minute later she regretted it. She almost ran back to the hotel entrance to get another cab to the airport. There's still time, she thought. But in the end she was able to restrain herself.

As she headed home, memories of her time with Martin welled up in her heart, and the scenes played out vividly before her eyes. So much had happened in these twenty days! The weather was still blazing hot with no relief in sight, but Martin had already gone. Tears streamed down Ah San's face. She thought of Martin's large, gentle hands, and how they held her smaller ones as they walked along the bustling streets. At that very moment, Martin was looking out the window of his taxi at all the people rushing about under the scorching sun, and he was thinking of Ah San. He knew that he would never see this woman again as long as he lived, and the pain was like a knife twisting in his heart.

Martin sent Ah San two letters after he left, but Ah San never replied. That unfamiliar address in France written on the envelope was a world away from her. She knew it was in the remote interior of Europe, with a pure bloodline that hadn't changed in hundreds of years, and that its eternal and enduring setting remained a faithful outpost in France. She had nothing she wanted to say to Martin, and nothing she could say could make a difference, anyway. What about love? Forget it. It was just an extravagance, nothing more than playing around with emotions. Neither Martin's enthusiastic warmth nor his sadness and distress could move her heart. She didn't understand what it was he really wanted. When he compared their relationship to two planets that could only ever meet once in all of eternity, in one eternal moment, Ah San smiled and said to herself: What's an "eternal moment?" When she broke down this phrase, he—Martin, and also Bill—were eternity, while Ah San was the moment. Ah San tore up Martin's letters.

But one thing really infuriated her, and she couldn't get over it: She could no longer paint. Martin's complete rejection at such a critical juncture really got to her. Martin, she thought, you're not taking responsibility! She had built a house through much hardship and labor, and Martin had come along and knocked the whole thing down. He should pay her back with another one, but he didn't. He just gave her a few pats on the butt and left, leaving Ah San alone to face the pile of ruins. When Bill left, Ah San could still paint, but when Martin left, she couldn't even do that. Although she didn't love Martin the way she loved Bill—this was the result of her own comparative analysis—Martin had done much more to ruin her life.

Finally the weather cooled down a little. The sounds from the katydid that clung on the outside of Ah San's window gradually tapered off, and the sunlight became lighter and clearer. All around her apartment, new buildings sprang up from the flattened ground. A tower crane stood in the distance, and on hazy evenings the light on its working arm would shine through the haze to Ah San, like an eye of the night. There was a sense of purity in this scene, but also a feeling of emptiness.

In the afternoon, rainclouds gradually gathered in the sky, and a dragonfly flew in the room; the sky suddenly turned dark, and its wings flickered as it flew around in what now looked like the dim evening light. Ah San thought of Martin's notion of "original." She calmly extended a hand out into the darkening atmosphere and nearly felt the breeze off the dragonfly's wings brush past her palm. Was that "original?" It was now almost as dark as night, with rainclouds filling the entire sky; the air pressure was so low it was even getting hard to breathe. It was about to rain, and faint thunder could be heard rumbling behind the thick layers of clouds. But the next minute, the edge of the rainclouds could be seen; sunlight started to shine through, and the sky once again brightened. Only then did it become apparent that the rainclouds were quickly blowing by, and because the area covered by them was so large, it was a long time before they finally cleared away. The lightning never came, the heavy rain fell somewhere else, and the dragonfly had flown away. The illusion of coming close to something "original" had also passed.

Ah San lied on her bed staring out the window. The room was piled up with paintings she hadn't sold, which also represented a recent history of art from the past few years. No one came to visit; everyone knew that she'd been seeing a French art dealer, which had immediately sparked rumors that she was going to France.

By now, Ah San was considered the kind of girl who only went after foreigners, and Chinese guys had given up trying to pursue those kinds of girls. This was why no Chinese guy had ever tried to woo Ah San. She lived her life within a mysterious circle outsiders could not enter. No one had any way of knowing the actual details of the daily lives of these women—sometimes they were in luxury hotels eating fresh oysters that had just been flown in; other times they were eating instant noodles in a far-flung apartment in the city's outskirts, lighting candles because the electricity had been cut off. Their latest fashions hung on the whitewashed walls, covered by a protective cloth; their stylish shoes lay scattered over the floor, a pair here, a pair there.

With nothing to do, Ah San wanted to go find the Author. But she seemed too ashamed—this new chapter had come to a close too quickly and wasn't even worth discussing. She thought back to that evening in the Author's sitting room, when her performance had led the Author to expect something of her. She didn't end up going to see her.

After lazing around like this for two months, Ah San was completely broke. Only then did she rally her spirits enough to go find a way to make some money. Across from the Shanghai Hotel was a shop selling things for tourists, and the boss was a friend of hers who had once purchased some of her watercolors and oil paintings—mostly still lifes and depictions of scenery. Back then, because she had just become very successful, she was naturally a little upset she'd gotten such a low price. But now, after thinking it over, she had no choice but to go find her. She bathed, got dressed, made her final packet of instant noodles for breakfast, and then left to get on the ferry.

The clear, bright October sky stirred Ah San's spirits, and a brisk breeze swept away the stale night air. Ah San's complexion wasn't bad; everything that had been weighing on her had now settled down, and she looked as if she were ready for a fresh start. She was even already thinking about what her next works would be. When she left school, she thought she'd never again paint still lifes, but now that she was unexpectedly presented with some still-life scenery, she found herself getting a little excited. She saw the buildings of Puxi with new eyes. The green area along the river was filled with old people doing their calisthenics, along with some children. After going through such a turbulent period, she had been starting to wonder if there really was such a thing as a peaceful life. Now, however, the scene before her eyes gave an affirmative answer. Ah San happily thought to herself that after visiting the tourist shop, she'd go try to squeeze a meal out of the Author—yes, she'd try to take advantage of her this one time, and make her take her to a really nice restaurant.

She hopped on the trolleybus, and the whole street scene made her happy. The shops had just opened, and the first crowds were rushing in. The ground had just been sprinkled with water, but in the blink of an eye it had already dried. This all helped to lighten Ah San's mood, so that by the time she made it to the tourist shop and discovered that it had changed hands some time ago, she wasn't that upset. The new owner was a middle-aged woman who didn't know Ah San's friend, so Ah San rattled off a wide-ranging list of names in the hopes of establishing a connection. In the end, only one name elicited some vague recognition—one character was different in the name of the person the shopkeeper knew, and Ah San admitted that she had perhaps remembered it wrong. Now, they could start talking.

It was then, however, that Ah San noticed that the shop was no longer selling any oil paintings or watercolors, but only some painted tiles and a few particularly gaudy paintings on glass. She asked the shopkeeper why she no longer sold oil paintings or watercolors, and she said it was because she couldn't get a good price for them—the artists all wanted a high price, so she said forget it. How about if I paint some for you? Ah San asked. I've never seen any of your paintings, the shopkeeper replied sternly, so what do I have to go on? I'll paint one for you, said Ah San, but you have to give me an advance. The shopkeeper laughed: If I've never seen your paintings, how can I give you any money? Ah San said: So-and-so is my friend, and they're your friend, too—can't you have a little faith in me? With this joke, Ah San turned around and left the shop, saying to herself: Even if you want my paintings, I won't necessarily sell them to you.

As Ah San stood on the tree-shaded street, with the dappled light of the autumn sun shining through the leaves of the parasol trees, her body and mind felt relaxed. Her freshly washed hair fell down to her waist; pulled together it was no thicker than a finger, but when it was let down it spread out in thousands of silken stands. The cool, smooth feeling of her hair spread to her entire body. She was wearing an old pair of jeans cut off at the knee and ragged around the edges; a black, high-collared sweater with the openings of the sleeves' cuffs beginning just below the neck, leaving her shoulders completely bare; and sheepskin sandals on her feet with a skinny heel and a cut-out pattern in the leather. Her style was quite original, and everyone who passed her on the street turned around for another look.

Where do I want to go now? Ah San wondered. The question didn't leave her floundering, though; her mind was steady and clear. No, she wasn't floundering at all—it's just that she had nowhere to go.

She stood under the shade of the trees for a while, unable to come up with a plan. She felt so relaxed that a smile floated to her face. Behind her, the owner of the tourist shop looked out at her through the glass door, as if she were also waiting to see where Ah San would go—she'd pegged her as a certain type of person. Operating a shop here day and night had made her quite knowledgeable about the world, and few people could escape her judgment.

The tips of Ah San's hair waved slightly in the breeze; she had weighted it down with a small glass bead to keep it from blowing around too much. One of her high-heeled leather cut-out sandals extended down to the edge of the street, like she was testing the temperature and current before wading into the water. To see her posture from behind, she looked like a dancer holding a pose on stage; but then her body made a sudden movement, and she strode across the sidewalk toward the hotel across the street. A smile appeared on the shopkeeper's face—it seemed that Ah San had not done anything unexpected.

Ah San entered the lobby, looked around, and sat down on a sofa. The morning scene in the hotel was busy with both cleanup and preparation. The cleaning staff was busy sweeping and mopping, and the front desk was dealing with a number of guests who were checking out, their suitcases all set over to the side. The cafe was empty, as was the shop, which had just opened. Compared to the sunlight shining outside the glass doors, the light inside the hotel appeared dim and spiritless. Ah San sat on the sofa with one leg crossed over the other, looking calm, but like she meant business. Her eyes scanned nonchalantly, yet politely, over all that was going on in the lobby; she had certain expectations, but she was in no rush. Her gaze landed on the empty café—she and Bill had gone there one evening, and the young pianist from the music conservatory had been playing absentmindedly, jumping from one song to another.

Just then someone came by and asked if the seat beside Ah San was taken. Ah San reined in her gaze and, with a cold expression on her face, wordlessly turned her body to the side to indicate they could sit. The person sat down. By that time all the sofas were full and people had to sit facing one another, although they all avoided making eye contact, as if they were enemies. A simply dressed older couple was sitting across from Ah San, but they were quickly led away by a woman from Hong Kong wearing lots of jewelry. The woman's Cantonese sounded like she was arguing, and the expressions on the old couple's faces appeared shy and distant as the three of them headed toward the elevator. Two men immediately took their spots. A middle-aged man was sitting in the stuffed chair to the left of Ah San—his manner seemed okay, but it was ruined by the gray suit he was wearing. To call it a suit was being generous—from the area over the shoulders and down to the cuffs, it looked more like a Mao jacket. A fake leather briefcase was placed on his lap, and both eyes were staring straight ahead without moving. The person sitting in the stuffed chair across from him, which was to Ah San's right, had just the opposite appearance—his head kept turning so much it was as if it were on a swivel, and although he was sitting down, he gave the impression he was eagerly looking forward to something. Several times an excited light flashed in his eyes, and he started to wave and call out, but then at the last minute he realized it was the wrong person.

Ah San noticed that a group of sofas arranged in a circle in front of her were not fully occupied. Some of the foreigners over there would rather stand than be scrunched in together on the couch—even some who had originally been sitting would get up and move away as soon as someone sat down too closely beside them. Ah San thought angrily that even when they were driving, Chinese people didn't allow any open space on the road and would fight over it tirelessly. Now she discovered that they were all sitting together in a circle, closer than a family—it was a ridiculous scene that made her want to get up and leave. On second thought, though, she wondered why she should be the one to leave, and not some of the others. So she sat back down. When she raised her head and looked around again, she noticed that new people were now sitting around her—even the person beside her had been replaced by a young woman around her age.

The scene in the lobby started to liven up. People were coming and going more frequently, and the café over to the side now had some guests who were speaking loudly, adding to the hubbub. The escalator started moving, taking some people up to the restaurant on the second floor. This surge of activity passed, and the lobby once again quieted down. But it was different from the previous calm, when things hadn't really gotten started yet; now, everything was poised and ready. Ah San didn't know when the sofas beside her had all become empty, or when the café had calmed down; the escalator continued to operate even though no one was on it. Things at the front desk had also tapered off, and the receptionists each stood with their hands clasped behind their backs; the cleaning staff was getting into all the nooks and crannies; and a foreign child was sliding around on the mirrorlike surface of the floor as if it were an ice rink—in the blink of an eye, they were gone. Ah San remained at ease and kept a low profile—there was only one thing that upset her, which was that her stomach was growling so loudly; on such a quiet afternoon, she was nearly afraid that the doorman not far behind her could hear. A man sat down on the sofa across from Ah San and looked at her with a bold, provocative glint in his eye; Ah San pretended not to see and didn't move a muscle, and when he didn't get the reaction he was looking for, he got up and left in a huff. Ah San sensed that the cleaning staff and other young female workers in the lobby had taken notice of her, but with that man's departure, they would now have to revise their opinions.

After a while, she stood up and walked over to the shop. She glanced over the silks and the jade, moving slowly as she went. Everyone was either out eating or sightseeing, so this was a rather lonely stretch. Although her stomach was rumbling, Ah San's mood was not in the least bit dampened. She liked this place. It may only be made of glass, but it enclosed a whole separate world. She felt that this building was a glass dome of fate, and everyone under it had a kind of covert relationship with one another; when the right moment came, that relationship would become clear. She walked over to the escalator and suddenly turned around and said with a smile to the foreigner who was one step behind her: After you. The foreigner politely said: After you. Ah San held firm: You first. The foreigner said "thank you" and walked in front of her to get on the escalator. Ah San stood two steps below the foreigner as he slowly made his way to the second floor, and she watched as he went into the restaurant. She lingered around the shops on the second floor, examining all the Ming- and Qing-style furniture and porcelain.

She didn't come upon anyone else.

When she made her way back to the lobby, she found that her original spot was now occupied by several Japanese people, but she was happy to change places—she walked over to another group of sofas and once again selected one meant for two people. This time she felt even more at ease, and also a bit livelier. She dispensed with her previously cold, blasé attitude and put a warm, lovable smile on her face—one that made it look like something was making her so happy she just couldn't suppress it, and that the reason she was sitting there had to do with this happy event. The giant clock in the lobby had already struck one, and those who had finished their lunch rode down on the escalator. Another group of foreign tourists arrived and poured into the lobby, and the front desk was once again put to work. The foreigners' heavy perfumes temporarily filled the air. Ah San liked this sort of atmosphere—although it was a bit chaotic, there was always another wave of excitement about to arrive. She no longer felt hungry. She said "hi" to an old woman in the group who was looking around for a place to sit and rest her feet, and the woman gave a "hi" back to her, happy to be so warmly welcomed upon arriving in this country. Ah San asked her where she was from, and she replied: The United States. She wanted to continue chatting, but the tour guide called them together, and the woman had to go back and join the group. Ah San watched with feeling as she hobbled away, and called after her: Have a nice trip.

Just then, she heard a man's voice beside her say in English: Excuse me, miss. At first she didn't think he was addressing her, but then she heard him say again, more loudly: Excuse me, miss. At this she turned around and saw a man with an Asian face standing behind her, wearing a T-shirt that said "New York" tucked into his jeans. He had a fair complexion with neatly coiffed hair and a refined smile on his face. Are you talking to me? Ah San asked in English. He nodded, and Ah San said: Is there something I can help you with? With a smile, he said: Would you mind telling me where you're from? Ah San tilted her head and said: Guess. Japan, he ventured. Ah San shook her head. Hong Kong, he tried again. Ah San shook her head once more. America, then, he said. Ah San replied: It's a secret. The man smiled and walked around to the front of the sofa and sat down beside her. She smelled the minty flavor of his chewing gum, cool and fresh.

Ah San had already determined he was a foreigner of Asian heritage—Chinese guys rarely had such a fresh face, tidy hair, and polished smile. She also noticed how sturdy, yet delicate, he was. Ah San waited for an invitation, perhaps over to the café. In her eyes, this was just basic courtesy if a man was wanting to get to know a woman. He, however, seemed to forget there was such a thing as coffee, and went full steam ahead with his chitchat. They talked about how beautiful Shanghai was, how the Bund was a bit like New York, how people were very open-minded, and how international everything was. Ah San then purposefully disagreed with him on everything, saying that the city was dirty and cramped and the people were rude—they'd step on your foot and then curse you for not watching where you were going. He then assumed a very historical perspective: That's because the ten years of the Cultural Revolution destroyed all culture. Ah San retorted: Wasn't the Cultural Revolution, as the name suggests, supposed to benefit culture and build a new civilization? As the man patiently explained the basics of the Cultural Revolution to her, Ah San thought: This guy has been listening to too much propaganda. She knew that this kind of foreigner existed, the kind that "understood"

China better than the Chinese themselves. She feigned interest as she listened. She also acted as if they were on familiar terms, so that the women at the front desk would think she had finally met the person she had been waiting for—an old friend.

When he had finally finished, Ah San said in a mocking tone: To hear you talk, you sound just like a Chinese person. Modestly, he replied: I am Chinese; Ah San waited for the next phrase—"even though I was born overseas"—so she could then go on to mock his Chinese mind. Instead, though, the sentence that followed was: I was born in Shanghai. Ah San was shocked; looking at his smile again, it seemed to carry a bit of cunning. Her face fell, and she leaned back and straightened her body. I'm also Chinese, she said. Born in Shanghai. He stood up, and, still maintaining a warm, polite smile, said "goodbye" and disappeared. Ah San thought to herself: He went to so much trouble over his appearance, but still didn't have the sense to treat a girl to coffee. Then, on second thought, she suddenly wondered if he had perhaps been waiting for *her* to invite him out for coffee! Ah San felt it was all absurd, and stupid. The two of them had carried on a whole conversation in English, down to the final "goodbye," as if they were a couple of foreigners. At this point Ah San felt a little dispirited, realizing how unsuccessful most of the day had been. Irritated, she stood up, gave the extra-long strap of her tiny purse a fling, and headed outside. But before she had taken two steps, she heard someone behind her call: Excuse me, miss! This time it was real American English. A bit flustered, Ah San stopped in her tracks.

A foreigner was quickly walking over to her—he was an older man with a kind face, just the sort that could be either your father, or, just as easily, a lover. This was the good thing about foreigners—with their Hellenic features, there was always a romantic undertone; no matter what the person's background, there was always the possibility for romance. Ah San waited for the man to get closer as she prepared to ask: Can I help you? But instead, he asked Ah San: Can I help you? Ah San was caught off guard and blurted out: Treat me to a cup of coffee. She sounded a little angry when she said this, taking out her frustration with the previous situation on this old man—why did he have to come up to her just as she was walking out the door? Great, said the old foreigner. Then he asked Ah San where they should go. Ah San hesitated for a moment, not really wanting to go back into the hotel; it would be better to change venues. So she took him to a neighboring hotel, where they went up to the second floor and sat at the café.

This hotel was much smaller and had fewer guests—they were the only two people in the café. Ah San ordered a slice of cake; she no sooner laid eyes on it than it disappeared into her stomach, so she ordered another one. Without batting an eye, she had devoured three pieces of cake. The old foreigner watched her eat with a bemused smile, and asked her how she managed to stay so skinny if she ate so many sweets—it must be some kind of magic. Ah San didn't respond. She remained a bit standoffish, having not quite yet shed her anger. The man once again praised Ah San's beauty, especially her hair—it was really as fine as silk! As he said this, he reached out a hand to stroke the bit that fell over Ah San's shoulder. Ah San flicked her head, and her hair flipped over to the other side. Although he only ended up feeling the air, the old man wasn't angry, and only smiled more kindly. By this point, Ah San felt she'd shaken off most of her anger, and her mood started to brighten. She opened up a napkin, took out a pen, and did a quick sketch for him. She barely looked at him; to her eyes, all foreigners looked basically the same—except, of course, for Bill, and also Martin. She picked up the napkin with her drawing on it and held it in front of the old foreigner's face. The old foreigner was as delighted as a child, and said it really must be magic. Ah San said: I can do lots of magic like this—if you want some, we can discuss a price. The old foreigner said: Such wonderful magic should be kept at the Met. Ah San responded to his clever remark in kind and said: Then please help me pass this along to the Met. She folded the napkin up as she said this and solemnly placed it in his hand. They both laughed.

My name's Charles, said the old foreigner, from the United States. My name's Susan, said Ah San, from China. Because this last part was unnecessary information, they both laughed again. Now they were on friendly terms. Charles went on to tell her that he lived in Los Angeles, where he ran a gas station. His son and daughter were both grown up, with one living on the east coast, and the other on the west; his wife had passed away last year. Originally he and his wife had agreed that when they grew old, they'd sell the gas station and take a trip to China—he never thought that death would be one step ahead of them. Only when his wife died did he realize that the future would never actually arrive, and that he would always be living in yesterday. A year later, he sold the gas station and came to

China—although his wife would never be able to make it. Ah San listened with rapt attention; she began to pity this old man and dispel the feeling of enmity inherent in this kind of meeting. Charles pulled a heart-shaped pendant out from his collar, opened it up, and showed Ah San a photo of his wife. Ah San moved her face closer, but she didn't see the photo; instead, her eyes moved past to see the spots and wrinkles on the old man's neck—he really was old. Ah San sat back up and expressed her sympathy. He went on to talk about his wife—she was an old-fashioned woman who worked hard her whole life, raised two children, helped her husband, and managed the housework. The reason she had wanted to come to China was for the pandas—she was an animal lover with a big heart.

As Ah San listened to him ramble on, she began to grow a little impatient and anxious, unsure of what would come next. But then things abruptly came to an end. The old man suddenly wrapped up his monologue and called for the check. Then with a beaming smile he told Ah San that his tour group had gone to buy souvenirs that afternoon, but he wasn't interested. When he saw Ah San, he thought that maybe this young woman wouldn't mind listening to him talk, and he was very grateful for her time. Shanghai was really a nice place with such friendly people—you could see them smiling everywhere. Now he needed to go back and rejoin his group for dinner and an acrobatics show, which was supposed to include pandas. Ah San was at a loss for words and didn't quite know how to respond, when Charles added: But Susan, you really know how to eat cake! Nearly forgetting who "Susan" was, Ah San stood up with him, and they both walked out of the café.

The last thing remaining for Ah San to do that day was to go see the Critic to collect an old payment they had both forgotten about—after that, neither would owe anything to the other.

It was hard to say if this experience in the hotel lobby had been a success or failure. The important thing was that Ah San needed to be very clear with herself about what she wanted—was it really just to drink coffee with foreigners? Of course, the answer was "no." But drinking coffee was a good start; as for what came next, who could predict? And if another one like Charles came along, she wouldn't refuse. Heaven only knows if he was really called Charles, which is more than could be said for whether Ah San was really called Susan. But at any rate, the experience with Charles proved that at least it was possible to get things started—once that happened, there was always a way to proceed toward a result. With this thought, Ah San felt relieved.

Ah San slept in late the next morning, and it was already three o'clock by the time she made it across the river to Puxi. This time, she breezily entered the café, ordered something to drink, and started looking around with fresh interest. It was a period of high activity in the lobby. The café was nearly half full, with people sitting in groups of two and three, some chatting loudly, and others more softly. The only person there alone was Ah San, but she maintained a composed and cheerful expression, as if the person she was waiting to meet would be showing up at any moment. From the shadowy corner where she sat, looking out toward the brightly lit lobby was like looking out over a rowdy audience before the opening act of a play—and she was on stage. The curtain hadn't yet opened, and the lights hadn't come on, but the performance was getting ready to start. Ah San felt very calm. Someone walked by her, but they weren't the type she was looking for, so she remained aloof. The people around her had nothing to do with her—they were all talking about their own affairs and drinking their own drinks. But it was these people—their quiet conversations, the drinks in their cups, the smell of the coffee, and that little bit of light—that created a warm, almost familial atmosphere, distracting Ah San from her loneliness. It was so nice sitting here like this! She forgot about her painting, and about Bill and Martin. That was because, aside from the warm, homey atmosphere, there was also a certain reserved sense of decorum that allowed private memories to remain separate.

A foreigner walked by, looked Ah San over, and gave her a smile. Ah San promptly responded, but nothing happened. The man walked by and sat down in a corner; a little while later, he was joined by his Chinese boyfriend. So he's gay, she thought to herself.

Ah San was pleased with herself for being so familiar with the whole scene—not like the middle-aged woman over to the side who seemed so timid and ill at ease, and who was dressed so inappropriately, wearing a silk dress feebly draped over her thick yet droopy shoulders. She was sipping her coffee from a spoon, which was another faux pas. With her there to serve as a contrast, Ah San felt even more confident—she was really well suited to this. Another foreigner came by, probably a German—serious, uptight, and arrogant, Ah San surmised. He was by himself and sat down at a neighboring table across the aisle. A waitresses came over with a drink menu, and without really looking at it, he simply said the word "coffee"; he then proceeded to take out a cigarette. It was all so natural. Ah San stood up, walked over to him, and asked: Sorry, sir, but may I have a cigarette? Of course, he said, and passed the pack over to her. Ah San took one out, the man lit it with his lighter, and Ah San returned to her original seat. They smoked on their respective sides of the aisle, neither one looking over at the other. Then his coffee arrived. The waitress set it down and passed right between them as she walked away. It seemed as if everything was slowly coming together, which was reflected in the fact that they both appeared a bit stiff.

When Ah San had finished her cigarette and pressed the butt down in the ashtray, the "German" came over and offered the pack of cigarettes again: Would you like another? Ah San politely declined. They both looked at each other and smiled, and their expressions relaxed.

Where are you from? Germany? Ah San asked. America, he replied. I was wrong, she said. Why did you think I was from Germany? he asked. Because you looked so serious, Ah San teased. The American gave a big laugh. Ah San thought to herself: That's about right—Americans can be amused by the tiniest little thing. When he stopped laughing, the American asked: Do you know many Germans? No, Ah San slowly replied. I used to have an American friend who was completely different from you, so I assumed you weren't American. Where did your friend go? the American asked. Ah San brought her fingers together and then popped them open with a "poof," indicating he had vanished. The American demonstrated his sympathy. No, said Ah San, slightly raising her eyebrows to introduce a different perspective. Chinese people have an old saying—the feast must always come to an end. The American disagreed, saying: But what if it's not a feast? What if it's love? With a smile, Ah San replied: Love? What's love?

They chatted like this across the aisle, eventually reaching the topic of love. They both became more excited, with lots they wanted to say, but once they thought it over for a few moments, nothing came out of their mouths, and they stopped talking.

After this pause, Ah San asked: Are you in Shanghai for sightseeing? The American said he was there for work as a language instructor at a university—it was Sunday, so he had gone to the bank to change money, and then come here. He asked what Ah San did, and she said she was an artist. He asked where she studied, and she said she'd already quit. Why? he asked. No reason, Ah San replied. Then she said: Did you know? Your Sylvester Stallone was expelled fourteen times during his thirteen years in school. The American laughed.

Ah San was pleased with this sort of conversation—there was something unique about it that came close to the happy feeling of creating something. It wasn't a pursuit of truth; it had nothing to do with truth—to the contrary, it was more like dreaming. It's what she'd had in the early days with Bill. As she became nimbler and more skilled with her English, and as the conversations became more colorful, this feeling grew stronger. Now that this person from another country, totally separate from her, was right here, she needed to pay close attention to his pronunciation and the way he put words together—this would give her the materials to construct a dream world and give it something tangible. She was being very talkative—for every word the American said, she said three. Soon she was the only one talking, while the American just smiled and listened; he clearly didn't have as much to say as Ah San. He seemed like a simple person—he was lonely working abroad, so he naturally welcomed the opportunity to talk with someone.

After some time had passed, the lights over at the bar turned on, and it seemed like something was about to happen. The bartender's face under the lights made him look like he was on stage. That distastefully dressed woman had long since left with her companion and had been replaced by two young women, sitting there facing one another silently with their drinks. Suddenly Ah San offered the suggestion: Why don't we go have dinner together? The American smiled—he had been afraid this woman would stop talking and bid him farewell, leaving him not knowing what to do with himself for the rest of the evening. Great, he said, and went on to add that he knew a small restaurant nearby with excellent spicy tofu. So they each got their checks and stood up to leave. Ah San could feel those two new arrivals staring at her back as she walked by, while the bartender kept his head down and busied himself with something, not once looking up.

They each got separate checks at dinner, as was the American way. Although Ah San didn't have any money to spare, she at least had a feeling of equality. As they ate, the American told her that his wife and children were still back in the states, and that if he continued his job there, he would bring them over. Ah San was not in the least bit interested in his family affairs, and she thought to herself: I'm not exactly planning on marrying you—yet the indifference of her expression only increased the American's confidence. As they left the restaurant, the American took her hand and said: Let's start a new feast! Ah San thought back to what she'd said earlier about the feast coming to an end, and she ventured a laugh. These Americans always appeared a bit foolish, but they always came out with a clever response when it counted most. Without taking his hand, Ah San looked up at him and said: What feast? Very earnestly he replied: The one that you said will always come to an end. Unable to withstand Ah San's stare, he turned away and said: I'm very lonely. After a pause, Ah San said: I'm lonely, too.

Later, they went back to his room at the university where he was teaching.

It was an old apartment that had recently been renovated, and the modern décor made it look even older. That synthetic wallpaper, that flimsy wooden casing around the curtains, that lotus-shaped wall lamp at the head of the bed—and especially those new fixtures in the bathroom, like the low shower pan and the pedestal sink—all looked a bit awkward and forced in that room with its high ceilings, heavy door, and wooden shutters. Ah San looked up at the cheap light fixture hanging from the ceiling, in the middle of a circular design left over from before the renovation. She smelled the room's particular scent—a mixture of men's cologne mingled with butter and toast, and it reminded her of her days as a tutor in the Qiaohui apartments, which was already so long ago. She thought of Bill.

The American was attracted to Ah San, and her sexual forwardness exceeded his expectations; compared to her, he was cautious and conservative. For a time, he even thought she was engaged in that kind of business. But he was a bit confused by the fact that Ah San had never mentioned any payment, and that even at dinner they had each gotten their own check. When Ah San put on his oversized bathrobe and went to take a shower, he sat there awkwardly wondering if he should give her any money. Finally, he decided he wouldn't mention the issue unless she brought it up first. But Ah San never brought it up; when she came out of the bathroom she was focused exclusively on tending to her wet hair, sitting cross-legged on the bed with several cool droplets of water still sprinkled over her. Her body looked tiny in his big bathrobe, and particularly alluring. The American suddenly felt it was all a bit unfair and began to feel a sense of pity toward her. He apologized and said she would not be able to spend the night; not only would the security guard take notice, but they were still strangers, after all. Ah San cut him off and said she knew, and when she was finished with her hair she began to get dressed. Once she got herself ready and was about to leave, he stopped her and, his face blushing, said: Sorry, I don't know if . . . and handed her a green American banknote. Ah San smiled and mumbled something to herself as she tried to figure out how to respond, and the American's face turned even redder. Ah San raised her hand, swiftly grabbed the money, and turned to leave. The American stopped her once more and asked if he could see her again. He was free next Sunday, and he would go to the same hotel where they had met today.

When Ah San left the faculty residence building and made her way out to the street, it was already twelve o'clock, and the last ferry had left—where could she go? But this didn't worry her; she was in fine spirits as she strolled along the empty streets of this rather remote part of the city. A cargo truck rumbled by, causing the ground under her feet to shake. Humming to herself, she continued walking around aimlessly. Her bare, freshly washed arms and legs felt cool and smooth, as did her hair, which had now partly dried. A late-night bus sped past her and pulled up to a stop just ahead without even opening its doors. Ah San started running and shouted: Wait! Just as it started moving again, the doors opened. She hopped on without even looking to see what bus it was or where it was going, and the doors snapped shut behind her.

Now Ah San's life seemed back on track. On Sunday afternoons she'd meet the American and they would have dinner—he, of course, would pick up the check—and then they would go back to his apartment in the faculty residence. These regular meetings certainly did nothing to stop Ah San from visiting cafes in the lobbies of other hotels—and if she received an invitation, as long as it was a foreigner she didn't find completely revolting, she would kindly accept. Not only did this help pass the time, but it also helped her search for a better opportunity. What kind of opportunity? Ah San still wasn't sure. At any rate, her experience in the lobbies was a start, and as a certain rhythm began to develop, her goals would start to become clearer, too.

One thing, though, was very clear, and that was that she needed to avoid any messy situations. In the midst of this steady stream of meetings in the lobbies, she was always able to keep one basic and relatively stable relationship going. First was the American, but then his wife and kids arrived, so their weekly meetings had to end. By that time she had already begun seeing a high-powered Japanese businessman, but the truly intimate part of their relationship didn't get going until things had ended with the American. This relationship didn't last long, mostly because he was just a transitional partner for Ah San. She didn't like Japanese guys—she thought they were even less romantic than Chinese ones. She referred to the period of time she was with him as her "War of Resistance Against Japan," and used her fluent English to temper the arrogance he had from coming from a country with such a strong economy. Ah San was also the clear victor in the bedroom, where he would obediently submit. Her most ruthless and decisive move came just as he was beginning to feel he could never leave her—she abruptly dumped him for a Canadian.

These types of stable relationships, though, were never dependable in the long run. One could never put too much faith in these kinds of encounters. Neither party would ever reveal their real name, and although Ah San would do her best to move things forward, it was often to no avail. The guys weren't usually interested in getting to know her, nor did they think that what they'd be getting to know was real. They mostly only engaged in boring small talk, but once they did get on slightly more familiar terms, they would start saying things that went a bit too far. At these points, Ah San's English wasn't quite good enough to ward them off, and if she handled things wrong, she could end up falling into a trap. She had no way of knowing when there was a double meaning or hidden connotation in what they said, and they also used some slang, which left her in the dark. She also came to realize that most of the foreigners who liked to pick up girls in hotel lobbies weren't the most upstanding people. China was the same—the boring guys were the ones who would go out on the street to pick up women. Then there were these foreigners who were in China for the long term either for business or some official appointment—their lives were quite dull, and some of them were particularly uninteresting. This rather surprised Ah San, who thought that such common, vulgar thoughts couldn't be found inside these noble Hellenic heads. So she would always start out making a good faith effort to understand them, and only when she really fell for one of their tricks would she finally wake up. But she was unwilling to admit this depressing situation to herself.

Although Ah San always hoped for a stable relationship, things didn't always turn out as she wished. The men she met rotated like a merry-go-round—it was actually not that easy to find someone like the American who wanted to meet once a week. This made it easy for Ah San to remember all of his good points. At their final parting, it was clear that this middle-aged man was reluctant to leave her. Of course, though, Ah San also understood that was all there was to it—even if she wanted to take it one step further, she couldn't. The American had a tight line of defense, which was his way of dealing with things.

In this way the hotel lobbies allowed Ah San to look behind a mysterious curtain. In the dimly lit cafés, those quiet, intimate conversations carried on by foreign couples—once they could actually be heard—were all just a bunch of boring, insipid clichés. Sitting there now, Ah San only needed to glance out of the corner of her eye to know what they were doing, and what their next step would be.

Ah San was also able to distinguish between those other women. Like her, they were also there looking for an opportunity; they harmed Ah San more than anyone, making her feel like she was under attack. She never considered herself to be one of them, but everyone else remained unconvinced and saw her as no different. One time she was sitting in the corner of a lobby waiting for her new friend when a member of the cleaning staff came over to wipe the windowsills, tables, and legs of the sofas. She was a woman around thirty years old, who kept her head down the whole time with a stern expression. As she was cleaning something beside Ah San, she suddenly raised her head and said with a smile: Two girls just went after the same foreigner, and now they're fighting. Ah San looked in the direction she indicated, and there on another sofa she saw two women flanking a Middle Eastern–looking man, who was tightly squeezed between the two of them. Although she couldn't hear anything or see their faces, she could tell from the way their bodies were positioned that they were engaged in a battle. By the time Ah San turned her head back, the cleaning woman was already wiping things down somewhere else. When Ah San thought back to the woman's tone and expression just then, and why she wanted to tell her this, it appeared that she thought Ah San would understand this sort of thing, so she immediately took offense. Looking again at her dumpy figure from behind, Ah San really felt disgusted.

These women were polluting the atmosphere of the lobbies and the meetings that happened there, and some of their filth was starting to get on Ah San—sometimes her friend would bring one of his buddies along, and they would go pick up one of those women and bring her into the mix. To show that she was different from them, Ah San would play the role of the host, translating for them and inviting them to order something to drink. Yet she could also see that she still received the same level of welcome and enthusiasm as they did. She wanted to demonstrate that she had more of a special understanding with her friend—one time, for instance, she went ahead and took a cigarette from his pack. But this just made the two other girls do the same thing, while her friend happily watched. At times like this, Ah San felt really humiliated, and she was barely able to remain calm. In the end, she always descended into a chilly silence, building a wall to block out the enemy.

Now, however, Ah San no longer needed to go to hotel lobbies to have an uninterrupted stream of foreign friends. Foreigners in China were actually all connected in a giant web, and once you gained entrance, each thread would pull another. But encounters in the lobbies still held their own attraction; they began without any prior knowledge and always involved something unexpected, so it was possible to remain hopeful. At the same time, her experiences in the lobbies left Ah San feeling frustrated. She was constantly establishing new relationships with foreigners and constantly having them fall apart. It all eroded her self-confidence, and she nearly forgot what she was hoping for. But one thing was clear— she couldn't live without foreigners. While she was aware of their certain shortcomings, she still liked them; they made everything look different, and they made her look different.

These days it was difficult for Ah San to stay in her apartment, looking at her paintings and her cheap furniture accumulating dust and cobwebs, and her kitchen that was piled full of trash, with the plastic bags from instant noodles lightly swirling around over the floor. There was something about this setting that really matched her state of mind, and also made her a bit afraid. She didn't want to stay in this apartment; she felt like she needed to escape. So she escaped to the hotel lobbies, with their foreigners, foreign languages, lamplight, candlelight, glassware, vases with roses—it all fused together to form a curtain she could hide behind. It seemed there were some things, like foreigners, that the less she understood them, the more hope they gave her. This corresponded to that murky, indeterminant sense of hope.

To avoid her apartment, Ah San began spending her nights elsewhere. She would follow a foreigner down the hall, the carpeting swallowing the sound of their footsteps. Then they would hang a "do not disturb" sign on the door and softly close it. She would get a drink from the refrigerator in the room, take a shower, wrap herself in a bath towel cinched around her chest, and sit cross-legged on the bed watching international news on closed-circuit TV while responding to any conversational inquiries coming from the bathroom. She was already so familiar with this scene that it was just like going home. Peeking out through the sheer curtains, she could see the city streets down below in patches of light and dark, with several clusters of lights making the darker places appear especially black. Ah San knew that she was in one of those patches of light, in what looked like an illuminated honeycomb.

These standard hotel rooms were no different from one another, and they all looked about the same. This gave Ah San the misperception that they had the same stability as a real home, and this was now where she was perched. She would wash her silk underwear and hang them to dry on the pullout clothesline above the bathtub, and she would arrange the toiletries she happened to bring with her along the ledge under the mirror, creating a peaceful, homey appearance. The foreigners themselves were also not that different from one another, and after only a night or two, Ah San couldn't tell them apart. As a result, Ah San was unable to distinguish between the love she felt for them, and she would end up using them as the basis for her daydreams.

From her experience, Ah San knew she was the kind of girl foreigners were attracted to, and that she compared quite favorably to the girls in their own countries. The enthusiasm and compliments she received from these foreigners made her think of Bill; there was even one who compared her to "a cat with nine lives," just as Bill had once done. Gradually, her memories of Bill began to drown in this series of similar experiences. Martin, however, was an exception—no one ever turned up who was anything like him, and certainly no one brought up anything like his idea of "originality." In all of her experience, then, Martin clearly stood out. Sometimes, Ah San would think: If it wasn't for Martin, would she still be continuing to paint, and would she be selling her paintings?

Ever since Martin, Ah San wouldn't let anyone else love her. This was one drawback of the meetings in the lobbies—as soon as they started, they were already doomed. Looking around her, those younger, more modern, and even more openminded young women all looked like they had never experienced this thing called love. Out of self-respect, Ah San would also not let herself think about love—her attitude was something like: You don't love me, so I love you even less! What's so great about love? She thought: I can't love anyone else, even Martin, because. . . because I love Bill.

Because there was no possibility for love, it all seemed counterproductive, and Ah San began to hate these foreigners; she would often come up with mischievous ideas to take revenge on them. When they were dining together, she would order the most expensive dish on the menu, along with the most expensive wine. When they got to their room, she would go directly to the minibar without waiting for an invitation. She especially liked doing this when she was with a particularly stingy cheapskate. Another fun trick she liked to play was to tease them until they were burning with desire, and then leave. She felt she could already handle these little games with ease, and she was successful every time. She was also better now at understanding English slang and double entendres, and she had learned some other clever phrases as well, with the express purpose of helping her manage those sleazy come-ons. She couldn't help but be a bit pleased with herself, and sometimes she couldn't restrain herself and took things a little too far.

And that's when things could go wrong.

Actually, counting them up, there had already been a stretch of days when Ah San had not gone to a hotel lobby. She'd met a Belgian man who was single and lived in the same Qiaohui apartments where she used to tutor. She thought he seemed like an honest person, and also rather conservative. Things had changed over time, and Ah San had begun to warm up to the conservative ones because she knew it was probably only with this type of person that it would be possible to find love. While she wasn't holding out any hope for love, and while she still stuck to her same method of meeting guys in hotel lobbies, this one was really different. She had met him by chance in a lobby—it was by chance in the sense that all her other meetings had an ulterior motive and were engineered by her savvy calculations. He had gotten up and forgotten his wallet, and Ah San had run after him to return it—that's how they met.

She'd not prepared for this encounter, and it made Ah San think back to the wise words the Author had once given her: If you try to grow flowers, they won't bloom; but if you randomly stick a willow twig in the ground, it will grow into a huge shade tree.

Her outfit that day gave her some help. She was dressed very simply in a white shirt, a cotton print skirt, and white canvas strap-on shoes; her hair was parted in the middle and done in two braids, just like a middle schooler. The Belgian exchanged a few words with her and discovered how fluent her English was, with almost no accent. He asked what she did, and she said she was an artist, which also gave him a good impression. This was very important to Ah San, so in order to maintain her good impression, she even returned to her place in Pudong and took the ferry over every day to meet him, just like a normal girl in love. Only after two weeks of this did she finally go see him at the Qiaohui apartments, which also made her seem like a normal girl in love. The Belgian's apartment surprised her—she never thought the life of a single man could be so neat and orderly. Once she got there she wasn't given any hints that she should stay the night, so when the evening news came on TV, she left. The next time it was the same. Another two weeks passed, and finally the Belgian held her in his arms. After that, everything happened that should have happened. Everything proceeded so systematically that Ah San was further led to believe that this could be a proper relationship. Although there wasn't quite enough romance, that only seemed to indicate a more realistic result.

What Ah San found in the Belgian's apartment was a very domestic scene. Pots and pans hung neatly on the white-tiled walls of the kitchen; in the bathroom a white cabinet was stacked with fluffy towels all washed with fabric softener; a wicker basket sat in the laundry room full of clothes waiting to be ironed; and on the refrigerator a fruit-shaped magnet held up a chart of daily expenditures. It was then that Ah San saw very clearly what she was hoping for. It was very simple—it was a home, a home like this Belgian had.

Ah San saw the Belgian's apartment as her own home. She even bought a few things for it herself, like a flower vase and a tea mat. She hoped that after another two weeks, another new formation would take hold. But this new formation was not the one she had been hoping for. The Belgian's girlfriend from back home was coming for a visit, so he asked Ah San not to come by anymore. Only then did Ah San understand that this was just the love affair of a European in China, and that two weeks was just an episode. She didn't express one ounce of resentment; on the contrary, she tried to show only that she had known all along. They parted amicably on the street, Ah San hailed a taxi, and, without a second thought, she gave the driver the name of a hotel.

Ah San entered the hotel, and its exuberant atmosphere rushed over her. A nocturne by Schubert was coming from the piano, and the lamplight surrounded a darker area that was lit by candles—this was the café. The receptionist at the front desk was busy either checking people in or out, and the bellhop was pushing along a rolling luggage cart. The elevator went up and down. Ah San had put the Belgian to the back of her mind, which now contained only one thought—have a good time. Her heart was filled with excitement as the scene in the lobby beckoned her; she could even see the clear lamplight reflected in her own eyes as she thought: This place is still wonderful! No one was beholden to anyone else, and everyone took equal part. The people walking by her had smiles on their faces, as if they were all members of the same family. It really was one big family! The propertied classes and the proletariat from all over the world had come together here. A smile appeared on Ah San's face as she made her way through some of the more restless groups in the lobby. Conversations in a variety of languages floated by her ears. There was some kind of gathering here every night, and anyone who wanted to could come.

Ah San went over to the café. It was packed, with candles flickering on all the tables. People were sitting close to one another having quiet conversations, and the music from the piano switched to a minuet—it was that familiar one with all the staccato notes going up and down, which sounded sort of artificially happy and satisfied. Ah San went over to a table by the entrance occupied by three foreigners and asked: Do you mind if I sit here? She pointed to an empty chair, and without waiting for them to answer, she sat down with a big smile and offered them her More cigarettes. The waitress came over and she ordered a White Russian—that rich, sweet cocktail that tasted like coffee candy. Then she said: Good evening, gentlemen. They all looked a bit surprised. She asked them where they were from, and one of them said England; she said her name was Susan, what were their names? They each reported back: Charlie, Ike, and James; now they were all acquainted. They were all handsome young men, with either brown or blond hair, and eyes that were either blue or gray—that standard look of the Aryan race. Any of them could be the leading actor in a film. They just didn't seem to like to talk that much—but why? It looks like they still don't trust me, Ah San said to herself. So she smiled even more amiably.

Is this your first time in China? Ah San continued: China is a vast land with a multitude of riches and an ancient civilization—but you must have learned this from your geography books, right? Ike shook his head—he looked to be a bit younger than the other two, and also a little less experienced, so she used him as an entry point. Have you heard of Wu Zetian? she asked. She was a queen, just like your Elizabeth. How about Jiang Qing? Seeing the confusion in Ike's eyes, Ah San chuckled and said: Okay then, you tell me what you know. The young man blinked a few times and said: Yellow Mountain. Oh, very good! Ah San praised him. He smiled like an overgrown child. Ah San looked at him affectionately and said: You remind me of my boyfriend—his name is Bill. So, she'd brought up Bill. The three of them listened intently and didn't interrupt. As she spoke, in the shadows under the table she moved her bare knee up against Ike's; Ike withdrew, and then was still. Bill is extremely kind and gentle, Ah San finally concluded.

Would it be possible for me to get another drink? Ah San asked as her eyes scanned over their three faces. The three of them exchanged glances, and one of them raised a hand to call the waitress. Ah San ordered another White Russian, and then passed it over in front of Ike and urged him to try a sip: It's really good. Ike hesitated. His eyes moved back and forth between Ah San's face and the glass, until finally he took a drink. Great! Ah San said before taking a drink from the same spot as Ike. Ah San was feeling relaxed and lighthearted, and also very chatty. When she listened to her own voice, it sounded soft and clear. The expression in Ike's eyes seemed to grow increasingly sincere, and he began to look excited. Now, he began talking. He said that back home, he'd seen a Chinese film called *Yellow Mountain*, which stirred his interests. As Ah San listened, she laughed to herself—these foreigners all had such one-track minds. If someone mentioned pandas, then all they wanted to talk about was pandas; if it was Yellow Mountain, then they could only talk about Yellow Mountain—they had no sense of what small talk was.

Ike was drinking beer, which gradually began to take effect. Ignoring the looks he was getting from his two friends urging him to slow down, he became increasingly drawn to Ah San. But because he was so shy, he only showed it very timidly and hesitantly, and with a touch of shame; red-faced and glassy-eyed, he kept wanting Ah San to take a drink of his beer. Ah San said to herself: Look, even his flirting is single-minded—mention beer, and then all he can think about is drinking beer. Ah San toyed with him a bit, not saying she would drink, but not refusing, either; as soon as he saw her place her lips to the edge of the glass, she turned her head away and still didn't take a drink, and Ike was unable to suppress a broad smile. Several times her hair brushed against his neck, increasing his excitement.

At this point, the other two suggested they return to their room, and despite Ike's protests, they called the waitress over for the check. Ah San had had enough fun and enough to drink, and she was ready to leave. Although she was a little tipsy by this point, her mind was still clear enough to perceive that Ike was being a bit belligerent, while his friends were being very inflexible—it was a recipe for trouble. What should she do? She certainly did not agree with their approach to continue forcing the matter. Unsurprisingly, Ike wouldn't let her leave. For better or worse, she encouraged him to get up and leave the café, and she took his arm and led him over to the elevator. The two older ones said goodbye to Ah San and went to take Ike from her, but Ike wrapped his arms around her and wouldn't let go. The elevator attendant held the door for them and waited for them to get in, but they formed a huddle and wouldn't separate. Ah San tried to be as soft and gentle with Ike as she could, urging him to let go. The other two were clearly getting angry and impatient, and one of them tried to drag Ah San out of Ike's embrace. The whole situation had become very unseemly. Some people stepped around them from behind to get in the elevator, and the door shut and took them up. The elevator attendant stood calmly to the side and waited for them to get themselves under control before she opened the door again. But they were locked in a stalemate.

Their awkward positioning began to attract attention. Other foreigners, especially the Japanese, minded their own business and kept their heads down as they walked by, pretending not to see anything; the Chinese, however, who always enjoyed a good scene, all craned their necks to watch. Ah San started to panic, knowing that things were getting out of hand. She looked imploringly at the one trying to drag her away and said: Let's just go up first, and then we'll talk. She hadn't thought this would anger him even more—he had no kind feelings toward Ah San, who had just shown up out of the blue and inserted herself into their evening. The more she tried to explain, the more he thought she was just trying to get into Ike's room. It was their first time in China, and they had no understanding of this socialist country still in the process of opening up. They had been on edge the whole time, and now their fear of being violated had become a reality. In the end, he actually called the police.

By this time, everything in the lobby had returned to normal, and the piano was now playing "Auld Lang Syne" from the movie *Waterloo Bridge*.

The cypress tree had eventually moved out of sight, and the bus now came to a halt. The door opened, and the young female police officer got off. Then, one by one, so did the labor reform prisoners. As Ah San stepped down from the bus, she felt someone give her a push from behind, nearly causing her to fall before she even got a foot on the ground. When she turned around to look, she saw it was the woman from before who had been making those obscene gestures. She met Ah San's gaze as if nothing had happened, and Ah San stared back at her. Once they had gotten off the bus, they split into the groups they had been divided into before they left, each now led by their respective correctional officers, their section chiefs, who had been awaiting their arrival.

The bus was unloaded, and they each carried their own luggage into the giant compound, which was located in the middle of a vast stretch of fields. The afternoon sun shone softly, and aside from this group of new arrivals, no one else was there. Dark, shadowy mountains rose above the walls of the compound, and because the weather that day was so sunny and bright, the horizon was clearly discernible; even the few white, wispy clouds that persisted appeared clear and distinct. Ah San and two other young women, including the one who had been trying to provoke her, constituted a section. Ah San was wearing a straw hat with the brim pulled so low her face was completely covered by the shadow. Their section chief walking ahead of them was tall and thin, and dressed in an officer's uniform; she wore no hat, and a single, unadorned braid hung down her back. She didn't once look back, seeming perfectly confident that everyone was obediently following behind. They walked deep into the compound, up to the entrance of a small lane, where she turned in and walked up to an iron gate. She took out a key and opened it; inside was a courtyard surrounded by rooms on three sides. A woman sat knitting in front of one of the doors, and as soon as she saw the section chief, she stood up. The section chief told Ah San and the others to find an empty bed, get settled in, and have some lunch. Taking into account their long hours on the bus, they were allowed to rest until two o'clock before going to the factory to start work. While the section chief was speaking, the woman who had been sitting there got up and fetched them three thermoses of hot water and three boxed meals.

Ah San looked at her watch and saw that it was already past one. She spread open her blanket and sat on the edge of her bed without touching the food in the metal box. The two others were already getting to know the one who was already there; when they asked her why she wasn't in the factory, her answer was "residential manager"—she was responsible for managing the lives of the prisoners. As they began to eat, their metal spoons clinked against their metal boxes. While they were eating, one of them began to cry, saying how much it would hurt her parents if they knew what she was eating. The residential manager tried to comfort her, saying that it was like this for everyone in prison, and that her parents, after all, were in Shanghai—how would they find out? The woman who had tried to provoke Ah San laughed coldly: You know how to swallow your punishment, right? If you don't swallow your punishment, you won't get anything to swallow. What she said sounded rude and unwarranted. Ah San looked over at her and thought to herself that this would be the first one to give her trouble. She and Ah San hadn't been in the same detention center, so the first time they had ever seen each other was on the bus. Ah San didn't know why she was being targeted as an enemy.

Ah San lied down on her bed and stretched her body out straight with her hands forming a pillow behind her head. She stared at a sunny patch of ground outside the door, where she saw a shoe brush lying alongside a water dipper, both exposed under the beating sun. Although it was October, the sun here was still fierce. A few flies were buzzing around, and there was a stench of spoiled food in the air. The other three were at the end of a bed talking quietly about something, as if they were trying to keep it a secret. Then it was two o'clock.

Ah San's new life had begun. Before coming to the labor reform camp, she had written the Author a postcard from the detention center asking her to send a blanket and a few daily necessities. The Author came to the detention center and, using her celebrity and connections, was permitted to meet with Ah San alone in the office. When she got there, she didn't immediately recognize Ah San with her hair cut short—and then once she did recognize her, she couldn't get any words out. After a pause, Ah San gave an embarrassed laugh and said: Now, not only do people leave your sitting room and go off to America; they go off to prison, too. Thanks for rewriting history, the Author sarcastically replied. After sitting there for a while, the Author reached into a large backpack and, one at a time, pulled out a blanket, a pillow, a washbasin, and a towel; she placed them on the table and then gave Ah San the backpack as well. She said she'd already dealt with her apartment and was temporarily storing Ah San's things at her place; she took the liberty of giving a few things that were too big for her to carry to the neighbors. As for all of Ah San's old paintings, after thinking about it for a while, she finally had the Critic come with a car and take them away, but she was sure to have him make out a receipt. At this point, Ah San interjected: What's the point of giving them to him? Just burn them and be done with it. The Author ignored her and pressed an envelope into her hand. Ah San looked in—it was five hundred RMB. Someday I'll pay you back, said Ah San. The Author said there was no need—her voice sounded hoarse, and she was on the verge of tears. Ah San furrowed her brow and stood up to go back in. It wasn't easy for me to come here, said the Author. And now look at you—wanting me to leave after a few minutes. Do you know why I didn't want my family to come? asked Ah San. Because I didn't want to see them cry—and now you're here crying for them. You're really hard-hearted, Ah San! exclaimed the Author, biting her lip. With that, she got up and left.

Now, Ah San's new life was spent sewing tags into the back collars of sweaters. The tags needed to be sewn on with two kinds of thread—the one facing out was a woolen strand of yarn, while the one facing in was a thread of silk, and there could be no puckering. Not many people could get it right, so a lot of them needed redoing. Ah San, though, caught on right away.

This sort of work was hard won by the production team leader, who had managed to wrestle it away from one of Shanghai's TVEs—township and village enterprises—although a management fee had to be paid as one of the conditions. A deadline to make a shipment was looming, and because they couldn't negotiate anymore, they needed to do something to get ahead of the problem. Because this was such a difficult sort of handiwork, much of it was done poorly and had to be redone, which took extra time and meant they had to add extra shifts. The production team leader didn't sleep for nearly a week—her voice went hoarse, her eyes were bloodshot, and blisters formed on her lips. Nowadays, the labor reform camp had to assume sole responsibility for its profits and losses; the output from the fields was obviously limited, so they also needed to take advantage of these industrial opportunities. The cadres needed to mobilize everything they had—the labor reform prisoners as well as their social connections—in order to get them, and they often came along with harsh terms and conditions. Because the jobs they were able to bring in came from various realms, and they each required a specific type of training before they could be done—on top of which there was a constantly rotating workforce—there was no way to develop any technical training. Everyone was a novice, so this consumed a huge amount of time and energy. As soon as the production team leader saw the size of the order for the sweaters, she knew she was getting taught a lesson. The factories of the TVE clearly couldn't handle it, so they passed it on to the labor reform camp knowing that, as the intermediary, they would still get the management fee. Every step of the process involved some difficulty, and the production team leader would always have to step in and handle it herself, so she was continually correcting and reteaching. Now, with the appearance of the intelligent and dexterous Ah San, the production team leader was thrilled beyond belief. She was practically ready to worship her, and she made the slow and clumsy ones bring Ah San tea and wipe her face with a damp towel—she didn't want her to move an inch away from the sewing machine.

Ah San, for her part, found happiness at the sewing machine. The woolen sweaters moved swiftly and obediently through her fingers, and in the blink of an eye she'd have another one finished. The people folding the sweaters could barely keep up, and they had no choice but to step up their pace. The anxious pace of work in the factory infused this compound quietly tucked away in the hills with some vitality. Everyone passed the time here by keeping their heads down and working. As the sky outside gradually darkened into night, the lights would come on, and the food truck would already be waiting outside. But no one even stopped to eat, nor did they have much of an appetite. They were like machine parts on a spindle that just kept going.

Ah San wasn't thinking about anything—it was like she'd been there for a decade or two rather than just a couple days. Everything went along extremely smoothly and efficiently.

Ah San even rather enjoyed this work—it simplified everything and filled the time, and it made the whole experience a little less difficult to bear. Sometimes, she would suddenly raise her head to discover it was dark outside; yet inside it was as bright as day, with the sound of machinery filling her ears. It was a scene that actually, ever so slightly, warmed the heart. It was laying down on her bed that she tried to avoid. As soon as she was on it, she would feel like there wasn't an ounce of energy left in her body, and she would dread the coming of the next day. She was even reluctant to go to sleep—she relished this precious time that was so careless and stress free. But before she could think much about it, sleep would be upon her, and she would enter the dream world. In what seemed like the blink of an eye, the whistle would blow. The sky would still be dark, and she would groggily gather herself together and go to the factory, where the lights would already be on, and the production team leader would already be at it. Everyone lost track of the days and confused morning with evening as they sat in a fog at their machines. After their initial bout of fatigue and despondence, their energy would return, and the previous day's rhythm would resume. Physical strength, like a reservoir, was always replenishable. Then, the sky would turn light.

By now Ah San had become the technical director—wherever there was a problem that couldn't be solved, Ah San went over and figured it out. When the production team leader glanced over at her, it was with a practically ingratiating look in her eye. One of the most frustrating things about being the production team leader was that she was unable to choose her workforce. But this woman Ah San—it was as if she had dropped down from the heavens. Because she was so partial to Ah San, she unconsciously became rather protective of her. When Ah San grew long, manicured nails, for example, she seemed not to notice. But when one of her roommates discovered it, she reported it to the section chief, and Ah San had some work points deducted as punishment.

Ah San knew who had reported her.

Back in her old residence at Shi Liu Pu, there had been one occupant everyone knew—her nickname was "Noodles" because she only charged as much as a bowl of plain noodles in broth. This gave her low standing among the prisoners in the labor reform camp. Ah San's sort, however, who did business with foreigners, held the highest standing. Next were those whose clients came from Hong Kong and Taiwan, and then the ones who worked for independent businessmen in the private sector. Noodles's clients, however, were mostly shipbuilders from northern Jiangsu province. This made her extremely jealous of Ah San. But simply hating Ah San wouldn't be enough to provoke her like this. There was another reason.

Just as Noodles's backstory had spread among the inmates, some gossip had spread about Ah San, too. She had once, in her own defense, said to one of the processing officers: I don't accept money. Just like that, Ah San also got a nickname—"Freebie." Noodles didn't really believe it, and felt that Ah San was just a lying hypocrite; however, she wanted to believe it so she could look down on her. So whenever she picked a fight with Ah San, it was also a kind of probing. But probing what? It seemed as if—and even she herself couldn't really say—she was trying to see if she and Ah San could be friends. This sort of feeling was both simple and complicated, and even carried with it a crude sort of honesty.

Ah San knew about her nickname, of course, but she allowed it to quietly make the rounds without so much as batting an eye. She didn't bother to kick up a fuss with anyone. Actually, when she had said the line "I don't accept money" to the processing officer, she immediately regretted it. How could she expect some young guy who had just graduated from a technical college, with a serious face yet barely a layer of fuzz on his upper lip, to understand all of this, when even she herself had difficulty understanding it? Actually, there was no point in saying anything; there was no way to change any of it, and everything that should have happened had already happened. At the end of the day, it was all in the past. Things weren't as good as they could be, but they certainly weren't as bad as they could be, either.

Staring at the dark mountain range in the distance produced a feeling of loneliness—the tea fields were also lonely, and the cypress tree was the loneliest of all.

At first Ah San didn't pay attention to Noodles, but those nasty little things she did disgusted her. Noodles also didn't do anything to really offend Ah San; because Ah San was the production team leader's favorite, it wouldn't have been worth it for Noodles to really go after her, so she could only irritate her with little things. For instance, she'd steal the water from her thermos, mess up her bed so she'd lose work points, hide her things so she couldn't find them, or do her best to spread baseless rumors. Finally, Ah San decided she had to retaliate in some way. She also didn't want to cause a stir; after all, they would still need to keep interacting with one another, so why create an enemy and make the days that much harder to bear? The retaliation would have to be completely effective in teaching her a lesson, so that afterward she would stop her antics for good. Ah San lay in wait for several days, and finally her opportunity came.

That day they had just finished sending out a shipment, but the new order wouldn't arrive until the next day, so under these unprecedented circumstances, everyone took an afternoon nap. As everyone was sleeping, Ah San drifted in and out of consciousness as she usually did when she napped; suddenly, she sensed a ray of warmth pass over her eyelids. When she opened her eyes she saw a flash of light, so she began searching for its source. Finally she realized that it had been the light reflected by a small mirror, which was on the top bunk diagonally across from her where Noodles slept. Ah San smiled to herself and quietly got out of bed. The even sounds of breathing filled the room and made that bright, sunny afternoon seem unusually peaceful. Ah San walked over, stepped on the lower bunk, and roughly threw back the blanket: there was Noodles, hiding with the small mirror and plucking her eyebrows.

Noodles's face went completely red, and she ingratiatingly passed the tweezers and mirror over to Ah San: Would you like to use them? Without taking them, Ah San only stared at her and asked with a smile: What do you think should happen now? Noodles lowered her eyes: You should probably go report me. Ah San said: I'm not going to report you; if the team leader docks you some work points, what do I get out of it? Everyone's here as punishment, and we all want to make our days a little easier to bear, so why go making enemies? With that, she forcefully threw the blanket back in Noodles's face and got down off the bunk. Noodles stayed there with the blanket over her face, not moving a muscle until the whistle summoned them up from their naps. That night passed without incident. So did the next day. On the third day, Ah San was at the knitting machine working on a certain kind of patterned sweater: There were only a few machines that could be used for this; all the others were used for supplemental tasks, like sewing together pieces of cloth, arranging colored threads, or transporting products. Noodles, of her own accord, brought a glass of water over for Ah San, who took a sip and realized it had been sweetened with honey. Ah San responded with a "thank you" and blushed like a bashful child. That evening, Ah San found a note under her pillow with a few crooked characters scrawled on it, addressing her as "Sister": Sister, I'll be loyal to you. Feeling both amused and disgusted, Ah San threw the note away.

It was typical for the inmates here to form partnerships, and almost everyone had paired off, arranging themselves next to one another when they could. From morning to night they would pass notes to each other, and before the lights went out in the evening, everyone would lie in their beds writing letters on their pillows—if they weren't writing to their families, they were pouring their hearts out to each other. It was a way of both looking after their own well-being and coming to terms with their loneliness. Ah San found it revolting. Because of her arrogance, and also because the production team leader held her in such high esteem, no one had expressed this sort of interest in her; now, however, Noodles had sought her out. She almost regretted her counterattack that day—this sort of outcome had been totally unexpected. Compared to the way things were now, she would almost rather still be the object of Noodles's petty bullying. She now avoided Noodles even more than she previously had for fear of inviting more of her toadying behavior.

But Noodles persisted. She was quite stubborn, and once she decided to be on good terms with Ah San, her mind was set. It was just as she had pledged in her note: I'll be loyal to you. Ah San's thermos had already come under her management, and if she missed the chance to go wash

Ah San's clothes, she made sure to collect them and fold them neatly on Ah San's bed. In the evening when she made instant noodles, she would always make some for Ah San as well. When they lined up outside for their exercises, she would often look over at Ah San from several spots away and give a knowing smile.

At first Ah San's tactic was to ignore all this, but when she could no longer bear the constant kindness and attention, she had to tell Noodles directly that all she wanted was for her to not make any more trouble—there was no need to be so attentive, and she really didn't deserve such treatment. She didn't expect Noodles to respond with such a serious expression and say: Sister, you're clearly still angry with me from what happened before; I've admitted I was wrong, so why can't you forgive me? It's not that I haven't forgiven you, said Ah San. We've wiped the slate clean between us. Saying this is the same as not forgiving me, said Noodles; her eyes became red as she spoke, and she looked as if she were about to cry. Annoyed, Ah San quickly said: It's okay, let's just pretend I didn't say anything. After that, everything continued on as before, with Noodles continuing to wait on Ah San, and Ah San continuing to ignore it.

As long as one didn't think about it too much, life here was relatively easy to get used to. Because there was a regular pattern to daily life and it was highly regulated, Ah San's complexion actually improved—the circles that had been under her eyes for so long finally disappeared, and her body grew stronger. Sometimes, when the production team leader summoned her to discuss a technical problem, and she got permission to walk out through the iron gate of her section and into the open expanse of the main courtyard, she even had a sense of freedom. What's so bad about it all? she wondered. Things are pretty good like this. Within these four white walls surrounded by green mountains, any talk of hopes or desires was nearly out of the question, and she felt relaxed. Ah San wasn't like the other girls, who would get all worked up over a bunch of chicken feathers and garlic peels. They were always publicly and privately comparing who was better looking, whose families were better off, and who'd had more boyfriends, always looking for some way to gain an upper hand. Ah San could only laugh at how boring and stupid it all was—even after falling into these circumstances, they were still concerned with such trifles and couldn't see reason. How could anyone know that she was actually in more danger than the rest of them? Unlike them, she was not releasing her desires little by little; instead, she suppressed them, and they began to accumulate. Who knew when they might explode and create an incident?

When they weren't that busy at work, they'd get off around seven. After getting washed and ready for bed, when there was still fifteen or twenty minutes left before the lights went out, Ah San would move a small stool over to the doorway and sit looking out at the greenish-blue night sky. This made her feel at peace. Now she could think about some other things, but what was there to think about? She really had no idea, so she didn't think about anything and just looked up at the sky. It was a sky that didn't exist in the city—there was nothing obscuring it, and there was no pollution—nothing but a wide, open expanse. So *this* was the sky. It encouraged boundless thought. There wasn't much time to spend gazing, but those few minutes before the lights went out were just enough to settle her thoughts without letting her enter a state of empty boredom. She was exhausted. As one yawn followed another, she would get up and go back in the room, crawl into bed, and almost immediately be fast asleep.

Things continued on like this, and before long Spring Festival was approaching. Because Ah San had been such an outstanding worker, the leaders decided that she should be allowed to receive a visit from her family during the holiday. When she got the official notification, instead of mailing it to her family, she quietly tore it up, and no one ever noticed. When Spring Festival arrived and Ah San had no visitors, no one thought anything of it; many of these girls' families were so angry they had sworn never to see them again. For an official invitation to be mailed out and receive no reply was hardly anything out of the ordinary. Noodles, however, was there to stick her nose in things. On the first day of the lunar new year, everyone was gathered in the assembly hall waiting for the film department to come put on a movie when Noodles squeezed in beside of Ah San and said in her ear: Sister, why wouldn't you let your family come see you? Ah San turned her head to the side to avoid Noodles's hot breath. This woman always made her feel dirty, and she was unable to suppress her disgust. Don't worry about it, okay? said Ah San. Has your family disowned you? Noodles was still earnestly pressed up against Ah San's ear, expressing her sympathy without taking the slightest notice of Ah San's reaction. Ah San decided to ignore her; she didn't respond, and Noodles didn't follow up with any more questions. Ah San thought it was over, but then after a pause, Noodles, sighing with heavy emotion, unexpectedly spat out two words: Those bastards!

Over the following days, Noodles was so attentive to Ah San it almost seemed like tender affection. She would prepare food for Ah San, and as soon as Ah San had finished eating, she would have her tea ready. When it was time for Ah San to go to sleep, she would have the blanket spread out for her. Ah San would crawl under it and close her eyes, trying to shut out the image of that face plastered with mushy sympathy. She could sense that Noodles was gathering up the clothes she had taken off and was placing them neatly on the chair. She even tiptoed over and carefully tucked in the corners of Ah San's blanket. Because it was a holiday that evening, everyone was over in the section chief's office watching television, and they were the only two left—one lying down, and one sitting. Ah San tried to breathe as lightly as possible as she lay on her back under the covers, not feeling the slightest bit drowsy. She was both angry and worried, not knowing how she should bring an end to this ridiculous "unrequited love."

Spring Festival was over, and although they were stuck in the monotony of this vast, empty environment, there was still some sense of spring. The dark, shadowy mountains in the distance turned emerald green, making them appear a bit closer, and the different colors of the trees created distinct shades of light and dark. The surrounding tea fields started coming into leaf, spotted with tender green buds. The breeze carried the fresh, invigorating scent of grass, and the sun shone brilliantly, especially in the evenings, when the colors of the sunset filled the sky with seven or eight alternating hues. When all of this was taken together, it created a buoyant atmosphere that stirred the spirits.

Because of this stirring, more things happened.

First, two girls started fighting over someone using the wrong tin cup. This sort of thing was always happening, but this time—no one quite knew why—one of the girls suddenly became enraged and flung the bowl of soup she was holding straight in the face of the other one, and the next minute they were tangled up in a fight. The production team leader heard the ruckus and ran over, and when her shouting had no effect, there was no choice but to get some others to physically pull them apart. After they had been separated, they continued screaming at each other, each one going for the lowest blow, digging up all the issues they had bottled up in the past and using them now as weapons for attack. Finally, they were both put in detention and the matter was laid to rest. The whole incident seemed to be over, but in fact it was only the beginning. Not even two days later, several more incidents occurred, one of which even involved an inmate who tried to harm herself; using a piece of broken glass from a teacup, she had cut her arm and drawn blood. This time, they even had to use handcuffs. These sorts of violent acts seemed to infect others like a disease, and they quickly spread to all the other sections. The more they spread, the more violent they became. Everyone wanted to make a show of themselves and have a breakout performance. It was an extremely chaotic period—all day long it was like a bunch of chickens and dogs running around. Sometimes a fight would break out in just the few minutes it took to walk from the factory floor back to the dorm. When the commotion was over, it became unusually peaceful; all the shouting and crying was done, and they once again became well-behaved girls, whimpering and sniffling as they climbed into bed to calm down. The problem was that as soon as the eastern sky had darkened, the west began to light up—once things had settled down here, they were just getting started over there. When would it all end?

In these early days of spring, everyone was lacking self-control—they were each like an arrow poised on a bowstring. At the same time, no one felt safe, afraid that they might be the next to come under attack. The section leaders were even more nervous than the inmates, so they would sometimes be more permissive in an effort to appease them: they'd put on a film, or improve the food, or have individual heart-to-hearts, or meet with them more frequently. But this was just like adding oil to the fire and encouraged them to run even more wild. It was a frightening and dangerous time; no one knew what each day would bring. People who were normally friendly with each other suddenly acted like strangers, and everyone grew very awkward and began avoiding one another. The production team leader called a meeting with the inmates who were deemed to have "strong self-control"—Ah San being among them. They were mobilized to maintain the normal order and produce a stabilizing effect in their respective dorms. But the incidents kept happening one after the other, and the results were increasingly violent. Finally, one of the inmates successfully resorted to the most drastic behavior—she swallowed a pair of scissors. The ambulance came that night and took her to the hospital; the sound of the engine was so deafening it lingered in the ears for a long time afterward, making the night in this hilly region suddenly seem that much quieter and emptier.

That night, everyone held their breath as they tried to suppress the fear pounding in their hearts. While they had always heard talk of this sort of thing happening, this was the first time anyone had seen it with their own eyes. That girl wanted to die on the spot, they all thought to themselves. Her clothes, blanket, bowl, and chopsticks were all quietly placed back in their original spots; they looked so tragic and sorrowful sitting there, already tinged with the scent of death. Everyone lay down in their beds, but no one closed their eyes. When the moon rose during the latter part of the night, it was unusually bright, and the courtyard was bathed in its white light. Ah San got up to use the bathroom and paused for a moment in the courtyard. The air she inhaled was fresh and moist, and she felt some relief in her heart. She had the vague sense this was the peaceful feeling that follows an episode of violence. She even had the thought that this peaceful evening came in exchange for the girl's life.

Just before morning, however, news came that the girl had immediately undergone stomach surgery, and that her life was no longer in danger; after a week, the stiches could come out and she could leave the hospital. Everyone once again returned to normal, as if nothing had happened. The events of the previous night became insignificant, and the fearful atmosphere dispersed like a cloud of smoke. This gave rise to a new saying—not even swallowing scissors can kill you. Once before, someone at the labor reform camp had swallowed a sewing needle, and to this day it was still in their stomach. Not only was she doing just fine, but she had finished out her sentence and returned to Shanghai, where she was now selling clothing on Qinghai Road! Fine, that was all in the past now. But the unsettled mood returned just as it was before, with one incident after another.

These disturbances had now become part of daily life, and no one really batted an eye. It seemed that as these incidents attracted everyone's attention, their level of intensity continued to ramp up. But the reactions they were able to elicit were no longer so serious. Everyone acted as if they were just watching a spectacle, joining in with cheers and playful laughter; each event became more and more of a farce. Ah San found it all quite irritating, and her irritation gradually replaced her feeling of disgust. One day there was another fight in the dorm, and everyone began pushing and shoving the two parties involved without even really knowing if they were trying to separate them or egg them on. Ah San flung open the door, walked out, and stood in the courtyard with her arms crossed, waiting for it to be over. Shortly afterward, Noodles also came out and said very sympathetically: It really is annoying. As usual, Ah San ignored her. After a little while, Noodles suddenly came up next to Ah San's ear and asked mysteriously: Do you know why they're fighting? Ah San didn't answer. Noodles continued: Spring is here, and the rapeseed is in bloom, so it makes everyone crazy.

Ah San couldn't help but give a look of surprise, which nearly made Noodles break out in song and dance. She redoubled her efforts and went on in an exaggerated tone: There is only one cure for this sickness, which is—as she said this, she made a gesture with her hand. Ah San had seen this gesture before, when she was on the bus on her way to the labor reform camp. She spun around in disgust and walked back to the dorm. At first Noodles was confused, but then her face turned red and she shouted angrily at Ah San's back: What makes you so great? Is giving foreigners [X] so special? Her shouts became louder and shriller, piercing the stillness of the whole courtyard. For an instant everything grew quiet, and even the fight underway suddenly stopped. It was as if everyone realized something new and more exciting was about to come on stage, so they tactfully withdrew from that venue and moved on to the next.

Ah San burst into the room and slammed the door with a bang that reverberated throughout the courtyard. The pregnant silence that followed only encouraged Noodles more. All of the injustice she had suffered and suppressed for so long now came surging forth. All she had gotten in return for her sincerity was Ah San's cold, expressionless face—how could she bear it any longer? She shed a river of tears, and then pointed at the door Ah San had just slammed and began cursing.

To make friends with Ah San, Noodles had gone against her true nature. She tried her hardest to please her. Ah San didn't curse, so Noodles didn't curse; Ah San was cool and indifferent toward others, so Noodles was cool and indifferent toward everyone other than Ah San; Ah San refused a visit from her family, so Noodles even threw away the one opportunity she had to see hers. She secretly imitated Ah San's mannerisms and style of dress. Although each inmate was only allowed three outfits per season, they were still permitted to wear their own clothes. All of Noodles's efforts, however, were for nothing—Ah San didn't notice a thing and remained aloof. But what made her so special? Wasn't she drinking the same soup as everyone else? Only Noodles knew the resentment she felt. If she didn't think about it, fine—but when she did think about it, she wanted to kick and scream.

All the filthy language she had kept inside for the past few months now came pouring out. Without even needing to think, the words just naturally came tumbling out—they seemed so fresh and new, making her so happy she even became a bit innovative. Everyone gathered around as if they were watching her perform. She became more pleased with herself as she went on, trying to get more of a reaction, resulting in gales of laughter. Her tears had dried, and a smile appeared on her face. There was only one thing she regretted—why didn't Ah San come out to face the attack? This made her angry all over again and want to provoke Ah San even more. Her curses basically centered around two topics: One was the difference between giving Chinese guys [X] and giving it to foreigners, and the other was the difference between taking money or not. Her argument was completely off the wall, yet not entirely without reason. From time to time, when she felt she was really making a point, she would repeat it over and over, like she was some kind of virtuoso.

She really hurled some filthy language! The young, unmarried section leader couldn't bear to listen, so she covered her ears and reprimanded her. She was already so worn out and exhausted from these past several days that she didn't feel like doing anything more than scold her, so she just tried not to listen.

Noodles got herself worked up with all of her cursing, and she was feeling quite invigorated. She still had so much she wanted to say! It was nearly too wonderful to express. Her eyes glistened as she stared off into the distance. She didn't notice a thing as the crowd in front of her moved aside to clear a path for Ah San. Her face pale as a ghost, she walked right up to Noodles and slapped her in the face. For a moment, a loud ringing filled her ears, and Noodles couldn't hear anything; only then was she able to faintly make out the image of Ah San standing in front of her. Ah San looked as if she had hurt her hand with the slap, and she was rubbing it on her pants. Then she raised it once more and slapped her again. This time she hit some teeth, and Noodles's mouth started to bleed. Noodles rubbed her mouth, and when she saw blood on her hand, she understood. It's hard to say whether she was angry or happy. Ah San had finally fought back. She had ignored her and ignored her, but in the end, she paid attention to her. Sounding a little like a spoiled child, she began to sob.

Once Ah San got started, though, she couldn't bring herself back under control. She raised her arms and beat Noodles again and again. She could feel that her hands were wet with Noodles's blood, tears, and spit, which made her more disgusted and want to hit her even more. She felt people pulling her arms and grabbing her around the waist, but she found a boundless reserve of strength—no one was going to keep her from beating Noodles. Venting her anger also gave her a surge of happiness—she had held it in for so long! Her calm, unperturbable demeanor had all been an act, deceiving others as well as herself. She was now learning firsthand the reason why this spring, when the rapeseed flowers were in bloom, everyone had been picking fights. It was actually a very good thing, and it helped solve some larger problems. She couldn't really see Noodles's face, which by now was nearly unrecognizable—but Ah San didn't stop! When her hand made contact with Noodles's body, it disgusted her. She was now getting her payback—how dare Noodles make her feel so disgusted!

Everyone was stunned. No one had ever thought Ah San would also act out; they had all just assumed, along with the section leaders, that she was one of those with a strong degree of self-control. Even in this kind of place she had maintained her dignity. Although people felt that she put on airs, they certainly didn't reject her; moreover, as the production team leader's favorite, they weren't about to give her a hard time like they did with others like her. Everyone kept a respectful distance. Now they rushed forward and tried to pull her away, but when they met with her indiscriminate, flailing attacks, they had no choice but to retreat in laughter. This laughter provoked Ah San to a critical level, causing her to forget that she had gone beyond the bounds of a serious fight and was now just being frivolous, as if she were just keeping at it for amusement and didn't expect anyone to take it seriously. Her attack was now without a goal, and whomever she could reach would do. The courtyard was in an uproar as everyone ran around laughing, playing a game of hide-and-seek with her. Finally, Ah San had exhausted her strength and lay down grimly on the cement floor of the courtyard, twitching from all of her physical exertion. The afternoon sun was like a hammer, ruthlessly pounding her chest.

From that point on, Ah San refused to eat. At first, to keep her from harming herself, the production team leader put her in handcuffs—but then realized her hunger strike might be in protest to the handcuffs, so she took them off. But she still refused to eat or drink, and just lay on her bed. When everyone went off to the factory, only Ah San and a guard remained. At first the guard tried to make small talk with her, but after getting no response, she eventually got bored and just sat by the door. The sun was shining warm and bright, and a strange insect was crawling over the floor. Come look at this, said the guard. There's something weird over here. I promise you've never seen anything like it! But when no response came, she could only sigh; she didn't say anything else. When everyone returned from the factory that evening, they saw Ah San's lunch tin sitting untouched beside her bed, and they all tried to be as quiet as possible, as if there were a gravely ill patient in the room. Women from the adjoining room also came over to poke their heads in and have a look around; some even sat at Ah San's bedside and sighed as they looked at her. A pile of food accumulated by her bed that included every type of snack one could buy from the convenience store, and those who had just received visits from their families donated the special foods and drinks they were given. It was as if these offerings might tempt Ah San out of her hunger strike and get her to start eating again.

Only Noodles kept away, hiding by herself in the furthest corner and not daring to come near Ah San's bed. Her face was still bruised and swollen from Ah San's pummeling. She had originally intended to refuse food along with Ah San, but whether that would have been to show she wasn't afraid of Ah San's hunger strike, or to express her support for Ah San, even Noodles herself couldn't tell. Whatever the reason, it wasn't enough to keep her at it for very long—she could bear neither her empty stomach nor the scolding from her fellow inmates and the production team leader, so she just started eating again. The production team leader came over a few times to encourage Ah San to get something in her stomach, but when Ah San didn't pay her any attention, she got angry. To Ah San's face, she said: Then you can deal with the consequences yourself! But in her heart she was worried, and decided she'd give it one more day and then send her to the hospital to get an IV.

Ah San slept. She didn't really feel that hungry, but she fell into a state of deep reflection. She wondered how she had been able to calmly endure this kind of life for so long. How had she kept going for over half a year? She thought back over it all: attaching tags, the knitting machines, sewing patches, packing up, loading the truck, unloading the truck; drills, sitting in classes, eating out of a metal box, cutting her hair and fingernails short; having only three changes of clothes per season, the inmates' filthy language, their love notes to each other, their jealous rivalries; and of course Noodles' toadying and sucking up . . . all of it. It all made her so disgusted and depressed, it would be better to just die!

When the thought of death crossed her mind, she calmed down. She looked back on her nearly thirty years of life, and many people and events appeared clearly before her eyes. As these people and events drew near to her right then and there, she felt a slight tinge of excitement. She had experienced many ups and downs and gotten a taste of the pleasures life had to offer. Although she had been unable to hold on to them, it was as the saying goes: Don't hope for eternity; just hope to have once had something. Wasn't this the case for everything? All of life was to have once had something. Calculating her gains and losses in this way, Ah San felt satisfied with her life. She had the overwhelming feeling that death was really not so frightening, to the point that it didn't even make her feel sad; actually, she was slightly happy.

Her mind was crystal clear, and her thoughts were active—it was like feeling talkative and spirited after a few drinks. Several times when she slept, her mind stayed on track, marching forward with quick, tiny steps and carrying her through a series of images that were all lively and vivid. She let go of any sense of responsibility and felt directionless and free. Everything anyone said to her became just puffs of wind past her ears—she wasn't in the least bit interested, and to listen would be wasted effort. She was just fine like this, really just fine. Now, as she closed her eyes, she saw the distant, shadowy mountains rising above the high walls of the compound, turning a brilliant green under the enchanting springtime sun, as gleams of light darted around like wild honeybees.

On the morning of the fourth day, Ah San was taken to the hospital.

To keep her from pulling out the IV, her arms were fastened to the bed so she couldn't move. But she didn't really care, and she didn't listen to anything anyone said to her. As the glucose solution entered her body, her mind became more sluggish, and thinking became more cumbersome. At the same time, her body began to feel restless and somewhat revived. She started to feel hungry. At mealtime, the smell of food in the room roused her hunger, and her ears actively tried to home in on other people's conversations and do their best to understand. But then she was overcome by a wave of drowsiness, and as she fell asleep, the conversations gradually faded away until she could no longer hear them.

She slept for a long time. When she woke up, she realized that a good bit of time had passed, and she slowly started to understand her situation.

She discovered that the room was quite dark—not because it was night, but because the sunlight was so dim. The other patients in the room were quietly laying in their beds. Her ears were filled with a soft, gentle humming. Then she saw the door to the room open; someone came in and leaned a dripping wet umbrella by the doorway. She realized it must be raining outside. The person walked over to her—it was the production team leader.

The production team leader walked over to her bed, stared at her for a while, and said: Okay, you've done it now; you've saved face. Is that still not enough? After a pause, she added: With all my pressing responsibilities at the production team, I've still come to see you, and everyone knows about it—is it enough for you if I lose face? Ah San avoided her eyes. The production team leader continued: You should at least help me save a little face—and help the government save face as well. They both found this last phrase amusing and couldn't help but smile a little. Although they quickly got their expressions back under control, the atmosphere had nevertheless been lightened a bit.

The production team leader flopped down in a chair beside Ah San's bed and extended her legs, tucking her hands underneath her thighs and holding her shoulders up. Stretching herself out like this, she said: I know that every one of you feels you've been wronged, sent out here to suffer in the middle of nowhere, and you don't know how to get back at us. After two or three years, though, you'll all be back in Shanghai doing whatever you want. But what about us? We have to stay here— aren't we being wronged, too? I know I shouldn't be talking to you like this—you don't need to understand us. We only need to understand you. But we're all just people, and we always need to let each other know how we feel. When she reached this point, the production team leader suddenly began to feel depressed, but she fixed her gaze straight ahead and pushed those thoughts out of her head.

Ah San looked over at her. She noticed there wasn't a single wrinkle on her youthful face, and her eyes were bright and clear; her skin just wasn't very good, with a sickly pallor from lack of sleep. Ah San thought to herself that the production team leader actually wasn't that bad looking, although the uniform didn't suit her.

All of a sudden, the production team leader laughed and said: One time when we were talking to a prisoner, she was telling us how this guesthouse in Shanghai did this kind of business, and that guesthouse did that kind of business, until finally she just said: Team leaders, don't ask me what guesthouses I've been to; just ask me which ones I haven't. What were we supposed to say? The production team leader looked over at Ah San, and their eyes met; after a moment, they each looked away. The production team leader looked around the room—the other patients were all laying in their beds with their eyes closed and seemed to be asleep. The room was very still; a light patter of rain could be heard outside the window. The production team leader asked: Do you know what makes it possible for us to keep on living here? Ah San shook her head. It's because here, we're better off than everyone else. The production team leader looked into Ah San's eyes and saw not only her strength, but also a look of imploring, as if to say: I've given you my dignity—won't you let me save face?

Ah San's hunger strike ended that evening, bringing the total time she refused to eat to six days. She felt a little embarrassed as she took her first bites of food, as if everyone were laughing at her. But nobody was paying any attention. From beginning to end, the whole episode proceeded just as one might expect—nothing really notable or unexpected occurred. This made her feel even more embarrassed. She acted as if the food she was eating had been stolen; she finished a bowl of rice porridge, lied back down on her bed, and wished that everyone would forget about her. This was the first time she had really gotten to take a good look around the room, and she noticed that it was cleaner and more peaceful than the average hospital room—the patients were all prisoners, so there was no one coming in to visit. All together there were eight beds lined up side by side, slightly offset from one another so that the occupants could gaze at the trees outside the window. The leaves on the branches concealed a streetlamp crafted with a flower petal design reminiscent of the city.

Dinner was served at four-thirty in the afternoon, so the evenings seemed unusually long. It was then that the atmosphere in the room livened up a bit, with the clear, soft sounds of the other patients chatting reaching Ah San's ears.

Their discussion was about a prisoner who had escaped from the men's labor reform camp that was located the furthest out in their district. The night before last, the authorities had sent out three police cars to search for him, but they still hadn't found him. Ah San gazed out the window at the gradually darkening sky; the streetlamp had come on, but because there wasn't quite enough electricity, it could only emit a dim, yellow light. She wondered why she hadn't heard any sirens. Her mind then wandered back to her initial arrival from Shanghai, and she saw that lone cypress tree standing on top of the rolling hills, which remained in her field of vision the whole way.

Another day passed, and the production team leader came in a delivery truck to fetch her. Ah San sat in the bed of the truck, getting jostled around as they drove. The tips of the wheat planted on the higher ground had all turned golden, and the rice shoots were already poking up in the lowland paddies. The tea leaves were green and glossy, and the hills near and far had become fresh and verdant. Stands of trees rose intermittently, forming green protective screens. Even the cypress tree became part of this scene, along with a few others scattered here and there. A few white clouds floated by overhead, and then dissolved into the bright blue sky. A new sense of vitality arose in Ah San's heart as she squinted her eyes to shield them from the dusty wind. The fields stretched out before her far into the distance, where they eventually became the narrow line of the horizon.

Life once again resumed as usual. A mountain of work had piled up in the factory, so each work day ended later and even began cutting into their classes and morning calisthenics. Things in the dorm were still in the same state of unrest, although the frequency of incidents had begun to decrease, which seemed to indicate that the main wave was subsiding. As summer approached, everyone's restlessness was gradually replaced with laziness and sluggishness, and they became quite reserved. As for Ah San, it was just as the production team leader had said—she had saved face. Everyone now seemed to see her with new admiration and respect. Noodles, however, didn't dare come near her and stayed as far away as she could, which made Ah San quite happy. So the days were now much more bearable than they had been, but Ah San's state of mind was different from before.

Now that she had gotten used to all the new aspects of life here, and had finally released all of the physical and emotional tension that had accumulated in this harsh reality, Ah San realized how unbearable this life really was. It was as if she had finally opened her eyes and seen everything clearly. At first, Ah San had only been present as a bag of bones; now, her spirit had returned. She thought to herself: It's only been a little over half a year, and there's still more than a year left—how I am supposed to get through it? Ah San felt distressed; she couldn't sleep at night, and all sorts of thoughts went floating through her head, nipping away at her patience. She knew she shouldn't think these thoughts, but she couldn't seem to help it. Her face thinned down until her chin became pointy and sharp. For each meal she would only eat about as much as a cat, and she often felt dizzy. She worked so hard it was like she was punishing herself; her hands were more like tools than hands, attending to all sorts of tasks. One close look into her eyes revealed how she was suffering. Her gaze became penetrating, and her eyes emitted a scorching light. She spoke less than she did before; a full day could go by without her producing a sound. A vague, oppressive feeling emanated from her, and wherever she was, the atmosphere would become strangely depressing.

In such a mechanical existence, however, everyone became simple-minded and numb, and no one noticed the changes in Ah San. The only person who did notice was Noodles, who avoided Ah San like a mouse avoiding a cat. Actually, after that major incident, Noodles felt even closer to her. It was as if their hand-to-hand combat had eliminated the barrier between them, even though on the surface she never got anywhere near her. Now, Noodles could tell everything Ah San was thinking. Only she could tell that it was all too much for Ah San to bear, and she was genuinely worried for her. She knew that if things continued on like this, Ah San wouldn't make it. This was no way for Ah San to pass her days.

Ah San had no idea that when she was experiencing her worst suffering, there was one person who was suffering even more. When Ah San was nearing her wits' end, a plan slowly took form in that person's mind.

After work had ended that day, Ah San remained in the factory going over some work that needed to be redone. Noodles asked if she could stay and help Ah San; the production team leader agreed, and Ah San pretended not to hear. Once everyone else had left, Noodles immediately rushed over to Ah San and said: Sister, you have to run away! She was nearly trembling with excitement as she presented her great idea. Stunned, Ah San raised her head and looked up at Noodles's face, which had come up right next to hers. It looked incredibly pale under the fluorescent lights, and Ah San could see the enormous pores in the crevices at the sides of her nose, along with a bruise on her forehead, which was thanks to her.

Sister, you have to run away! Noodles lowered her voice as she repeated this, although it still echoed throughout the quiet, empty factory floor.

I know you're different from the rest of us—you can't stay in this kind of place. Run away! Go to the south—everyone down there is from somewhere else, and they won't make you report your household registration, so it'll be really easy to blend in!

Ah San calmed down and evaluated what Noodles was saying, trying to figure out whether or not she might be right.

Based on what I've heard from a few who've been locked up here for the second or third time, every year people escape, and some of them have never come back; they go out the main gate and head for the mountains behind the prison, where they find a place to hide and wait until dark; then they go down over the mountains where there are a few peasant homes. If you give them money, you can spend the night there, and then the next morning you can make your way to the highway and hitch a ride on a truck, which can take you to the train station. Really—I've gathered all this information for you. The peasants are desperate for money, and if you give them a little extra, they'll take you right to the station—just don't tell them you've come from here. Actually, even if you don't tell them, they'll still know, but this way they don't have any responsibilities. If you want to escape, I'll help you get everything in order; it would be best to do it under the cover of night.

Ah San slowly moved her eyes away from Noodles's face and lowered her head as she turned back to her work; the whirring of the sewing machine started up once again. Noodles's face fell, and then she muttered: If you don't believe me, fine—but everything I've said is true. She left Ah San and retreated to one of the corners, where she sat on a cardboard box hugging her knees and staring out the window, looking like she was lost in thought. Her expression became sullen and serious, as if she had just been greatly hurt.

In the middle of the night, when all was quiet, Ah San lightly turned over, reached her hand into her pillowcase, and tore off a patch that had been sewn on the pillow. She felt around inside the kapok-fiber stuffing until she found a roll of money—it was the five hundred RMB the Author had given her. Although she hadn't thought about how she might put it to use, she felt she might have a special need for it at some point, so she never reported it to the production team leader. Now, as she held this roll of bills in her hand, she knew exactly what she must do. Lying there in the dark, she couldn't help but smile.

Ah San prepared for her escape. She began forcing herself to eat more in an effort to gain strength. She carried a bottle of insect repellant with her in preparation for her time hiding in the mountains, so that she wouldn't be eaten alive by mosquitoes. She had long been familiar with the path from her section quarters to the main courtyard, which she had walked many times to go discuss work matters with the production team leader. She also understood that on Sundays, the section leaders all went to the main headquarters, leaving only one person behind to supervise. She had even cleverly hidden away an exit pass from one time when she was called to go meet with the production team leader—the guard at the main gate had been busy dealing with some new arrivals and had forgotten to collect it from her. Excitedly, but calmly, she made these preparations. There was never a moment when she wasn't thinking of her plan of escape, running through it a thousand times in her head. When she thought of a part that made her anxious, her face would flush and her fingers would tremble slightly. But no one noticed, and even Noodles had stopped paying her any attention—she had become quiet and dispirited, and it was rare to hear her causing any commotion; she was always just hunched over her work.

Ah San waited for the right moment. She knew this was by far the most crucial part of her plan, and that the right moment wasn't something that could be determined through deliberate consideration, but was something she would just have to feel. She calmly waited for it to arrive. It should be a kind of spiritual arrival, and when she held her breath and concentrated she could nearly feel its approach. The days ticked by one by one; the weather gradually grew hotter, and the days became longer. In the evenings, bright stars twinkled overhead, casting down their snowy light, and the moon shone bright and hot. Everyone was gripped by fatigue and yawned all day long. For Ah San, however, her mind became clearer and her eyes grew brighter with each passing day, yet she kept herself calmly under control, waiting for her chance.

When she got up that morning, the sky was clouded over, and by afternoon a light mist began falling. It was Sunday, and that morning the production team leader was still in the factory with everyone working an extra shift. In the afternoon, she announced they would be calling off early and then left, leaving only the section chief on duty. By three o'clock everyone was struggling—some were nodding off, their heads drooping down little by little, and whatever work they had in their hands dropped to the floor. The sound of the sewing machines also became less steady and more sporadic. The gray, overcast day made everyone feel depressed. But in no time at all they had endured for another hour, and the section chief called off work. Everyone got up and put away the tasks they had been working on, moving as quickly as they could to rush out the door and be the first to the sink to wash their clothes and hair. Ah San, however, said: Section Chief, I'll stay here a while and finish up before I go. The section chief said okay and told her not to forget to turn off the lights and lock the door when she left. Just then, Noodles raised her head and looked over at Ah San with a glint in her eye, an irrepressible smile spreading over her face. Their eyes met, and for a moment neither of them turned away as they exchanged looks of mutual understanding. The smile stayed on Noodles's face as she walked by Ah San and meaningfully placed a hand on her sewing machine; it seemed as if she were waiting for a response. If she weren't so thoroughly disgusted by Noodles's body, Ah San might have reached out and touched her hand. But, she didn't. Noodles passed by her and didn't look back, but the image of her glowing smile lingered resolutely in front of her eyes for a long time afterward.

Everything proceeded just as Noodles had said, and it all went just as smoothly. Night fell early that evening; around six o'clock it had already started getting dark. Gray skies covered the misty mountains, almost as if there were a layer of protection between heaven and earth. The rain was steady but not that hard, just enough to thoroughly envelop Ah San's body with its moisture. The sound of the rain filled every space, so that it also acted as a layer of protection. The drizzle was so fine that Ah San

would nearly be unable to see it were it not for the glittering, crystal droplets sliding off the leaves and tips of the grass.

Ah San began to make her way down through the mountains. Thanks
to the rolling hills, the roads down out of the mountains weren't that
steep, and Ah San could barely even sense their slope; only after walking
for a bit and then looking back could she tell whether she had been going
uphill or downhill. As Ah San made her way over a thick area of grass, she
looked down and suddenly noticed that the grass where she was stepping
had actually already been trampled, although it was not very obvious.
Could it have been the last person who escaped? Well then, continuing
along that way must be right. Yet when she deliberately tried to find the
path, she couldn't see it.

Ah San raised her head, and the water droplets on her eyelashes slid
back into her eyes. She could dimly make out a vast stretch of hills towering over the faint form of the cypress tree. Suddenly, the form morphed
into a person. Was it Bill? Or Martin? It was Bill. When she thought of
Bill, Ah San's heart was instantly filled with a pathetic sort of joy, and she
thought: Bill, do you know where I am right now? She used Bill to boost
her confidence and make her believe that none of this was ordinary, that
it would not just come to some ordinary conclusion.

There was no one else on the hill—only Ah San and that cypress tree.
She walked on blindly, with the path obscured by the mist and the coming night. But she wasn't concerned with the path—she just mechanically
pressed on, diligently putting one foot in front of the other. When she
shivered and her teeth chattered, it almost sounded as if she were laughing. She forgot about the time; all she knew was that it must be the next
morning. When the lights of a cottage appeared in front of her, she nearly
couldn't believe her eyes—it was a scene she thought would never tran-
spire. When she stopped walking and gathered her wits, she realized that
the light was actually quite nearby, about a hundred meters away. Only
now, at this moment, did she feel a jolt of fear, and she panicked: If these
people go and report me, what will I do? Her legs felt like jelly, and it
was only with difficulty that she made it that next hundred meters. She
made up her mind: If the people she encountered did anything to raise
her suspicions, she would leave immediately. With this plan in mind, she
calmed down.

As she approached the light, she smelled the scent of food, along with the grass, kindling, and charcoal burning in the cookstove. She suddenly realized it was actually still the same evening, around dinnertime. No matter how late these people ate, it most likely wouldn't be past eight o'clock. She examined the dwelling; it was a one-story house with a row of three rooms in the front made out of brick with tile roofs, and two earthen rooms with thatched roofs on each side. On one side was the kitchen, where the fire had already been put out and the lights were turned off, and on the other side was a storage room that abutted a pigpen; there was no courtyard wall. The door to the main room was closed up tight, as if no one lived there, but some faint lamplight could be seen coming from the two windows on either side. As Ah San approached the door, she stepped on a pile of chicken droppings and nearly fell—a soft cry escaped her lips, but she regained her footing and went up to knock on the door. A woman's voice responded, asking who it was. Ah San said: Sister, please open the door. The woman again asked who it was. Ah San said: Sister, please open the door, I'm just passing by. The woman was quite stubborn, and insisted on asking who it was. Ah San knocked again, and a voice shouted back: If you knock again, I'll call for help—there are police over at the labor reform camp! It was only then that Ah San realized that anyone living in a single dwelling out here by itself so close to the labor reform camp would naturally be quite fearful.

Ah San stopped knocking, but she felt exhausted and was unable to set off again. She slowly walked along the wall of the kitchen to keep herself from slipping and made her way around to the rear of the main room. There she found a window with long eaves extending out over it, so she sat down under the eaves and rested her feet while she tried to devise another plan.

She curled up in a ball, hugging her knees to her chest and tucking her head down—everything that had happened felt like a dream. She was so exhausted she felt like she could die. Sleep came over her; she would wake up and catch herself as she started tipping over to one side, and then continue on sleeping. The whole earth and sky was permeated by the gentle sound of the rain, and everything was soaked—it was as if she were in a different world. She gradually figured out how to sleep sitting up, so she didn't tip over anymore. She forgot about the cold and the rain, and she was overcome by the warm, sweet embrace of sleep. It was like she was sleeping in a bed. She saw Noodles's face gradually draw nearer to her, and she saw the bruise on her forehead, which caused her to flinch and wake up.

Now she was completely awake, and she could clearly hear the chirping of small insects. She was a bit surprised; she felt that the scene in front of her looked entirely different. She refocused her eyes and discovered that the rain had stopped, and the moon had moved out from behind the clouds, casting its bright, white light over everything. The haystack in front of her, which had been totally soaked in the rain, was now glowing with a pale, yellow light. She placed her hands on the ground to prop herself up more comfortably, and unexpectedly felt one of her palms come up against something smooth and round. When she lowered her head to look, she saw that it was an egg, half buried in the mud.

She lightly scraped the mud away and dug out the egg, thinking it was a delicacy from heaven—eating it raw would satisfy both her hunger and her thirst. As she lovingly looked it over, she noticed that it was small and translucent. Its thin, flesh-colored shell looked so delicate and fragile, and it was marked with a trace of blood.

This is a virgin egg, Ah San thought. Just then, she noticed a warm feeling in her palm—it was the soft, pure, humble heat from that young mother hen's body. My God! Why had she wanted to cover up this egg—so that no one would see it? Ah San felt a stab of pain in her heart, and a number of thoughts rushed through her mind. As she held the egg in her hand, she lowered her head and wept.

First draft, September 11, 1995
Second draft, October 17, 1995

MATCH MADE IN HEAVEN 天仙配

The village head of Xia Kilns was very worried. Day and night he racked his brains: How could this be resolved?

It all began with the digging of a well. And mentioning the well first requires mentioning the village spring, the lifeblood of Xia Kilns. This spring trickled down from the mountains into Xia Kilns, nestled there in the mountain's folds. If a crow were to fly high over this mountain crevice, drop an egg in a crack between the rocks, and be unable to find it again, that would be Xia Kilns. Yet the town had persisted for many generations. In ancient times, the kilns had been charcoal ones. In those days, the mountains were green, and the spring flowed through the lush forest that covered them. Every slope and ridge was dotted with kilns burning charcoal. This meant that in the summer, Xia Kilns was enveloped in white smoke, as if a cloud had fallen out of the sky and settled among the folds of the mountain. From the village's name, it should be obvious that the family running the kilns was named Xia, but that was only in the beginning. Later, the Sun family arrived in the village by following the path that was used to transport charcoal down the mountain, and the Xias received them warmly. At any rate, day in and day out, from spring to autumn and from winter to summer, the spring gushed through the thick forest that covered the mountains, and the sound of its gurgling filled Xia Kilns with a heavenly music. Many generations passed, and the Xia and Sun families grew and flourished. The kiln chimneys crowded closer together atop the rolling slope, until the mountain was all dug up. Gradually and almost imperceptibly, the forest became sparser, the soil grew poorer, and the stream began to dry up. That's when the dispute over the kilns began. First, documents to file a lawsuit were sent to the local authorities. At the time, both the Xia and Sun families were well off, with enough money to pay court fees and hire lawyers. But the lawsuit soon became a bottomless pit, swallowing up all the gold thrown into it. After more than ten years, during which time a number of magistrates grew rich off the two families, the case was dismissed. Then the two sides resorted to violence. Both families were prosperous and large, and they relentlessly attacked one another for several years, until the Suns eventually drove the Xias off the mountain. This is why no one named Xia lives in Xia Kilns anymore. After so many generations, all the trees were eventually cut down for firewood, and one by one the kilns sat cold and unused. Since the whole area was now just dirt, it was put to use for growing crops, which sprouted up in clumps and dotted the land like donkey shit. Nowadays in Xia Kilns, not even the trace of a kiln can be found. The spring has been reduced to a small trickle no wider than a finger, thinly clinging to the mountain rocks as it drips over them. A few times it had even threatened to dry up altogether, which is how the business of digging the well came about.

Digging the well was the village head's idea. After the village committee discussed the matter, funds were raised and a specialist from the county's department of agriculture was brought in. Equipment was purchased, and each household contributed labor according to its size and landholdings. The sound of drilling soon reverberated through the peaceful air of Xia Kilns. By this time the mountain was already bald, and the houses squeezed in its folds were made of stone foundations, mud walls, and thatched roofs. They were crowded so tightly that the front eaves of one dwelling abutted the rear eaves of another, and villagers had to turn sideways to pass between them. The drill ran day and night—people stopped to rest, but the drill did not; the lights went on and children ran around playing beneath them. It was such as lively scene, as festive as New Year's! The village head walked around with his hands clasped behind his back, issuing instructions left and right—who expected anything bad to happen? By all appearances everything was moving along merrily. The specialist said they could hit water within the next day, and not a single person uttered anything unlucky or had an inauspicious dream. Each day was sunny and clear. But as they were clearing away rocks, the single sprout of Sun Hui's family, Sun Xixi, was buried in the bottom of the well. The village head would rather it had been himself.

Sun Xixi was eighteen that year. He had graduated from high school the year before but had not tested into college, so he was preparing to study for another year and try again. He was bright-eyed, broad-shouldered, and tall, and he also liked to wear suits, which made him look like he had just stepped out of a movie. Starting in middle school, girls would write him love letters, and some even came to his home to raise the topic of marriage, but he rejected them all. His only goal was to attend university, which he thought was his only way out of Xia Kilns. Leaving the village was a common goal among the local youth, who felt that all the government aid provided to Xia Kilns was pointless. Things like bringing in electricity, allocating special funds, and teaching them how to raise Angora rabbits were not getting at the root of the problem. There was only one real solution: to pick up and move away from this barren chunk of land. They'd heard that at one point twenty years ago, the government had initiated an effort to move Xia Kilns to level ground at the foot of the mountains, but the village ended up staying put. Some people left and were gone for about a month, but returned once they had spent their relocation allowance. Hearing this made the young people in the village nearly explode, and some of them even went to the village authorities to inquire about the policy. The authorities replied that this was no longer possible, since the land had already been distributed, and the population on the plains had increased in the past twenty years—where would they fit now, and who could spare land to give away to outsiders? To get out of Xia Kilns, a person would have to struggle on their own. As an educated and intelligent youth, Sun Xixi's determination to leave the village was greater than most others his age. Now, though, not only was he unable to leave the village, but he also had to remain buried in Xia Kilns, in the bowels of the mountain.

Sun Xixi was an only child. His parents had him late, when they were in their forties, and all their hope for continuing the family line rested on him. Perhaps as a result of that bygone era, when the Sun and Xia families were fighting over the kilns, the residents of the village placed particular emphasis on producing male heirs. Without enough people, how could the Suns have overcome the Xias to rule the mountain? People can eke out an existence on a barren mountain, but if there are no people, then the mountain may as well not even exist. People are the basis of existence. The people of Xia Kilns did not fear poverty; as long as they had sons, they were rich. If there was a little one crawling around the courtyard with a wiener dangling between its legs, and if there was a coffin ready and waiting under a grass covering in the side room, then that meant there were ancestors and descendants, and a dependable source from which to build a respectable life—everything else would be fine. Because of this, every year Xia Kilns owed a huge pile of money in fines for exceeding the family planning policy, and to be perfectly honest, the village's poverty was partially a result of these fines. How else could the village head have lost his party membership, which he carried with him from his time in the army? So the youths here all had their marriages arranged quite early, with the grooms' families famously offering generous betrothal gifts out of fear that no one's daughters would be willing to move to such an impoverished village. This accounted for the other main reason the village was poor. Sun Xixi's parents had long since stuffed away a particularly large amount of money under the mat on the kang for this purpose, waiting for the day a marriage could be arranged. Sun Xixi, though, had no interest in this and only cared about attending college. As the only son, he was always the focus of his parents' attention, and was also used to getting his own way, so it was a tricky situation. Although on this particular issue he would not listen, he was a good son in every other respect, always easygoing and filial. In fact, when it came time to contribute labor for digging the well, their family would have met their quota even if only his father, Sun Hui, had gone by himself. But Sun Xixi said no, he would go help his father do the work. Sun Hui felt his son had died in his place, and it broke his heart.

Now that his child was gone, Sun Hui gave the wood he had acquired last year to his son. He had originally intended to use these boards to make his own coffin—how could he have known when he was storing them away that his son would end up being the one to rest on them? He felt responsible for his son's death, that he had set him on the path toward it last year when he had procured the wood. It was truly unbearable! After the funeral, the old couple tidied up and drank pesticide. Luckily, someone saw them before they were finished and wrested the bottle from them. They were sent to the hospital in town that same night, and their lives were saved. Although their bodies recovered, their hearts could not, and they existed merely as empty bags of air. Seeing this lonely elderly couple laying side by side on the kang, the village head wondered how he could restore their spirits. For three days and nights he mulled it over, and then finally he thought of something.

What he thought of actually went back several decades to the battle with General Hu Zongnan. The village head was born in the fifties, so he'd heard about it from the old folks. They said that during the time when Hu Zongnan was attacking the Shaan-Gan-Ning Border Region, a young, wounded female soldier turned up in Xia Kilns. They didn't know what regiment she was from, but in any case it had been scattered by Hu Zongnan's forces. She had a wound on her belly—she'd followed an old path dating from the bygone days of the charcoal trade, and had actually crawled her way to Xia Kilns and burrowed into one of the haystacks belonging to Sun Lai's family. Back then, Sun Lai's grandmother had just married into the family as a young daughter-in-law, so she would rise early to fetch grass to start the cooking fire. When she went out to the haystack that morning, she found it stained completely red with blood. Then she spotted the small, pale face of the female soldier, eyes closed, nestled in the hay. The female soldier remained in Sun Lai's family's haystack for seven days and seven nights, during which time all the local villagers went to see her. At first they wanted to take her into the house, but as soon as they tried, blood ran out of the hole in her stomach, so they didn't dare move her. Nor did they dare feed her, because as soon as she ate or drank anything, pus would ooze out of the wound. She was unable to speak, and when they asked her questions it was unclear if she heard. She just slept, occasionally opening her eyes to peacefully gaze at the sky—that narrow sliver of sky over Xia Kilns, squeezed between the mountains. Her eyes were particularly large and dark, her lashes long and thick. She gazed at the sky for a while, and then once again closed her eyes. She seemed to have only a single breath left in her, yet it wouldn't release. The villagers all cried. Perhaps she was unwilling to part from this life, they thought.

She was so young, and she hadn't yet had the opportunity to experience life. Everyone got together to put up a shelter over the haystack to protect her from the dew, and they surrounded her with blankets, which made her appear even smaller, like a baby. On the evening of the seventh day, she finally drew her last breath. Right before that, she opened her mouth and called out a single "Ma." Her voice was so clear and crisp it sounded as if she had never been wounded, but then she immediately closed her eyes, and her face became slightly flushed with a dewy glow. The villagers thought of her mother, wherever she was, who must be worrying about her daughter. How could she ever know she had ended up in Xia Kilns? When the female soldier uttered this "Ma," it was as if she were calling out to the village of Xia Kilns! Everyone got together and collected some random pieces of wood—although by this time the village kilns had ceased operation, there were still a few trees around. After gathering these materials they gave her a proper sendoff, burying her in the cemetery on the hill at the entrance to the village. She was small, as were the coffin and grave, and her resting place looked like a little mound of dirt. Every year at the Qingming Festival, someone would always be sure to add a fresh layer of dirt over her grave.

The village head now thought of this female soldier. According to the story, she was a nice and attractive young woman, with a pointed chin and large, black eyes. If Sun Xixi were given a posthumous marriage, he thought, it would at least provide some comfort to the old couple. He also thought of how Sun Xixi had his heart set on attending college as a way of going somewhere, anywhere, away from Xia Kilns, which was now no longer a possibility. The young female soldier, though, had arrived from some other unknown place—maybe even a big port city. She had joined the army and had likely received some education, so she would probably be acceptable to Sun Xixi. What's more, both of these young people had died under tragic circumstances—the former by facing the enemy, and the latter, well, in the blink of an eye his life was just snuffed out, and there was no returning. They were both just beginning to blossom, and hadn't yet started their lives. In his imagination, the village head saw the young female soldier with her big eyes, staring up at the sky over Xia Kilns without a hint of resentment or complaint. These two poor youngsters would surely love each other dearly. Tears gathered in the corners of the village head's eyes, and his heart began to ache. After a long pause, he shook his head and said to himself: That's it, you've really got it! Although he'd lost his party membership, he had received a proper education and was, after all, a materialist. But then, he thought, maybe idealism is the best way forward—it can comfort the soul, and no matter what happens, that comfort will always remain in the heart.

Xia Kilns held the ghost marriage on behalf of Sun Hui's family. They dug up the grave of the young female soldier, moved it next to Sun Xixi's, and set up a tombstone for the new husband and wife. Because they didn't know the female soldier's name, they made one up and called her Fengfeng, which made her sound doted on. She had suffered so much and been so lonely, the villagers thought, that it showed there was now someone to care for her. They made a bridal chamber out of paper and glued some white "happiness" characters on it, and inside it they put a bed, a dresser, some blankets, a TV, a refrigerator, and a phone; in addition to donkeys, horses, pigs, and sheep in the courtyard, there was also a car. All of this was then burned along with some paper money. Funeral musicians were hired, and they played for the better part of the day. Several tables of drinks were set up, and everyone who was anyone attended the banquet, even including the specialist who had been called in to engineer the drilling of the well. In the middle of the feast, the village head, tearing up, said to Sun Hui and his wife: From now on, you go about your lives and the children will go about theirs—everyone will be just fine. After that, Sun Hui and his wife were at peace. That's not to say they weren't still heartbroken; heartbreak is still heartbreak, and they still cried from time to time, but they were at least able to get through the days. One by one the days ticked by and the seasons changed; before they knew it, three years had passed, and the fresh grave was no longer fresh. Then something unexpected happened.

It was almost noon that day when the jeep drove up to Xia Kilns. It was unable to fit through the village gate, so at that point the three people in it got out and walked. The first was Deputy Mayor Wang, a familiar figure from the nearby administrative town who had visited Xia Kilns several times before. The first time was to take disciplinary action against the village head; the second time was to distribute relief funds; and the third time was the first evening after electricity had been installed in the village, when he stayed overnight with the village head. The other two no one had ever seen before, but they had the look of cadres from the city. There was an old one and a young one, both with glasses on their pale white faces and wearing black leather jackets. Deputy Mayor Wang waved at the children who had gathered to watch the excitement and told them to go tell the village head that guests had arrived. With that, a whole string of children disappeared over the ridge like a puff of smoke. By the time the group of visitors, with their varying gaits, had ambled over to the home of the village head, he had already managed to kill a chicken and was waiting for the pot to boil so he could remove the feathers. The child who had been sent to buy cigarettes at the co-op had also already returned, and the village head was standing in the courtyard ready to greet the guests. Deputy Mayor Wang introduced his two companions to the village head as they entered the room: The older one was Old Yang from the county's department of civil affairs, and the younger one was Little Han from the county's cultural bureau. It was an early spring day, and the weather was still quite chilly, so everyone gathered around the warmth of the stove, which was heating some water for tea. First they chatted about the weather, and then they talked about the planting and the harvests. Then everyone fell silent for a moment, and Old Yang pinched out his cigarette, coughed, and started to speak.

The first thing Old Yang asked the village head was his age. The village head replied that he was a year older than Deputy Mayor Wang, which meant he was born in 1954, the year of the horse—that made Deputy Mayor Wang born in the year of the sheep, correct? Old Yang then asked if there were any elderly people in his family. The village head replied that his mother had died when he was seven, and his father had passed away last year. Then Old Yang asked who the oldest people in the village were. The village head laughed and said: Old Yang, whatever it is, if it has to do with Xia Kilns, you can just ask me—I might not be able to say much about the previous five thousand years, but I know a lot about the past hundred. As soon as the village head said this, an unhappy look spread over Old Yang's face. Deputy Mayor Wang tried to intervene, saying that the elderly villagers were not used to seeing outsiders, and that they wouldn't be able to speak very clearly anyway—it would be better to just ask the village head, and if he couldn't answer, then they could go find some old people. At that, Old Yang got to the point: In the spring of 1947, did or did not one of our wounded soldiers come to Xia Kilns.

The village head's heart pounded, but his mouth continued to function: Of course, I know exactly what you're talking about, I've heard the old folks talk about it ever since I was little. During the time of Hu Zongnan's invasion, a wounded soldier arrived here after crawling along the old path for transporting charcoal. Old Yang exchanged a glance with Little Han and asked: Was it a man or a woman? The village head's heart pounded once more as he wondered: Why on earth are they asking this? His answer was vague: There couldn't have been that many wounded soldiers who were women. Old Yang said it looked as if they'd better go find an old person. When the village head heard that, he knew he had to come out with the truth: It was a woman, that's why I remembered it! Old Yang sat back down and asked how old she was. If she were a soldier, said the village head, she couldn't have been that old. This time Old Yang stood up more decisively, and Little Han rose as well. They asked the village head to take them to interview some elderly villagers. The village head's family members, having just prepared food for the guests, now feared they were about to leave. The noodles have already been rolled out, they said, and the chicken's been cooked—everyone can talk together here, so why not eat before leaving? The village head wouldn't let them go, and Deputy Mayor Wang also spoke up on his behalf, saying there was plenty of time to have a meal before going out to find the old people. So the two men had no choice but to sit back down, temporarily shelving the topic and returning to small talk. As he drank and ate the spicy chicken, Old Yang's face began to redden, and his eyes took on a glassy appearance. He seemed to be softening up a bit, and when he spoke it was no longer so harsh. The village head encouraged him to drink more while secretly trying to work out why they had come. Judging from their questions, they all seemed to be centered around that young female soldier, and were not just random inquiries. Were her family members now looking for her? But nobody had heard a peep from anyone for so many years—why would they come now? If her family was looking for her, what was their background, where were they from, and what were their intentions? If they were to discover she had been married posthumously to Sun Xixi, how would they take it? The village head felt uneasy and didn't want to think about it. At several points he let his mind wander, and when he was asked a question he just mumbled something noncommittal. Then he gathered his wits and realized that would not do—he would have to take the initiative to figure out why exactly these men had come, and then figure out a way to deal with them. If he kept evading their questions like this, he might be able to avoid one or two, but what about fifteen?

So the village head decided to reintroduce the topic himself. He started from Sun Lai's grandmother discovering the female soldier's head poking out of the haystack, and went on through that evening of the seventh day, when she opened her mouth to call out a single "Ma" before closing her eyes. Finally, he delivered the profound conclusion that with that final "Ma," the female soldier was recognizing Xia Kilns as her mother, so the village has taken her as its own child ever since. The table fell silent as everyone became drawn in by the story. After a long while, Old Yang finally said it sounded like it must be her. After another pause, the village head cautiously ventured: It must be who? Old Yang looked him in the eye and said: The revolutionary martyr Li Shuyu. He then proceeded to lay out the whole story from beginning to end.

Li Shuyu, born 1930, Jiangsu province, had attended the Jinling Academy for Girls, where she first aligned herself with the revolution. She vowed to join the Communist Party and went to Yan'an with her boyfriend. Shortly after they arrived there was a strategic withdrawal from Yan'an, and as they were crossing the Yellow River the enemy attacked from the rear. She got wounded and fell behind, and that was as much as anyone knew. According to the last comrade who saw her, it was in this district that she had been injured. After 1949 her boyfriend transferred out of the army and was assigned to various leadership positions in a number of different provinces, and now he was retired. Although he had married and had children, he never let go of his first love from so many years ago, Li Shuyu. This was especially true in recent years, as he had begun writing his memoirs. As the events of the past resurfaced in his mind, he decided he should try to find out what had happened to her, so about six months ago he sent a letter to the county's department of civil affairs. Little Han here was responsible for recording the party history of the district. He had visited the site of every significant battle that had occurred that year and made inquiries, but to no result. But then several days ago he had received another letter ordering him to keep investigating, saying that an injured soldier couldn't have gone far, and that she had to be in this vicinity. So he had to comb the area once more, visiting each locality regardless of whether or not any fighting had occurred there. That's how they had now ended up in Xia Kilns, the most far-flung and remote area of the township. They had set off from the county seat in a Santana, but as they approached Xia Kilns they'd had to stop at the police station in town to exchange it for a jeep. As they bumped and bounced their way along the road, they came upon several places where rocks had slid down off the mountain-sides; at these points they had to get out and either move the rocks or push the jeep—only then did they finally reach Xia Kilns. They were not very hopeful at first, and had never expected to find such results—it was truly a case, as the saying goes, of wearing through iron-soled shoes searching for something, and then finding it easily by accident! Old Yang was now both happy and drunk, and he had become quite the chatterbox.

Hearing this, the village head was at a loss. He just couldn't connect the female soldier—that pitiful young woman in the haystack!—with the name "Li Shuyu." Although many decades had passed, and only a few people in Xia Kilns who had actually seen her were left, her memory was still very much alive. On top of this, her recent ghost marriage to Sun Xixi made her seem even more present, although now the image in people's minds was not of her in the haystack, but of her snuggled up against Sun Xixi's chest. But who was this "Li Shuyu?" What did "Li Shuyu" have to do with any of this? The name sounded like that of a revolutionary martyr, just as Old Yang had said, and he could imagine it as the name of an important person printed in a newspaper or book. Xia Kilns had been hiding the identity of this important person! The village head felt like he was dreaming. While still in a fog, he went along with Old Yang's sugges-tion that they go pay their respects at the graves of the martyrs. So they pushed back their bowls, stood up, and headed out.

The alcohol had started to go to his head, making the ground under-foot seem slightly unstable, and his body and mind seem nimble and light. The afternoon sun was shining brightly, creating a lazy atmosphere. The village was very peaceful: The pigs snorted in their pens, and the chickens quietly pecked at their food with an occasional cluck. The village head led the three visitors along a ditch that passed by Sun Hui's courtyard. It was empty, but some grain was spread out on a mat to dry in the sun, and a string of eye-catching red chili peppers hung from the doorframe, giving the impression that a little spirit had returned to the old couple's lives. As they walked past the courtyard, the village head remained at a loss. Gradually they approached the large hill at the entrance to the village, where generations of Xia Kilns villagers had been buried. Seeing the graves, the village head's mind cleared up a little, and he wondered why they were going there. His feet mechanically stepped around the grave mounds and headed toward Sun Xixi. There was no turning back now.

The four of them stood in front of Sun Xixi's grave. There was a double mound, with two names carved on the tombstone: Sun Xixi and Fengfeng. The village head looked up at the bright blue sky. He saw apple trees growing on the slopes in the distance, their short brown branches spreading over the ground. The Qingming Festival had not yet arrived, but a few people had come early to tend the graves, some of which already had fresh layers of dirt shoveled over them. There was also a new grave with a white streamer waving over it. The village head gazed around at their surroundings, and then looked back to the three puzzled pairs of eyes. He gave a sheepish grin and lowered his head.

That's when the village head's days of torment really began. At first there was no action, as if the whole episode had never taken place. After the jeep drove away and disappeared out of sight, there was no Old Yang or Little Han to be found. Then after a few days, a rumor made its way to the village. Someone had heard that the family of the female soldier was planning to come and move her remains to their hometown. They also heard that her family was very powerful and influential—some said they were from Beijing, some said Shanghai, and some even said Hong Kong or Taiwan. When these rumors made their way to Sun Hui and his wife, the old couple went to the village head to ask if this was really the case. The village head felt it best to keep them in the dark for the time being. Who could say for sure what the situation was, anyway—had anything actually happened yet? Maybe Old Yang and Little Han had found the real Li Shuyu somewhere else, and the female soldier was still just a female soldier. So he told the old couple no, it wasn't true. But if it really were the case, they asked, what would happen then? Without really thinking, the village head blurted out: Well, so what? It wasn't wrong to find a husband for this revolutionary martyr, and Sun Xixi was an upstanding young man. When students were sent down to the countryside, didn't they marry peasants and settle down in the villages? At this, the old couple breathed a sigh of relief and left. Thinking back over what he had just said, the village head also felt a little better himself. As the days continued to pass quietly, he felt even more confident about the situation—everything's fine, everything's fine, he kept telling himself. Just as he was really starting to believe it, the mail carrier delivered a message from Deputy Mayor Wang, summoning him to town the next day for a talk.

The village head teetered down the road on his bicycle, heading for town. He felt very uneasy and had no idea what awaited him there. Volunteer workers sent by their villages often lined the roads performing repairs; since it was Sunday, most of them were students off from school. Their faces were pale from sitting in the classroom all day, and they wore either jeans or other good clothing, which they were afraid of getting dirty. They couldn't help being clumsy at their work, and they often stopped to chat about current affairs or joke around. As they heard the bicycle approaching and turned to look, their faces still wore smiles, revealing rows of bright white teeth. The village head was shocked—he thought he saw Sun Xixi. The sun was scorching his back, and his whole body was sweating. At some points along the way he had to get off his bike and push it, and sometimes he even had to carry it on his shoulders. The wheat growing on the plains at the foot of the mountains was several inches high, and the mountains had a faint tinge of green. Had Deputy Mayor Wang called him to town to tell him something good or bad? Before, when he'd lost his party affiliation, he had been summoned to town for a talk. But then a few other times he had also been called to town to receive relief funds. At any rate, he knew deep down what this talk was about. As he neared the town, his conviction grew stronger.

Because it was Sunday, the town offices were closed. The village head continued along the brick path past the offices and walked into the back courtyard. Two single-story structures stood in the courtyard, emitting the clanging and chopping sounds of food preparation, along with music from a TV. This was where Deputy Mayor Wang lived. Deputy Mayor Wang was squatting on the ground fixing a bike, which had been disassembled and spread out all over the place. An old, worn-out tire was soaking in a basin of water. The village head was about to squat down in front of Deputy Mayor Wang, but just at that moment the deputy mayor stood up, spread out his big, dark hands, and said: I'd like to hear your explanation for giving the female revolutionary martyr a ghost marriage. Raising the topic this way made the village head feel more at ease, and he responded playfully: My party affiliation has already been taken away, and now you're trying to take away my human affiliation! Deputy Mayor Wang was not amused, and he looked the village head straight in the eye and asked: How do you suggest this be handled? The village head grinned, and Deputy Mayor Wang continued: They've sent a letter saying next month they want to come see the grave. What are you going to show them? The village head, grinning no longer, raised his head to look at Deputy Mayor Wang, who appeared slightly sympathetic. Go back, he said, dig up the grave, and put up another tombstone. The village head panicked and said he couldn't dig up the grave. Deputy Mayor Wang asked: If you don't dig it up, then what? The village head said that if they dug it up, the old couple would drink pesticide again. Hearing that, Deputy Mayor Wang squatted down again and started fiddling with the old tire in the basin, as if he were washing pig intestines. He was also from the countryside, and he knew that digging up a grave was no small matter. The village head also squatted down and stuck his hands in the basin as if he were helping, then told the deputy mayor the same thing he'd said to Sun Hui that day. Well, said the deputy mayor, this ghost marriage isn't appropriate because the ages don't work out. Well, said the village head, don't you know that when you go down to the House of Yin, you stop aging? Otherwise, why would a lifespan be referred to as a yang principle? You're willing to say this to *me*, said Deputy Mayor Wang, but are you willing to say this to them? Why don't *you* tell them? asked the village head, gesturing with his chin. Deputy Mayor Wang pulled the basin away and stood up silently, his back to the village head. Left squatting there with his two empty, dripping hands, the village head looked incredibly awkward. After a while he slowly rose to his feet and said: I'll be going, then. There was no reply— Deputy Mayor Wang was angry.

Over the next few days, the village head walked up to Sun Hui's courtyard several times, but he always ended up turning around. The red chili peppers hanging from the couple's doorframe burned his eyes. They really weren't that garish, and were likely just there to help get them through the days; with the slightest bit of carelessness they could so easily be knocked down. He also walked up to the edge of the well several times and looked down. From far away in the dark depths he saw the shadow of a person silently looking up at him. It's true, he thought. The fewer complications the better! The rumors circulating through the village had stopped, and this time things were unusually quiet—only the village head sensed that something was off. The Qingming Festival arrived, and when he went to add dirt to his ancestors' graves, he saw that Sun Hui and his wife were also there burning a whole stack of paper, including some paper children's clothing, hats, and shoes. He pretended not to see, but Sun Hui's wife called out to him, catching him off guard. Village Head, she said while wiping away tears, these two children should add another to the family. That's right, that's right, the village head responded vacantly. He quickened his pace, wanting to get away from her as fast as possible. But she stayed hot on his heels, murmuring behind him: If we take in a daughter-in-law, then we should also add a child. That's right, repeated the village head. They continued into the village, one in front of the other, before finally splitting off on separate paths. Only then did the village head slow down. He drew his hand into his sleeve, tucked the shovel under his arm, and sauntered home. In his mind he settled on a plan.

A few weeks after Qingming, just as Deputy Mayor Wang had said, some people arrived. It was an old man and an old woman, both with gray hair but very straight backs. They had the look of high-ranking officials, and were accompanied by some cadres from the county-level administration. Deputy Mayor Wang, Old Yang, and Little Han were also there, but this time they were bringing up the rear. The village head was immediately notified upon their arrival, and he nearly tripped over himself as he rushed out to welcome them. As he greeted those in front, he patted around for his cigarettes but was unable to locate his pocket. At this point he noticed his hands were shaking, and his mouth was quivering so much he couldn't produce a complete sentence. The two old people, however, were very nice, and they each shook his hand. His heart was trembling as he led them down the path to the village committee building, but he was then overcome with a different sort of mood. Despite the old couple's official attire, their gray hair, wrinkles, and sagging bags of flesh beneath their eyes made them appear not so different from the old peasant farmers, especially the man. The village head was touched by their kindly dispositions, and he now began to feel not so sure about the plan he had hatched that day on the Qingming Festival. They don't have it so easy, either, he thought. When they made it to the village committee building, they found that the door had already been opened, the floor had been swept clean, and hot water was already waiting for them to make tea. At first they sat down and made small talk about things like the population, the harvest, fines for underproduction, and the student retention rate. When the real topic came up, it was the old woman who spoke.

She spoke a crisp, standard Mandarin, which made her sound like a young woman presenting on television. For her opening line, she said: Many thanks to the citizens of this district for looking after our revolutionary martyr. She then continued on to say that comrade Li Shuyu was Mr. Fan's friend during his youth, and that they both participated in the revolution together. Even after this many years, not a day goes by that they don't think about her. As the village head started to relax a little, he suddenly realized that these were not the parents of the female soldier, but her peers. The man, then, must have been her lover. That meant that if the female soldier were still alive, she would be around the same age as this old woman, wearing the same sort of clothing and referring to them as "the citizens of this district" in the same crisp Mandarin. The village head now found the whole thing slightly less touching, and he even began to feel a little uncomfortable. Continuing this train of thought, then, what did this woman amount to? Hadn't she just weaseled into Li Shuyu's rightful place? Li Shuyu had died, of course, and Mr. Fan had to get married at some point, but what was this woman doing here spouting off like this if he was still so attached to his old flame? She shouldn't have come with him, really. The village head's discomfort turned to dislike, and his resolve, which had begun to waver, was now bolstered once more.

When the old woman was done talking, everyone grew quiet and waited for the village head to say something. The village head gave a single cough and slowly lifted his gaze. My sincerest apologies, he said, but it seems there may have been a slight misunderstanding. Everyone's eyes bulged as they stared first at the village head, and then at Deputy Mayor Wang, Old Yang, and Little Han. The three of them turned bright red and opened their mouths to speak, but they were stopped by a firm hand gesture from Mr. Fan, indicating that he wanted to keep listening to what the village head had to say. So he continued: Last evening, when we heard that the higher-ups were coming, we called a special meeting of all Xia Kilns residents who were over seventy to inquire further about what happened. Some of them said they couldn't really remember, while others said they did. They said that the young female soldier in Sun Lai's family's haystack wasn't actually a soldier—they didn't know where she was from, but she had been out gathering firewood when she lost her footing and slipped off a cliff. She managed to save her life by hanging onto a branch, and then crawled her way to Xia Kilns by following the old path that had been used for transporting charcoal. Because it was right at the time of Hu Zongnan's offensive, some people connected the two events when they retold them. They also said that for the first few days the young woman was still able to talk—she'd call out "uncle" when she saw a man and "auntie" when she saw a woman. And she seemed to have a Shanxi accent, so that doesn't match up either. Because this is about a revolutionary martyr, it's a government affair, and we can't allow for the slightest error—otherwise, we would be disrespecting the revolutionary martyr Li Shuyu! The old man's face turned deadly serious, and he remained seated without moving a muscle. The village head realized that up until this point, the old man hadn't really said anything. His wife, proving herself to be more than just a pointless accessory, launched into the deputy county magistrate, who had accompanied them: Is this how you do your jobs? As soon as Mr. Fan learned of comrade Li Shuyu's whereabouts, he got so excited he couldn't sleep for several days, and his blood pressure went up. The deputy county magistrate's face alternated between blushing and draining of color. All he could do was turn to Old Yang and Little Han to ask for an explanation, who then turned to Deputy Mayor Wang, who finally turned to the village head. Although the deputy mayor didn't utter a word, it was clear from his eyes that he was cursing all the village head's ancestors as far back as he could go. The village head ignored these signs and averted his eyes to look outside, where the villagers stood quietly watching the scene. Scanning the crowd, he saw neither Sun Hui nor his wife.

The old woman spoke up again: Mr. Fan knows you're all superstitious and have performed some sort of ghost marriage, but he's not upset—he knows that peasants require a long-term education. All he would like is to move Li Shuyu's remains to the martyr's cemetery for a peaceful burial, fulfilling the hope he has held onto for so many decades and providing a lesson for future generations. He had no idea your basic task here would be handled so sloppily, with no sense of responsibility! The village head remained calm and didn't listen to what the old woman was saying; instead, he simply watched her mouth, wondering how it could spit out so many words without interruption, like beans hopping around in a frying pan. Suddenly the old man issued another firm hand gesture, and the old woman immediately stopped. He stood up and said: Let's go see where the girl is. His voice wasn't very loud and his words were sparse, but the village head trembled as he followed suit and stood up. He once again saw something familiar in the old man's eyes, under which hung those two bags of drooping flesh. This sense of familiarity conveyed an incredible degree of what felt like mutual understanding. The village head once again became uneasy. Obediently he led everyone out of the village committee building, and all those who had been gathered outside the door cleared a path for their exit and watched them leave.

As the village head led them on their way along the drainage ditch, sunlight filtered down in slender rays between the eaves and intermittently illuminated their faces, which were all very somber. Behind them, keeping a certain distance, followed the villagers of Xia Kilns. Beyond the eaves and rooftops rose a bald mountain cliff, the top of which was white as snow under the shining sun, completely barren. It was a different world up on the cliff, but what kind of world was it? The procession reached the courtyard of Sun Lai's family, where Sun Lai, his wife, and his two parents stood waiting. They gestured to show the visitors where the haystack had been that year, as well as what the courtyard had been like, indicating what had changed over the years. The southern wall had been moved out several feet, and the gable had been extended, so the present appearance was a bit different. As they spoke they attempted to shoo the chickens away from the center of the courtyard, eliciting some clucking. The visitors formed a circle around the empty space, imagining the haystack that had stood at this spot sheltering the young female soldier. With a long face, the old man listened as Sun Lai's father told how she had spent seven days and seven nights in the haystack. He also said that, according to his mother, he had been born two years after the female soldier's arrival. The village head squatted down outside the circle and said nothing. The voice of Sun Lai's father sounded as if it were drifting in from some distant place. He repeatedly referred to "the young female soldier," and the information he recounted contained a number of gaps. But the old man didn't question him, nor did the village head attempt to correct him. The village head knew there was no fooling the old man—he might seem a bit dull, but he actually saw the details of everything quite clearly. There was another thing about this old man, though, that struck the village head as dull—a dull sadness.

The procession then followed the old man out of Sun Lai's courtyard. The village head had no choice but to follow behind and proceed toward the cemetery near the village entrance. The old man held his hands behind his back and lifted his head to examine the surroundings. He looked at the courtyard inside the gate, the pigs in their pen, and the grain drying on the ground. When a small child pressed up against his legs, he patted their head. His face relaxed a bit, and was no longer pulled quite so taut. Whatever dullness he had carried with him now seemed to soften, allowing him to move more freely. As the late morning sun shone down on the old man's gray hair, the village head thought of how many days and months had passed. They had passed on this old man's head, and they had also passed in Xia Kilns, but the young female soldier was still the young female soldier. The group arrived at the cemetery high on the hilltop and stood in front of the double grave of Sun Xixi and Fengfeng. The dirt that had been added for the Qingming Festival was still damp, and the mound of earth on the grave was still new enough for a piece of pink paper to still be sticking out, catching the eye. The old man stood in front of the grave for a while, then turned around and glanced over the villagers standing around him. He lowered his head and reached into his pocket to take out a small wallet, and out of the wallet he withdrew a photograph and handed it to one of the old men standing in the crowd. Take a good look, he said. Was this the woman?

The old villager took the photograph and looked at it for a long time without making a sound. Then he handed it to another old man who was older than him. The older old man also looked at it for a while in silence, and then he handed it to an old woman. She passed it on to another old man. The picture circulated through the crowd and eventually found its way to the village head. It was an old, yellowed photograph not much bigger than a finger, but the image was still clear. The top half of her body faced the camera directly, and her face was that of a student, with bangs cut evenly across her forehead and an old-fashioned jacket with a stand-up collar. Her lips were pursed—she was not smiling—and her eyes were jet black. The young female soldier he had never met suddenly leapt out before his eyes, and he felt as if he had known her for years. Starting from nothing in his mother's womb, he had grown up from a bare-assed monkey into a middle-aged man. But the young female soldier always retained this same face, just like in the picture—silent, not smiling, and with jet-black eyes. This little injured sparrow! The village head's eyes grew moist. He handed the photograph back to the old man, and saw that several of the old villagers were also wiping away tears. The village head paused and, with great effort, swallowed the lump in his throat. In a raspy voice, he said: For so many years, the people of Xia Kilns have taken her as their own daughter. The old man, also in a raspy voice, said: She was an atheist who believed in communism. With that, he looked down at the ground and remained still. At this point the village head knew he'd lost— the old man was simply more stubborn.

That evening, the village head stepped over the threshold of Sun Hui's home. He knew that if he didn't cross this threshold, the old couple would have no peace the whole night. In fact, they would have no peace for as long as it took for the village head to pay them a visit. As soon as they saw him, they understood, and their tears began to fall. Sun Hui's wife kept wiping her eyes until they were all red and puffy, as if they'd been pickled in tears. After crying for a while, she then got up to make tea, but the village head stopped her. These past few days, he said, I have been meaning to come talk to you, but I didn't have any spare time, and to be honest, I was afraid of making you cry, so I put it off. But if I didn't say anything, it would remain bottled up inside me and make me sick. Village Head, said Sun Hui, everyone knows you didn't have much of a choice in the matter. The village head cut him off: Wait, he said, And first listen to what I have to say. Several weeks ago, before the Qingming Festival, I had a dream, and it now seems clear that it was sent to me by Xixi's wife. What did she have to tell me? She said that she and Xixi had a good life together, and passed their days in harmony. But the Jade Emperor had unexpectedly selected her to be reincarnated. In her previous life, you know, she hadn't really had the chance to live, and she spent more time in suffering than happiness. Those last seven days were especially tortuous, and yet she wanted to live! So go, I said to her. You go first, and take Xixi with you the next year, so that you can once again be husband and wife. Elder Uncle, she said, you don't realize how remote Xia Kilns is, squeezed into the folds of the mountains. With no water and a road that's barely passable, the Jade Emperor is unable to pole his boat in to fetch me! Elder Uncle, she asked, could you send me out of there? At this point, the dream ended. At first I didn't take it to heart—it was just a dream, wasn't it? But after a while—well, not that long afterward, really—the higher-ups came, specifically searching for this woman and wanting to move her to the cemetery for revolutionary martyrs in the provincial capital. I was shocked—wasn't this a response to that dream? Wasn't this the Jade Emperor sending people to lead her out?

The next day, the village head sent someone into town with a letter for Deputy Mayor Wang, saying that everything had been taken care of. After three days someone would come for the remains, and he would handle everything; the officials needn't worry.

That day, a team of three jeeps driving in a row arrived in Xia Kilns. As they entered the village, a crowd of people could be seen busying themselves on the top of the hill. White smoke was rising up and blowing away in the wind, along with some bits of paper, burned black. An order was passed up from the rear jeep to the two in front, and the jeeps stopped about two hundred meters from the village entrance. There they waited, and nobody got out. Nobody in the cemetery up on the hill noticed the jeeps, and they continued going about their business. On orders from the village head, they burned four piles of paper on the four corners of the grave of Sun Xixi and his wife. While the paper burned, they kept repeating: Aunt and Uncle, Uncle and Aunt, I'm leaving now, and I thank you for all the care you've given me over the past three years. We got along so well—I'm going now, leaving behind Xixi and the baby, and I have to ask for more of your help. When they had finished chanting, they started to dig up the grave. They probed the area by sticking shovels into the dirt, and once they got their sense of direction they began to really dig. They burned some more paper, this time for Xixi, and spoke some comforting words while also encouraging him to be a strong and independent man. Smoke enveloped the charred bits of paper that hadn't been burned and carried them up into the air like a cloud of black butterflies. After being subjected to so much recent activity, the old boards of the coffin had already broken apart, and the village head collected the remains into an urn, along with several handfuls of dirt from the top of Xixi's coffin. It was not until he stood up that he saw the jeeps parked at the village entrance. He held the urn in his hands and wondered how it could suddenly feel so heavy if all it held were some bones and dirt. Fengfeng, he said quietly, this is to send you out of the mountains. He walked down off the hill and made his way to the road. Finally someone got out of one of the jeeps.

It was Mr. Fan, who was holding a piece of red cloth as he waited for the village head to approach. He wrapped the urn in the cloth and took it from the village head. A number of other people then got out of the jeeps. The old woman wasn't among them, which made the village head feel slightly more at ease. The moment the old man received the urn, the village head sensed that the young female soldier had suddenly became old—as if she had suddenly become the same age as Mr. Fan, with gray hair and saggy bags under her eyes. Several decades passed in a flash, and in the blink of an eye they were gone.

The old man got back in the jeep, followed by Deputy Mayor Wang, Old Yang, and Little Han, and they left. The village head stood there watching them slowly drive away down the mountain road. Behind him, the people continued their work, piling up a new, high mound on Sun Xixi's grave, adding fresh dirt, and burning another wreath of paper. On the gravestone, Fengfeng's name had been painted over in red, indicating she was still in the yang realm of the living, but that her resting place was already prepared and waiting.

1998

A Girls' Trip 姊妹行

When Fentian and Shui first set out, no one in the village thought it was a good idea. These girls were too wild and prone to bold actions without really thinking them through—if they weren't careful, they'd be kidnapped. When the villagers said this, though, no one actually thought they'd be proven right.

Fentian's boyfriend was a soldier stationed in Xuzhou, and when she received a letter from him inviting her to come for a visit, she asked her friend Shui to come along. This is always how it was with young couples in the countryside—the girl would invite one of her good friends to accompany her, like a young lady bringing a maid. Not only would this avoid arousing suspicion, but it would also help prevent things from becoming too awkward between the couple, so this "third wheel" was actually quite welcome. In keeping with conventions, Shui was single and a couple years younger than Fentian. They both liked to have a good time, so they agreed to go to Xuzhou together. In fact, Fentian's boyfriend had planned things out quite carefully and mailed them a roadmap before they left. Early in the morning they would get the bus at Hanji and take it to Dawangji, where they would then get a coach to Caocheng, arriving around three in the afternoon. Then at five o'clock they would catch the train to Shangqiu in Henan province, spending that night on the train and arriving in Shangqiu the next morning. When they got to the station, they would call Fentian's boyfriend using the number he'd written on the map beside the two characters for "Shangqiu." Beneath that, in tiny handwriting, he explained how to use a pay phone—it was necessary to have some coins with them, etc. When he got the call that they had safely reached Shangqiu, he would be able to relax. They would also need to tell him what tickets they'd gotten to Xuzhou, so he would know which train they were on. When they arrived, he would come with one of his army buddies to collect them at the station. He placed particular emphasis on the words "army buddies," which projected a fresh image of someone who had grown up and entered society. Although Fentian's boyfriend was ten months younger than her, he was much more steady and grounded, which is why she agreed to this proposed marriage. He was from the same village as her father's sister, so it was this aunt who had made the match. Since things were more open now than they had been in the past, the two had already met and walked around Hanji together; needless to say, Shui was there, too. When he returned to his unit, Fentian and Shui saw him off. So although they didn't really know each other that well, they weren't complete strangers, either. This was also one of the reasons Fentian accepted the invitation.

One could say that Fentian and Shui basically stuck to their instructions on the map, they just varied slightly on some of the details—actually, these weren't even really variations, but accommodations. Even though these accommodations were made according to the circumstances, they still demonstrated the girls' nature. It was inevitable that somewhere along the line one of the accommodations would lead to an incident, so it's not an overstatement to say that they were to blame for their later misfortune. That day, they did actually go early in the morning to catch the bus at Hanji, but they didn't walk there; they hitched a ride on a two-wheel tractor. Not long after leaving the village, they heard the tractor rumbling up behind them on the dirt road, and they recognized the driver—it was their middle school classmate Xiao Xiao from the neighboring village, who had now opened his own brickyard. So naturally both parties greeted one another, and the girls climbed up on the dump trailer and bumpily made their way to Hanji. They got the bus, which was also driven by an acquaintance of theirs—Lin, another former classmate, who drove the bus along with his cousin. When they boarded the bus, they sat in the front seats and chatted with their old classmate all the way to Dawangji. He invited them to lunch at a small restaurant beside the bus station and ordered some peanuts and cold *fenpi* noodles to share, along with three servings of dumplings each. Although they didn't have any alcohol, the three classmates became quite worked up reminiscing about the old days, and all of their faces reddened with the animated conversation. Then they parted ways, with Lin heading back toward Hanji, and the two girls getting on the coach to Caocheng. This portion of the trip felt a little lonely, which was perfectly normal, since they didn't run into anyone they knew and nothing unexpected occurred.

Because they had gotten up early, and also because they had been so excited, the two girls were now feeling tired, so they settled in and dozed off. In the time it took for a nap, they reached Caocheng. However, night had already fallen. Caocheng was a county seat, so the streets were much wider, there was a lot more traffic, and people seemed a little more uptight; before they had even gotten out of the bus station, they'd already been pushed and shoved a few times. But this didn't put them off. On the contrary, it only roused their spirits: They found the scene quite impressive, and they knew that Xuzhou would definitely be more impressive than Caocheng. The bus station was nearly right next to the train station, and they went over and located the ticket window. Just as they were digging out their money, a woman who had been squatting near the window stood up and told them she had two tickets to Shangqiu. Her husband and son had been intending to go there that evening, but they'd eaten something bad and suddenly got food poisoning, so now they couldn't go. Fentian and Shui wondered if this person might be a ticket scalper like they'd read about in the newspaper. The woman immediately guessed what they were thinking and told them she didn't want a penny over the original cost. It's just that if she went to exchange them at the ticket window they would charge a service fee, so she didn't want to lose out. Warmhearted girls that they were, Fentian and Shui didn't like to see anyone in a tight spot, so they took the tickets and checked them over a few times. The woman said she would see them over to the ticket inspection gate, just to verify they weren't fake. If she was going to these lengths, what was there left to doubt?

Later on, Fentian had her suspicions about this woman: Did she have any connection with the group that kidnapped them? The more she thought about it, the more she felt it must have come down to that cell phone, and not have had anything to do with the woman. So, while this interlude may appear a little suspicious, it actually doesn't amount to anything—didn't they get on the train without any problem? The train left on time, and the last stop announced on the loudspeaker was indeed Shangqiu. They got to Shangqiu right at the time when Fentian's boyfriend said they would, just as dawn was beginning to break. They left the station, bought their tickets, and started looking for a pay phone. They asked several people where to find one, but no one knew for sure, and they were sent on a few wild goose chases. Fentian was getting anxious, so she went up to someone and asked: Where on earth can we find a phone around here? The person stopped and looked at Fentian, then reached into their pocket and pulled out a phone, saying: You can use mine. Later, what Fentian criticized herself for most was going up to this person. How could she just randomly go up to people on the street? This gave the impression she was not very discerning. At the time, of course, she didn't think about it that much, and she took the phone. She didn't know how to use it, though, so the person helped her enter the number and then told her when to talk. At first the voice coming through the phone didn't really sound like her boyfriend's, but as she listened more, it did. She told him they had made it to Shangqiu and bought their tickets, and she told him what time they would arrive. He said that when they got off the train, they should exit the station through the underground passageway, and he and his army buddy would be there waiting for them, "if we don't see you, we won't leave." This last phrase carried an easygoing freshness, indicating that he was really living a free and open life; it sounded a little strange to Fentian, but she also liked it.

After a day and night on the road, the two girls weren't the least bit tired, nor did they feel there was anything to fear in this strange city with its unfamiliar people. Although they hadn't seen much of the world, they had read some books, and they'd gained some understanding from them. So they remained calm and composed as they pushed and shoved their way through the chaotic square in front of the train station, buying some *baozi*, water, and a few magazines to read on the train; they even bought a sack of bread to give to Fentian's boyfriend and his army buddy. They saw a few strange people and a few strange things, but they didn't find them suspicious, only amusing. Because they were in a happy mood, and also because they were away from their village and there was no one around they knew who could reproach them, they didn't restrain their laughter. For a while, they laughed at basically everything they saw. At one side of the square, for example, a row of desks was set up with people sitting at them. It was clearly a place to register for something, but register for what? The name of a vocational school was written on a sign, and the topics of study included growing bean sprouts, raising earthworms, and fixing noodle makers, but no one was going up to register. Of course, this made them laugh. There was a young person wearing a green military uniform for no apparent reason, complete with shoulder straps and copper buttons, who looked like a soldier but with hair down below their ears and almost to their collar, like some foreign military personnel. This, too, made them laugh. A little while later another person appeared in the same uniform, and then a third and a fourth, until they realized there were lots of young people dressed like this all around them. This made them want to laugh even more. From this point on, whenever they looked at each other, there was always something making them laugh. They had always been a couple of giggly girls, and sometimes people would get irritated with them and say: Laugh now because your days of crying are ahead of you! No one expected they would be proven right.

They waited happily at Shangqiu Station, and when it was time, they boarded the train, the whistle blew, and they were on their way to Xuzhou. They were taking a slow train that stopped at every little station. Although it seemed like the train would start moving again before it even came to a complete stop, new people would enter their car, while others who had just been in the car were now left standing on the platform under the station sign, receding into the distance as the train slowly pulled away. As this went on, the sun shining through the train's windows gradually moved farther away until it became a small reddish yellow ball shining down on the fields, which had already been cleared in the autumn harvest. They appeared open and vast, while the stations where the train stopped seemed small and isolated. But because of the mood they were in, they were completely unable to appreciate the journey or this feeling of loneliness that had suddenly arisen. Instead, they just grew more and more irritated with sitting, commenting that taking the train was harder on the lower back than doing manual labor. Because it was a slow train providing local service, there was a constant turnover of passengers: just as they became familiar with the face of an older man, for instance, he got off, and just when they started chatting with a small child, he had to get off the train with his grandmother. There were a few other passengers who appeared to be on for the long haul, but they didn't look very friendly, and the girls weren't willing to strike up a conversation. Sometimes their car was packed, and sometimes it would empty out; at one point the two of them occupied seats meant for a group of four, and they sat facing each other and imitated the men they saw who seemed well-versed in train travel, taking off their shoes and putting their feet up on the seats across from them. When they took off their shoes, they discovered their feet were a little bit swollen and gave off a strong smell of foot sweat mixed with leather. They stretched out their legs, straightened out their lower backs, and rested their chins on their chests, making them look very comfortable and lazy—after all, they didn't know anyone around them, so who cared? The two of them laughed as they sat facing one another and engaged in some rowdy conversation. They had become used to the train's frequent stops and starts, and they were no longer so interested in the new people who got on the train; by now, they felt they were seasoned travelers. Just then, the train pulled up to a station that caught them off guard.

Looking out from the window of the train, the scene on the station platform seemed chaotic. Beyond several sets of tracks lay a wide expanse of fields, factories, and highways. A wall around the platform made it feel like a proper station, and three large characters appeared on a cement sign: 徐州西 Xu Zhou West. They wondered if this could be Xuzhou; they had been expecting something a bit more impressive for Xuzhou Station. What was the meaning of "Xuzhou West?" Still, they felt pretty certain that aside from this station, there should still be one for "Xuzhou," in the same way that in addition to the "Wang Village Central" stop, there was also one for "Wang Village." But before they could feel completely sure, three people came rushing up alongside the train, clearly searching for someone along the platform and knocking on the windows. When they came up to the two girls lying down and staring out the window, they shouted louder: Are you Fentian? Both of them sat up at once. What followed was a mad rush to put on their shoes, get their luggage, gather up the food and magazines on their tray tables, and shove their way into the aisle. The train had already started moving again as they stepped down onto the platform. The two girls just looked at each other, too surprised to speak and not understanding what had just happened. The train sped up as it went off toward the east and disappeared in a cloud of white smoke; by the time the cloud dispersed, there was no trace of the train. As they began to collect themselves, they noticed that the platform was quiet now, and that beyond the station walls, three tall cement smokestacks reached into the darkening evening sky. Only a few people remained on the platform. The three young men who had come running after them were all dressed in military uniforms. These uniforms were the second point in Fentian's later reflections: How could she so easily put her trust in uniforms? She had only to think back to Shangqiu Station, where they saw all those long-haired youths in the green uniforms, to know that nowadays any kind of person could wear any type of clothing. But they believed them!

The three of them said that they were army buddies of Fentian's boyfriend, and Fentian was also convinced by the words "army buddies." But the same rule applied: Couldn't anyone be saying this stuff? They said they were his army buddies, and that he'd been given an urgent task to carry out, so he sent them to come collect Fentian and her friend at the station. Furthermore, Fentian's boyfriend had suddenly realized he had forgotten to specify it was Xuzhou West where they should get off, so he specifically asked his pals to go in the station to get them. It was a risky plan—if they hadn't been right there waiting for them, they would have missed each other. How could the three of them have gone back to face Fentian's boyfriend? The three young men divided up the luggage, and Fentian and Shui followed them out of the station without having to carry a thing. The station didn't have much space in front of it, and as soon as they exited they were out on the street, which was full of cars zooming by alongside people walking and riding bikes. Car horns mingled with the sounds of motorized bikes, and even some two-wheel tractors puffed out smoke as they went along. The sky suddenly seemed to grow a shade darker; although the sun was still clearly visible hanging over the road, it was a grayish white. The noisy din, the coal smoke in the air, and all the sudden changes left the two girls a bit dazed. At one point, when Fentian hesitantly turned her head and looked behind her, one of the young men, very politely and in the manner of an "army buddy," raised his hand and gave a gesture indicating "please proceed." So, she kept walking. They started up a jeep, in which the driver was already waiting; two of the three men sat in front with the driver, while the third sat with Fentian and Shui in back. Then they set off. The vehicle made a quick U-turn, kicking up a cloud of dust, and drove off in the direction of that grayish white setting sun. Just then, a curious thought flashed across Fentian's mind: They had been traveling from west to east, but now they were heading back west—didn't this mean they were driving back in the opposite direction? Later, this observation would help guide Fentian on her way.

In the end, Fentian never was able to learn the name of the place where she served as a wife. In a low-lying area like the palm of a giant hand were clustered a few dozen one-story houses with brick walls and tile roofs. Perhaps because the land dipped down, the bricks weren't laid straight, and the tiles were crooked. Fentian never set foot on the ground, so she didn't know what kind of ground it was; she only knew that in every courtyard and on every roof was a sheet of plastic, and on the plastic were tobacco leaves. Presumably it was a kind of tobacco, although it wasn't really being handled like tobacco: The leaves became wet with the dew and were all a bit soaked, and they gave off a moldy smell. Their color was a greenish black or greenish purple, and they covered the entire little village, giving it even more of a worn-out appearance. The people also looked worn out, and most of them had droopy expressions. They swallowed their words in the backs of their throats when they spoke, and their accent sounded very honest and simple. Their clothes were gray and drab, which was especially true on the days it rained: On those winding, muddy streets, legs, feet, and bodies went every which way, like they were all turning to mush in a big pot. Fentian leaned against the door and looked out at the dreary village, feeling very depressed. Beneath the stove was Liu San, the man who had bought her, and his mother was there cooking something. The floor was covered in bits of grass and beans, and Liu San was crouched down on top of them, nearly laying on the floor as he blew into the stove to stir up the flames. The more he blew, though, the smokier it got. The stoves they used in this place weren't right, either. The flue came out the back of the stove and curved all around, going up to extend just a little bit above the roof. This was probably to help warm the room and to keep from burning so much grass, but didn't it make it harder for the smoke to escape? The ceiling was low, at least three bricks lower than Fentian's house, and the rafters had also turned black from smoke. It was more like a cave than a room. As Fentian watched Liu San's mother clumsily go about her chores, she didn't lift a finger to help—it all sickened her. Liu San's mother didn't dare talk to her, and she lowered her eyes and quickened her step whenever she passed by. The way Liu San walked was very similar to his mother—it made them look like they had short legs, although actually they didn't. Maybe it was because they had always lived in such a cramped place, but not only did they walk like they had short legs, but they were also all hunched over, as if their elbows had fused with their waists. Liu San would not dare look at Fentian. He would get up early and go out on the land with his father, while Fentian would cover her head and keep sleeping. When they returned in the evening, it was still Liu San's mother who would bring them a basin of water to wash their hands, faces, and feet, and she would also set the table and dish up the meal. Fentian would have either already eaten, or she would take her food into the other room and eat by herself. When she sat in the room, it was like she had seized the territory, and Liu San wouldn't dare enter. In the evening, this room still appeared relatively bright under the lamplight, and it made Fentian feel a bit calmer than she did during the daytime. She sized up her surroundings: The floor was cement, old newspapers had been pasted to the ceiling, and the walls had been whitewashed with lime. There were a few pieces of furniture, including a large wardrobe, and a section of mirror, which was an oily yellow, had been placed on the door. There was a bed surrounded by some mosquito netting. The weather was just turning toward winter, and this netting seemed to convey a sense of extravagance, demonstrating the ability to take a wife. There was also a table with drawers, which had a few items placed on top, including a mirror, comb, and face cream. In the corner was a stand with a wash basin, and some curtains were hung over the window. A few corners of the bed frame, the table legs, and the wardrobe still displayed some of the old cloth and newspapers they had been wrapped in. Fentian thought: This furniture had been prepared a long time beforehand, just waiting for me! This thought did not soften her heart, but instead made her angrier—how could she have to come to occupy such a stupid, irritating room?! She heard Liu San's mother in the main room encouraging him to come in, and then admonishing him, and then Liu San defending himself. They both mumbled when they talked, and Fentian couldn't hear them clearly—it was like there were only tones and no consonants. Later on, after Liu San's mother went in the other room, only Liu San was left in the main room. She could hear him shuffling around, not daring to enter. Only after the last embers in the stove had gone out and the stovepipe had gone cold, doing nothing to ward off the nighttime chill, did he tiptoe in. This person wasn't like a man at all. Fentian grew nervous and broke out in goosebumps.

Not daring to take off her clothes, Fentian kept them on under the blanket. Nor did Liu San have any intentions of touching her. He slept on the opposite side of the bed, also wrapped tightly in the blanket. The nights in this village were so quiet that not even the bark of a dog could be heard. Fentian's whole body felt parched and overheated, like she couldn't get enough air. She even wished this man would provoke her so she would have reason to kick him, scratch him, and spit on him. But he never moved a muscle and stayed wrapped up even more tightly than Fentian, lying there like a big stone lump. Aside from its blank numbness, this lump had perseverance and resolve. This, when combined with his stupid intransigence, added an element of fear for Fentian—it seemed impossible to get through to him. A few times, Fentian boldly gave him a kick with her foot, but he didn't move. Fentian couldn't take it anymore, so she jumped up and stood on the bed, kicking the big lump and trampling on it until she finally knocked it off the bed. On the surface, the scene could have appeared like young newlyweds fighting but very much in love, and the sounds of movement on the bed comforted Liu San's mother. Fentian, however, felt like she was about to go crazy. She dejectedly sat down on a pillow, while the lump remained perfectly motionless for who knows how long, slumped in a dark, indistinct pile on the floor under the bed. Fentian got off the bed, put on her shoes, stepped over the lump, and walked directly to the door. She had forgotten that the door was locked from the outside, and that it remained locked until Liu San got up in the morning and called for his mother to open it. She banged on the door a few times, but to no response—it was as if the whole village were dead. She returned to the bed, feeling cold. Shivering, she crawled back under the blanket and wrapped herself up tightly, and without realizing it she fell back asleep.

Many nights were passed like this, alternating between hot and cold, dreams and wakefulness. Winter came, and at some point the tobacco leaves were gathered up from the roofs and courtyards. The last bits of green disappeared from the tree branches, the edges of the fields, and the roadsides; the village looked a bit tidier, though even more drab. Fentian was still not allowed out of Liu San's house, and nobody came to visit. She would sit on a stool by the door and watch the people out on the street. There was little rain on these winter days, and the street became rock hard and pale in color. Liu San's mother had burned all the grass and switched to coal. She used an old broken bellows to fan the flames, so the room was now filled with the dry, grating sound of the bellows opening and closing. Coal smoke filled the air, and the sunnier the day the more it felt like they were choking in the filth. No one spoke to Fentian, and she didn't talk to anyone, either—she had basically become mute. But she had always been someone who loved to talk and laugh!

After several clear, cold days, the weather strangely warmed up again and a haze appeared, which grew thicker by the day, clearly indicating it would soon snow. Liu San and his father were making plans to leave home. From the family's sparse conversations, Fentian gleaned that they were going to a neighboring village to work in the kilns, and that several men from their village were going as a group. Although there had still been no visitors to the house and the family members rarely spoke, there was still a palpable restlessness—their dreary lives were about to get a shake-up. Liu San's mother set up a griddle to make *jianbing*, and the smells of pulp and beans mingled with the coal smoke. She also washed their bedding after removing the old wadding, and then filled it with new cotton. As she closed it up again, one stitch at a time, bits of thread and fluffy white stuffing floated around in the air. Father and son went to the expense of buying some alcohol and had a few drinks with each meal, while she served them bone broth and eggs with scallions. The room once again had an atmosphere of abundance. All of this helped lend an air of liveliness to this poor, withered peasant family. The night before they were to leave, Liu San seemed to indicate he would have his way with Fentian—but for this muddleheaded person, all he could muster was a night of tossing and turning. Fentian was so nervous she spent the entire night wrapped up tightly in the blanket, sweating and listening to her heart pound. In the end, the night passed without incident. Breaking from her normal routine, Fentian didn't linger in bed after Liu San got up; unable to lay there any longer, she rose before Liu San. This gave the two older ones the impression that she had given him some sort of special sendoff. Fentian sat on a stool by the door as Liu San brushed past her to fetch the pot of water warming on the stove. He poured it into the basin and used both hands to splash it on his face, sputtering as he gave himself a good wash. For the first time, Fentian noticed that he performed his tasks with a certain vim and vigor that was usually concealed by his wooden expression. She noticed how the back of his neck had turned red from scrubbing, as well as a patch behind his ears, and that steam was rising from his tousled hair. This was the final, and only, impression he left on Fentian.

When Liu San and his father left, a number of other men from the village went as well. It didn't really seem like there had been a decrease in men so much as an increase in women. The women seemed to be out and about a bit more than usual, sometimes stopping in the middle of the street and having a good long chat. The sounds of their voices rang out, and their clothing was a little brighter than what the men wore, making this dreary little wintertime village slightly livelier. Liu San's mother still kept within an inch of Fentian, but the scene that Fentian saw from her perch by the door had changed. A light snow fell, covering the village in a thin layer of white that made it look clean. Shortly afterward, however, the snow grew dirty as it melted and got trampled, and the resulting patches of gray and black returned the village to its dilapidated appearance. The sun gradually began to peek out through the haze. On this particular day, there was suddenly some movement out on the street— actually, it was really just two or three people running off to the southern end of the village. Fentian couldn't help but get up and look out to see what was going on, but Liu San's mother, who had been drying tobacco seeds in front of the doorway, turned around and rushed over to her. This woman, who was always hunched over and quietly shuffling here and there, suddenly became as quick and nimble as a beast. Though still so stooped over she was nearly crawling; she swished over in front of Fentian. She stretched out her veiny hands and grabbed Fentian's ankles as if she were trying to press them down into the ground. This gave Fentian such a shock that she lost her balance and reached out to grab hold of the doorframe. Without loosening her grip on Fentian's ankles, Liu San's mother threw back her head and let out some raspy shouts. Fentian saw her eyes were wide open and filled with a mix of fear and viciousness; her beastly appearance delivered Fentian yet another shock. Responding to her shouts, two women came running up from outside and held down Fentian's arms, one on the right and one on the left; with their combined effort the three women pushed Fentian back inside the door. Fentian was suddenly sure that something had just happened in the village, and they were afraid that Fentian would show her face. A few more people passed by the front yard, headed south on the main street below the embankment of their elevated courtyard. A locust tree stood to the south where the road split, and behind its leafless branches there seemed to be some sort of disturbance. Fentian held on to the doorframe with all her might and refused to go back into the room. The three women, however, kept their grip on her arms and legs, which made it difficult to keep her footing. Fentian changed tactics: She loosened her grip and leaned forward, turning a somersault with her hands nearly clasped behind her back. She flipped over Liu San's mother's head, rolled over twice on the ground, and slid down off the courtyard's embankment. Before she realized what was happening, she was out on the street. Running down the hard-packed dirt road, she headed south, with the three women shouting behind her. She couldn't understand what they were saying, but the desperation in their voices frightened her. She ran up to the locust tree, but no one was there; single-story brick houses stood to the left and right, but there was no sign of movement. The disturbance seemed to have already passed—or maybe it had never even occurred, and Fentian had simply been mistaken. As soon as she left the room, Fentian realized she knew nothing at all about this village and had no idea where she was. The three women following her had split up as if they were casting a net, ready to head her off from any direction. At this crucial moment, Fentian heard the honking of a car horn, faint but clear. She determined the sound was coming from the east, so she turned and began running in that direction. In her path was a well, and beside it stood one of the women recruited by Liu San's mother, her arms open and ready to catch her. Fentian ran straight toward her, and when the woman reached out to stop her, she was nearly shoved into the well. Fentian felt a boundless strength at this point, along with an incredible happiness; she felt like she could fly. The car honked again, and she heard the sound of the motor starting up. She could already see the green roof of a jeep parked under another embankment that abutted the street.

She scrambled up and finally spotted a group of people. She was shocked to discover how many were living in this quiet little village.

Everyone was clustered in front of a single-story brick house with a tile roof. Among them were two women, dressed as if they came from the city, and a uniformed police officer; they were leading a woman along with them as they shoved their way out of the crowd. Fentian had seen this woman a few times. The first time was out on the street; she'd thought she was the daughter of one of the village families, although she didn't quite look like the locals—she had a broad forehead, and her eyes were very large. When she passed by Liu San's home and raised her eyes to look up at Fentian, she gave the impression she was quite clever. The next time Fentian saw her, she noticed that the front part of her jacket was sticking out like she was pregnant—only then did Fentian realize she was a young married woman. Now her condition was even more apparent, and the two official-looking women were supporting her underneath the arms as they led her out. Fentian had a good idea of what was going on. She rushed forward and scrambled down the embankment, nearly falling in front of the jeep, and then proceeded to open the door and get in. When those people got the other woman in the car, Fentian explained that she had also been kidnapped, and she begged them to take her with them. At first they wanted to question her some more, but the situation didn't allow them to linger. The villagers were surrounding the jeep, and although they were just silently standing there, who knew what would happen next? They had no choice but to squeeze in together and shut the door. As they began driving, the crowd made way and let them pass. The jeep accelerated, and they hit a bump that sent them airborne; they landed, then hit a few more bumps like that as they flew down the road. Everyone breathed a sigh of relief, and Fentian began shaking. As she trembled, she saw the other woman glancing at her through the dark interior of the jeep, her pregnant-looking face making her eyes appear even larger and more penetrating. Later, when Fentian thought of her, she realized the woman was probably younger than her, yet so determined. She had been kidnapped from much farther away in Sichuan and had figured out a way to free herself, incidentally saving Fentian in the process.

Fentian had left home just after the harvest, and by the time she returned it was almost the Spring Festival. She'd been gone for less than three months, but it seemed like no one in the village recognized her anymore. When people saw her they would give an awkward smile and politely allow her to go first if she needed to pass by. You've returned? they would ask, but as soon as it came out of their mouths they knew it wasn't the right thing to say. Fentian hadn't gone off to get married, so what was this "return" supposed mean? Visiting her parents? Villagers who had gone elsewhere for work would return home for the Spring Festival, and everyone would excitedly ask them about the places they had been. Some people, who were either too naïve or simply had a slip of the tongue, would ask Fentian, "How are things in Xuzhou?" Realizing their mistake before she could respond, they smiled and beat a hasty retreat. There was also a greedy child who stuck out his hand to ask Fentian for some candy, since those returning to the village would always bring back some candy for the children and cigarettes for the adults. Someone came and dragged the child away. Even Fentian's mother acted like she didn't recognize her own daughter. Once, when Fentian was walking in front, she inadvertently turned her head and caught her mother staring at her back; unable to look away in time, her mother's face reddened out of awkwardness. Another time, Fentian felt a strange sensation as she was sleeping, and she opened her eyes to find her mother hovering over her, anxiously looking at something. Fentian had a faint idea of what was going on—she was examining her. The old folks have a lot of sayings about the differences between married and unmarried women, and it was this difference that was on the minds of the villagers whenever they saw Fentian, unspoken beneath their expressions. On this point, Fentian wasn't worried, saying to herself: It doesn't matter what anyone says, except for one person! And who was this person? Her boyfriend. With this thought, she couldn't help but feel a little pride: She had done right by him, and had done nothing to make him lose face—how she had endured, day after day and night after night! Sometimes Fentian felt like she should make this clear to people, but what could she say? The whole situation was so complicated she didn't even fully grasp it herself, and she was unable to make heads or tails of the whole mess. If she herself hadn't been the one involved, she wouldn't believe such a story. The only person she could count on to believe her was Shui. But where was Shui?

Fentian visited Shui's family a few times to explain what happened and offer her apologies. She felt entirely responsible for what had happened to Shui: If she hadn't gone with her to Xuzhou, she would have never been kidnapped. So, after returning home, Fentian found Shui's family the most difficult to face. She brought a few bundles of bean starch noodles with her, making clear that they were from her brother, who had opened up a noodle factory with some business partners. She couldn't help but adopt the villagers' general feeling that for someone returning home under her circumstances, it was inappropriate to bring gifts. Shui's parents listened expressionlessly as Fentian spoke, and by the time she reached the part in her story where they got off the train at Xuzhou West, they started asking irrelevant questions. How was her brother's noodle factory doing? Had they been able to pay their fees to the local collective fund? Clearly, they were trying to cut Fentian off. She didn't get the feeling they were placing much blame on her, but that they were having trouble with something else. It was quite clear they felt ashamed, which made Fentian think of her own family's reaction. As she left Shui's house, she felt that someday the whole truth would come out, and her boyfriend would confirm her purity. She had already written him a letter, which had taken her no small amount of effort. At first she felt it should simply explain the situation, but as soon as she started to do that, it sounded like she was trying to defend herself, which made her feel horribly wronged. Fentian was a strong young woman, and throughout this whole ordeal she had only concerned herself with how to handle it and had never really felt wronged. Now, though, things were different. It felt like her boyfriend was standing right in front of her, and just as she was about to say something, she would swallow it back. She resentfully thought to herself: I haven't done anything wrong, so why do I need to be providing explanations? Strangely, this feeling of resentment softened her mood. In the end, she ignored the whole thing and simply said: Due to unexpected circumstances, our meeting has been delayed. She said she was doing well and asked after him, and finally ended by asking: When can you come back? After writing this line, Fentian let out a sigh and thought to herself: Now it's all up to you! With the thought that she still had someone to depend on, a tender feeling entered her heart. But this was immediately followed by another thought: Who could Shui depend on? What would Shui do?

So the next day, she went back to Shui's house. This time, she told them the story of the young woman from Sichuan—how secretly, when her captors weren't watching, she'd mailed a letter to her family back in Sichuan, who had then contacted the local Women's Federation and the police in an effort to free her. Fentian then followed this by saying to Shui's parents: You can get in touch with the Xuzhou authorities and tell them where your daughter was kidnapped—they'll definitely be able to rescue her. Shui's parents listened with rapt attention as Fentian told them about this brave young woman, and they didn't interrupt her once. When Fentian offered her suggestion, however, Shui's father said: But isn't a marriage still a marriage? Fentian replied: Shui must be waiting for you to save her! After wiping away her tears, Shui's mother said: That young woman from Sichuan had a cruel fate. Once again, Fentian left Shui's home feeling dejected. Shui was two years younger than her, she thought, and was usually not very serious. Would she be able to hold up? Then she thought of the young woman from Sichuan, with her sallow face and big bright eyes, and her confidence was renewed.

On the fifteenth, Fentian's aunt showed up. Seeing her aunt made Fentian hate herself for not having made any progress, and her face flushed red. It also obviously made her think of her boyfriend, and the fact that she should have received a letter by now. She became angry, which made her arms and legs seem heavier as she went about her tasks. Setting out the stools, pouring the tea, and poaching the eggs—it was all done with a crash and a bang. Her aunt, who should have been angry, wasn't angry at all, although she was very uneasy seeing her niece like this. When Fentian had finished her tasks and seemed to have blown off some steam, her mother sent her out to the market to buy a live fish to prepare for their guest. Fentian got on her bicycle and rode out from the center of the village and onto the highway. The market was a small one located about two *li* away, but because the Lantern Festival was approaching it was quite busy. There were some rabbit lanterns for sale with light yellow bodies, big red eyes, and wheels underneath their wooden frames. Fentian bought two: one for her nephew, and one for her aunt to take home to her little cousin. Then she hated herself for trying to curry favor with her aunt. Yet when it came time to buy the fish, she still picked a nice big energetic one, which caused her to hate herself once more. She hung the vigorously flopping fish from the handles of her bicycle, along with some stewed meat, pig's trotters, roast chicken, white liver, and a bag of haw jelly cakes to make a filling for the traditional Lantern Festival dumplings. On the back of the bike she placed the two rabbit lanterns, one on each side. Propelled by her disgust, she quickly peddled back to the village. Her aunt, though, had already left. Her mother's eyes were red from crying. Her father had a smile on his face, but he was even more painful to look at. As soon as she laid eyes on this scene, Fentian had a good idea of what had happened. She got off her bike, propped it up, and began removing the items from it one by one. After rolling up her sleeves, she grabbed the fish by the tail, threw it down with a slap on the ledge around the well, and yelled: Kill the fish! The blade of the knife sent fish scales flying up like sparkling flakes of snow. Fentian managed everything for this meal herself—eight platters, eight dishes, and Lantern Festival dumplings. The dumplings featured several different fillings, including sesame, haw jelly, and sweetened lard, all shaped to the same size and plopped in a basket. When evening fell, Fentian lit the rabbit lanterns, and her little nephew pulled both of them around the courtyard. As their wooden wheels went click-clacking over the ground, the scene appeared quite lively, if not also a bit lonely.

With the brief appearance of Fentian's aunt, the villagers knew that Fentian's boyfriend had dumped her, and they all looked at her with pity. But Fentian now seemed happier than she had been, becoming more talkative and laughing more heartily. As she laughed, she'd look the other person over, as if to say: Who dumped whom? If this had been before, people would say she was crazy: Laugh now because your days of crying are ahead of you! But now, nobody would dare say this about her; even thinking it seemed like a curse, so they tried to not even let it cross their minds. As a result, people couldn't help but avoid her, and if they happened to walk past her, they would avert their eyes. This really angered Fentian, so she would intentionally make eye contact with them and start talking and laughing, even going as far as to seek out people in their homes, where she would then sit herself down to start talking and laughing. It was as if she wanted to force people to admit there was nothing wrong with her. When she ran out of homes to visit in her village, she rode her bike over to the neighboring village and called on her old classmates there. While news of Fentian's situation had spread quickly, it was all just hearsay—so when she showed up in person, people were understandably caught off guard, thinking to themselves: She's actually here! At this point, Fentian became a figure unlike any they'd seen before. Every time people saw this "classmate" of theirs, her face would have a strangely hopeful expression. Yet in the midst of all this activity, Fentian felt lonely. What could she say?

What could she say to make people understand? So she soon left the class-mates in this village and went to the next classmates in the next village, but unfortunately the situation was not much different. Her parents didn't say anything about her running all over the place, and just let her go. Her older brother had gone to the noodle factory, and this time her sister-in-law had gone along as well, leaving behind her little nephew. Everyone was busy keeping the wheat hoed and watered, but her parents didn't send this idle daughter of theirs out to help. Fentian, however, propped a hoe over her shoulder and went down of her own accord to that three and seven-tenths *mu* of land. Angered by the situation, she grabbed the tool out of her father's hand and walked out the door by herself.

The wheat had shot up quickly, and the field was a deep green. Fentian's family had gotten a good piece of land on the sunny side of a hill. There were lots of hills in the area, and so it mattered quite a bit whether a field was on the shady side or the sunny side, as did its distance from a source of water. Fentian's family's land was right next to an irrigation ditch, so as soon as they harvested the wheat, they could flood the field to grow rice. Under the official output-linked agricultural production respon-sibility system, Fentian's family was given this plot of land the same year she was born. That's why they named her "Fentian," meaning "divide the fields." That's also why they doted on her and ignored her brother, and why her sister-in-law was not very happy—luckily her brother was able to cover up this last fact, and things never reached the point of open conflict. In general, they had always been a happy family; now, however, things were completely different. As Fentian stood alone in the field of wheat sprouts, she felt like this plot of land stretched on forever, extend-ing upward to touch the sky. Between the sky and the land, there was only her. The past few days had gone by in a whirlwind, but now things had calmed down. Fentian listened to the sounds of the hoes working the earth and the insects scurrying in all directions after being awakened from their winter sleep. The sun shone on her face, then moved to the top of her head, and then her back. Gazing out over the freshly hoed field, it looked like a dark, black layer of oil had been spread over the ground, making the sprouts appear even more crisp and green. As the sun set, bathing the field in its final rays, the blacks and greens all changed to yellow. By the time Fentian had hoed out to the edge of the field, dusk had already come, and a thin layer of gray had descended. She picked up her hoe and went home.

A light breeze blew over the field, and as she walked out from the rows of wheat, the wavering sprouts whispered softly.

The next morning, Fentian rode her bike over to Hanji. The sky was not yet completely light, but already there were cars and two-wheel tractors out on the road, filling her ears with the roar of wind and motors as they whizzed by. It did not cross Fentian's mind that this was the same road she and Shui had taken on their way to Xuzhou—everything had changed too much since then. She rode up to the bus station in Hanji and got a bus to the county seat. There were no empty seats left, so she sat on a burlap sack of peanuts. She got off the bus at the county seat and, after asking directions, made her way to the government offices. Once there, she asked for directions to the Women's Federation. Fentian was received coolly by the two female cadres sitting in the office, but they very quickly became engrossed in her story and put down whatever they'd been doing to give Fentian their full attention. This was the first time Fentian had ever given a complete account of her experience, and she surprised herself at how clearly she was able to present things, as if she had already told her story many times before. In fact, she had never even once run through the whole thing in her mind. She was also surprised at how calm she was, as if she were recounting events that had happened to someone else. Of course, the attentive attitude of the two female cadres encouraged her.

When she had finished talking about the whole ordeal, she then talked about how the proposal had been broken off. Finally, she presented a request to the two female cadres: Might they be able to, under the authority of the Women's Federation, write a letter to her boyfriend urging him to retract his previous decision? The two cadres were completely sympathetic and agreed at once, even promising that if they couldn't get in touch with her boyfriend, they would communicate with his unit; for the time being, of course, they had to leave him a little face. Fentian left the government offices and felt like having a stroll before returning to the station. On the bus home, she sat on a sack of fertilizer. This was the first trip she made to the county seat, and after this she would make a second, a third, and many more. She soon became familiar with the route, as well as the route to the government offices. With each trip she made, her hopes regarding the situation got dimmer, and the enthusiasm of her two comrades at the Women's Federation gradually decreased.

They sent a letter to Fentian's boyfriend, and not long afterward they received a reply. It said that while he was very grateful for the attention this organization from his hometown was paying to his personal situation, his relationship with Fentian was still in the stage of getting to know one another, and that no decision had previously been made. Furthermore, both parties were equal in this relationship, and it couldn't be said that one of them had dumped the other. For now, he felt that they were both still very young with their whole lives ahead of them, and that the most appropriate thing to do would be to postpone the issue of marriage. This nearly convinced the two comrades at the Women's Federation, but they persisted and sent another letter emphasizing the reality of such arrangements in rural customs: They had already exchanged betrothal gifts, so in everyone's eyes they were engaged, and he should be mindful of the pressure this placed on a woman's reputation in this environment. They also emphasized Fentian's position as the victim in recent events and hoped that, in accordance with his responsibilities as a member of the military, he would be sympathetic and look after her.

Fentian's boyfriend quickly responded with another letter showcasing his rhetorical skills, which seemed to demonstrate his enjoyment of this sort of back and forth. In the letter, he expressed his opinion regarding several issues raised by the Women's Federation: The first was on the necessity of changing prevailing habits and customs, and the second was on love, incisively pointing out that sympathy was not the same as love, and that to confuse the two would be unfair to Fentian. The Women's Federation then sent a third letter, which showed how exasperated they were getting—it threatened to get in touch with his army unit. This resulted in a polite but stern criticism from the boyfriend: It's better to persuade others through reasoning than to force them through administrative orders. Her comrades in the Women's Federation let Fentian read every letter, and after finishing each one, she would express her own views. Her reasoning was much more convincing and eloquent than the letters from the Women's Federation, making these two comrades feel weak and useless. Really, though, they had been roped into the middle of a situation that had no clear solution. They sincerely felt that Fentian and her boyfriend were a couple; it was just a shame that heaven wouldn't allow it and this situation had to arise, ruining the happy fate of their marriage. In the end, they did send an official letter to the young man's army unit, which responded in kind with its own official letter. It said that after conducting an investigation, they determined that their soldier had only a romantic relationship with Fentian that did not reach the level of marriage. The letter went on to point out the clauses in the marriage law regarding free love, which tactfully refuted the criticisms of the local Women's Federation. Her comrades at the Women's Federation gave Fentian a copy of this letter, indicating that the matter had now come to a close. Fentian remained unconvinced and returned to the Women's Federation several times, but her comrades there started avoiding her, and then went into hiding. Finally there came a day when Fentian was met with a locked door, so she angrily left.

Only one final opportunity remained for Fentian: wait for her boyfriend to return home to visit his family. Last year it had been decided that he would come home in July or August. In her heart, Fentian still wondered: Could he really be this heartless? She needed to say this to his face in order for her to finally be convinced. The wheat grew taller, putting forth ears and filling out. This was especially true for the wheat in her family's plot on the sunny side of the hill, which matured earlier than everyone else's, its awn glimmering in the sunlight. A southwest wind blew for three days, and then one morning, once the wheat was no longer wet with dew, they took the sickle to it. As soon as those crisp stalks of wheat met with the blade, they fell in even swaths. Fentian cut the wheat all by herself, while her father threshed it in the courtyard and her mother took charge of preparing the meals and tending to the old pregnant sow. When the wheat ripened, so did the melons and other vegetables in the garden, their vines having climbed high up the trellis. The villagers got together and hired a stonemason to set up two large millstones at either end of the village in preparation for milling the wheat. The neighboring village opened a grain processing plant, but the residents of this village, especially the older ones, preferred stone-ground flour, complaining that machine-milled flour tasted like motor oil. The village and surrounding fields were filled with a festive atmosphere. In due time, the wheat was harvested, threshed, and dried, and the sounds of the millstones could be heard from one end of the village to the other. The old sow gave birth to twelve piglets, and a month later someone came to purchase a few. When Fentian saw what was happening, she drove the one she liked best into the house so it would not be chosen. She secretly gave the piglet a name, which was the same name as her boyfriend. As she corralled the little pig, she silently scolded: So-and-so, where are you going? Where will you run when you're facing the chopping block? Sometimes she would catch the piglet and hug its roly-poly little body, and then let it go, thinking to herself: So-and-so, you son of a bitch, you can't escape! When it was almost July, she went to visit her aunt and presented her with some fresh buns she had just steamed. At the end of July she went again with freshly harvested eggplants and onions. In the beginning of August she went yet again, this time bringing along her beloved little pig with its stubby nose, long torso, and voracious appetite. She hugged it one last time and set it down in the courtyard, where it sniffed all around until it circuitously sniffed its way to the pigpen. Her aunt awkwardly watched this delightful little creature and said: Fentian, he didn't come home. Fentian turned around and left, her bike rattling as she pushed it out through the gate. Have some guts and quit hiding! she shouted in her head as tears streamed down her cheeks. She lifted her head and let the wind blow directly in her face. A few times her bike jolted as it passed over the ruts in the road, but she didn't slow down. From the time this whole mess began, she had yet to cry! Now, she wanted to sob bitterly.

Several days later, Fentian left home. She told her parents that a classmate of hers had opened up a straw weaving factory in Heze, and she was going there to look for work. She also asked for the money from selling the piglets, and her parents didn't object. The last time she left home it was a disaster, but what would become of her if she were to never again leave? It was very clear to them that Fentian was not happy staying at home, and that she felt unsettled; they weren't sure what to do with her. Their daughter was an adult now, and a very strong-willed one at that, but now that she had reached such a dead end, they didn't really have any control over the situation.

One morning in August, although it was still early, the summer heat was already scorching. Luckily a brisk breeze was blowing. Fentian put on her nephew's canvas sunhat and tied her hair up in a bun, which made her look like a pretty young girl. She was facing the sun so she was forced to squint, making her expression seem quite determined. She went to Hanji to get the bus. A two-wheel tractor came up behind her and the driver called out to her a few times, wanting to give her a ride. She didn't respond, so the driver assumed she hadn't heard and drove on by. The bus she got at Hanji was headed to Dawangji, and at Dawangji she got a long-distance bus to Caocheng. As the bus left the station and went around a corner, she saw the little restaurant where she and Shui had eaten dumplings with their classmate Lin. It was a rudimentary structure, covered on top with some asphalt roofing felt. A striped nylon awning stuck out beyond the eaves, and under it were some chopping boards and short stools. The people who ate there were always either just about to take the bus or had just gotten off—around them sat their bags and luggage, and their faces were covered in dirt. No matter what time of day it was, there were always people there eating. This is also a characteristic of people who are traveling: whenever they have the opportunity to eat, they eat. The bus made its way to Caocheng. The sun was high in the sky, and it was roasting inside the bus, but once it picked up some speed, a breeze started blowing through. Some small factories lined the road, puffing out smoke that stretched part way up into the air and then dispersed in the sunlight, disappearing without a trace. At Caocheng, she got on the train. She was traveling the same routes at the same times as she had before with Shui, but one thing that had happened before didn't happen this time: there was no woman trying to sell her tickets. This trip was much less remarkable than that first one, with nothing unexpected cropping up; this time, though, she had a sense of resolve that seemed to guarantee she would reach her goal. Fentian didn't strike up a single conversation along the way, nor did she sleep. As the scenery out the window sped past her eyes, some doubts began to creep into her mind: she was following the exact same route they had taken before, but why did everything look completely unfamiliar? The trees, the fields, the houses, the sideroads, the people on the streets—it all seemed muted and distant. When the train got to Shangqiu, even the clamor of Shangqiu Station felt removed. As Fentian made her way through it, with people and luggage colliding amid angry shouts, she felt as if she were in a different world that had nothing to do with her. The recruitment station for the vocational school offering instruction in growing bean sprouts and raising earthworms was still there, but it was now a different season, and the people had changed their attire: they now wore sun visors with a blue plastic bill in the front and a white elastic strap in the back. From time to time, these hats could be seen sticking out from the crowd, reflecting the sun. By now it was the next morning, and the sun was already beating down fiercely on the square; there was no breeze, only the smell of sweat. Fentian wasn't in a hurry, and she installed herself by a cement flower bed and patiently waited for her train. She was already used to being on the road, having now accumulated some experience; she didn't need to think about it anymore, but could just go with the flow. When she finally got on the train, her car was rather cool and spacious, and once the train began moving the wind started blowing in so strongly she had to put the window up halfway. Although she hadn't slept that night, she didn't feel the least bit tired, and her eyes were wide open as she gazed out the window. She appeared calm on the surface, but inside she remained on high alert. This world seemed so peaceful, but somewhere—you could never tell where—unthinkable danger was lurking! The sun moved from the south side of the train car to the north side, and then back again. As it alternated from side to side, and as the train alternated between stopping and starting, that fiery red ball gradually moved to a distant place over the fields; because the air was clear, its edges were very distinct. Fentian got off the train at Xuzhou West. Not that many people got off the train there, and she followed them out of the station and onto the street, where she stopped. She raised her head and looked all around, feeling a bit lost. It was already around five o'clock, but because the days were long, the sun was still rather high in the sky. When she looked up at that blazing red disk, it appeared a little smaller than it just had out the train window, and also a little more yellow, but its light was just as searing, with a heavy sort of heat. Fentian was surprised to realize this was the first time throughout the whole trip she recognized something familiar. Although its color, light, and positioning were all a little different from what she had seen on her first trip, it was still the sun! Her memory suddenly became clear.

She remembered thinking at the time: they had been traveling from west to east, but now they were heading back west—didn't this mean they were driving back in the opposite direction? They had then stopped for dinner at a restaurant along the side of the road, and the name of that place was "Miss Xia's Restaurant." Those three army buddies had told the two of them that although they said their unit was in Xuzhou, it was actually located several *li* outside the city, and they wanted to make sure that Fentian and Shui would not go hungry. The owner, probably Miss Xia, seemed to be familiar with them. Actually, it was then that Fentian had her second suspicion: People in the army usually came from all over the country, and army life was highly regulated—how could they all know this woman who owned a roadside restaurant? But she hadn't given it that much thought. As they ate, she sat facing the door, and noticed that across the street there was a neon sign glowing with the words "Ding Lou Baths," which was quite striking against the gradually darkening sky. Now, after thinking things over as she stood at the side of the street, she returned to the station and went up to the ticket counter to look at the street names on the list of fares. She could always go ask someone, but hadn't she tried that before? It wasn't that she didn't trust anyone, it's just that there was always the possibility that someone might be trying to take advantage of her. There was no "Ding Lou" on the list of fares. She wasn't in a rush, so she stood on the side of the street as she ate a bun she'd brought from home and drank a bottle of water she purchased. As she stood there eating and drinking, people kept coming up and trying to solicit business from her. Some wanted her to go eat at a certain restaurant, or stay at a certain inn, or give her a ride, but she didn't respond to any of them. The ones who wanted to give her a ride asked her where she was going, but she wouldn't say for fear of revealing she was alone in an unfamiliar place. Who knows—maybe "Ding Lou" wasn't the name of a place. There was, however, one driver who drew her attention. He was holding a sign and shouting "Headed west, headed west" as he walked by, and on the sign was a list of places that included one called "Yu Lou." Fentian thought that maybe she had misread the sign, mistaking the character for "Yu" (于) as the one for "Ding" (丁). At any rate, she thought, he was heading west, so she could look for things she remembered as they drove along and get out of the car at any point. So she decided to go with that driver. Only two or three other people were sitting in his minibus, so he was naturally unwilling to leave yet, and continued looking around for more passengers. The sky had grown dark, and the coal dust in the air reflected the light from the streetlamps, weakly illuminating the night and making everything appear faint and indistinct. The driver wouldn't turn on the interior lights, so the passengers' faces were masked in darkness, their features completely obscured. Fentian wasn't afraid; she no longer even knew the word "fear." She sat quietly in the seat next to the door, recalling that the restaurant had been on the south side of the street, with the neon sign to the north. Out the window, she saw countless minibuses parked along the uneven ground, their drivers all shouting for business. In the darkness of the night, it didn't seem noisy; everything appeared clear and open in the vast expanse between earth and sky.

When Fentian saw the neon characters for "Ding Lou" suddenly appear against the purple darkness of the night, she felt herself go weak. After she got out of the minibus and started walking the half-*li* back toward the green and red sign for the "Ding Lou Baths," she finally understood: the character for "Ding" (丁) was originally "Yu" (于), but one of the lights had burned out, so "Yu" was missing a stroke. Just as she had expected, there was a restaurant across from the neon sign. The door was open with a patch of light extending out, and inside stood a woman who was very young and definitely not Miss Xia. She walked up to Fentian and stood in front of her. It was a little strange, of course, for a single woman to be showing up at that hour. Fentian smiled and stepped through the door; although she hadn't gotten a good look at the restaurant's sign, she was certain this was the place. Hesitantly, the woman asked her: Something to eat? Without answering, Fentian walked directly up to a table and sat down. Yes, it was this table, with that plastic tablecloth printed with peonies and aquatic plants—just what these two plants had to do with one another was unclear. The young woman brought over a menu, but Fentian didn't take it, and instead asked: Where's Miss Xia? Clearly uneasy, the young woman asked: Miss Xia? What Miss Xia? Fentian didn't try to argue, but responded with a restrained smile and said: I've arranged to meet with Miss Xia, so I'll just wait for her here. The young woman left and soon returned, saying: There really is no Miss Xia here. Fentian didn't pay her any attention and just kept sitting there. There were no customers in the restaurant, and trucks could be heard driving out on the highway, their tires humming loudly against the pavement. No other vehicles stopped. Fentian was the only person sitting there, and behind her—probably either the kitchen or some guestrooms—all was quiet. In the midst of this silence, the young woman brought over a pot of tea, so Fentian had some. After this standoff had gone on for about half an hour, the young woman came out and said: Our boss says it's quite late, and we have some rooms in the back for rent. Fentian said: Your boss? I'd like to meet her, please. Almost in response, a woman appeared in front of Fentian; she apologized for the waitress's poor treatment of her and asked if she could bring her anything hot to eat or drink while she rested. Fentian examined this woman, who seemed to look nothing like "Miss Xia."

Actually, though, she didn't really remember what Miss Xia looked like, but she decided this must be her. She looked up and greeted her: Miss Xia. Miss Xia looked shocked but quickly recovered, putting on a bright smile and saying: Call me whatever you'd like! My employees wouldn't dare call me this—it was my childhood name! Fentian asked: Do you recognize me? Miss Xia said: Yes, of course, how else would you know to call me Miss Xia? Fentian saw that she was being evasive, so she cut straight to the point: Last fall, three soldiers—when she said "soldiers," she smiled again—three soldiers and two young women ate at Miss Xia's restaurant, and left about two hours earlier than it is now. Those two young women were kidnapped and taken to two separate places. One of them was able to escape—that was me. Fentian stared directly at Miss Xia's face, which again changed expression in a cunning way. Fentian continued: The other one was my friend, and I would like to rescue her. I've already registered the case with the Women's Federation and the police, and I can get in touch with them at any point. By the time Fentian had finished, Miss Xia had already calmed down. She had seen a lot in her time as a single woman running a roadside restaurant—what hadn't she experienced? She very considerately asked: What county was your friend taken to? What town? What village? Fentian answered: I don't know. Miss Xia sighed: Well, this is going to be difficult. Fentian said: You mean you don't know, Miss Xia? Miss Xia clearly perceived her mocking tone, but she didn't return it, and instead replied calmly: I don't know. Fentian didn't know what to say next, so she paused and said: I'll stay here. Miss Xia very warmly said: Stay—please stay, and you can go in the morning. The next morning, however, Fentian gave no indication that she intended to leave, and she ended up staying for another night. She stayed put for the next several days. Actually, Fentian didn't know where she should go or what she should do. But from Miss Xia's perspective, this young woman seemed to be very calculating, and whatever her plans were, she must have her reasons for staying there. This made Miss Xia uneasy.

Because Fentian didn't have anywhere to go while she was staying at Miss Xia's inn, she just sat in the restaurant all day. Her so-called guest-room was extremely cramped, with one big bed squeezed in and hardly any other space. The room was clean, though; the walls were freshly whitewashed, and purple curtains hung over a window in the back. A table was shoved under the window, with a cup, a mirror, and some other items on it. Hidden behind the door was a stand with a washbasin, along with a towel and a box of soap. A woven mat for summer sleeping was spread on the bed, and the pillow was covered with one as well. The thin blanket had also been recently washed and starched—all around were the detailed, considerate touches of a female innkeeper. As Fentian stayed at the inn, she gradually began to pick up on a few things. At each mealtime, the waitress in the restaurant would go out to the road to try to drum up business, but not many vehicles would ever stop, and the ones that did were usually returning customers. They pulled off the road, parked in the empty space to the side, and walked in the restaurant as if they were already quite familiar with it. Miss Xia and the waitress would come out with their warm greetings of "Older Brother Zhang!" and "Older Brother Li!" One of them would bring some tea as she greeted them, and the other would go to the kitchen to get busy chopping and frying—it was almost like it was their own brothers coming home. There were also some "older brothers" who didn't eat anything but went straight to a certain room in the back; the waitress would follow them and then disappear, leaving only Fentian and Miss Xia in the restaurant. Neither of them spoke, and things in the room were suspiciously quiet. Once or twice, Fentian caught the eye of an "older brother," who would ask: Are you new? Miss Xia would immediately cut him off and lead him to a table further away from Fentian. She had a lot on her mind and couldn't see that Miss Xia was afraid of her. One day it rained, and the cars whizzed by over the shiny, wet pavement. Their drivers were all probably anxious to get home, and not many people stopped for a refreshment. Fentian stared out at the rain, and Miss Xia stared at Fentian. By evening, Miss Xia couldn't take it anymore, so she followed Fentian to her room. First she used a cloth to dust off the bedframe, the small table, and the few objects on it. Then she asked: Where were you and your friend separated from one another? Have you heard anything about where she could have gone? I can help you find her if you give me a little information! Fentian gazed at Miss Xia and tried to gauge what she meant. Miss Xia was probably twenty-eight or twenty-nine—somewhere close to thirty—and she had a large frame with permed hair that looked like a bunch of noodles gathered up high on the back of her head. She wore a bright red dress with shoulder pads, and standing there under the lamplight she looked like the Buddha's warrior attendant. Fentian was sitting almost completely in Miss Xia's shadow, but her eyes were shining brightly, which gave Miss Xia goosebumps. With a bitter grin, Miss Xia said: I really can't help you. With that she made to leave, but from behind her Fentian said: I don't believe you don't know! Miss Xia turned around and asked: Know what? Fentian replied: Shouldn't you say? Miss Xia responded in turn: Say what? Fentian asked: You mean you don't know? Actually, they were each thinking about the other: What is it she knows? The room was so small that as they stood facing one another, each could nearly feel the other's breath on her face. Miss Xia said: How should I know? Do I owe you something? Fentian said: If you don't know, you don't know—what's there to get so anxious about? Miss Xia retorted: Who's getting anxious? Fentian said: You—you're getting anxious! Miss Xia said: It looks to me like you are. Fentian laughed: Yes, I'm anxious. Miss Xia also laughed: Yes, it really looks that way. Fentian nodded and said: I want to be anxious. Miss Xia also nodded: Then you just go ahead and be anxious! The two of them stood there looking at each other for a moment, and then Miss Xia opened the door and left. Fentian followed her out with her eyes and silently applauded: That's right, just run away!

The two of them continued this standoff, their hearts each weighed down by their own issues. Fentian was reaching the end of her tether, but luckily she had no misgivings, and as far as "he" was concerned, she had already risked everything. Miss Xia, of course, had some misgivings. With a guest like this staying at her place, how could she go on with the kind of business they usually conducted there? So, in comparison, Fentian occupied the stronger position. After their standoff had continued for a few more days, Miss Xia once again followed Fentian into her room and sat down shoulder to shoulder with her on the edge of the bed. With a sigh, she asked once again: Where was it exactly that you and your friend were separated? Do you have any information about where she might have gone? Although it was the same thing she'd said before, this time it carried the sense of an apology. Fentian didn't dare answer, afraid she would reveal that she really didn't know anything at all, and that Miss Xia also had something she wasn't saying. Miss Xia said: Look, with you here, how are we supposed to do business? It sounded a bit like Miss Xia was confiding in her. Fentian responded by saying: Haven't I been paying my bills? She sounded a bit like a stubborn child. Miss Xia couldn't help but laugh: Yes, you've paid your bills—who said you hadn't paid? After a pause, Fentian spat out: I just want to find my friend. Miss Xia said: But where is she?

Fentian said: Even if I have to dig six feet under, I'll find her! Miss Xia interjected: What kind of unlucky talk is that?! Fentian knew she'd said something she shouldn't have; her palms broke out in a sweat and her heart started pounding. Miss Xia slowed down her speech and said: Who knows, your friend might be doing just fine. With that, she stood up and left the room. For the next two days, they didn't speak. By now, nearly a month had gone by. Fentian sat in the restaurant every day, like neither a guest nor the proprietor, which confused the customers and actually prevented a few of them from coming in. National Day was approaching, and the police strengthened their efforts to maintain order and crack down on crime. So for the past several days police officers had come by to look around, ask a few questions, and take down some notes. When this happened, Miss Xia became extremely nervous. One day, an officer asked to see Fentian's identification. Miss Xia, who had been carrying a pot of tea, forgot to set it down and just stood there holding it. She watched as Fentian took out her ID and answered a few questions—nothing she said touched upon her search for her friend. The police left after they finished their routine business. Miss Xia carried the teapot and teacups out of the room and then returned, only just realizing she had something in her hands. She stopped and gently set them down on a table, saying: I see you've made up your mind to ruin my business. I really don't understand how I've ever wronged you, but that's fine—I'll close up shop and go out of business. Just leave! Fentian said: My mind's made up—I won't leave until I find my friend! This made Miss Xia explode: What does finding your friend have to do with me—why rope me into this? Just get out of here. Moving out of her way, Fentian said: I'm not leaving! The two of them chased each other around the table a few times, and although they were serious, it looked a bit like they were just having fun. Fentian said: Maybe we should go have a talk with the police. Miss Xia said: Are you serious? Then go now before they've gone very far! She grabbed Fentian's hand from across the table and tried to drag her, but Fentian flung her off so forcefully it made her stumble. Neither of them really wanted to go to the police. For Miss Xia, in her line of business, the less interaction she could have with the police, the better; for Fentian, she was afraid that going to the police would reveal not only that she had never registered with them, but that she also had no evidence or clues. The two of them stood there for a minute and then left, one continuing to run her business and the other continuing to stay there.

A few days later, Miss Xia came to have a talk with Fentian, saying: Tell me more specifically about those three men that brought the two of you here—what they looked like and how old they were. If I'm going to help you, I want to do what I can. Fentian said: You mean you need to ask me? You should know. Miss Xia sized her up for a moment and said: If you're going to make it impossible to talk to you, then just leave. Fentian was actually starting to waver, and wondered whether or not she should cooperate with Miss Xia. But who could tell what kind of person this Miss Xia really was? Maybe she was just testing the waters, and wouldn't take Fentian seriously once she knew she had no information. Fentian passed the next two days in this uneasy state of uncertainty. The following night, after Fentian was already in bed, Miss Xia knocked on the door, entered, and placed a note on top of Fentian's blanket: From what I've gathered, this is the location—they say a young wife turned up there from out of town. Tomorrow morning, go and check it out—if it's not your friend, there's nothing else I can do. Then she added: Whatever you do, don't tell anyone you heard this from me—people in our business shouldn't talk about what we see here. She pulled the door shut and left, leaving Fentian sitting alone in her blanket. She felt like she was dreaming—it took her quite some time to regain her senses.

Early the next morning, Miss Xia arranged for a truck driver to give Fentian a ride and saw her off like she was sending off a Buddha. This "older brother" had stayed at the inn the night before, and there seemed to be a certain degree of affection between him and Miss Xia—when it was time to go, he tugged on her gold earrings and hopped up into the driver's seat. He drove fast and didn't speak to Fentian the whole way, and after about three or four *li* he stopped the truck and indicated she should get out. Fentian looked around as she stood at the side of the road. There were some cars coming down the road, and after waiting a little while she hailed a bus and squeezed her way in. The road beneath them gradually gave way to dirt and became quite uneven. After bumping along for a while they came to a stop, and Fentian got out and walked the rest of the way.

The sun was now high overhead, and kindling smoke hung over the village as people began lighting their cooking fires. Fentian wasn't hungry or thirsty. She had already decided that if this young wife turned out not to be Shui, she would return to Miss Xia's inn and remain there, confident that Miss Xia would have some information about Shui. As she walked through one village, and then another, the smoke from the midday cooking fires rose, and then disappeared. In the calm of the afternoon, she would occasionally hear the contented sounds of a chicken or a dog. Following what was written on the note, Fentian walked into a courtyard—in that instant, she had the feeling she was back in Liu San's home. Actually, though, the two places didn't really have anything in common. This home was a little better off than Liu San's—there were chickens pecking on the ground, and there were a few trees in the courtyard, including peach, pear, and persimmon. The clothes drying under the trees were also a bit brighter in color. Furthermore, this courtyard was located in a whole cluster of courtyards, unlike Liu San's place, which was up on an embankment by the road. Yet Fentian felt this was very much like Liu San's courtyard. Her heart was beating light and fast, and she felt a little dizzy.

A young wife was sitting in the courtyard breastfeeding a newborn, and she looked up when she heard someone enter. The sun was very bright, and the whole ground was covered in light and shadows. The woman looked as if she were sitting in the shadow of a flower, her face appearing very small and white. The two of them stared blankly at one another for a moment, and then Fentian called out: Shui—and Shui started crying. Fentian knelt down in front of her and asked: How have things been for you here? Shui said: Not good. Would you like to leave with me? Fentian asked. Yes! Shui pulled her nipple out of the baby's mouth; the baby's forceful hold stretched out Shui's nipple until it was quite long. Shui gathered up her clothing, set the child down on a cotton blanket spread over the floor, and stood up to leave with Fentian. By the time the child's crying attracted the attention of Shui's mother-in-law, the two young women had already exited the courtyard. Shui's mother-in-law at first didn't understand what was happening, but then, after a moment of shock, she realized what was going on and began shouting and chasing after them. Shui returned the insults, and both parties hurled filthy curses at one another until Fentian made Shui stop yelling and quickly pulled her along. They followed the path Fentian had taken into the village and made their way to the highway, where they hailed a minibus. It was a long and winding journey. Night had fallen by the time they made it to Xuzhou Station.

This was the actual Xuzhou Station, not Xuzhou West, and the lamps in the square were all shining brightly, lighting up half the sky. It was only at this point that Shui thought to ask Fentian: Where are we going?

Fentian said: To Shanghai. Shui followed Fentian through the masses of people that filled the square. When they'd bought their tickets and made their way to the waiting area, Shui let out a wail and began crying, sobbing for her child. Fentian told her: Stop crying! Shui promptly stopped. The two of them found the line for those heading to Shanghai and got in it, and others immediately continued lining up behind them; long lines had also formed to their left and right. The two girls were absorbed into this sea of people and disappeared.

2003

THE RESCUE TRUCK 救命车

There was a period of time completely hidden from his memory. The last thing he remembered was racing through the *longtang* alleyways, a mighty army following close on his heels—a "mighty army" that consisted of his brother and the other neighborhood boys. He ran straight to the back gate and stopped in front of his grandmother, who stuck a finger down his back collar and asked: Why is there no sweat? Their grandmother kept tabs on their health by checking the backs of their necks. If she found them sticky and wet with sweat, there was no problem, and she would release them to continue running around; if they were smooth and dry, however, they were definitely coming down with something. This was a method she had developed from her experience raising two generations of children, and it was never wrong. After his grandmother checked his neck, he still retained some jumbled impressions, making the cutoff of his memory not so definite, but actually quite fuzzy—like the fibers in a lotus root that remain joined after it's been broken.

Those fragmented memories were dominated by a deep sleep, which mingled with his grandmother saying things to his mother, as well as his mother complaining to his grandmother and scolding his brother. At one point either his mother or grandmother grabbed him by the arms and took him to the hospital, where he slept on a bench while he waited after getting registered. A few times his mother tried to get him to sleep on her lap, but at his age he was neither physically nor psychologically suited to sleeping in his mother's embrace, so he struggled free. A cold thermometer was stuck under his tongue, and it quickly came out scalding hot. When he put his feet on the ground he was unable to stand, so he squatted down until finally his father lifted him up on his back. Pills were put in his mouth, only to be retched up again in their original form; they were ground up into a powder and poured into his mouth with water, where the mixture swirled around in the back of his throat. He was surrounded by the fumes of alcohol, pungent smells, and a piercing cold. . .

When his grandmother inspected the boy's neck, he already had a fever. Fevers are usually not particularly frightening for a child, and even when they get up to thirty-eight or thirty-nine degrees Celsius, they still might not even realize it. This time, as his temperature climbed from thirty-eight to thirty-nine, his grandmother naturally could not ignore it, and she immediately sent him to bed. Upon lying down, his fever, which had at first remained low, began to shoot up. By the time his parents came home from work, the child, wrapped in a quilt on a July day, was burning up like a hot coal. When they checked his temperature again, the mercury in the thermometer nearly reached the tip. His mother complained that his grandmother shouldn't have bundled him up in a quilt on such a hot day, while his grandmother countered that fevers have always been treated by sweating them out. In the end his grandmother was unable to overcome her forceful daughter-in-law, who removed the quilt. The child looked like a skinned rat, his whole body red and trembling. His mother was left with no choice but to cover him up again. After thinking it over for a little bit, they decided to go to the hospital.

Despite his high fever, the poor child was still able to stand up by himself while his mother and grandmother dressed him in a sweater. Then they left the house for the hospital, where they registered him at the emergency room, which was full of adults and children with fevers, most of whom were diagnosed with colds. They'd be given injections to reduce their fevers and prescribed some medication, and the fevers would come down. Although the days were long at that time of year, dusk had already descended and the streetlights had come on; night was quickly approaching. The summertime heat of the day had begun to abate, and the breeze brought a slight coolness. The injection the boy had received began to take effect, and he became slightly reinvigorated. When asked what he wanted to eat, his answer was noodles; when asked what he wanted in the noodles, his answer was nothing. When his grandmother suggested a bowl of *yangchun* noodles in broth, the boy stubbornly responded: I don't even want the *yangchun*! Clearly he had not fully regained his appetite and only wanted to eat something light and bland, although he didn't realize that *yangchun* was merely a nice-sounding name and had nothing to do with the actual contents of the dish. His mother and grandmother exchanged a smile, allowing them to reconcile after their squabble.

Before he had eaten half the bowl of noodles, the boy laid down his chopsticks and quickly crawled back under the quilt. He would repeat this action many times: His fever would go down and would venture out of his quilt, but then it would return, and he would go back under. It was as if the fever were some sort of external attack, and he was a small animal under threat, crawling back to the safety of his nest. He was completely unable to determine where the danger was coming from, but he would do everything he could to escape it.

He'd been to the hospital, gotten a shot, taken the medicine, and returned under the quilt for the age-old method of sweating out the fever— the only thing left to do now was wait. Waves of hot and cold came like the tides, according to their own laws of motion. The night passed, and he woke up the next morning with renewed vigor. That evening, he was particularly calm. The boy's brother was much better behaved than normal and went to bed early. The adults relaxed a bit after their initial alarm— they tucked the sick child under the quilt, and laid a towel on his brother's belly. Then they lit some incense to repel mosquitoes; the pungent smoke spread over the wooden floor, swirling around the table legs and lingering around the foot of the bed. This peacefulness contained some hidden hope, which ushered in some happiness. It was all part of the normal ups and downs of family life, in which small crises and their solutions strengthened bonds and brought the family closer together.

Because they all went to bed early, that night was longer than most. The boy's younger brother woke up a few times, and in his bleary state he perceived the yellow light of the lamp and the soft murmuring of their grandmother, who was helping his brother drink some water, take his medicine, and go to the bathroom. The younger one was used to getting some attention, but tonight he simply turned over and kept sleeping. Children are all sensitive creatures, and when they feel that things aren't normal, they know something's going on—so, subconsciously, he wanted to avoid whatever it was, while maintaining hope that maybe, when he woke up, things would be back to normal. The light from the lamp flickered in his eyes, and they were once again overcome with sleep, leaving his feverish brother there under the lamplight while shadows played on the wall. The July evenings were quite warm, and a gentle breeze blew over them as they lied on their bamboo mats. The heat was not sticky, and the air became so light that faraway smells and sounds were able to drift by and then disperse. A certain energy floated in the stillness. Some green insects flew around under the lamplight and crashed into one another, then suddenly disappeared into the darkness. Sleep enveloped the night.

As expected, the morning brought a fresh atmosphere: The boy's fever had somewhat abated, demonstrating the effectiveness of the injection, staying hydrated, and sweating it out. Yet he remained listless and was unwilling to get out of bed. He continued to sleep. His parents went to work as usual while his grandmother did the shopping, cooking, and laundry. She instructed the boy's brother to remain in the room and report any movement to her. The little one played with toys on a bamboo mat spread on the floor; they were nothing more than some wooden knives and guns, playing cards, and marbles, most of which had been broken or damaged in fights with his brother. Now that the one who usually fought with him over the toys was sick, and he could play with them as he pleased, his interest decreased. The room was so still he became fearful and drew up to the side of the bed. His brother was still sleeping, and he could hear his breathing. Something seemed not quite right, so he called for their grandmother, who dropped what she was doing and rushed over. She checked the back of the sleeping boy's neck, as well as his forehead, and found that he was a bit warmer than before; he was sleeping soundly, though, and there didn't seem to be any major cause for concern. As she was about to leave, she saw the younger brother looking up at her pathetically with big, round eyes.

So she got a few cookies out of a container and gave them to him, praising him for his report. He ate the cookies by himself, with no one bothering or threatening him, but he was unable to enjoy them as much as he normally would. The morning passed peacefully like this.

By the afternoon, the boy's fever shot up, and his body was once again burning like a hot coal. When his grandmother called to him, he gave only a vague response without opening his eyes. It didn't feel right to let him keep sleeping, so she called to him again, and once more he responded without opening his eyes—he was already in a deep sleep. His grandmother was a bit startled by this and was reluctant to leave his side, so she sat by the bed. With no one else to fight for their grandmother's affection, the younger one took the opportunity and climbed into her lap. Young and old sat there quietly watching the boy sleep. His breathing was very quiet, and it seemed like he was really out, but when they tried softly calling to him, he would still answer, as if he weren't really asleep. But when they asked if he wanted a drink of water or something to eat, he would only respond without any movement, like he couldn't really wake up. Twice their grandmother put down the younger one and helped the sick one sit up by leaning him against her arm, but he would just slide right back down again. She didn't actually realize how heavy a child of six or seven could be, and she was nearly pulled down with him—he simply didn't have any strength to support himself. She didn't need to take his temperature to know that his fever had gone up. After a while, she wrung out a cool towel and put it on his forehead. Fevers were common for children, but this time was different. Again, their grandmother had raised two generations of children, and she was relatively confident in her knowledge and abilities. While applying a cool towel to the boy's forehead, she brought over a basin of warm water to wipe over his body. When she opened his shirt and exposed his chest, she saw that, at some point, several bright, rosy red spots had appeared. Her next thought was measles.

Her first move was to get the younger one away from his brother, since he had never had measles. As for the older one, he'd had them once before, so normally he shouldn't be getting them again, but the spots he'd gotten that first time weren't standard in their appearance, as if they had never fully emerged. Now their grandmother started to wonder: Had he actually had measles before, or not? She lowered the bamboo blinds, cutting off the sunlight and creating a gloomy atmosphere. The grandmother looked over the boy's entire body and discovered a few more red spots on his belly. She paid particular attention to the area behind his ears, but found nothing; according to her experience, this would be the first place for the spots to appear. What's more, the boy didn't have a cough or runny nose—only a persistent fever, so it remained unclear. This time she was really stumped. She had done what she could: She kept cool towels on his forehead, and she forced him to sit up and have some thin rice porridge and water, and then go to the bathroom. The boy was very obedient and unusually sub-dued, which made everyone anxious. He was fast asleep when his par-ents arrived home from work, and the cold compresses appeared to have brought his temperature back down. His parents were young and optimis-tic, always looking for the good in a situation, and their attitude naturally helped the boy's grandmother calm down a bit. This evening was a little more relaxed than the previous one, as the household had now adapted to the fact that one of its members had fallen ill.

The next two days also passed under these alternating feelings of un-easiness and peace. Whenever the boy's fever appeared to go down a few degrees, it would quickly shoot right back up again, hovering around forty or even forty-one. One evening, when they called to him, he didn't re-spond. When they tried again, he responded, but the person he addressed was his playmate next door: I'll find you no matter where you hide! He had clearly returned to their chasing game—was he talking in his sleep, or was he hallucinating? The evening passed uneasily, with his mother and grandmother taking turns keeping watch at his bedside. At one point he reached his hand out in front of him and grasped the air as if there were something there. This frightened the boy's mother and grandmother, and they debated whether or not to go to the emergency room. But it was very early in the morning, before the first buses started running, and there were no rickshaws to be found, so they had no choice but to wait until sunrise. His mother was generally an impatient person, so waiting like this was like torture. She wanted to hold her son's hand, but he wouldn't let her, and he stubbornly broke free to continue stroking whatever invisible thing he saw in front of him. On this night, he departed from his peacefulness of the past few days and became agitated, crawling out from the quilt and then back under again. Very slowly, the sky grew brighter. The in-cense had all burned down and several mosquitoes were buzzing around, their tiny wings lightly yet rapidly beating along with the air currents.

They first appeared gradually as faint shadows, and later their needlelike mouthparts became visible. The red light of dawn appeared, ushering in another midsummer day. They heard the door to the back alley open, and the industrious women of the *longtang* began coming and going. The boy's father lifted him up on his back while his mother went ahead to hail a rickshaw, and his grandmother stayed at home with the younger one.

This time they were gone for quite a while, and it was almost afternoon by the time the two adults could be seen bringing the child back to the *longtang*. A blood test had been taken at the hospital, and the boy was diagnosed with typhoid. Then he was given an injection and ordered to stay in bed on a liquid diet. As soon as they heard the word "typhoid," everyone jumped with fright. While they had previously erred on the side of caution, they would now have to be extremely vigilant. Everything that entered the boy's mouth—whether it was watermelon juice, mashed vegetables, thin rice porridge, or soy milk—would first have to be filtered through a cloth. All of the family's bowls, chopsticks, and towels would need to be heat sterilized in a basket steamer. The younger boy had been kept away from his older brother ever since measles had been suspected, but now it became even more imperative that he stay out of his brother's room. Sometimes when he was bored stiff, he would just stand in the doorway and stare from a distance at his brother lying on the bed. Because the disease was being treated with medication, and also because it was beginning to run its course, the patient clearly took a turn for the better. His fever didn't completely go away, but he regained some energy. At this point he opened his eyes and looked over at the person standing in the doorway. The two brothers, on opposite sides of the door, stared helplessly at one another, as if they were worlds apart.

During the period of the boy's illness, the first days of autumn had begun to draw near, and although it was still hot, a cool breeze had begun to make the heat less stifling. There were often thunderstorms in the late afternoon, and the scorching sun would suddenly be covered by black clouds. The sky would turn dark and thunder would begin to rumble, and a gust of wind would blow inside and swirl around the room. Then they would hear the rain start to fall. The storm would come racing through like a stallion, and before long the clouds would part and the window panes would be glowing a golden red with the setting sun. The table would be set with autumn vegetables, wild rice stems, and soybeans, all a tender white or green, along with purple water chestnuts and taro root. The sponge gourds and eggplants had become too old by now, and no one would touch them. A new game was also being played in the *longtang*, although it was more a result of changing trends than the changing seasons. At some point the boys had abandoned the *longtang*, and it had become the domain of the girls, who made up a new rhyme to sing: "little rubber ball, rolling to and fro; on the ground it falls, sixty-one flowers grow." The first part of the rhyme was pretty good, with the somewhat obscure word for "to and fro" (趱, *xue*) used correctly. The second part, though, was rather clunky—*longtang* rhymes were always half-baked like this.

As the boy's health gradually improved, he would sometimes be allowed to sit up, and his brother would be permitted to enter the room and sit on the edge of the bed to play. Boys are generally less talkative than girls and aren't that used to playing around with words, so they will often just fall into silence. This time, the brothers sat together silently folding paper, using pages torn out of last semester's notebooks. The older one folded a dart for the younger one to throw, and soon it was whizzing all around the room. Owing to weak throws and poor folding skills, the darts usually just fell softly to the ground, until the whole floor was covered in them. The two boys played quietly, while behind them in the kitchen their grandmother cooked and did the laundry. The sounds of water rushing out of the faucet and food frying in the skillet drifted over to them, along with sound of their grandmother's voice—it seemed that some of their friends had come over to visit, and their grandmother had sent them away.

But this sort of scene didn't last that long. It seemed like everything had been going along just fine. The boy was still resting in bed, he was still on a diet of liquids and soft foods, and the woman from the neighboring *longtang* was still coming twice a day to give him his injections; by the time she had administered the last of his medicine, the situation had definitely improved. Then suddenly one afternoon, he got a sharp pain in his stomach. This child was quite tough—or maybe all children are this way—and because he thought there was no way to ease the pain, he just tried to bear it. He didn't make a peep, and simply bent over at the waist and started writhing, rolling from one side of the bed to the other. At a few points he cracked his head on the bedframe, which made an alarming sound. The next minute he was once again burning up with fever. His grandmother panicked and called over the woman from next door, who helped her call the boy's parents. In no time at all they came rushing home, nearly tripping over themselves in their haste. The boy's father immediately hoisted him onto his back, and his mother followed behind holding his two flailing legs. His grandmother gathered up some random items and grabbed the younger boy by the hand, and the whole family went off to the hospital.

When they arrived, it was, as always, full of people. First they went to the division of internal medicine, and then over to surgery. Then it was decided the boy would have to stay overnight, so they went to the inpatient ward. In the midst of the chaos, the parents still had to worry about the grandmother and youngest boy following behind them getting trampled or contracting some disease. They tried to send them home, but they were unwilling, choosing instead to sit and wait calmly in the courtyard. Although the part of the hospital that faced the street was not wide, once you entered the building, it kept going and going. If you made your way to the very center, you'd come to a round flower garden surrounded by several benches. The grandmother and her grandson waited here. When they first sat down, the setting sun was still casting its final rays of the day, and as it gradually set, its remaining light was particularly clear. Neither of the parents were anywhere to be seen, and if they were to try to look for them, with the hospital's countless doors and windows, they wouldn't even know where to start. The grandmother felt like an ant trapped in a hot skillet and was unable to calm herself down. When she thought of the little one with her, she couldn't help but pity him for being so ignored and patient. So, she got up and took him to the street outside the front of the hospital, where she bought him some ice cream. Then they returned to the bench to wait.

The crowd in the hospital had gradually thinned out. The outpatient services had closed for the day. Everyone who had been waiting to fill their prescriptions at the pharmacy counter had left, and the janitors had begun mopping the floors. A gardener who had come by to water the scarlet sage in the flowerbed picked one of the blossoms and gave it to the child, showing him how to smell it and enjoy its light, sweet scent. Somehow, receiving this attention from someone made the grandmother feel more at ease. Dusk settled over the area like rising floodwaters—at first, it was still light enough for the grandmother and her grandson to still see each other's facial features, but they soon became obscured. The windows in the hospital fell dark, except for one side of the building where they were all lit up. It was not enough light to reach the courtyard, which, strictly speaking, was little more than a small opening in the building. Instead, the courtyard had its own single lamp, which had just come on, casting a light so faint that the pair remained in the shadows. Still the ones they were waiting for had not returned. At one point the little one looked up at his grandmother, his eyes gleaming through the darkness with a questioning look. She responded by gently stroking his face.

A while later, after several trips inside the hospital to look around, they could see there were fewer cars and people on the street out front. The grandmother and her grandson were the only ones who remained in the courtyard, making it feel broad and open. Finally, at last, two figures appeared down the path between two buildings. As they stepped into the light from the windows, the pair of them could tell that the two approaching forms looked familiar. When they drew nearer, it was confirmed: Without a doubt, it was the boys' parents. Their father didn't have anything with him, and their mother had something soft and light balled up in her hand; when they got closer, they could see it was the sick child's clothes. The younger brother stared blankly, then broke into tears and wailed: Brother's not here! This was the first time since the whole ordeal began that anyone had expressed their feelings, and the adults around him were all filled with sadness. His words seemed extremely inauspicious, and furthermore they were the words of a child—according to the old superstition, unfortunate utterings like these were prophesies. The boys' parents belonged to the modern era and likely didn't think much of it, but their grandmother went pale with fright. But regardless of their generation, everyone's faces fell as they realized they would be returning home with one less than they'd come with. The younger brother sobbed for a while, and when he calmed down, the group sullenly made their way home.

The grandmother didn't sleep well that night—she was thinking of an event in the child's past. But what past could a little beansprout like him have to recall? Well, once she thought about it, there were a few things. She thought back to the time when the boy was just a month old and she was holding him in her lap, sitting by the doorway enjoying the sunshine. A monk of some kind—she couldn't tell if he was Buddhist, Daoist, or what—entered the *longtang* wearing shabby, faded clothes and speaking with an unfamiliar accent. Under the new political regime in the 50s, most religions had disappeared, and the Buddhists and Daoists had gradually dispersed; who knew where this one had come from? With his eyes fixed on the baby, he said: This child is one of the heavenly constellations fallen down to earth—you must take him to a temple to see an arhat in order for him to achieve peace. At the time, the grandmother thought he was just saying some propitious-sounding things as a way of begging for alms, and she didn't take him seriously. But now, as she thought back, she regretted her attitude. Her eyes stayed open the whole night, and before the sun had risen she got up and headed out the door.

Where did the grandmother go? She went to the Fragrant Aloeswood Pavilion. The pavilion held a Ming-dynasty bodhisattva carved out of aloeswood that had supposedly floated in from the sea during the reign of the Wanli Emperor; hundreds of years later, the treaty port was opened and the area had flourished. Although it was quite early when she arrived, the stand selling candles and joss sticks was already set up, and several people were already burning incense and kowtowing. She went over to make her purchases, intending to buy a whole pile of offerings. On second thought, she began to worry that it would displease the bodhisattva if it looked like she was placing too much importance on the child's life, so she opted for a much smaller selection. She went up to the place of worship and kowtowed three times, and then three more times. The first three kowtows were meant to compensate for the previous years, while the following three were meant to beg for protection in the present. She got up, went over to the donation box, and happily shoved in a large bill. On the way back she passed the city god temple, so she went in to the Daoist pavilion, where she kowtowed and donated some more. Now she could feel at peace. By the time she made it back home, she realized just how early she had gone out when she discovered that everyone was still in bed.

Because of the medical treatment, and also because of the family's sincere hope, all the news from the hospital was good. Each day was better than the one before it, and in no time at all two weeks had gone by. The day for the boy to be released from the hospital had come. Only one word could describe how the family felt: "grateful." They were grateful he had come home safe and sound—not only that, but also that he had both returned to his life and come back into theirs. The day before, his mother had gone to the hospital and asked him what he wanted; because he had suffered so much, and because he was coming home, she wanted to prepare a gift for him. As the child thought about it, his mother encouraged him: Anything you want! The child answered: A rescue truck. That was the common local name for "ambulance." He had always liked vehicles. There was a shop at the entrance to the *longtang* that sold toys and stationery, and he had always paid close attention to the wooden cars and trucks displayed in its window, yet he had never thought of actually getting one for himself. For someone who lived such a plain, ordinary life, he knew that most of what he saw in the world around him was only for looking at—it was a life of restriction and knowing one's place. But the less you try to think about something, the more you want it, and now the opportunity had suddenly presented itself. The reason he wanted the "rescue truck" was because it was the biggest vehicle there, and its doors were halfway open, indicating they could open and close. He also liked that it was all white with a bright red cross on top. While the adults felt that this "rescue truck" wasn't exactly the most auspicious object, now that the boy had explicitly said he wanted it, they could get it for him without having to feel any misgivings.

The next day it rained—a light, continuous shower that evoked the phrase "the chill that follows an autumn rain." The boy's mother brought the "rescue truck" with her to the hospital when she went to collect him. The moment he received the truck in his hands, he seemed to go into a slight trance. It was bigger and heavier than he had imagined, which could have also been because the illness had sapped his strength, and he had to exert some effort to lift it. The first thought that went through his head was about his brother: Should he let him play with it? The boy had lost a lot of weight while he had been sick, and the expression on his face was rather serious, so as he held the white truck in his hands, it looked as if it were a solemn occasion.

As he followed his mother out of the hospital room carrying the "rescue truck," he heard her thank the doctors and nurses as she bid them farewell, receiving their encouragement in return. He endured having countless hands rub his head as he remained silent. Finally they exited the inpatient ward, went down the stairs, and walked out of the building. They got into a rickshaw, and as they settled in, he held the "rescue truck" on his lap with both hands. The driver put up the canopy and lowered the rain flaps, which were attached around all sides of the rickshaw, and still tiny streams of rain trickled in through the cracks. The small space they were sitting in was dark and cool, and filled with the acrid smell of oilcloth. All of his suspended memory picked up again, and the world became reinvigorated.

2007

THE TROUPE

文
工
团

1. Liuzi Opera

In its previous life, this regional Cultural Workers' Troupe of ours had been a Liuzi opera troupe. After being displaced by the "new culture," Liuzi opera seemed to be in full decline—an ancient and rare dramatic form that had become obsolete. We had never seen it ourselves, or even heard a line of it sung. Some said it had its origins as palace entertainment, possessing a subtle richness and lofty style that made it truly an elite form, though too elite to gain the popularity needed to withstand the test of time. This explanation always sounded a little overblown. It was hard to imagine that this dusty place with its rough people had any kind of highbrow opera, when a loud wooden clapper would be a much more suitable form of expression. But who knows? This place also has history—armies vied for control of the area in an endless succession of battles that destroyed the city many times over.[1] The tombs from the Han

---

1. This Cultural Workers' Troupe is based in Xuzhou, in the northern reaches of Jiangsu province.

dynasty show evidence of this. So as for whether or not Liuzi opera really did originate in the palace, it's hard to say.

We did once have some slight contact with Liuzi opera. It was the fall of 1976—the Gang of Four had just been overthrown, and the troupe was coming up with a skit to perform in the small event to be held that evening. The one playing Zhang Chunqiao was an older actor who always carried a fan with him. He could dance out in front and do flips in the back, as well as a whole series of tricks. Whenever he appeared on stage, he was sure to be a crowd pleaser. His steps and hand gestures were clear and distinct, his rhythm always smooth and flexible, and his performance lively and concise. Clearly it was not something that could be attained through impromptu imagination, but instead came from rigorous and standardized training. Although our skit was nearly a disaster, his portrayal of Zhang Chunqiao helped save the day. After talking to the older members of the troupe, we learned that this actor specialized in playing the martial type of *chou* role,[2] with a fan as his preferred prop. This accorded with what I would later discover in a dictionary of theater under the entry for "Liuzi opera," which meticulously laid out the division of roles. The male ones included those of *jingmian, jiazi, xiu, wu,* and *baihu,* and the female roles were *qingyi, hongyi, guimendan,* and *laodan.* The painted-face roles, furthermore, were divided into red and black, and the *chou* roles into civil and martial.

Flipping through the dictionary many years later was the first time I ever really learned anything about Liuzi opera. Actually, I discovered that the local rumors I had heard about it were not unfounded, and everything seemed to have some basis in fact. Its origins could be traced to the Central Plains during the Yuan dynasty, at which time there was a flourishing of *qupai* tunes to which folk verse and short *ci* poems were set. These included songs like "Suo Nan Zhi," "Beside the Dressing Table," "Sheep on the Mountainside," and "Children Playing." The Ming dynasty saw an even greater abundance of these poems and verses, and it was out of this that Liuzi opera was born. During the Kangxi period of the Qing dynasty, Pu Songling used this form of verse to write the lines of "Nao Guan," which has survived in Liuzi opera under the title "Teaching with the Gentleman." The popular saying in Beijing during

---

2. *Chou* is often translated as the "clown" role. The following technical opera terms are all standard types of roles in traditional Chinese opera. The colors of painted-face roles indicate certain attributes of specific characters.

the mid-Qing—"Liu in the east, Bang in the west, Kun in the south, Yi in the north"—demonstrates the prominent position Liuzi opera once held. It was right around that time that opera troupes from Anhui province were brought to perform in Beijing, when Peking opera was still in its swaddling clothes.

The entry then went on to describe what I had heard about the richness of Liuzi opera's arias and the loftiness of its style. It was a form of *qupai* drama, composed of both Liuzi and folk verse. The folk verse set to *qupai* was soft and pleasant, capable of subtly conveying complicated emotions. Yet it was freer than *kunqu*, another form of *qupai*, because it allowed for the insertion of seven- or ten-character lines into the long-and-short verse *qupai*—a practice known as "*guaxu*." It was a transitional form in the development of *banqiang* from its origins in *qupai*, which was part of the general transition from elite to popular. This demonstrates the relatively broad expressive capability of Liuzi opera, and it may even be considered one of the major operatic forms. Calling it palace entertainment might be a bit of a mischaracterization, but it's certainly understandable. According to the dictionary, during the first week of the second months of spring and autumn, when sacrifices would be offered to Confucius at his ancestral home in Qufu, Liuzi opera would be performed at his family mausoleum. The site had performers who were specifically trained in Liuzi opera, and professional actors would often come to study with them. During the height of Confucianism in the Qing dynasty, these sacrifices were a grand celebration, and the performers who took the stage were certainly among the most well-known and illustrious. Confucius was so highly regarded that his family mausoleum was considered a holy site, and the peak of the temple roof was only three bricks shorter than the Hall of Supreme Harmony in the Imperial Palace. So, mixing up the Temple of Confucius with the Imperial Palace is a relatively natural mistake.

This is the full portrait of Liuzi opera I got from the dictionary. It appears to have been a particularly flourishing form of opera, and it doesn't say what conditions led to its decline. There's still a troupe that specializes in the Liuzi lute in our area, as well as one that specializes in the wooden clapper—but during the reforms of the sixties, the Liuzi opera troupe became part of the Cultural Workers' Troupe, which specialized in song and dance. The "Cultural Workers' Troupe"—both its name and what it entails—can trace its origins back to the Chinese Revolution as a militarized form of artistic expression that spread to every army unit all over China. That's when Liuzi opera began to die out. By the time we arrived in this area in the early seventies, it had already disappeared, like something that only belonged in the previous century. For a whole style of opera to vanish in such a short period of time was rather alarming. With evergreen pines and emerald cypresses towering in the sky over Confucius's ancestral home, and the rhythmic beating of drums and gongs joining with the lingering sounds of the stringed instruments, the scene must have been utterly magnificent, emanating outward for hundreds of miles and into the future. But where have these verses and melodies gone today?

Liuzi opera was finished, and the troupe became the Cultural Workers' Troupe, or more officially, "The League for Cultural and Artistic Work." Compared with the time it took for Liuzi opera to disappear, the period of the group's construction was much longer. It seems that for the entirety of its existence it struggled to find direction, and it never really had any clear goals. "Culture and art" was too broad of a concept, and it presented this new organization, based on the old opera troupe, with some difficulty in its orientation. There was no way to confirm what it was actually supposed to be, so it always just seemed like a hodgepodge. Nothing ever really went smoothly—it was always one thing after another. There was a contingent of holdovers in the new troupe from its old Liuzi opera days, and we referred to them as the "old guard." They were actually just in their late twenties or early thirties, only about seven or eight years older than us, but it seemed like we were from different generations. We were separated by the chasm of different eras.

2. The Old Guard

Sometimes, the members of the old guard in the troupe's band would suddenly break out into a few bars of old melodies, exchange knowing looks, and erupt in playful laughter. Presumably, those were the melodies of Liuzi opera. They were clearly recalling some things from their shared past that we knew nothing about. A certain barrier always remained between us, despite the fact that we spent nearly all of our time in each other's company. This sort of living situation was probably passed down from the old troupe. We all lived like one big family in a courtyard residence, always together, morning till night—yet we had no idea what they did or what they were thinking. From our perspective, their lives were completely different from ours. They were from a previous era that had already disappeared and had no hope of returning. In the new kinds of performances we put on, they mostly played the random bit parts of soldiers or bandits. They had been trained in martial arts from a young age, but in the new forms of song and dance, there was no real way for them to use their skills. The voices they used on stage were also not very appropriate for modern songs, and when we sang together, they always sounded abrasive and out of place. The situation in the band was slightly better. They all played the pipes or the bamboo flute, and they weren't bad, sometimes putting together some solo and ensemble performances of folk music. At the same time, they also practiced a selection of Western instruments—those who played the bamboo flute, for instance, took up the Western concert flute; those who played the reed pipes studied the clarinet; and the percussionists learned the timpani. Together, they were able to form a small Western-style concert band, which demonstrated a remarkable adaptability. Although their execution was far from perfect, the results were certainly passable. The band's director was a graduate of the art institute, and he placed particular emphasis on the central role of the conductor; his biggest complaint was that everyone ignored him. The old guard really did ignore his conducting, yet they were always in time with one another and never missed a beat. The ones who got off beat were us—the ones staring at the conductor with rapt attention. The old guard may not have been much to look at, but they were certainly able to deliver. In other words, they were like soldiers who really knew how to fight. During dance performances, the dancers would often leave props or pieces of costumes lying around on the stage, and since there was no way to collect them, they would get in the way and trip everyone up. The old guard, however, knew how to clear them off the stage without the slightest deviation from the rhythm. When we put on musical dramas, the graduates of the art institute took the lead roles, but they were always having issues— sore throats, congestion, and any number of small vocal cord problems. The old guard playing the supporting roles, however, were always able to fill in at a moment's notice, relentlessly belting out the parts from beginning to end, regardless of how it sounded.

Most of them had joined the opera troupe at a young age to begin studying their art, and if it hadn't been reformed, they would now be in their prime. Instead, they were relegated to the fringes. They were all still young and adaptable to change, and they were hardworking and diligent in their efforts to study new things. Their professional study at a young age, however, had left its mark on them. To look at them, they appeared as if they were part of a totally different group, and in the end they were never really able to integrate. Everything went okay behind closed doors—we did live together, after all. There were some we saw all the time, with whom we spoke often and were quite familiar, and their differences were not apparent. But outside of our residence, things were different. One year, there was an event featuring Cultural Workers' Troupes from all over the province. Our troupe came with a program of folk music performed by the old guard, who were all wearing identical costumes made especially for the occasion. Compared to the attractive members of the other troupes, our performers looked unrefined, crude, and clumsy. Their out-of-place appearance caused the audience to snicker, and the whole troupe couldn't help but feel embarrassed. Actually, it was hilarious. They performed with the utmost seriousness. The grand scale of the venue in the provincial capital made them uncomfortable, and they drew their faces taught with concentration, like tigers eyeing their prey. But actually they just looked like they were staring ahead stupidly. They didn't resemble anything like a modern Cultural Workers' Troupe—they were more like traditional musicians at a wedding or funeral. In this setting, they were completely isolated and alone. If they were a little more perceptive, they would have seen that the overall atmosphere of the event was actually quite lighthearted. They didn't have an ounce of lightheartedness, and it was difficult to watch.

They had nothing of the manner and bearing of modern "cultural workers." In general, people looked up to the members of these troupes, and some of the more unconventional young men and women would emulate their style. They were a group that was steeped in the new culture and stood out from the crowd; they were cultured, stylish, good looking, and energetic. What's more, they all resembled one another, standing tall and proud like cranes among chickens. As for the old guard, you couldn't tell them apart from regular people on the street. They were tradespeople, just like blacksmiths, cooks, and shopkeepers. For them, it was just another job—studying performance didn't make them anything special. Yet the theater does, in the end, have its own unique attributes.

It's somewhat nihilistic and detached, a bit like watching a fire rage from the safety of the opposite shore. But for them, it was just another way to feed themselves, one occupation among many. They were a bit coarse, and the pretty ones among them had an unrefined beauty that was no different from the other attractive women on the street. They appeared extraordinarily common, even more like locals than the average local, wholeheartedly embodying their particular customs. This is why they seemed like such misfits at the provincial extravaganza—they didn't have the slightest whiff of an artistic demeanor.

Supposedly, when passing through the lower reaches of the Yangtze River, the Qianlong emperor described his visit with eight words: barren mountains, filthy water, shrewish women, unruly people. This eight-word description turned out to be basically true. The customs of this place really were crude and violent—just a few wrong words and a fight would break out, no weapons needed other than fists. These sorts of incidents were commonplace. Almost without exception, the members of the old guard displayed this sort of fierce temperament. My first summer after joining the troupe, I saw a female performer dump a full tub of water right in the face of a lighting technician in a dispute over the bathroom. For summer bathing, there was a small bathhouse in the corner of the courtyard, complete with a cement platform and drainage system. Because both men and women used it, there was a constant struggle over it. That day, the lighting technician had actually arrived first, but he realized he had forgotten to bring anything with him, so he left to go get his stuff. As soon as he left, the female performer seized the opportunity and slipped in. The lighting technician was a former soldier from the countryside who was not yet familiar with the harshness of the locals, and he let loose some coarse language. Without missing a beat, the female performer dumped the tub, completely drenching him. More incidents like this arose from romantic entanglements. The women here were all fiercely committed to defending their honor, and they were not in the least bit concerned with things like self-restraint or poise, nor were they afraid to show their true feelings. It might sound laughable now, but it was really an emotionally charged situation at the time. If a male performer were acting on stage with his ex-lover, his current lover might rush up on stage and cause a scene—screaming, shouting, punching, ripping clothes—until the roles were switched out. In the theatrical division of the troupe, men and women were in constant contact with one another, and the general atmosphere was quite permissive, so these types of affairs happened all the time. It was as if everyone had had a fling with each other at some point, and these heroic dramas were then acted out on stage. It was a case, as they say, of the water and soil of a particular place nourishing a particular kind of person—they hadn't received much formal education, and they were all very authentic, red-blooded products of this land. Perhaps it is also because Liuzi opera, as a traditional art form, is so closely connected to this region that it accentuated and even exaggerated the local flavor of its performers, showing their harmonious and inextricable relationship with the land that reared them.

The Cultural Workers' Troupe was a product of the new revolutionary literature and art and symbolized the new society, so this presented the old Liuzi actors with an enormous transition. All day long they could be seen happily laughing and joking, but who could tell how they really felt? After the graduates from the art institute entered the troupe—along with those cadres who had been transferred from the army's cultural division, and the intellectuals who had been "sent down" as a result of the repeated movements in the socialist revolution—the old guard was surrounded by these newcomers. Day by day, their look and behavior appeared cruder by comparison. The wind, frost, and dust gradually dulled their faces to the point where we could no longer tell what they really looked like, and scandalous stories about them circulated among the troupe. They once set up a tape recorder on the bed of a female performer on her wedding night, and the next day they played her the recording. This woman was also a member of the old guard, and she was not exactly known for her prudence—she supposedly had ambiguous relations with a number of people. Choosing her as the target of their practical joke couldn't help but reveal their secret fascination with her. Of course, this joke was disgustingly vulgar. But if we take out the element of modern technology—the tape recorder—and just look at the basic substance of the situation, it's nothing more than the thousand-year-old folk custom of "eavesdropping on the wedding night." From this perspective it seems perfectly natural and even demonstrates a lighthearted and generous attitude toward sex. But, either because of the tape recording or the more urban environment, the prank was ruined and turned into something filthy. Civilization, after all, involves pollution—it defiles nature. This practical joke did major damage to the old guard's reputation. It left a bad impression that persisted throughout several waves of newcomers, eventually becoming an entrenched view they were unable to cast off. Inevitably, history was about to pull these washed-up members of the old guard off the stage, and no one would even notice how lonely they would look.

In the beginning of the seventies, after restructuring and a prolonged period of subsequent floundering, the Troupe finally ushered in its golden era. The "golden era"—that's how people would later refer to this unforgettable time. The troupe adapted a multiact opera from Hunan called *The Serf's Halberd*, which was based on Hunan folk songs. The melodies were familiar and easy to imitate, and when a Western orchestration was added, the arias sounded truly excellent. What's more, a male soprano arrived from Shanghai, rounding out the phrase, "the right time at the right place with the right people." This male soprano was a 1965 graduate of the Shanghai Theater Academy's performance department. Because of a health issue, he did not receive a placement upon his graduation, and the subsequent onset of the Cultural Revolution further delayed this process until he simply became unemployed. He loved singing—he had studied under a well-known voice teacher, and he was quite good. Both the Shanghai Chorus and the regional military song and dance troupe had expressed interest in him, but because of some problems with his family background, it never went anywhere. Seeing he was completely dejected, a friend introduced him to our troupe in an attempt to cheer him up. It just so happened that we were rehearsing *The Serf's Halberd*. Not only did his singing voice dominate the entire troupe, but his face bore a natural resemblance to that of a Greek hero. Without hesitating, we decided to invite him to play the male lead. His performance was nothing short of sensational. Word of his superb voice spread like wildfire, and many came to see *The Serf's Halberd* just to hear him sing—he really gained quite a reputation. His understudy was one of the old guard from the Liuzi opera days. His stage presence and voice were not bad, but he couldn't compare to the man from Shanghai. One time he was allowed to stand in for him for a performance, but as soon as he opened his mouth, he was met with hissing from the crowd. Shouts of protest drowned out his arias, and no matter how hard he tried, he couldn't win over the audience. At any rate, when the first scene was over, the curtain closed, and a frantic search was made backstage for the Shanghai man. They were able to get him dressed and made up in time, and the performance was saved. From then on, this member of the old guard was an understudy in name only, and he reverted to being just another member of the troupe. After suffering this defeat, he kept a low profile and gradually fell into silence.

But things did not end here. *The Serf's Halberd* grew more popular with each performance, and word continued to spread. We went on tour for several months and performed to packed houses before finally making our triumphant return home. The audience in our city could hardly wait—people were clamoring for another performance, and every day they went to the ticket office to inquire when it would be. So, after taking a short break to rest up and regroup, we got back on the stage. The posters went up, the tickets were sold, and we waited for the big day to arrive. Just then, the man from Shanghai received a telegram from home asking him to return immediately to begin teaching at a certain middle school. His father had found him this position, which was for a substitute music teacher. To someone like him who had been out of work for so long, this was naturally an important opportunity. He immediately gathered his belongings and boarded a train back to Shanghai, abandoning the expectant audience and leaving the troupe high and dry. His behavior really ought to have been forgiven—in Shanghai at that time, finding a job was by no means easy, and he had been very anxious to get one. But his decision incurred everyone's anger, and when nothing ended up materializing for him in Shanghai and he returned to the troupe for help, no one wanted anything to do with him. An embarrassed and confused look spread over his beautiful, Hellenic face, and you had to feel some pity for him. But at this point, no one could help him—he had no idea what an enormous taboo he had violated. Throughout its transformation from a traditional opera troupe to its present form, our troupe had stubbornly held on to a certain old-fashioned notion: that the audience would always be the performers' basic providers. "Basic providers"—what a weighty term! For years, people had sung the praises of a certain performer who, right before he was about to go onstage, received the news of his father's death. When the curtain opened, he swallowed his tears and took the stage with a smile on his face. Our troupe couldn't forgive the Shanghai man's behavior, and there was no reason that could ever suffice.

The natural conclusion to this situation was the only one there could be: the understudy who had been booed offstage had to get back up there—reclaim the territory, so to speak. More jeering and cursing his mother was inevitable, but when the sky is falling, you have to prop it up, and retreat is not an option. This shows the thick skin of the old guard— they were particularly able to withstand the audience's taunting. No matter how fierce they may have been offstage, once they were up there, they'd do whatever was needed without a word of protest. One time during a small performance of miscellaneous folk arts, a member of the old guard was halfway through his clapper story when his belt broke. He threw the bamboo clapper aside and used both hands to hold up his pants. The person at the side of the stage operating the curtain couldn't see very well, and although he pulled the curtain closed as soon as he realized, it was too late to avoid the embarrassing spectacle. A roar of laughter rose up from the audience, which shook the roof and seemed like it would never die down. The performer collected himself, picked up the clapper, and continued right where he had left off. The audience once again erupted in laughter, making the seasoned veteran turn beet red. But there was no turning back, and he could only continue his clapper story through to the end. This was the old guard; this was the meaning of "artistic integrity." This was what they had studied from the time they first entered the opera troupe, what their instructors had physically beaten into them. No matter how many transitions the troupe underwent, they would remember this lesson and pass it down until they finally left the stage and quit the profession. In our dilapidated courtyard, where Liuzi opera had been passed down from master to student for generations, the screws on the dance barres had loosened, cracks had split open in the floorboards, the rafters were draped in cobwebs, and the rotting beams were speckled with dark spots of mold. Even if another reform were to come along and replace the orchestra with *qupai*, the old guard would continue to maintain the dignity of their profession. They were truly unbreakable! *This* was the old guard.

As the years went by, along with all of their unpredictable events, the old guard gradually blended into the group, and their loneliness was alleviated. Yet there were some things that could never be understood. Deep down in the bottoms of their hearts, perhaps even they themselves had forgotten, but forgetting is not the same as not existing. If one day they happened to come upon a *sanxian* lute, or a set of *sheng* pipes, or a bamboo flute, they could pick them up and produce a few tunes with no problem because they were the tunes they knew in their hearts. Everything that is buried deep may once again rise to the surface. It was only through the old guard that we could really come to know each other.

3. The Courtyard

To one side of the East Rail Station, which hummed with activity day and night, was a small street called Two Horse Road. It was a cobblestone street lined on both sides with tightly packed dwellings, which appeared to have been there for ages. At the end of the street was an unremarkable side gate, where our troupe lived. The style of the courtyard's construction and arrangement revealed the changes it had undergone over time. It was shaped like a square, with housing on all sides, and because all the windows and doors opened on to the center of the courtyard, it was difficult to tell which direction you were facing. Entering through the side gate and passing through the reception room would bring you to the gable wall of a two-story cement building. The floors, doors, and window frames were all made of wood, and the cement steps that led to the second floor were located at the front of the outside wall. It all looked a bit rudimentary. Detached and on the right side stood another two-story building, and the two of them formed what was certainly not a right angle. The toilets and a room for storing props were located along the narrow path between the two buildings. The building that stood at an angle was a bit wider and longer than the other, and it was also a bit nicer. Its walls were made of stone, as were the pillars of its covered walkway, and it even had an arched doorway and window frames that were made of stone as well. Everything inside was made of wood, including a raised mezzanine, which was very authentic. I suppose this was the main building in the whole courtyard, and it faced south, I believe. It was also the first one built in the courtyard—all the others came later, so it was the most old-fashioned. The floorboards were a bit loose, and the large cracks that had opened between them gave easy access to a giant colony of mice. The windows wouldn't shut very well, and the roof also leaked badly. People said the buildings around this courtyard were put up by the Japanese during the occupation and used as a command headquarters. If that's true, then this building must have been the main one. That other cement building was clearly added later as a supplemental structure—its appearance was much simpler, and it didn't feel quite as old fashioned. It was the same for the building on the western side of the main one, which we'll just call "the western building" for now. It was also a supplemental, two-story cement structure that looked pretty much like the one on the eastern side, though slightly smaller.

Also on the western side was a row of simpler, single-story buildings. The canteen, the practice room, and the lighting room—as well as that site of contention, the washroom—were all located here. Perpendicular to this was another row of simple one-story buildings, which included the administration office along with the homes of some of the troupe members' families. The collection of buildings in the courtyard also included the dormitories for singles, students, and families, as well as the studios for the dance team, the performance team, the chorus, and the band. So our courtyard encompassed all manner of life—young and old, chickens and dogs. Whether we were at work or at rest, eating, drinking, shitting, or pissing, it all happened here. Surrounded by these four rows of one- and two-story buildings was the rehearsal hall. It had a small stage that took up about one third of the area, and the remaining two-thirds was used as practice space, with barres and mirrors attached to three of the walls. No matter what this courtyard had previously been used for, this rehearsal hall had clearly been built specifically for a performance troupe, and it was this hall that indicated the true character of the courtyard. It stood in the center, surrounded by everything else. But it also made the courtyard appear much more cramped, turning all the space around it into paths. Even so, on a hot day there was still enough room for the band to practice outside.

It was this courtyard that bore witness to the paltry career of our troupe. It never really enjoyed any comfortable period of stability, and the good times were always a flash in the pan. Year after year it remained in this same pitiful state. As if able to sense the ups and downs, the courtyard itself seemed to grow melancholy. In the winter, it got so cold you couldn't so much as stick your hand outside; in the summer, it got so hot the dogs couldn't keep their tongues in their mouths; in the spring, it was so damp that all the costumes mildewed; and in the fall, it was so dry you could hear the wood splitting and cracking wherever you went. It was truly steeped in sorrow: You could tell this from the cascade of water running off the eaves on a rainy day, and from the frost on the roof tiles. It couldn't talk, but it could understand our hearts. When we went out on tour, living almost like vagrants—eating and sleeping poorly, loading and unloading the vehicles, setting up and taking down the stage, looking forward every day to our return home—it was as if the courtyard understood, quietly waiting with bated breath for us to come back. In the evenings, when all the other courtyards were brightly lit and fragrant smells of dinner were in the air, only our courtyard remained in an anxious darkness. After several months on the road and feeling exhausted from the long and dusty journey, you could really sense the courtyard welcoming us home. The cobblestone street was all smiles, and if it were evening when we arrived, the windows around the courtyard would also break into bright smiles as they lit up one by one. With all the lights ablaze, the whole courtyard would become as festive as New Year's. By the time the sun was high in the sky the next morning, freshly washed clothing would already be hanging around the courtyard to dry, like the flags of every nation fluttering in the breeze. In the course of one night, the courtyard's vital energies would return, and it could begin to see all the pain and suffering we had endured on the road. Seeing this seemed to put it more at ease than not seeing it, because, in a sense, it could experience our suffering along with us. No matter how dilapidated the courtyard may have been, it was still our refuge, our nest. Every day we were out on tour, we longed to return home—and the home we longed to return to was this courtyard.

Each day before the sun rose, you could hear the sounds of someone poking the fire and clearing out the ashes. The nimble footsteps of the old man who tended the furnace could be heard pattering all over the courtyard. In the practice room, the soft soles of the performers' shoes produced a sensual effect as they brushed over the floor and thudded against it. Cautiously and with a mute, a trumpet played the "Neapolitan Dance" from *Swan Lake.* Then the chickens and dogs would start up, and the courtyard would be filled with all sorts of noises. The area around the sink was the most active, with washbasins and cups for tooth brushing clinking against one another, water gurgling out of the pipes, and the clanging and banging of pots, dishes, and utensils. Joining in the racket were the sounds of people practicing solfeggios—*yee-yee, ya-ya*—straining to project their voices up through their foreheads until their noses buzzed. Some people would be joking around; some would be practicing by imitating others' examples; a group of sparrows would take flight. The canteen would bustle with food preparation. No other courtyard had as much activity as this one; things got hopping at the crack of dawn. After this vigorous beginning, a period of calm would follow, as if the whole tempo had slowed. The dance team would begin practicing to the simple and slightly stiff accompaniment of the piano, which kept an even rhythm that seemed composed and unhurried. A quick passage on the violin would periodically come into focus, carrying with it a brisk and lighthearted feeling. In another room people were reading newspapers, and during the breaks in the piano music a few lines could be heard getting read out loud. There were fewer people in the courtyard when the family members of the performers went off to school or work, and the chickens would also leave the courtyard in search of food.

The days were actually quite peaceful, and could even be considered carefree, but that was only when looking at them on an individual basis—taking a step back and viewing them in a slightly broader perspective, things didn't look very optimistic. The future of the troupe was our perpetual concern. It was a lot like a poor family's house with leaks all over the roof—it was impossible to patch them all. So those fleeting, carefree moments were really quite poignant. The canteen always prepared meals on a schedule, there was always enough hot water in the pipes, and there would always be a sunny day after the rain. In the middle of the night, industrious farmers would come in from the outskirts of the city to collect the waste from the toilets, and in the morning they would always be clean. On the days we didn't perform and had nothing to do, we'd suddenly be moved to rehearse something: Let's do "Gathering Medicine" again, we'd say. "Gathering Medicine" was a song and dance routine performed by the Cultural Workers' Troupe from Jinan that originally came from the Yi ethnic group in the southwestern provinces. It told the story of some miraculous events, and the music was really excellent—just within the capabilities of our band. So it was part of our repertoire, and it was also something we liked to do for our own enjoyment. Just hearing the first notes of the music cheered our hearts and made us forget our worries. The more troubling our days were, the more we attempted to find joy in our sorrows. The busiest times were often some of the best for the troupe, when we would practice day and night in preparation for an upcoming performance. The night sessions presented a particularly stirring kind of scene, with the lights of the rehearsal hall shining brightly,

along with those of the canteen, where a midnight snack was being prepared. The sounds of tuning notes, auditions, and the director's instructions all blended together in a continuous dull roar. The noise would then
die down, and a brief period of silence would ensue, followed by the first
notes of the opening prelude. In that moment, this almost unbearably
dilapidated courtyard would seem so impressive and grand—by far the
greatest and most outstanding on all of Two Horse Road! So this courtyard also witnessed our moments of pride. Although there weren't many,
we still had them.

Our courtyard saw very few good days and many bad ones. Accordingly, it grew more and more haggard. The main building became more
dilapidated: the stairs were on the verge of collapse, the floorboards were
completely rotten, scrubbing the floor upstairs made it start raining down-
stairs, the ceiling sagged, and the whole place was covered in dust and
smelled like mouse droppings. As for the cement buildings on either side,
deep cracks appeared on their gables, which were clearly slanting—yet
this didn't stop more people from moving in. Large rooms were partitioned into smaller ones as people got married, members of separated
couples were able to have their spouses come live with them, and new
students arrived. People moved into the prop room next to the toilets and
the windowless bathhouse. In the rehearsal hall, a part of the stage was
cut off, and two families moved in, and then another part of the stage
was relinquished. Finally, the practice room was also partitioned up until
it became basically a maze of apartments. Kitchens and bike sheds of all
sizes were put up in the empty spaces around the courtyard until it became completely filled with these shoddy structures, as if we were trying
to patch over all the holes. It was almost unbearably shabby and makeshift. Around this time, our troupe's situation went from bad to worse,
with little hope for the future. The troupe and the courtyard depended
on one another for survival, and we shared a common fate. The courtyard became so unpleasant it was barely tolerable; simply entering it was
dispiriting. The unlucky fate of our troupe was written all over it. After
consecutive days of rain, the courtyard would become a pit of mud, and
once it stopped and the blazing sun reappeared, large intersecting cracks
would form in the earth. Just as our troupe had to keep pushing through,
so did the courtyard. Later, after the reorganization and consolidation of
cities and prefectures, our troupe merged with the municipal song and

dance troupe, and this courtyard, located within the area of the East Rail Station's renovation and expansion, was demolished. The station square was bustling with activity around the clock, but if you were to find a few moments of calm, bend over, and hold your breath, you would hear the muffled sound of crying. And if you followed the sound of that crying, you would find the courtyard, weeping.

4. The University Graduates

The majority of the university graduates came from two institutions, the provincial art institute and the arts division of the provincial normal university, mostly majoring in voice. Throughout the course of its tortured existence, the troupe always diligently worked to develop a certain goal, which was opera. Actually, this began with the graduates' arrival; our troupe thought it would give us an opportunity to stand out and excel. Hardly any other prefecture-level cities had troupes with the vocal capabilities of ours, which had a good number of properly trained singers. Once these stars entered the decision-making levels of the troupe, it was only natural that they would actively work to promote this vision. To vocal performers, what could be better than opera? In this midsized city, in addition to us, there was another troupe of the same nature, the municipal song and dance troupe. This new troupe was formed in the context of the national surge in model operas, and from its very inception it had a clear mission: to replicate the ballet *The Red Detachment of Women* with complete accuracy. The city had allocated a massive amount of funds and personnel for this revolutionary project, allowing them to advertise and recruit on a national scale. And so, the perfect orchestra was assembled, and fantastic dancers were brought in. Their performance was a complete success, and in the course of one night they rid the city of its vulgar atmosphere and ushered in the winds of modern progress. But after that, their circumstances took a slight turn for the worse: The city sneakily withdrew nearly half of the resources it had initially promised, leaving the song and dance troupe in a tough position for a time. The biggest problem this posed was how to handle the educated youth from Shanghai who had moved from their posts in the countryside—sending them back to their rural production teams would likely be the same as sending them to their deaths. But the crisis passed. The song and dance troupe was re-structured, and it was still the best. Dancers and an orchestra made up the basic foundation of a song and dance troupe, and in this regard, our troupe could only gaze up from below. Ours was a troupe that had transitioned from old to new, and the integration of the old members remained a thorny issue. Our prefecture was primarily rural, our funds were limited, and our household registrations were restricted. So, we had no choice but to seek an alternative route.

To call what we performed "opera" was a bit of an exaggeration, and to use the word sounded like bragging. Let's just start with the script—in those days, how many operas even were there? As far as *The Serf's Halberd*—the success of which thrilled us so—was concerned, not only were we actually quite lucky, but we also basically ended up taking it as the main goal of our lives. It seemed like our troupe was always worried about getting good scripts; bad ones had caused us to suffer a number of losses. We searched for them all over, and wherever there was rumored to be a good one, we went running after it, but all to no avail. We also put a lot of effort into writing our own, and we actually produced a couple, but the results were mediocre: the plots and the arias were all a bit pathetic, and after just a few performances we were unable to sell any more tickets. Luckily for us, no one back then was talking about economic results. One time, we set our sights on a script from an opera house in another province, and we dispatched a whole scouting contingent to go observe, study, and copy the musical scores; after that, we could assemble a cast, apply for a budget, and finally get things off the ground. Just as our troupe was kicking into full gear with rehearsals and preparing our performance schedule, the entire nation suddenly began criticizing a Shanxi opera called *Three Trips up Peach Mountain*. The plot involved a story about a horse, and happened to be very similar to the new opera we had been preparing. It might not sound like much, but to our troupe this was a huge blow. After a significant period with no performances or new material, we had basically been freeloading, and the Cultural Affairs Bureau began to complain. We had put forth no small effort to right our ship, and the turning point had seemed just on the horizon—we never expected such a setback. Having spent all of our funds and gotten nothing in return, the troupe was once again at a loss. This event did provide us with something, though, and that was a warning: that the political situation presented danger on all sides, and we should not act without careful consideration. After this, the troupe became overly cautious. Where we were once able to make progress, albeit with great difficulty, we were now completely stuck. It seemed that ever since our decision to pursue opera, our luck had taken a turn for the worse.

The troupe's leader was an aging man who looked like the stereotype of a party branch secretary, always dressed in a black coat and carrying a pipe and tobacco pouch. He was a kindhearted but unlucky secretary who was melancholic and rarely spoke. Judging from his age and qualifications, he should have been more than just the secretary of a Cultural Workers' Troupe, yet it looked as if this could be his last appointment. He had nothing left to look forward to. He had absolutely no ambition to push the troupe to any great accomplishments that would allow him to achieve glory in this, his final post—he simply wished to pass his days in peace and smoothly finish out his revolutionary career. In addition to personal and political factors, he may very well have also suffered from a bad fate, but in any case, he was overly cautious and indecisive, always fearful that something would go wrong. He seemed destined to head straight for ruin—the more cautious he was, the more storms he was forced to weather. One time, after an incident, the old secretary came upon one of the old guard in the toilets and said something very depressing to him: that there wasn't even a place for him to go die. When word of what he had said got around, we couldn't help but feel sad. The old secretary became even more gloomy and reserved, and he appeared to grow older and wearier by the day. One beautiful sunny day in March, we found him still bundled in that same black jacket. Not long afterward, he was transferred away from the troupe. No one knows where he went, and we never heard anything more about him.

Opera was our troupe's perpetual torment. How could we make it work? "Opera" in the sense that we meant it was actually quite far from the Western notion; it was a form created from the new style of revolutionary literature and art. The earliest example was *White-Haired Girl*, while slightly later examples like *Sister Jiang* and *Red Troops on Honghu Lake* were a bit more influential and seemed to draw more upon traditional Chinese opera. The music in *Sister Jiang*, for example, was based largely on Sichuan opera, while *Red Troops on Honghu Lake* modeled its music on Hubei opera, with all the arias sung in *banqiang* style. Yet in its overall dramatic form, this type of opera approached the freer style of modern spoken drama, as its plots unfolded through the use of spoken vernacular dialogue, with the music only really serving to express emotion and enhance the atmosphere. In short, when it was time for speaking, there was speaking, and when it was time for singing, there was singing—there were no formal restrictions, and it was all arranged according to what was most convenient. It was very much in line with the demands of revolutionary literature and art, which was geared toward the actual needs of the masses. All of the Western-style opera houses in the country were established after the 1949 liberation, as opera was a socialist art form that clearly encompassed the characteristics of the "new culture." For a troupe like ours, which had originally been a traditional, old-style one, to switch to Western-style opera was simply conforming to the development of history.

We often wondered: Why didn't the revolution's standard bearer, Jiang Qing, choose Western-style opera to conduct her revolutionary artistic experiment? If she had, the fate of our troupe might have been different. It was probably because ballet and Peking opera were classical forms of Western and Eastern art, respectively, so adapting them would prove both interesting and satisfying. New Western-style opera already carried the imprint of former revolutions, and a standard bearer like Jiang Qing couldn't eat a bun someone else had already chewed. There's also another explanation: that she adapted Peking opera in order to create China's own operatic form. I'm not sure how dependable this reasoning is, but it does contain one compelling fact. When various forms of traditional Chinese opera were grafted onto model opera, there were no hints of Western-style opera. So Western-style opera never enjoyed the divine providence of model opera, and it could only advance unsteadily. Taken together, the Western-style operas from that era, with the occasional exception, were all pretty crude. Its time had actually already passed, and our troupe was just covering old ground. In other words, we lacked an understanding of the times and were swimming against the current.

That year, we learned an opera from Jiangxi province called *Model Village in the Mountains*, which told the story of a revolutionary base area during the war. The plot and music were so clichéd that no one really felt one way or the other about it. Actually, our troupe made a strange decision to move everyone to the outskirts of the city for rehearsal and perform for the peasants. This seemed very much like self-exile, and our reasoning was a bit pathetic—it was like saying to the powers above, "we're bad, so maybe we should just leave." There was obviously also an element of "suffering hardship to strengthen our resolve," as if holding ourselves captive out here would make us produce a solid performance. We wouldn't see a single soul until we had something to show for our efforts. To accomplish this, we had to borrow some people to strengthen the orchestra and chorus. After amassing our troops, we set out and went to a place called Wei Village. The village lent us some old warehouses and sold us some carts we could pad with straw for bedding, so we built a stove and set up camp. Life was hard. We weren't accustomed to living like this—our bodies became covered in welts, there was no way to bathe, there were no shops or movie theaters to visit in our free time, and those who had families couldn't bring them along. But compared to the frustrating defeats our troupe had suffered in the city, this was nothing.

Life in the village was peaceful, and it lifted our spirits. Singing and playing the lute in the open fields had a kind of dramatic feeling that was certainly enough to satisfy our petty bourgeois romantic sensibilities. When the wheat ripened, the rippling fields mirrored the scenes of abundant harvests we sang about in our songs. We didn't mind if the peasants secretly laughed at us. We picked wildflowers from the banks and furrows and gathered them into bouquets, which gave us a moment's beauty before withering. In the end, the days we passed in Wei village were delightful. Because the air was fresh, life was simple and pure, we felt at peace, and our appetites increased significantly. Based on its resources and food supply, the kitchen often made something it called "crispy fish." The dish, which could keep for a long time, took a carp about the length of a finger and boiled it in layers of bok choy. After adding hot peppers, aniseed, and vinegar, it was particularly delicious. Sometimes on Sundays our friends from the city would come visit us—for them it was just a weekend outing, but for us, it was a chance to get some foods we couldn't otherwise get in the village, along with some fresh excitement. When the sun began to set and we would see them off on their journey back to the city, our feelings of friendship would seem even stronger, and we would have our most heartfelt conversations. As we watched their figures gradually disappear into the evening rays, our hearts were filled with a sweet sort of melancholy. Our rehearsals proceeded smoothly. The demands of the director and the conductor were very high—they were particular about each and every detail, hoping that we could produce a real success. To be honest, though, that production didn't really have anything worth looking into so carefully; from the very beginning, you could already predict the insipid conclusion. But wasn't this the entire reason we had come to Wei Village? Compared to everything else we did there, this performance was the most dull and boring.

News of the Tiananmen incident of April 5, 1976, came to us while we were there. The troupe's new secretary had us gather in front of a broken wall as he related to us the official documents regarding this "counter-revolutionary event." His complexion did not look good; he seemed preoccupied and uneasy, even a little weak. Of the leadership assigned to our troupe, this secretary had the most political sensitivity. His family name was Lu, and he was a section chief in the bureau, so everyone called him Section Chief Lu. He had a feeble constitution and had developed diabetes during one of our troupe's more trying periods. He didn't talk much and very seldom held meetings, but he could get things done. For example, he had enabled our troupe to recruit more students, he had decided on the script for *Model Village in the Mountains*, and he had come up with the funds to go rehearse in Wei Village. It was hard to tell what he saw or what premonitions he had as he told us about the incident. What effect could some event in Beijing have on our troupe, tucked away here in Wei Village? But his heavy, worried expression drew a dark cloud over our spirits. Within the entire structure of professional artistic troupes, ours was near the bottom of the barrel. We were situated in an interior, midsized city, and none of us were anything special—we were just trying to make a living. History seemed very far away, so as it advanced, it was hard to realize it had anything significant to do with us. A lot of things happened this year. On the day that Premier Zhou Enlai died, as we were preparing a performance to pay our respects, two groups that had joined together for the program started horsing around with a playful dialogue: Have you listened to the morning announcements? Yep. Have you had breakfast yet? Yes, rice porridge and fried dough, one of the old guard answered. It wasn't that we were unfeeling—it's just that great figures like Zhou were so far removed from us, and the fate of the nation so abstract, while our daily lives were concrete, vivid, real, and tangible. Out here, the old guard were more straightforward and sincere than the intellectuals. This time, though, the Tiananmen incident infused our days in Wei Village with a sense of unease, as if there were some particularly bad circumstances lurking behind it, and it made us nervous. The world was about to experience another upheaval—what would it mean for us? No one could say.

Our performance of *Model Village in the Mountains* went smoothly. Although it certainly didn't win us any special honors, when all was said and done, we still ended up with a new program, which allowed us to begin a new round of performances and rack up our appearances on stage. In those years, we were drowning in so many mediocre plotlines and musical scores that we nearly lost our minds. Very rarely was there a work that excited us, and everything we rehearsed and performed annoyed us. It really wore down our enthusiasm. This time when we went out to perform, it was the sweltering summer of 1976. It was a scorcher for the history books, as it was a prelude to the Tangshan earthquake. We were performing in the county seat at the time, staying in a loft above the theater. The thin cement roof trapped the heat during the day and didn't release it at night, so it was like sleeping in an oven. Because of this, we climbed down and slept on the stage, making our beds in a haphazard arrangement. It all felt a bit like it was the end of the world. In general, it seemed like everything went downhill that year: the weather went downhill, the situation went downhill, our repertoire went downhill, and our performances went downhill. The troupe's circumstances deteriorated by the day. After leaving Wei Village, we stayed on the road. Everywhere was gripped by the fear of another earthquake, which made returning to the city difficult, so we ended up throwing together an earthquake shelter in a corner of the prefectural administration's cadre school and staying there. We had no idea when these turbulent days would come to an end. In any case, it seems like things always have to get worse before they can get better—doesn't the saying go "out of adversity comes peace"? Sure enough, not long afterwards, the Gang of Four was overthrown.

Even if we weren't typically so concerned with current events, this time it was impossible to remain unaffected. The events were too big—they were earth-shattering events that would change everything. Everyone was able to see a light at the end of the tunnel, especially our hapless troupe. For years, it seemed, we had been waiting in the dark for our luck to turn around. Now, it looked like this could be it! We were so happy during those days. We took to the streets in celebration, and our usually very serious leader used his slogan banner to sword fight with some primary school students. The drums and gongs produced so many rhythms—were some of them the ancient sounds of Liuzi opera? It was at this time that we were rehearsing a skit about the arrest of the Gang of Four, which I mentioned above. Our hearts were happy, so we were kind to each other and everyone got along well, despite the fact that passing the winter in the earthquake shelter was not easy. Our blankets were covered in frost on both sides, and at night we had to take turns keeping watch: We would stand a slender-necked bottle upside down, and if it fell over, we would sound the alarm. But in the face of this great turn in events, ordinary pleasures appeared among all of our hardships. Living in the earthquake shelter was a bit like camping, and people were excited to be on night duty. We kept a fire in the stove all night long, roasting sweet potatoes, cooking porridge, boiling corn, and stir-frying soybeans, with the fragrant scents tickling our noses every night. In January of the next year, there was a large-scale mourning: A year after the death of Zhou Enlai, grief returned to the people's hearts. Our troupe came up with a program to commemorate the former premier, and for many days we were immersed in an increasingly somber atmosphere until the evening we performed. A year before, the same people had been joking around about eating rice porridge and fried dough. But that was then, and this was now—in each instance, their feelings were sincere. We were all just ordinary citizens who couldn't see the historical import of events when they happened. All we could do was follow our feelings.

Well, this great happiness and sadness came and went, and we were once again left with our day-to-day lives and work. But a turning point really had come, or at least that's what we told ourselves in the beginning. We decided to start rehearsing the banned opera *Red Troops on Hong Lake*, which was considered a classic of the new-style opera. Everyone loved the arias, and for so many years we had been able to enjoy them only in our minds. We approached our work with enthusiasm, enchanted by the beautiful melodies that had for so long been relegated to our memories. Rehearsing was in no way a chore; good things are naturally greeted with excitement, so we added more rehearsals. Every night the assembly hall of the cadre school was brightly lit, while the residents pressed themselves up against the doors and windows to watch us practice. We decided to withhold any announcement of our performance until the very last minute in order to pique their interest and catch the whole area by surprise. There was no real news media in those days, and the only way to spread the word was with a brush and a bucket of paste to stick the posters on trees, one by one. We waited until just three days before the performance to put up the posters, along with a large billboard in front of the theater, and finished our preparations to celebrate the opera's opening. However, at nearly the exact same time, the film version of *Red Troops on Hong Lake* arrived in theaters everywhere, and audiences flocked to see it. This opera really struck a chord with people—they wanted to see the real thing, but all we could give them was our knock-off version. In total, we only performed our *Red Troops on Hong Lake* eleven times, which included all the free tickets we gave out. This situation seemed to act as advance notice, announcing that from now on our troupe would be under attack from modern forms of entertainment. But this was only the beginning, and we were unable to see that far ahead and grasp the larger picture. All we could do was blame our own bad luck—it wasn't what we deserved. If not even the arrest of the Gang of Four could save us, what could? So while the whole rest of the country was welcoming the reform era with open arms, we could only curse under our breaths.

The university graduates came to our troupe full of youthful energy, more or less thinking they had achieved their desired careers. The first few to arrive were the most valuable, since at that time there weren't many art school graduates, and the few that did exist were as rare as phoenix feathers and *qilin* horns. They came with greater ambitions and were naturally more arrogant. But as more arrived, things evened out until they eventually formed their own group of intellectuals. They brought an updated artistic atmosphere to the troupe, transforming its older, more traditional appearance. This transformation actually proved to be unusually difficult, and it seemed like we would never see the light at the end of the tunnel. Success was only temporary, while the hardship was enduring. As their youth gradually left them, their dreams slowly disappeared. They got married and had children, and they would all squeeze into a room in the courtyard and set up house. From morning till night they would fiddle with a coal stove, and it seemed like the whole family was involved. They would cough and wheeze in the sooty smoke, holler at their children, and fight with their wives. Their appearance grew sloppier by the day: The shirts they wore in the summer were so torn up they looked like fishnets, and they shuffled to the market in cheap sandals and haggled with the vendors. They became petty, vulgar, and narrow-minded, each day growing more like the regular people on the streets. Their stage careers became nothing more than a way to make a living, having little to do with ideals or aspirations, and little to do with art. Some of these university graduates returned to their homes in the south. Our city was located in the northernmost reaches of the province near the Shandong border, while many of the graduates came from the more pleasant and fertile region to the south, where life was easier; doing the same work down there would be substantially better. The ones who remained could not resign themselves to their fate. They would search high and low for a work unit with better prospects and arrange a transfer. Our troupe was hopeless. The new graduates assigned to us would see this upon arriving and immediately start planning their exit strategies. Later on, they would hear about the unfortunate nature of our troupe before they even arrived, so they would ignore their assignment and not even bother to show up.

To this day I still remember once seeing the university graduates walking in a line down a country lane. The cars behind them were all honking, but they didn't care, nor did they pay attention to the oncoming cars. They looked so arrogant, as if a boundless future extended before them. They regarded everything with disdain and were anxious to change their realities. They looked down on the old guard, and they looked down on the troupe's leader. They really had, in fact, seen more of the world than others and were more educated; they had gotten to taste the richness of a more cultured life. In contrast to what they had experienced in their rather extraordinary youth, our troupe couldn't help but appear lackluster. But their glory lasted only for a brief moment and very quickly began to fade. In the dilapidated corners of our courtyard, they carved out a space for themselves. It was from there that their splendid, resonant voices would rise up—men's and women's voices sounding together in a Western style and lingering on the broken roof tiles above the courtyard. If you didn't already know about these university graduates, it would come as a complete surprise.

There's one person who must be mentioned now, or else he would be completely forgotten. He was one of the first university graduates to enter our troupe, as well as one of the first to attend an art institute after the founding of the new China, having graduated from the Shanghai

Conservatory of Music. He was originally assigned to the Central Conservatory of Music in Beijing, but in the effort to send cadres to live and work among the people, the Ministry of Culture assigned him to our troupe, which at the time was still a Liuzi opera one. Time slipped by—it's impossible to know the exact details of what all went on, but, as they say, the sound of honking lingers after the goose flies away. Disreputable anecdotes would pop up in conversation, most of which involved entanglements with the opposite sex and were clearly exaggerated and distorted to the point that they approached the form of folktales. In these renditions, he became a hilarious joke figure who always made a fool of himself. Yet one thing was not in dispute—he left our troupe because of a certain kind of slipup, and was brought down a peg; he ended up as a middle school music teacher in the county seat, which seemed like a punishment. At the same time as our troupe was bad-mouthing him, he was in his miserable dormitory at his school in the county seat bad-mouthing our troupe. According to his vicious assessment, our troupe was petty, crude, stupid, and stuck in its ways. His weak character manifested itself in an attitude that seemed serious and earnest with no sense of humor, like the type of person who was always just waiting to get angry. From the look of things, both he and our troupe had hurt each another. Both sides took it to heart and stewed over it. The situation wasn't good, but neither his drive nor his exuberance decreased in the slightest. Even if no one ever explicitly said it, the following phrase sums it all up perfectly: Eagles may sometimes fly lower than chickens, but chickens will never be able to fly as high as eagles.

As time went by, he remained stuck in that county seat, while we gradually progressed to the point of being a Cultural Workers' Troupe capable of putting on a large-scale opera like *The Serf's Halberd*. He was still able to criticize us based on his education and talent, and he basically said we didn't have a single redeeming feature—yet his criticisms were always on point. It was as if he was too far ahead of his time and had no way of alleviating his loneliness and anger. Some young, aspiring musicians sidled up to him and treated him like a god, asking him to teach them. While this pleased him, it also had the effect of emphasizing his failure, so he wasn't very nice to them and wouldn't take on a single one, effectively pouring cold water over their ambitions. When a particularly individualistic one among them remained determined to attend art school and even tested into his alma mater, the Shanghai Conservatory of Music, he completely cut off contact. At this, the others, who would never have any other hopes of studying music, finally realized the nature of the situation and quietly left him alone. With no one left around him, he waited for the next group of interested youths to appear. He got married, but his wife was from the countryside and remained there, so they lived separately. He feared loneliness yet refused to be a part of any group, and he suffered under the dual torments of pride and weakness, as well as anger. He ended up contracting a serious illness that left one side of his body paralyzed. At one point, those once aspiring musicians who had surrounded him in their youth paid him a visit, and they found him unshaven and lying on dirty sheets with an old photo album at his side. When he saw them, his eyes filled with tears, and he began sobbing uncontrollably. Having continually maintained his arrogance for several decades, he now collapsed into a blubbering mess— there was no way to pick up the pieces. After languishing in his sickbed for several years, he quietly passed away at the age of sixty. By this time, our troupe had already merged with the municipal song and dance troupe, and we were dancing to popular music and arranging our own unofficial gigs. Regardless of the anger and resentment that had been etched into our bones, no one was willing to take any responsibility or admit any fault. In the course of a thousand years of history, there wasn't anything worth mentioning—it was just a person and a troupe.

He was a northeasterner who had graduated from the Shanghai Conservatory of Music in 1954 with a degree in composition. He was also involved in the writing of *Happy River Chorus*, which went on to win first prize in the music competition at the Seventh World Festival of Youth and Students in Vienna—the highest honor received by a Chinese musical work at any international competition at that time. The department of composition had awarded his senior project, a symphonic poem called "The Stone Carp," the highest possible mark: a score of five.

5. The Students

Because of our troupe's location, we recruited students from eight different counties, most of them from the countryside. They were generally around twelve or thirteen years old, and had all left their parents to come to our troupe and live in that small, boxlike cement building just inside the gate. In a troupe like ours that had developed from its roots in traditional opera, the patriarchal structure of relationships in the traditional "Pear Garden" theater scene was long gone, but there remained a fairly affectionate family-like atmosphere. The members of the old guard called the students by their childhood nicknames, and if a student didn't have one, they would make one up—and they wouldn't be like the typical ones, either, with a "Little" tacked on in front of their family name to indicate a junior status, like "Little Wang" or "Little Li," which would have seemed slightly generic and impersonal. But there were also some exceptions. There was a girl named Yin (尹)—pronounced the same as the character *yǐn* (引)—which was a relatively uncommon surname, so everyone broke with the usual practice and called her "Little Yin." The pronunciation of these two characters together (小尹, *Xiǎo Yǐn*) sounded both cute and unconventional, so it became her nickname. The students in our troupe were treated very warmly, as if they were everyone's children. They would speak without thinking, and their behavior could be a bit wild, but no one would get upset with them. This was especially true for the girls, who would often display their little tempers. But by and large they understood how things worked, as if they had a natural understanding of social relationships and etiquette; although they were headstrong, they knew the boundaries and wouldn't overstep them. For the most part, they were simple, pure, and naturally kindhearted; whatever conflicts arose within the troupe, they would leave them to the leaders to sort out and not get involved. The adults all took them as naïve youngsters and didn't try to force their views on them. They were all quite obedient and hardworking, well aware of how fortunate they were to join our troupe. At that time, a lot of students from the cities were being "sent down" to labor in the countryside, but these students, at such a young age, had been able to come work in the city. Some of them would send their meager student wages back home to their parents to help support their families. Many of them had been the backbones of their schools' propaganda teams, and joining a Cultural Workers' Troupe had been their dream. Once they got to our troupe, they immediately took a liking to it. They found life in the courtyard both welcoming and fun. Every time they returned home for holiday breaks, they always had plenty of new and interesting stories to impress their families, and when they returned to the troupe, they would bring food and snacks from home to share with everyone. They added a feeling of innocence, along with an air of rural simplicity. With students always coming and going in the courtyard, our troupe felt much more alive.

They were really very loveable, without the slightest hint of the haughtiness or arrogance that afflicts so many adult members of artistic groups. On the contrary, they were all rather self-effacing, and felt that they were inferior to everyone else. Most of them were in the dance team—or it might be more appropriate to say that regardless of the reason they were originally recruited, they always ended up in the dance team. Many students entered the troupe under specific conditions, but then things would often change, and their special strengths and skills would disappear over time. What to do? Enter the dance team. From the trajectories of these students, one can see the confused and halting path our troupe took in its effort to transform from a traditional opera troupe into a Cultural Workers' Troupe, not really knowing where it was coming from or where it was headed. It was in this muddled, directionless state of affairs that these small children had the courses of their lives altered. So you can well imagine how random and uneven our dance team appeared. On top of this, the dance instructor, who had been in charge of martial arts instruction in the original Liuzi opera troupe, also decided to add a crash course in ballet, so you can guess the results. It seemed that none of the students could grow tall, but they could all very easily get fat. One time an instructor from the Central Dance Academy who was passing through the area stopped by to give a class to our dance team; she said that our students had all been improperly trained, and that every place they should have muscle, they were instead round and pudgy—so she recommended that they all practice "restraint." The class left everyone so exhausted they were all practically lying face down on the floor, yet they were still quite far from achieving any results! When the instructor left, everything once again returned to normal, and they kept on training the same way they had before.

The dance team was usually considered the face of a Cultural Workers' Troupe, and when people went to see one perform, what they really wanted to see was the dance team. Its members were always young, elegant, tall, and athletic. This was especially true for the women—their hair and clothing were very artsy, and they emanated all the exquisiteness of the female sex. At the province-wide exhibition for Cultural Workers'

Troupes, from the stage to the performers' lodgings, and even on the path in between, all eyes were on the beautiful, stylish women of the dance teams. Two teams stood out from the rest, and one was from the Suzhou Municipal Cultural Workers' Troupe. Women from Suzhou have always had an excellent reputation for their beauty; needless to say, the members of this team had been carefully selected and undergone artistic training. They were all slender, attractive, and graceful; any one of them could easily have played the part of the Luo River goddess. The other dance team that stood out was the one from our own city's municipal song and dance troupe, which had a different sort of character. Its members were all attractive, tall, and full of energy, and any one of them could have played Carmen. For both their dance team and ours to come from the same city placed so much pressure on the youngsters in our troupe! Faced with dance teams from all over the province at the exhibition, our team couldn't help but tremble from nerves. But in the end, the fact that they were able to maintain an appropriate amount of self-respect and humility under these circumstances was really quite admirable. It was an illustration of our youngsters' purity and sincerity—they would never become truly jealous because at the bottom of their hearts they were not only magnanimous, but also thick-skinned enough to take a few hits. When they heard people mocking our troupe, they simply turned a deaf ear. Practices, rehearsals, and performances all proceeded as usual. They were just girls—the little treasures of their mommies and daddies—so they were a bit shy, with sensitive hearts. They were also quite young and hadn't had much schooling, so it goes without saying that they weren't very accomplished. By consistently demonstrating their good-natured temperaments, they gave themselves an unexpected power. But no one really noticed this and just continued feeling superior. The youngsters in our troupe could really make one's heart ache.

Moreover, they weren't helped by their circumstances. The repertoire for the dance team was very trite—the arrangements were unimaginative and a bit random, the music was nothing new, and the orchestration was all jumbled. The lighting was arranged to shine straight down, leaving the backdrop scenery dimly lit and obscured—but the most baffling part of it all was the costumes. No one knew where they'd come from; they were neither folk costumes nor original creations. In one scene they would be playing rural youths, wearing Western-style shorts and silk shirts; in the next one, they would be doing a farm dance from who knows where with orange bandanas on their heads. It's not that they weren't putting any thought into it, it's just that they didn't get it right, and had no idea where the problem lied. In the end, it was all neither here nor there, neither fish nor fowl. To return to the municipal song and dance troupe, their dance team was "supporting the front": The women were pushing little carts of food to the soldiers during battle, and they were all wearing peasant-style smocks. But most notable was their hair: The girls wore long braids, while the married women had their hair done up in buns, with a wisp hanging down on each side by their ears, as was the custom for village women in the Huaihai region. It carried a simple charm that was both practical and sentimental, as well as beautiful, and it was all done intentionally. There were also the "duck farming girls" of the Yangzhou Song and Dance Troupe: Their hair was parted down the middle, with two fine braids tied with red ribbons dangling on either side of their foreheads, and a long braid in back hanging down to their waists; nearly half a foot was left at the end of this long braid, as was customary in the countryside of their region, and it conveyed a poetic feeling of "floating downriver to Yangzhou among the mists and flowers of May."[3] In an era that was so thoroughly cloaked in ideology, to see a few of these folk customs peeking through seemed so refreshing!

At the exhibition, our troupe's dancing gave us the most trouble; it was always just a bit off. But we were accustomed to failure, and anything else would have seemed out of the ordinary—this was the lesson we had to learn once we began taking in students. As we gloomily set off on our way back home, our mood was particularly well-suited to our troupe; as long as we were "gloomy," we were unable to imagine any other way of feeling. After we got back, we still woke up early to practice, and our lives resumed as normal; our troupe's old-fashioned sort of intimacy helped us lick our wounds. This sense of intimacy was not just a simple continuation of old habits, but in fact involved a subconscious desire to help each other through difficult times. Yes, we all depended on one another. While childish expressions had not completely disappeared from the students'

---

3. This line is from Li Bai's poem "Sending off Meng Haoran to Guangling" (送孟浩然之广陵).

faces, there was now added to them a familiarity with the vicissitudes of life. A few of them were even able to bear them better than adults. They just weren't as good at complaining as adults, but perhaps that was because they didn't feel they had as much right as the adults to vent their grievances. Sometimes it was hard for them to avoid feeling hurt. The adults more or less had the power of choice, but for the students, the choice had been made for them—and once they were selected, this was their life. Their young minds hadn't yet learned how to make calculations for themselves; they just earnestly went along with the fates they'd been handed, throwing their heart and soul into it and never slacking in their efforts. They never suspected that trusting in everything and not having a choice was actually the best thing for them. At their tender ages, they were thrown into our troupe's unlucky, deteriorating fate; there were a lot of things you shouldn't think about too carefully. But at the same time, our troupe did take them in and care for them. Like an old mother hen, that ramshackle courtyard opened its sparsely feathered wings and shielded them from the wind and rain. Although we weren't around when these children were born, we were there to watch them grow up. As I said, we all depended on one another.

During the years when everyone was learning model operas, our troupe's scouts were out in the countryside recruiting students when they discovered a boy who could play Li Yuhe. He was really adorable, with fair skin and a calm appearance, yet not without a certain heroic confidence, like a little rooster—and his voice was as clear and bright as a little rooster's, too. When such a sweet, beautiful child, his clothes covered in blood and his hands in shackles, sang "The Prison Guard's Summon, Like the Howl of a Wolf," his voice shook the sky. It was truly captivating; he was a child star that shone very bright. We recruited him and then went out and found him two girls—one to play Li Tiemei, and the other to play Granny Li. Both girls were the sort with small, doll-like faces, so we staged a "children's version" of *The Red Lantern*. One must admit it was a rather short-sighted move—we took in three people for just this one opera, which didn't even really pay off in the short run, much less the long run. Who had any idea what would happen when they grew up? To tell the truth, we got a bit overexcited and acted too quickly, and not without a bit of a gambling spirit—as everyone was intensely studying model operas, we were hoping to produce a breakthrough. At first the results weren't bad—our little Li Yuhe won over everyone's hearts, and word spread that our regional troupe had produced a real talent; he made quite a name for himself and became the center of attention. Though he was just a child, even if he were an adult with a deeper understanding of things, he wouldn't necessarily have been able to see past his own vanity or resist it. Everyone said his reputation was undeserved, and that it was all smoke and mirrors—but that all happened afterwards; what about at the time? At the time, it was really wonderful. But he was nothing more than a child from the countryside who had attended primary school, and who was lucky enough to be naturally endowed with good looks and a clear voice. He hadn't received much education, nor did he have much life experience or a very expansive field of vision, so he was quite unprepared to deal with the changes he was about to face. The good times didn't last long—just as his reputation was at its peak, something very tragic, yet also very natural, occurred: his voice changed. As a boy grows up, his sexless child's voice becomes the voice of a man. It's a unique transition particular to boys; the change for girls is much less pronounced. For boys it is really a transformation, with two completely different voices before and after. Their original voice disappears without a trace, as if it never even existed. The change takes place during a particular period, and then it's finished; all boys go through it. Their voices become husky, like a honking goose— they can't really raise or lower them very much, nor can they make them very loud or soft; they can only produce sound in one register. Yet they aren't really bothered about how they sound to others and continue to make just as much noise as usual. Then, as if out of nowhere, even their parents will be surprised to discover that their home has gained another mature male voice—the steady and powerful voice of a real man. It's a beautiful transformation that is all part of the miracle of growing up. Life progresses from tender to mature; this fact never fails to stir the emotions. The change is so clearly visible in boys, as if Mother Nature specifically entrusted them with this responsibility in the course of growing up.

For a boy so lucky and beloved as this one, he wasn't worried. He was just as happy and cheerful as always, calling and shouting in his husky voice, and taking advantage of everyone's love for him to stir up some trouble and play some harmless pranks. But then people started to feel unsure; his voice during this transition period was not a good sign. The members of the old guard were all too familiar with a "ruined voice";

they knew what the normal honking of a changing voice sounded like, and they knew when it sounded different. Sometimes there was still hope in these situations, and sometimes there wasn't, as was the case for this boy. The huskiness of his voice included a shrill, grating whistle that was almost unbearable. Now, his carefree, thoughtless attitude couldn't help but irritate people, and they started to let him know it. Having never experienced this before and feeling a little wronged, the boy responded by acting out even more. Once it became clear that his "ruined voice" was an irreversible fact, he had no choice but to leave the stage and become a loafer. Very quickly, this young star of the regional troupe faded into obscurity. When he kicked up a fuss, it was just so he could vent. He became a bit of a troublemaker and a nuisance, the kind that would howl and scream as soon as they stepped on a tack. The sudden change had left him completely unable to cope; he had no idea what had happened. He was confused, restless, angry, and afraid, and all of these emotions were expressed through one simple action: causing trouble. Actually, he had already developed into a young man, and his physique made him look a bit more mature than his actual age. Some scraggly hair began to grow on his fair, delicate face, making it look slightly dirty. His angelic, youthful form had suddenly vanished without a trace. The sound of him kicking up a fuss was so irritating, and his temperament was so difficult to manage, that no one quite knew what to do with him. Quite frankly, he had begun to fall out of favor—it wasn't that people were snubbing him; it was just that they couldn't love this disagreeable young man the same way they had loved him as a sweet little boy. People were sympathetic and pitied him, and still even loved him, although it wasn't that same doting sort of love as before. Their faces were unable to conceal their disgust, but it was because they were truly worried about him! Should they send him home? Would he be able to accept the decision? But that would also violate the troupe's principles of kindness and benevolence. We couldn't just throw him out and forget about him, yet there weren't that many options for keeping him with us—so we stuck him in the dance team. It seemed as if he had used up all of his nimble spirit when he was a child, and now that he was a young man, he was clumsier than most. That famous temper of his did not decrease one bit, and everyone took pains not to provoke him; but if a student couldn't accept the cards he was dealt, it would only land him in bigger trouble. That's when his period of suffering really began, and by the time it was all over, he was a completely different person, and we were living in a completely different era.

So what about the two doll-faced girls who joined the troupe with him? They were much more poised and discreet. They had always been hidden in the shadows of the boy's fame, so they were used to serving as background props. Although they were a little younger than him, they were more sensible, patient, and accommodating; they considered themselves protected by others and always exercised strict self-restraint. They were so well-behaved they made people's hearts ache, and they would tiptoe around like little cats. The boy's fate was also tied to theirs, and as they quietly observed his changing voice, they were even more worried than the adults who were responsible for him. After his voice went south, they patiently waited to see what the fallout would be. But there was no fallout, and they were assigned to the dance team. Because they had been specifically recruited for being small and delicate, which had given the audience what they wanted, their natural petiteness now ensured they were always placed on the fringes of the team, playing some minor characters from the Children's Corps.[4] But they were happy to do whatever they were asked and were very amenable to the change. On more than one occasion the troupe had considered having them transferred; jettisoning troupe members the way the prefecture's two traditional opera troupes did by transferring them to the district hospital or some other work unit would not necessarily be considered an irresponsible way of dealing with these children. Some of those transferred members had become typists, while others had become nurses in the operating room, so they'd had more opportunities for development and advancement than those who'd remained in the troupes. But when the two girls heard these proposals, they burst out in tears. They didn't give any reasons other than that they were attached to our troupe—it was the first place they had lived after leaving home at such a young age, and they were already used to it and felt so comfortable here. They knew the troupe, and the troupe knew them. They were a little unhappy, but that was fine; they were already used to it. The troupe was like a family to them! Their crying made everyone

---

4. This refers to the youth organizations established by the CCP during the Republican Era (the predecessors to the Young Pioneers).

else feel sad; some of the other youngsters started to cry, and the troupe members' hearts softened. Our troupe placed importance on feelings and didn't always do the most sensible thing, so it ended up unintentionally dimming the future prospects of these two children. They stayed with our troupe and stuck with it to the end, by which time they were full-grown adults and had become wives and mothers. As for the boy, he later entered a mental hospital; when he got better, he became a doorman in the reception room and distributed newspapers. He also got married and had children; the match was arranged by one of the troupe's old guard. At any rate, he ended up getting settled. Our troupe would never, ever discard an unfortunate child, even if things seemed to have reached a dead end. Unlike the municipal song and dance troupe, we would never recruit people only to later expel them. This was because of the code of benevolence and humaneness that had been passed down to our Cultural Workers' Troupe from its previous formation.

Some things it's best not to think about too carefully. If different arrangements had been made for these children, they might have had entirely different fates. To be honest, things didn't work out well for most of them. Many of the children in our troupe had some talent, but, as the saying goes, they were put in the wrong mother's womb. There was another instance that occurred while we were working on model dramas, although this time it was when we were doing the ballet *White-Haired Girl* instead of the Peking opera *The Red Lantern*. There was a child from the city's Railway Middle School who caught our troupe's attention—it was the girl who played Xi'er in the school propaganda team's production of *White-Haired Girl*. She was tall and slender, with graceful brows and large, round eyes. She taught herself all of Xi'er's moves and imitated them perfectly. For a time, our troupe and the municipal song and dance troupe fought over her. But our troupe was explicitly looking for someone to play Xi'er, while the municipal song and dance troupe was merely looking for a student to join their dance team. Maybe it was this difference that caused the girl to choose our troupe in the end.

She came from a family of train conductors and had grown up in a dorm for railroad workers; her life had been very simple. She was naturally optimistic and didn't have much in the way of brains, so she was easily tempted, and the promise of playing the lead role clouded her judgment. It was perhaps even more likely that she didn't make any sort of decision or choice at all, but rather just went with whichever side fought for her more strongly, letting nature take its course. This is the kind of foolish girl she was, although she did have a natural sensitivity when it came to dancing and music. When she wasn't on stage she was messy and sloppy, but once she got up there she was truly radiant—a real star. She had long limbs full of elasticity, coupled with exceptional strength and flexibility, and her face was small with a distinct silhouette that was well suited to the stage. She had an excellent sense of music that allowed her to provide improvisational accompaniment on the piano, and her voice was quite good, too. Once she started our troupe's particular methods of training, though, she soon lost her figure; it was just as the instructor passing through from the Central Dance Academy had said—she became pudgy. This made her head look smaller, giving her a pointy top and a squat bottom. But despite this development, she was still one of the best on stage. She had a natural loftiness and refinement that made it difficult for her to really integrate into the troupe; such was the stark difference between lead and supporting actors.

Our troupe then put on another model opera—this time the ballet *Ode to Yimeng*. You could say that this ballet was another golden era for our troupe. Riding the wave of model operas, our troupe was given permission to expand the orchestra and dance team. At that point, our orchestra surpassed that of the municipal song and dance troupe, which was also putting on *Ode to Yimeng* at the same time. We used the military tactic of strength in numbers—in addition to recruiting new members, we also borrowed even more musicians so that we nearly had a full orchestra with both winds and strings. We really practiced hard and held our breaths that we might be able to go head to head with the municipal song and dance troupe. Naturally, this girl from the Railway Middle School was our "leading lady." It had already been quite a few years since she had first joined our troupe to dance in *White-Haired Girl*, and since then she had played the leading role in several smaller productions and typed the captions for some others. This time, thank God, because it was a model opera that provided us with some guidance, our costumes weren't bad. The girl was dressed in a blue, floral print outfit characteristic of the Yimeng mountain region, and her hair was combed back in a bun; she was a towering figure, so genuine, mature, and gentle—she was truly beautiful. By comparison, the municipal song and dance troupe's "leading lady" seemed rather weak, even though she was better proportioned, more graceful, and had received better training. Actually, it was a bit of a pity that this girl was in our troupe; she could have definitely gotten a better opportunity and gone a lot further. The students in our troupe all seemed to share the same characteristic: They just handed their fates over to us as a matter of course and didn't give it any more thought. They spent their childhoods in our troupe, and they stayed with it to the very end.

However, once placed in the clutches of fate as they were, it was very difficult to get out. Perhaps the students understood this and simply felt that worrying about it was pointless, so they might as well just be happy. They were happy all day long and never seemed to get upset. If we didn't have them in our dilapidated courtyard, it would have filled up with worry and anxiety. Even when there were exceptions, the results were always the same. Take, for example, one particular girl who was good at performing. When our troupe was recruiting students, it was very easy for us to get excited over talented children, so we would feel inspired to make spur-of-the-moment decisions and forget to take our performance program into account, resulting in many awkward situations. This was one of our troupe's characteristics—it was like we were naturally lacking in logic and just did whatever we felt like. This girl was very beautiful and spirited, and she was an excellent performer, the kind that was full of passion and evocative in any role. Later on in her stage career, she gradually began to exhibit a trait that was rarely seen: She was a good thinker. Playing all those minor roles in our troupe's clichéd operas restricted her imagination and creativity. She liked to read and think, and she had both an original perspective and a great desire to learn. If she had been given an opportunity, she would have had some hope of success. It was very hard not to be moved by a child like this, and when she stared at you, you felt as if you'd been conquered; this helped us forget a very basic question: what exactly did we recruit her for? She didn't have a great voice, so she couldn't sing, at least not more than a few little numbers, so she definitely couldn't be in the opera division. Her body was also not quite up to snuff, so the dance team was out. Our troupe should have just left her where we found her, and something good would have quickly come her way. She really was one of our young talents, but she could only show it behind the scenes—she was the branch secretary for the Youth League, the "class monitor" of the students, and she held some other positions of this sort.

As previously mentioned, the students very sincerely handed their fates over to the troupe, and they never went looking for outside opportunities. In those years, opportunities were few and far between, and—how to put it—our troupe wasn't exactly an "opportunity." But weren't a lot of people envious of our status? Well, after she grew up a bit more, she began to feel anxious, and then actively began requesting a transfer. But what was the use in feeling anxious, or requesting a transfer? She started training even harder, practicing her movements and her singing, and fruitlessly hanging around the music rooms and practice rooms. She truly loved the stage and cherished the short amount of time she could spend there, and she was determined to keep improving. But it was all in vain; in the end, she would never be anything more than a bit player.

Years later, the universities resumed regular admissions, and also opened up specialized courses of study to help compensate for the lack of education over the previous years. The girl was twenty years old that year, and the provincial art institute opened up a specialized course in drama, which presented all of the performance troupes with an opportunity to receive advanced training; our troupe was able to secure a spot for her. This was an opportunity for her to choose a completely new path for herself, and at her age, it would probably be the last opportunity she would get—it was the last train leaving the station. This was the final thing our troupe could do for her. She excitedly packed up her suitcases and had them sent to the station, her friends held a farewell dinner for her, and early the next morning she boarded the train headed south to the provincial capital. Only when she made it to the university did she discover that because the course did not have full enrollment, it had been canceled; the notifications had been sent, but hers hadn't yet reached our troupe. Standing in the registration office, she burst into tears.

She was from a Cultural Workers' Troupe, so you don't need me to tell you how much she cried. She cried for herself, she cried for others, and she cried all day and all night; the floor of the practice room was damp from her sweat, and the paint was peeling off the dance barres. So that's how it went; as this episode came to a close, the out-of-tune vocal parts from all over the dilapidated courtyard joined in her crying, and everyone was in tears. In *The Hanging Branch*, a collection of folksongs from the Ming dynasty, there's a song called "Clay Figurine"—it's meant

to be sung for a lover, but it also seems to be well-suited to our troupe.
It goes as follows:

> Clay figurines, the two of us—mold one of me, form one of you, how do we
> look? Knead all the clay together and do it once more—mold a new one of
> me, form a new one of you; now I have a little you in me, and you have a
> little me in you.

6. The Self-Funded Apprentices

There was another group of people who passed through our troupe,
stayed for a while, and then quickly went on their way to continue making a living. They were usually full of hope when they arrived and dejected by the time they left. They initially hoped to remain in our troupe
and become members, but very few were actually able to do so. Bad luck
followed our troupe everywhere, but the reason people were still attracted
to us was that we were under ownership by the whole people.[5] In those
years, the arts were very popular, thanks to all the model opera troupes;
we also provided support for daily expenses, although obviously it wasn't
that much—two jiao per day, six yuan per month, which was considered
top-grade wages. In the eyes of others, we enjoyed a superior status. The
ones who sought out our troupe were always very admiring and envious.
Most of them were "sent-down" youths who were looking everywhere
for a way out. Some who came to our troupe left us as soon as they did
the math. Others who were a bit more patient and determined would stay
on without asking for any remuneration; they would participate in our rehearsals, trying to increase their skills and make a good impression while
waiting for an opportunity to come along. This sort came to be known
as "self-funded apprentices." At any given point in time our troupe had
quite a few, and if you counted them up from the beginning to the end,

---

5. "Ownership by the whole people" (全民所有制) refers to the highest form of socialist ownership, in which the entire enterprise is publicly owned and directly administered by
the state (which represents the whole people) according to the needs of the national economy.
See Henry Yuhai He, *Dictionary of the Political Thought of the People's Republic of China*
(New York: Routledge, 2001).

they would probably number more than our official members. Some of them really helped us out a lot—it was just too bad that the troupe had a restricted quota, and in the end we were unable to keep them. More than a few were incredibly dedicated and persisted for years; after several twists and turns we would sometimes be able to take them in, but then looking back on it all they would have to ask themselves with a heavy sigh: Was it really worth it?

In those years, young people faced a vast and uncertain future; if they received only the slightest nod, they would come rushing like moths to the flame. At the same time, they had learned at a young age to keep their hopes in check; they did what they could without thinking too much about the results, knowing that it would probably end in failure—but they could at least take comfort in the fact that they'd tried. There was the girl from Shanghai who had been "sent down" to Jiangxi province—someone had introduced her to our troupe, so she came to see for herself. Her father came along with her, but they didn't realize we had just gone out on the road to perform. So she and her father followed us—but it just so happened that the next day we had already left for another location. Without hesitating, they continued on to catch up with us there. It was July, the height of summer, and our troupe was staying in a crude, one-story building in the county seat; men and women were all together in one large room, mosquito netting hanging everywhere. The girl and her father split up and stayed with us in this collective lodging. The father was a well-known math teacher at a prestigious high school in Shanghai, but even in such humble conditions, he was able to maintain his tidy appearance and refined manner. He stayed in a good mood and seemed to have taken some interest in this hapless journey, chatting with the troupe members about some of his observations and impressions. His daughter studied voice and had a very proper appearance, petite and well proportioned; that evening we added a solo for her in our song and dance performance. She sang very well, and it was obvious that she had been well trained, but perhaps because of the setbacks she'd experienced in the previous few days, the results were mediocre. Our troupe was having a very difficult time deciding whether she should stay or go, but the girl and her father quickly indicated that they'd like to follow the troupe for a bit without requesting any sort of agreement. Allowing her to take part in a performance had clearly boosted their confidence.

The next day, the father left his daughter there and returned to Shanghai by himself. No matter how you looked at it, the scene was a bit tragic, yet both father and daughter appeared calm and composed. Maybe it was because of the situation, or maybe it was a kind of hereditary trait, but they were both able to look reality calmly in the face. The girl appeared quite willing to adapt to our unstable lifestyle, and she got herself settled in quite nicely. She had an eye for how things were done, and she treated people appropriately and knew the boundaries. This was a trait shared by nearly all of the "self-funded apprentices"; they were all very well behaved and had a survival mentality. By the time she had completed the tour with us, she had sung a few solos in our song and dance performances, and she had helped set up the stage and take it down—there was hardly any difference between her and the regular members of our troupe. She ingratiatingly told us her childhood nickname and encouraged us to use it, but no one really indulged her in this and just kept calling her by her regular name, complete with surname, which was like a subtle rejection. For some reason, she was never able to gain our troupe's affection. Sometime after returning from the tour, she was sent away. When it was time for her to go, she sobbed as she packed her suitcases, keeping her back to us the whole time. Actually, she didn't seem to take much of a liking to our troupe, nor was she holding out any great hopes, but a sense of failure was unavoidable. And who knew how many times she had failed before? At any rate, she kept herself under control the whole way through; there were only those final tears at the end, but they weren't enough to say she lost her composure. Beneath her delicate exterior was a heart that could take a beating. Later, we heard she'd eventually been accepted by a Cultural Workers' Troupe in a prefecture-level city in Anhui province; what's more, she had played the lead role in several major opera productions and become the backbone of that troupe. None of this was that surprising.

There were also those who left in tears, swearing they'd never look back, but then after a while they would glumly return and beg to keep paying their own way as apprentices. By the mid-seventies it was becoming harder and harder to recruit new people; our requests were repeatedly denied, and "sent-down" youths no longer had any hope of getting a transfer. But the art troupes did their own thing and were seen as little rays of hope in a hopeless situation. "Self-funded apprentices" were practically glued to Cultural Workers' Troupes, and it came off as a little shameless. These sorts of people were the hardest to deal with, and actually also the most hopeless; they would often force things into a stalemate. They'd put in all their time and energy, and even if another opportunity were to come up, they might still try to stay on. In the end it wasn't about finding a livelihood—it was about making even on their losses; it was about struggling against our troupe. It was hard for these situations not to produce resentment, and these "self-funded apprentices" always lost out in the end. This kind of patience and restraint had a way of distorting people's feelings. It was just part of the general oppression of life, and our troupe could not be held responsible.

Life was really hard in those days. Youth wasn't characterized by hope, but rather a concern for the immediate present; you had to grit your teeth and do your best to struggle through. There was nothing to rely on, so people had to keep searching. Being young was like being a headless fly randomly buzzing around and hitting whatever it flew into. There was a boy from Wuxi whose family had been transferred to the countryside; he was the youngest in his family, the only boy among many sisters, and he had a name that sounded like a childhood pet name—as soon you heard it, you knew he was his parents' special treasure. His oldest sister worked in the district office and arranged for him to come to our troupe as a "self-funded apprentice"; he had no special skills, and after coming to us he studied the three-stringed lute, the alto lute, and the violin before finally receiving some training in the pi-pa. He was hardworking and intelligent, and he came pretty close to mastering whatever he studied. But he was naturally a little mischievous and eccentric; it was hard to tell what was up his sleeve, and he pulled some stunts that really upset people. More than once our troupe wanted to dismiss him, but we couldn't circumnavigate his sister, who went around singing his praises, so each time we let him stay. But he was too slow in reforming his ways; before long several years had passed, and he had grown from a child into a young adult. By this time his face had turned dismal and gloomy, and he had become very standoffish; he often sat by himself, holding a small, handmade bow and producing a faint sound as he mechanically practiced fingerings. His eyes, tiny pupils surrounded by white, stared straight ahead; it was impossible to tell what he was thinking. He even became a little frightening—lying came very naturally to him, and he would make up stories and spread rumors. And the rumors he spread weren't just the general, run-of-the-mill kind, either, but were nasty things about the troupe's leadership. His sister in the district office had perhaps unwittingly revealed some of the goings-on behind the scenes, and he used them as weapons for blackmail. He would insert himself into all of our troupe's conflicts and try to use them to strengthen his own position, and sometimes he'd get results. He would wait for the situation to worsen, and then come up with some makeshift solution to alleviate the problem, pretending to have made some sort of sacrifice. He was attentive to everyone's interests since, as a "self-funded apprentice" with no status, he was of no real importance to the troupe. He was really quite confused, hindered by his own intelligence—dropping the rocks he was trying to move on his own feet, as the saying goes. But he could only get himself tangled up in so many of these sorts of incidents before the general attitude turned against him, which happened after two or three times. As he grew more and more depressed, he became filled with bad intentions, like spying on others' private affairs just for fun whenever the opportunity presented itself. After a while he started to lose sight of things, he himself not even understanding why he was acting like this, other than out of some instinct for revenge. Not only had the few opportunities to become an official member of the troupe passed him by, but some others who had come along after him had successfully gone through the process of officially transferring, on top of which, more "self-funded apprentices" had appeared. With such a grim outlook, he began to feel even more anxious, and he practiced his instruments from morning till night. That small, handmade bow never left his hand, and he was constantly going over his positions and fingerings. The result of all this was that he overworked his wrist and developed carpal tunnel syndrome. He first tried giving it a rest, but it didn't improve, so he had to get surgery. This made him extremely worried, and his face became sunken and withered as he waited for the wound to heal. He had a really difficult time getting through these few days, as if something horrible were about to befall him and every minute that passed were a matter of life or death.

Occasionally, however, he would reveal a more innocent side and suddenly become very happy, bounding down the stairs like a big child. He could also be quite witty, delivering one-liners that everyone found amusing, along with his strong accent. Sometimes he would intentionally try to make everyone happy to try to get on their good side. He yearned for affection; the girls would tease him and have him running here and there doing things for them, and he would agree to everything they said, his face lighting up to reveal a foolish grin. At these times, he appeared very loveable, and also rather pitiable. His malice would come periodically in waves, and when it subsided, he would actually harbor good intentions. When he was doing well, he was great, but when he wasn't, it was horrible— it was rare to come across someone so unpredictable, and we were completely unable to anticipate what he would be like from one day to the next. His situation wasn't great, which was at least partly his own fault, although he blamed it all on everyone else. At the crucial moments he would always come out with something hateful, driving away even those who genuinely sympathized with him. The time he spent with the troupe was certainly long and tortuous enough. Toward the end, everyone was a little scared of him, which made us afraid to officially take him in, but also afraid to send him away. The years ticked by under this ambiguous state of affairs. He had become pretty good at the pi-pa, and while you couldn't really say he had talent, his constant practicing had to have had some effect. In the general situation we could deal with him easily enough; after spending so many years in the band, he had gained plenty of experience. But he was never able to officially join the troupe. During the stagnant periods, he stayed relatively calm and seemed resigned to his fate, but as soon as there was the slightest sign of something happening, he would turn wild like a little animal and start making trouble. During those days, having a little hope was even worse than not having any at all—at least then you could feel at peace and continue to muddle through. What was really frightening was when a bit of hope did appear on the horizon. And why wouldn't it be? After a rather long period of not much happening, an old worker in the Cultural Affairs Bureau suddenly passed away, opening up an officially registered spot, which was allocated to our troupe. However, we had to complete the process of filling it before the new year, or we would lose it. By that time it was already the end of the year, with only a few days remaining. After waiting for so long, it seemed as if this spot was a last chance, and if we let it slip by, the opportunity would never return. Moreover, in a few days it would all be decided, and before there was even enough time to sleep on it, we would have to show our cards. In the end, of course, he lost. He didn't cry or cause a scene, but rather got down on the floor and started rolling around, from one side of the room to the other, and then back again.

Some "self-funded apprentices" were also there as a way of repairing the roof before it rained, so to speak. As their high school graduations approached, they knew that if they remained at their schools, there would be no way for them to avoid being "sent down" to the countryside. So they came to our troupe early, which seemed better than finding themselves on the back foot, but it was hard to say what the outcome would be; coming at the right moment beats coming early, as they say. The youngest of this group was twelve, having just graduated from primary school. Her mother was from Suzhou, and she had quite a lot of foresight—she still had another daughter at home, and she knew it would be hard to avoid having at least one of them "sent down," so she tried to make arrangements as early as possible. She used her connections to get this girl placed with our troupe, entrusting her to us and asking us to please look after her. She came to visit us almost every other day, sometimes bringing along a bag full of fruit candies from the south and leaving one on each of our beds. She often invited people over for dinner, all in hopes of improving her daughter's situation. From that point on, the child followed our troupe everywhere we went. The students in our troupe had all grown up by then, and we never took in any more after that; she was in the band, and the band members were all older, so she had no peers her own age. She was by herself in a group of adults, and she was exposed to a lot of gossip and less-than-refined banter, so she learned about the ways of the world before she was really ready; it was not a great environment for her to grow up in. Life in a Cultural Workers' Troupe could also be quite undisciplined, and she lacked any proper oversight. Because of her unstable position as a "self-funded apprentice," she needed to pay close attention to the behavior of others and the looks they gave her. She saw the ones who had a sweet appearance, stood by their word, and did as they were told, like little sheep—after those students grew up, our troupe never again had children like that, who were quite few and far between to begin with; people fell in love with them as soon as they laid eyes on them. She also traded on her youth while lording her pampered position over others. She wasn't actually able to lord it over that many, just the one she shared a music stand with. They were both "self-funded apprentices" who played violin in the back row, although the other one didn't play as well as her, or use her age to her advantage as well as she did; simply put, she was not as good at courting others' affection. She was also not quite as attractive, and her position was even more precarious; the troupe members often indicated their intention to dismiss her. The girl was able to see all this, and she became quite arrogant in front of this poor, hapless soul. She would squeeze so close to her in the orchestra pit that she was unable to pull her bow properly, and she never turned the pages of the music, as if her superior position entitled her to such behavior. That poor other girl felt that everyone was trying to kick her when she was down—even this young girl was acting so highhanded with her and treating her like she had no recourse. Why did everyone like that young girl and not her? So she threw herself into practicing the violin. But playing the violin isn't something that can come overnight. She grew so anxious she had trouble catching her breath, until finally she fell ill. As she lay there on her bed, she still wanted to practice. Her roommates took away her violin, and she became so upset she kicked off the blanket and punched the bed. By this point, she had gone out of control and become severely depressed; she could often be found crying silently. When the girl saw her like this, not only did she have no sympathy, but a smile even appeared on her face; she seemed to take delight in her misfortune. So this child turned cruel, much more so than any adult. She was still ignorant and hadn't yet faced any adversity in her own young life, nor did she understand the ways of the world, so her heart had grown cold.

Everyone was prone to change under these conditions. Basic survival was of such immediate importance that no one could pay attention to anything else. In this sort of environment, our troupe was a bit like Noah's ark, providing a safe haven in the midst of turmoil, a place of refuge in a sea of misfortune. When the floodwaters subsided, and the land once again rose above the waves, people left this place where they had taken shelter and rushed out toward the shining paths that lay ahead of them. The ark, however, was left to run aground on a riverbank and slowly rot, forgotten by everyone. Later on, this is just how our troupe was discarded. At the time people were distraught at not being able to join the troupe, but afterward everyone was elated to get out; they left to go enroll in university, join the army, or take up their parents' jobs after they retired, and the "sent-down" youths returned to the city. But those who had officially entered the troupe were now completely at a loss—many of the new policies didn't apply to them, so they could only look on as these new opportunities passed them by, while they searched for other ways to transfer out. The times had completely changed. These "self-funded apprentices" brought an uneasy atmosphere to our Troupe as they constantly cycled through as if on a merry-go-round, leaving behind a variety of memories both happy and sad; a few of the most tragic episodes would stay with us forever.

There was one "self-funded apprentice" no one could figure out. She was a middle-aged woman from a village in southern Jiangsu province, but she had the manner of a city dweller—she seemed to have seen something of the world and was a little more guarded than the villagers usually were. Judging from her face, she had likely been quite attractive when she was younger, although by this point time had made its mark. Someone had told her about our troupe, and she arrived claiming to be skilled in opera performance. At that time the troupe happened to be rehearsing *Red Troops on Hong Lake*, and we were looking for an understudy for the role of Han Ying. Whether it was singing or acting, she was supposed to be able to do it all, and be spectacular at it—but, at the end of the day, that was not the case. Because of her age, the troupe's leadership maintained an appropriate silence to avoid damaging her pride. A woman of her age going out and trying to make a living on her own like that must have had her reasons. Our troupe was always very understanding in these situations. While the outcome was more than clear, we just couldn't bring ourselves to ask her to go back home—the words just wouldn't come out, again for fear of hurting her. We even did one or two run-throughs of *Red Troops on Hong Lake* just for her, knowing full well it wasn't going to accomplish anything, although we acted like we were taking it seriously. She stayed with our troupe for some time; we even went to the local water authority to ask about performance times, and invited her to participate in a smaller performance of *Brothers and Sisters Clear the Wasteland*. On those clear, windy days, the sandy soil blew right into our mouths. As she strained her throat and sang with a rasp about how "the rooster raises his voice up in song," her dry wisps of hair fluttered in the wind and her face turned blue in the cold; it was nearly unbearable to watch. No one could understand why she wanted to do this—there was not a single thing about her that was well suited either to performing or the sort of life it entailed. She should be the kind of woman to wear stylish clothes; take good care of herself, as well as her husband and children; do some knitting when she wasn't busy preparing the three meals of the day; and chat with her neighbors about household affairs. If she really had to go out and find something to do, she should go work in a shop or a nursery school. Perhaps to show what a good fit she was for this artistic life, she tried to put on a lively, overly exaggerated display, but it wasn't appropriate for her age, nor was she up to the task. As to whether she would stay or go, everyone knew what the answer was—but did she? Who knows. With her age and experience, she should not have been clueless, and maybe she was just pretending to be; day after day she would get up and give it her best. But then finally one day, without a word to anyone, she quietly packed up her things and left. As soon as the troupe's leadership discovered this, they immediately sent someone to the train station to fetch her and bring her back. Both parties felt sad, each knowing the difficulties the other faced—it's just that no matter how willing they might have been, there was no way to help. The reason for bringing her back was not to make any sort of decision; she would have to leave at some point—it just couldn't be like this. On this point, everyone understood. Later, when she really did leave, she never tried to embarrass us by bringing up the fact that we had once kept her from leaving. When all was said and done, she was a mature adult who had met with some unfortunate circumstances, and she understood the situation.

Many people came and left our troupe like this, trying to strategize for their own survival. Many of these sad situations were quite difficult to watch; some were so ridiculous we couldn't even laugh. These kinds of experiences weighed us down and added to our dreary countenance. Our troupe didn't have a good fate; it was as if it were steeped in bitter water. To look at its members, most of them seemed unhappy and difficult to get along with. But because of this, they also had a deep sense of sympathy that was obscured by how they appeared on the surface. What was on the surface was just a clumsy, immature performance on a brightly lit stage with bad props. But in the area surrounded by the curtain rod that went around the stage on both sides and along the back, under the wobbly lighting that was threatening to fall down, amongst the dusty pile of stage props, and in the calm after the last sounds of singing and dancing had ceased—that was where the essence of our troupe was found. It was lying there hidden in the darkness, unnoticed by anyone; yet when it was approached, it would suddenly shine with its brilliant light.

7. Setting Out

Performing on the road was a vagabond life. All the lighting equipment, costumes, props, and instruments had to get loaded into boxes, and then onto a vehicle. Sometimes the vehicle was a truck, in which case it would take two of them. Other times it would be the freight car of a train, in which case the work would be divided into two stages. First, everything would have to be transported to the train platform, and then loaded into the freight car. When we reached our destination, it was the same—we would have to first unload everything into a truck, and then transport it to the theater. If the train with our freight car didn't show up on time, too bad—there was no telling how long we might end up having to wait at the station. If we had already sold all our tickets and the train didn't show up, it would be even worse. Luckily we were always somehow able to pull through at the last minute by the skin of our teeth, as if heaven were testing us. At other times, the train would arrive on schedule, but we couldn't find a truck, which was just as frustrating. Once, as it was getting time to load up the freight car, the truck still hadn't shown up, and it started to rain; the troupe scheduled after us then occupied the stage and started setting it up. Finding ourselves stuck between a rock and a hard place, everyone split up to go look for a truck. Finally some guy from the orchestra hired a donkey cart, and the owner came driving it up to us with his whip whistling in the air. Everyone said he was just creating more trouble, but we ended up having to use it. So that's what it was like making our dusty way from stage to stage, with never any time to settle down or take a rest—we were always either unloading the cart or waiting in the swirling coal smoke of the train station for our freight car to arrive. Our hair and faces were covered in dust and soot, and we were completely exhausted. When we were finally able to wrangle our things to the theater, we still couldn't rest; we had to set up the stage. The theaters were all different from one to the next, and some were better than others, so we were always having to arrange things differently. The lighting might need to be increased or decreased; it all required time and effort. By the time everything was finally in order, it would be late into the night; only then could we attend to our own affairs. Getting ourselves settled in was no simple matter, either. Some theaters had dormitories, but others didn't. In the theaters that also showed films, the women would stay in the projection room, while the men would go off to find someplace else. The entire floor under the lighting and within the curtains would be covered with sleeping mats. Our suitcases were piled up like a wartime street barricade, blocking off the corners to make separate little rooms for married couples whose partners both worked in the troupe, giving them their own cozy nests. These sleeping arrangements were why we usually went on the road in the spring or summer; winter was no good, since it was nearly impossible to keep out the cold. It was for the same reason that homeless people headed south—it made getting through the nights that much easier. Aside from the problem of finding separate places for the men and women, everything else was relatively easy to manage.

Because of the climate in our interior location, there was a long period of cold in the early spring. But once the weather turned warm, the days quickly grew hotter and hotter, and in no time at all we were sweltering in the summer heat. Loading and unloading the equipment under the beating sun was grueling labor. When it came time to perform, the stage was worse than a boiling pot; our masks were adorned with bright, shining colors, but behind them were streaming rivulets of sweat. By the end of the evening our costumes would be soaked through with sweat and the accompanying stench, and the only way to deal with it was to spritz them with *baijiu* liquor. When the curtain closed and the performance was over, our body heat would linger. Everyone would cram around the sink to get water for bathing and washing clothes; the kitchen would also be packed with people having a late dinner. If the audience were to turn and look back at the scene they'd just left, they would find it completely transformed. The place was packed with people holding bowls and eating their meals, or shirtless and washing themselves right there in the courtyard, bumping into each other and shouting curses; still others who hadn't yet gotten over their excitement would be singing at full volume. On the darkened stage after the lights had gone out, the first to turn in would have already spread out their sleeping mats, lit their mosquito-repellant incense, and be snoring in no time. The sounds of breathing would also come from the "cozy nests" in the corners, accompanied by some other ambiguous movements. And so it went—there were those who were calm and those who fought, and those who ate and those who slept; through the course of the evening, the troupe members were engaged in practically every possible activity. When the weather was really hot, awkward situations were hard to avoid, and we had to check our modesty at the door—that's when our troupe really cut a sorry figure. But finally the kitchen would turn off the stove; the laziest among us had hung up their last item of clothing to dry; the most excitable would no longer be able to keep their eyes open, and the movements in the cozy nests would cease. When everyone got settled into their spots and the lights of the theater were turned off, the moonlight would shine in through the open door, making everything appear clean and peaceful. The breeze brought a slight chill with it and dried the sweat on our bodies, and the dust in the air had settled, allowing us to breathe more freely. Sometimes, here and there, we could hear the sound of someone talking in their sleep, mumbling for a bit and then stopping. Sleep approached like a wave, and once it came over us, it washed away the suffering we'd endured under the heat of the day. But this was the season of long days and short nights, and after this brief pause to catch our breaths, the sun once again rose high in the sky, and the clamor of a new day started up again.

The hot weather brought illness with it—most commonly diarrhea accompanied by a fever. Sometimes several people would get sick at the same time, but there was nothing that could be done about it—when it was time to go on stage, they had to perform; when it was time for a scene change, they had to do the scene change. Backstage, people would often be lying on their backs, dazed and practically unconscious; then, when they heard their cue, they would jump up like a fish leaping out of the water to rush off and perform their part, returning when they were finished to lie back down in the same spot and reenter their daze. The heat, illness, hard work, rushing around, and being away from family for so long gradually ate away at everyone's patience. People started to become irritable, restless, and uneasy, which led them to cause trouble. This usually happened around the middle of our tour, once a number of issues had accumulated to a certain degree and surpassed whatever amount people could tolerate. At times like this, the theater became a powder keg, and the tiniest spark could touch off a wide array of problems. Some were verbal disputes, while others were full-scale, physical brawls that left the participants battered and bruised. Some people would cheer from the sidelines, and some would join in the fight; this would go on until the bystanders had had enough, and someone finally stepped in to pull the combatants apart. They would drag them before the troupe's leader, and without bothering to find out the facts of the situation, both sides would be severely punished. Getting into fights among ourselves didn't matter that much, but it became a problem when someone would gather their allies to go cause trouble outside the troupe.

One time, when the other party felt they had suffered some injustice, they went off, rallied their troops, and returned with weapons, ready for a fight. Because we were outsiders, there was no one to come help us; the only ones to show up were a few bystanders who wanted to see some excitement, and the look in their eyes seemed like they could eat us alive. The scene made our hearts pound with fear; we felt like we were being surrounded. The stage became like a city under siege. The guard at the gate was also one of the locals, so we had to hope he wouldn't betray us and aid his fellow villagers. The situation looked grim. But just when it seemed like they were going to attack, they didn't; they kept holding back until it started to become clear they were just toying with us, getting a kick out of seeing how scared we were. Once things reached this level, we realized we needed to pay closer attention to our behavior and not act so rashly. Huddled up in the theater, we waited until they'd finally had enough and withdrew their forces. But this moment of crisis had its benefits; it punctured our pride and took away any desire we had for troublemaking. The whole episode had resulted from an inflated sense of prestige, which had now been effectively tamped down. Although we felt a bit pathetic, our top concern was our own safety. We passed the next few days in a funk, and our hearts weren't really in it. The hottest days of summer were also upon us, and the noontime sun was so hot on the theater's cement roof that people kept flipping over on their sizzling sleeping mats like pancakes. Those who couldn't bear it any longer filled a basin with water and sat in it to cool off. The sounds of the cicadas, buzzing intermittently, rose up in all directions and created a din that filled the air. When the angle of the sun's rays grew a bit more slanted, the kitchen would begin serving the next meal, and the troupe members would start getting made up and ready to perform.

In order to break even with the hope of making a tiny profit, we would either not go on the road at all, or we would have to stay out for two or three months. Those female performers with children would have to bring them along. In the evenings the children would act up and start making a racket; complaining was unavoidable, but luckily no one wanted to make too much of a fuss over it, and by the next morning all would be forgotten. Space was quite limited for the number of people we had, and everyone had to be careful not to accidentally burn or scald one of the children in the kitchen. The children had to be watched over closely, adding to the burden. Because they were always being constrained, they felt wronged, and acted out even more. They usually managed to get by without too many problems, but when it came time to perform, there were too many things that required attention to keep a close eye on them. One time, a Japanese collaborator was fiercely marching across the stage to enter a village, but right at the crucial moment, a child appeared—he cocked his head, put his little legs into high gear, and raced across the stage from one end to the other. A roar erupted from the audience, and those on stage were too stunned to know what to do—they couldn't really call out to stop him, but they couldn't let him go, either. As if they were in a freeze frame, everyone stopped for a moment and waited for the child to run by; the soldier then continued approaching the village. These sorts of mishaps, however, didn't always involve children, and were sometimes caused by adults. Our troupe's cook was a huge fan of theater, and he was not very discriminating—whether it was traditional or modern, northern or southern, as long as it involved some stage lights shining on some actors speaking or singing in costume, he loved it. He used to have a more comfortable and reliable position in the district party school, but he transferred to our troupe just so he could watch the performances. Every time we were about to go on stage, he would follow us out and squat down to the side, remaining perfectly still with a long-stemmed pipe hanging out of his mouth and a misty expression gradually spreading over his face. When we were out on tour, the kitchen would be right next to the theater, and if you stood on your tiptoes you could see the stage; the cook would become completely immersed and ruin every late-evening meal. Once, when he was absorbed in the performance, he suddenly noticed another cook wildly gesturing to him from the other side of the stage, trying to get him to return to the kitchen and get to work. With a dazed smile on his face, he got up and leisurely walked right across the stage, the soles of his shoes knocking against his long-stemmed pipe. They were performing a modern opera that day, and his appearance, clothing, and movements were all actually quite suited to the scene being performed. The audience was actually fooled, thinking he was one of the characters crossing the stage, while the performers and everyone else backstage broke out in a cold sweat. After being on the road for so long, everyone could get a little woolly headed and lose their focus; things could get a bit messy, and mistakes were unavoidable. But in the end, we were always able to pull through, completing our tour as scheduled and returning home.

When we were out on tour, hard work and exhaustion were to be expected, but, like I said, no matter what, we were always able to pull through. What we feared most was making a mistake with our route, which would mean a mistake with our overall itinerary. We needed both a strategic acumen and the courage to make decisions. There were several in our troupe's leadership who knew our affairs quite well and formed a special taskforce—they were mostly members of the old guard who had lots of experience traveling from venue to venue and knew the surrounding areas well; they were also daring enough to leave some things to figure out later, after we'd already set off. While we were on the road, the leader of the troupe had to rely on them, discussing things over with them again and again before making a decision. Before setting out, the first thing to do was to get three venues lined up. Once we had these first three arranged, we had enough of a cushion to keep searching for the fourth and fifth venues while we were already out on the road performing. If we were overly cautious and got all of our venues lined up ahead of time, there was the fear that even some of the first three might fall through, to say nothing of the later ones; no place liked to make arrangements too far in advance, so we tried to avoid restricting ourselves too much—who knew when a better opportunity to sell tickets might crop up? It was always best to maintain our flexibility to respond to any changes as they happened. So we were really only ever able to line up the first three venues, and then figure out the rest from there. The tricky part was the direction in which these first three stops sent us, and this required some foresight. If these first three cornered us geographically, it would be very difficult to find our next place. If we changed direction midcourse, it would mean a major adjustment that would cost us a lot of time and money. It was also possible to become cornered in a cultural sense, and there were two ways this could happen. One was if we found ourselves in a big city, where the people had seen a lot of performances and were very familiar with them—it was hard to say how much interest a regional Cultural Workers' Troupe could generate there.

The other was in the areas surrounding a county seat, where audiences loved their local forms of traditional opera, but were largely uninterested in modern opera or other kinds of song and dance. Of course, we also had to take the economic circumstances into consideration—in a place where it was difficult to cobble together a livelihood, spending money to go see a performance was too much of a luxury, so it was unrealistic. Therefore, we had to stake out a middle path that was neither too fixed nor too open, but was calibrated to just the right level in the hope that we might hit the sweet spot and benefit all around. These first three stops played a huge role in determining the success or failure of a tour. Sometimes, as much as it pained us, in the interest of longer-term benefits we would have to abandon these valuable first three stops and turn around to draw up new plans. It was imperative to consider everything carefully and thoroughly before making a move. If something we hadn't anticipated came up, we could find ourselves stranded in the middle of nowhere, with neither staying put nor continuing on as viable options.

One year, in the spring, our troupe came up with an ambitious plan to go on a five-hundred–*li* tour that would take us to the provincial capital of Nanjing. We drew our encouragement from both the fall of the Gang of Four and the popularity of *Sister Jiang*. This was our attempt to get back on our feet after our failure with *Red Troops on Hong Lake* and put on another well-known opera. Everyone was filled with optimism during that period and felt that things must be getting better for a reason; it was really a happy time. In the joyful atmosphere of the national situation, our troupe became a bit muddleheaded, and we forgot to pay attention to the specific circumstances of our environment. Things actually started off pretty well for us, and we even performed consecutively in two different venues in the provincial capital. At that point, the film version of *Sister Jiang* had not yet come out, and the popularity of the similarly themed *Living in the Flames of War* no doubt helped increase interest in our *Sister Jiang*.[6] Because it was Nanjing, the

---

6. *Living in the Flames of War* (烈火中永生) is a 1965 film adaption of the 1961 novel *Red Crag* (红岩). *Sister Jiang* (江姐), a 1964 opera, takes its name from the main protagonist of *Red Crag*, Jiang Xueqin; it was later adapted to film and released in 1978 under the same name.

theaters were all up to standard, and our lodging was very nice. The atmosphere was quite different being in a big city, and the audience was very restrained and orderly. This buoyed our spirits, encouraging us to drop some of our less-refined manners and become a bit more sophisticated. We'd set out quite early that year, and the spring in the south is long; when we got there, the grass was growing and the sparrows were nesting. Nanjing: the ancient capital of the Six Dynasties, known all over the world for its history and scenery. During the day we would see the sights, and in the evening we would perform—our time there was so easy and carefree. It seemed like there was nothing to worry about. When we were finished performing in Nanjing, we continued south to Zhenjiang. Zhenjiang was also very nice. Beside the theater was a large bathhouse with a number of separate rooms and plenty of hot water, which you could adjust yourself; the knobs were on the floor, and the water ran out of the shower heads above. This was completely unlike the bathhouse in our city, which was dank, dark, and crowded, and where the water was sometimes hot, cold, or not even flowing. Bathing here really lifted our spirits. Across from the theater was a bakery. The desserts in the south were sweet, gooey, and delectable, and we couldn't get enough of them. Supplies were strained in those days; meat could only be obtained with ration coupons, and our meals were very plain, so this bakery was our salvation. We were also frequent visitors to Zhenjiang's famous three-filling soup dumpling restaurant. Spring in the Jiangnan region was warm with light breezes and gentle rains, and we were enjoying ourselves so much we nearly forgot about everything else. But things soon took a sudden turn.

The people we'd sent out from Nanjing to arrange our next venues returned without having any luck. At first we weren't too worried; we still had time. But our subsequent attempts continued to yield nothing. By the time we got to Zhenjiang, we split up our scouts to cast a net over a wider area. The results, however, were all the same. This actually shouldn't have been so surprising—with so many Cultural Workers' Troupes around, they were all heading to heavily populated areas like this. Back in those years, the troupes were all cycling through the same repertoire, and it was always the same set of performances. But more importantly, after the fall of the Gang of Four, the ban on traditional opera was lifted, as was the ban on a number of Chinese and foreign films,[7] so the theater schedules became packed—during the day they would show films, and at night they would host performances; sometimes, they would even stay open all night to show films that were just passing through. We went over the cities and towns on both banks of the Yangtze River with a fine-toothed comb, but with no success. The days flew by, and our time in Zhenjiang was up; we had to swallow our pride and negotiate with the theater to let us stay one more day and leave the next morning. We were now on a day-to-day basis, having to pester them each time. Every day we would sit behind the projection screen watching the films and receiving contemptuous looks from the theater staff. The next troupe would be arriving the day after tomorrow; their posters were already up all over the city, and the box office was selling their tickets. But we still had no place to go. The modern bathhouse, the bakery, the three-filling soup dumpling restaurant—none of it held our interest any longer, and we just wanted to get out of that city as quickly as possible. But where could we go? We couldn't just turn around and go back home because, to be honest, we didn't have enough money to get us there. We would have to perform our way back, venue by venue; that was the only way to keep from going broke. Watching movies from behind the projection screen was unbearable. On the other side of the screen, the audience happily enjoyed the film, and then happily went home. We, however, had to stay for film after film, not knowing where one ended and the next began. Finally, the Zhenjiang pulp mill agreed to take us in. It was a huge enterprise located in the outskirts of Zhenjiang, about twenty *li* away from the city, all on its own. As long as we agreed to put on a few performances for them, they let us stay there for free until we could find a new venue.

The pulp mill was located along the Yangtze River, and it had its own small wharf where only small reed supply boats could dock; reeds were the pulp mill's raw material. The scenery here was like a painting. The Yangtze was like a ribbon of white silk shimmering under the sun.

---

7. Before the landmark third plenary meeting of the CCP eleventh congress in December 1978, which ushered in Deng Xiaoping's economic reforms and liberalization, a number of pre–Cultural Revolution films had already become available to the public. See Yingjin Zhang, *Chinese National Cinema* (New York: Routledge, 2004), 222–28.

Mountains rose in the background, and tiny, unassuming blue and white flowers were blooming, sprinkled here and there. We climbed up the mountains at daybreak and looked out over the Yangtze. The river was quite busy, with boats sailing everywhere and the gentle sound of steam whistles filling the air. On both shores of the river were fields, villages, and factories with smokestacks puffing out white clouds of smoke that slowly drifted upwards and melted into the blue, cloudless sky. It was all part of a daily livelihood that was stable and dependable. It was all so tranquil; the sky and earth appeared vast and open. A feeling of melancholy arose and spread out in every direction. This was a rare moment of peace in the course of our travels—the constant clamor had ceased, and an unconscious sense of dread came over us. We were surrounded by a scene of happy lives and stable work, yet we were floating around like vagrants.

Although our fate had allowed us this period of reprieve at the pulp mill, misfortune hadn't let us entirely out of its grips. One night, all of the clothing was stolen from the men's dorm. Out of the entire factory district, out of the countless other family housing units and collective dormitories, the thieves had chosen us, and at one of our lowest moments. It was really a case of picking the persimmon when it's soft. After coming up against so many obstacles, though, this theft was hardly worth mentioning. We politely turned down the offer from the factory's security department to track down the culprits, and instead accepted responsibility ourselves for not being more vigilant. That's just how it had to be when we were living under someone else's roof. The theft was like a price we paid in exchange for the increased care the factory showed toward us. Because they had a guilty conscience, they arranged some sightseeing for us, gave us extra ration coupons for meat, and told us not to worry, we could stay for as long as we wanted. This was really a great comfort to us and helped lessen our anxiety. In this factory district, we were able to comfortably ride out our period of crisis. We were finally able to make contact with a theater in Chu county,[8] so we waited for the day we could go occupy the theater there. This began our return back to the north. By this time it was nearly

8. 滁县, in Anhui province just over the border with Jiangsu, opposite Nanjing from Zhenjiang.

summer, and we had entered the middle portion of our tour, which was the most arduous.

The time we spent stranded in Zhenjiang was actually a new beginning; the worst was yet to come. After the fall of the Gang of Four, the increased cultural freedom did not bring any opportunities our way; much to the contrary, the situation went downhill for us day by day. Thought had been liberated, and there was a feeling of freedom in the air. But we still had nothing to perform—or rather, everything we could perform had become dull and passé. In addition to practicing our old repertoire, we also studied some new material, such as *Ode to the Proud Poplar*, which had been put on by the Changsha Municipal Song and Dance Troupe to commemorate Chairman Mao's former wife Yang Kaihui. We also adapted some of the underground literature from the Cultural Revolution, like *The Second Handshake* and *The Plum Blossom Case of May 13*, but the results were mediocre. We were even so bold as to rehearse an actual comic opera, *The Lady and the Peddler*. Things started off going pretty much to plan, which was to transform our troupe into an opera troupe—but only then did we discover that the market for operas was not actually that great. The audience was sporadic; a performance one day was no indication of how it would be the next. In this new era of free choice, no one seemed to be choosing us. Wooden clappers, *liuqin* lutes, Peking opera, spoken drama, film—people wanted everything but us. Economics then started to play a determining role. If we hoped to support ourselves, it would be nearly impossible; if we hoped just to break even with our performances, that was also nearly impossible. If we wanted to minimize our losses, then the best option would be to stop performing. We had gradually become something that no one else needed; we didn't even need ourselves. But despite it all, we still wanted to—and were only really able to—go out on the road and perform.

Stranded far away from home, unable to retreat or advance—this became our daily fare. We kept making mistakes in our strategies; our judgment was off, and things would always go in the opposite direction from what we'd intended. In these trying circumstances, we had to choose the right times to amuse ourselves—we would play drinking games backstage, hold dinner parties, buy local specialties at the country markets, and have romances. We may have been thoroughly dispirited, but we were still able to have fun; we loved telling jokes, and laughter could be heard all day long, as if we were the happiest people on earth. At the same time, we started to dispense with the reserved and cautious attitude we had always maintained and became more reckless and impetuous. We even dared to drag our troops all the way to the international cultural capital of Shanghai. Although we were in dire straits while we were there, instead of getting anxious, we became increasingly cheerful and energetic. We visited Shanghai's parks and witnessed couples hugging and kissing out in the open, and we would playfully throw rocks at them. Not only were we not doing everything we could to go back home, we even invited our families to come join us and take the opportunity to expand their horizons. One time, as we were chatting after a meal, people started arguing over who could do the highest somersault, and they kept at it until they got up to compare, flipping back and forth in the narrow courtyard behind the theater. At that point, the party secretary of our troupe stood up and said: None of you are doing it right, watch me. With that, he cinched his pants, tucked his head down, and flipped himself over. For a moment everyone stood in stunned silence, as if some ominous kind of sorrow suddenly gripped their hearts. But then, just a moment later, the mood was shattered by an eruption of laughter. This secretary had been assigned to our troupe under the new formation, and he specialized in creative writing. He was sent in to take charge of our creative output with a particular emphasis on its intellectual content. He was definitely a writer, and he was full of democratic ideals. He was friendly, easygoing, and approachable, and he didn't put on any airs as a leader—but he had no idea what to do with our troupe. By this point we were really at the end of our rope, worried to the point that we weren't even worried any more, beginning to throw caution to the wind. With that big somersault, it was like seeing the backbone of our troupe come tumbling down.

Even so, we still had to stay on the road and perform. No one's heart was really in it anymore, and people kept leaving; those who left were better off than those who stayed, and those who stayed grew even more discouraged. To be honest, our troupe was at its last gasp. Yet every year, we still went out on tour at least twice. This is how we were able to keep going and extend our life! Although we were at our lowest ebb, our troupe would never completely lose faith. It was a bit like that simple life philosophy: A wretched life still beats a noble death. As long as we didn't die, we could go on living. It's the sort of outlook that arises only in the most difficult of circumstances and carries a sense of shameless perseverance. In those years when there wasn't a single grain to be harvested and the peasants struggled over the barren land, this was the irrational philosophy to which they clung; if life continued on for generation after generation, one never knew when it might once again produce a good result. This way of thinking was a characteristic of our troupe, and it was also the reason that every time things looked like they were finished, we were somehow able to keep on going. We kept believing that things could go back to the way they were, if only we could get over this threshold. Just think how many things we'd overcome in the past! But in the end, our troupe finally met its demise. We had persevered for so long, only to end up here. Only when we reached this point did we feel truly sad.

When the cities and prefectures were consolidated, our troupe was consolidated with the municipal song and dance troupe. You could say it was consolidated, but actually the other troupe was in charge, and we just became part of it. Everything was under their name; ours was erased, along with our existence. As the talk of consolidation turned from faint whispers to widely known rumors, and then from rumors to reality; as it went through various forms of discussion, negotiation and coordination, as well as various stages of working out the details, before finally reaching the extensive process of implementation, our troupe simply stayed out on the road performing, suffering all the difficulties that entailed. Although we could see the end was coming, we felt that we needed to see it through; this was our troupe's mission, its destiny. The final time we went out to perform, it was in the county seat of our own district—after that, we parted ways. After our performance, we smashed the lights, broke the supports, and divvied up the iron curtain weights to take home for various uses. We rolled up all the soft props into a ball, and did the same with the costumes. Suitcases were snapped open and shut, knocking against one another as they were thrown on the bed of the truck. After that, we left. The freight car on the train was filled beyond capacity, as if we were moving an entire village market. The chickens laid eggs while the fish went belly-up. In this noisy, chaotic fashion, our troupe ended its performance career.

Our district was comprised of eight counties. To the south was Tong-shan and Suining; to the north was Pei and Feng; to the east there was Pi, Xinyi, Donghai, and finally Ganyu, by the Yellow Sea. Our district, as well as its main city, was called Xuzhou. It was an ancient city, well-known throughout history; it was a vast region teeming with rice paddies, wheat, and cotton. The Grand Canal passed right through its center, as did the Yi River. Buried under the earth of this region were layers of ancient relics, stretching thousands of years into the past. A thick seam of coal also ran underground, the kind known as black gold, and it had been mined for the past hundred years. The people of this land liked to sing along with the wooden clapper and the *liuqin* lute, and their melodies were all crude and uninhibited. They also enjoyed legends about military heroes; Liu Bang, the first emperor of the Han, was their fellow villager. They held the acrobatic fighting of traditional opera in high esteem, as well as benevolence and righteousness; Confucius was their neighbor. Their speech sounded close to the dialects of Shandong province, but they came under the furthest reaches of Jiangsu's provincial administration. This was our district. Nowadays, some counties belong either to the cities of Lianyungang or Xuzhou, while others have become their own cities. However, in terms of physical geography, they still form a coherent tract, as closely related as lips and teeth, which brings to mind an old saying: Break the bones, and the tendons are still connected. This was our district.

First draft August 12, 1997
Second draft August 28, 1997